DARK SONNET

TOM
McCARTHY
&
BILL
DOHAR

DE PROFUNDIS BOOKS

Bill Dohar dedicates this book to his three sisters, avid mystery readers all:

Catherine Dohar

Maryam Paulsen

Betsy Kehres

Tom McCarthy dedicates *Dark Sonnet* to the light of his life: Clare

Contents

Cardinal College

Oxford, 1527

The cardinal's great chamber at night. Dark pours through the high leaded windows that look north into darker night. All is in shadow save the cardinal's table, a long board of sturdy English oak smoothed over centuries by the hands of a thousand monks.

Thomas Cardinal Wolsey, Archbishop of York and Lord Chancellor of England, waits and studies in silence the twelve clerics who sit at the table. Christ and His Apostles, he thinks without a blush. He watches them all, but no eyes meet his.

So it should be, for the twelve priests—his scholars, his college—stare in awe at the chalice on the table. The Cuxham Chalice, its gold and silver hammered and exquisitely shaped three centuries past, all to hold Christ's blood. Candlelight flashes off golden angles, amethysts and garnets. Shadow holds the rest.

At long last, the cardinal, in a great rustle of scarlet robes and a clinking of his gold chain of office, rises and the twelve black-robed clerks rise with him.

"Blood made this chalice!" he intones emphatically. He points to the Cuxham treasure, his words reverberating against the stone walls and vaulted ceiling. "And by your blood swear to its safekeeping. Guard this cup well and bind yourselves in secrecy—of this place, this treasure and your solemn purpose. Rule your tongues with a holy silence. He who breaks it, let him be broken and cast into the night of endless death."

1

Monday, May 1

1

In his seventeen years the boy had witnessed only three beheadings, but never of a child.

Until now.

They had been men from another province, thieves and butchers executed on the outskirts of his uncle's village in Iraq, and Rabi himself had been only a child when his relatives forced him to watch. Since coming to England, he thought he would never have to witness anything so terrifying and sickening.

A sudden wave of nausea sent a violent paroxysm through his entire torso. He bent over involuntarily to vomit, but nothing came up.

He closed his eyes and prayed to unsee what lay before him or somehow undo the last ten minutes of his life. To go back in time. Back to the pub and the endless trays of pint glasses he washed for university students to whom he was nothing, invisible, which is what he would like to be now. Back from this strange custom of May Morning, the one day of the year when Oxford pubs stayed open all night. He would not be here otherwise. But here he stood, barely, on rubbery legs, trembling. He reopened his eyes. He knew he could not go back. Could never unsee.

Looking nervously, illogically, around him for someone, anyone, Rabi wondered at what point in the last few minutes could he have evaded this gruesome scene. He might have gotten a ride home, if he had any real friends in Oxford. But he didn't. Not really. Not anyone he could call at 4:30 a.m. He could have resisted slipping past the "Keep Out" sign through the torn section of chain-link fence that surrounded the entire block to take his usual shortcut across the half-demolished Wilton Leys housing estate. The ruins of where people once lived was a place of bad luck and evil spirits, and still he had been defiant. All around him were low piles of broken concrete and rusting rebar surrounded by a hollowed-out four-story brick shell. Jogging slowly, he had chosen his steps carefully but confidently, proud of the physical prowess that allowed him such fluid movement over the uneven ground strewn with glass and awkwardly shaped chunks of construction debris. No one watched the site at night and couldn't catch him even if they did. The only sentinel was a single light high atop a crane that washed the ruined building with a feeble glow, made ghostly by the concrete dust that suffused the air. Thatcher Lane behind him still pulsed with music and the jarring sounds of revelers.

If it wasn't a matter of turning back time, he might have commanded his feet to carry him into a safer future, beyond this place and back into the anonymity of night, beyond the crane light and through the fence on the other side of the site. He would have been home by now.

But tonight—this morning—he noticed something that had made him slow to a stop. Low light was glistening off a broad, dark line running crooked along the pavement before him. He followed the shiny trickle as it widened to a semicircular pool beside a squared hole in the earth—an empty elevator shaft that workers had bordered with four poles strung with yellow DANGER tape. Avoiding the sticky black liquid, Rabi had stepped over the tape, then peered down into the shaft.

That was when time stopped and his world changed forever.

At the bottom, not four feet below where he stood, lay the sprawled and distorted figure of a young boy. He wore a football jersey, though it was impossible to see what color. The shaft was dark with blood sprayed across the walls, the same black that darkened the pavement near his feet. The boy's head had been separated from his body and placed to the right in the corner of the shaft. It was carefully cradled face-up between two bricks, as if to give the gelid, half-open eyes a last look at the Oxford night. Beneath a shock of blond hair caked with blood, the boy's forehead had been scored with a series of deep cuts. Rabi's gaze froze on the innocence of the disembodied face, if it could still be called a face.

4

Who could do such a thing to a child?

As he pulled his phone from his back pocket and began keying in 999, he noticed, ten feet away in the shadow just beyond the crane's light, something eerily familiar and almost as grotesquely incongruous as what lay in the bottom of the derelict shaft: a Muslim prayer rug. Rabi moved carefully around the perimeter of the shaft. He saw a small white disk placed in the center of the rug. Bending down to examine it, dawning recognition caused him to draw in his breath suddenly. He shook his head slowly. He knew now that he could not—must not—call the police.

He put his phone away. The prayer rug, the beheading—the whole display was sure to mean more trouble for the Muslim community. He wanted no part of it. He and his neighbors in Wilton Leys—immigrants callously derided or apathetically dismissed as outsiders—had come a long way toward something like assimilation. This could jeopardize everything.

He took a half dozen tentative steps in the direction of home before suddenly turning around and darting back to the rug. He picked up the delicate white disk and slipped it in the front pouch of his hoodie. His pulse pounding in his head, he slowly backed away. He wheeled around and broke into a run across the glass and broken concrete block. Reaching the torn bit of fence that marked the other side of the shortcut, he dived through it and sprinted away.

As he sped toward home, May Morning dawn edging the tops of towers and trees, Rabi heard the ethereal sound of a distant choir cantillating in a language he did not know. The *Hymnus Eucharisticus* from atop medieval Magdalen Tower. Casting a worried backward glance, he saw the silhouettes of spires, domes and finialed rooftops taking shape against the light of a new day.

Friday, May 5

2

The bus slammed to an abrupt halt, yanking Myles Dunn from a groggy doze. Passengers lurched forward. Several small bags toppled from overhead storage, their contents spilling into the aisle. The relative quiet became suddenly troubled with moans and anxious chatter. Myles glanced at his watch and realized that he'd been out for twenty minutes. The steady drizzle that had accompanied him since landing at Heathrow had stopped, giving way to broken clouds that he could make out above the steepled skyline of Oxford. They were on St. Clement's Street, just on the townie side of Magdalen Bridge. Gloucester Green, the bus station, was only a mile or so beyond that, but the bus and every other vehicle in front of it weren't going anywhere.

The driver picked up the bus microphone and with a harried voice—interrupted by the wail of a police siren heading into town from Iffley Road—informed the passengers that there was a "police action" on Oxford's High Street and the bus would be sitting where it was "indefinitely." This sparked a grumbling wave of concern and complaint through the bus, erupting into an outcry from a number of passengers, mostly along the lines of "What are we expected to do?" or "Now look what they've done." The driver appeared to be making a call on an official phone.

It was no secret why they were being stopped. Myles glanced again at the *Guardian* he'd picked up at Heathrow. No fewer than four stories on the front page had to do with the murder of young Peter Toohey, the headlines etched with fear-driven judgment: "Oxford Lad Martyred," "Who Beheaded the Altar Boy?" "Is Religion to Blame?" The articles detailed how the twelve-year-old boy was reported by his parents as missing when he failed to return home after a Sunday afternoon football game at an East Oxford municipal playing field. That would have been the eve of May Morning, a centuries-old all-night party for Oxford University students. Sometime early that Monday, a demolition crew at the Wilton Leys building site discovered the decapitated body and called the Thames Valley Police. There were rumors that a video of the boy's execution was on the deep web, and Thames Valley Police were said to be in consultation with Scotland Yard's anti-terrorism unit.

The articles went on to report that numerous Muslim clerical leaders had expressed their outrage over the slaying. Conrad Newell, a spokesman for the right-wing patriotic group, Britain Now, shouted at a press conference in Oxford that the entire deed—the beheading of a twelve-year-old altar boy and the gross disrespect shown to his body—was meant to be an Islamist slap in the face of English Christianity. Newell's crowd were advancing a conspiracy theory about a series of cuts on the victim's forehead, calling them "Muslim marks of terror."

Myles leaned back in the seat and closed his eyes, trying half-heartedly to quell the misgiving and foreboding that had plagued him since leaving for this hastily-planned and possibly ill-advised trip—and regretting its miserable timing. He'd heard something about the Toohey killing back in Colorado, so far had the harrowing news traveled. But if he had any idea how tense things were now in Oxford, he just may have stayed home in Highlands.

"Ladies and gentlemen," came the driver's voice over the microphone, "you can either stay put or I'm authorized to let you out here. However, it is strongly advised that you wait in the bus for your own safety. If you have luggage in the undercarriage, I'm required by law to take it to Gloucester Green. You can retrieve it there later." More groans and worried expressions. A few passengers stood and glanced at one another.

Myles tucked the folded newspaper into his backpack, grabbed his duffel from the overhead and made his way up the aisle. Other passengers watched him with a mixture of hesitancy and disdain, as if his choice to exit not only flew in the face of good sense but somehow contributed to their inconvenience.

As Myles reached the front, the driver looked at him incredulously. "You sure?" he asked, eyebrows raised as he gestured up ahead toward the bridge and beyond.

Myles nodded, and the driver shook his head before reaching for the lever that opened the door.

Stepping off the bus and into the cool humidity brought an assault to his senses. As far as Myles could see in every direction, the streets were packed with vehicles and people. Around him a crowd was staring across Magdalen Bridge in the direction of High Street, better known as the High. They looked distraught and panicked, hands to their faces. Securing his duffel bag over his shoulder, he began maneuvering through the stopped cars ahead of the bus. As soon as he could, he turned toward the bridge, his only way into the city from where he was. As he got closer, he could see that police cars blocked vehicle traffic from crossing, though pedestrians were being allowed to pass. The sheer volume made movement slow. He'd seen the city crowded with tourists and students, but never anything like this. Even the Cherwell's steep banks were scattered with people. As Myles approached the surreal scene, most of the faces, especially of those headed away from town, were lined with concern and fear—and a few with blood.

Myles knew from long experience exactly how to get to Ignatius College, but not under these circumstances. An otherwise reliable access to Christ Church Meadow and the colleges off the main south road to Oxford had police barriers in front of it. Crowd control, evidently, or requests from colleges to limit access to visitors. Or protestors.

It took him twenty minutes to cover the two hundred yards from the bus to the town side of the bridge. The Oxford he'd known was, like any university town, a mashup of all things lively and colorful and predictably weird, but with a centuries-old undercurrent of the staid and solid. Still, he'd never seen or heard anything like this kind of upheaval here. It felt more like Kabul or Basra—or for that matter any American city about two years back, post-George Floyd. The further he inched along, the louder it became.

With concerted effort and creative pushing, Myles pressed into the crowd on the south side of the High. He searched for any left turn he could make to the south and a less urban, less obstructed route. Though he didn't mind crowds and had attended more than his share of demonstrations for righteous political causes, he hadn't traveled 5,000 miles for this. His internal resistance to this trip was strong enough without needing further hindrance.

Two blocks ahead a particularly dense and obstreperous crowd occupied the middle of the street. Even from this distance, noise and chaos reigned: police sirens blared ahead; someone with a bullhorn led part of the crowd in an indecipherable chant; signs were hoisted up and down amid the shouting crowd. What was happening in the street ahead was reflected in the faces of pedestrians and bystanders. Some were visibly disturbed to be caught in the mayhem, while many others, on both sides of the street, formed a more dedicated, purposeful presence. Protest and counter-protest. Individuals were being swept along in the current, their freedom nullified in the tide of humanity that moved according to its own will.

As he pushed forward, Myles felt something or someone yanking at his duffel bag. He spun around with an arm raised in aggressive self-defense before realizing that an elderly man, stumbling under the force of the crowd, had grabbed at the nearest object—the duffel—to break his fall. Others were tripping over and stepping on the fallen man, whose cries of distress went unheard over the din. Before Myles could regain his composure or reach down and help him up, he himself was swept away.

Half an hour's jostling and dodging had brought him just a quarter mile. Normally the schizophrenic thick of Oxford's majestic medieval towers and its garish embrace of modern commerce, today the High was the center of a volatile standoff. Several dozen people circled the stone steps leading up to a corner building on the north side of the street. He could also make out some of the signs:

MUSLIM MURDERERS GO HOME!

IS-LAM IS WRONG

PROTECT THE INNOCENT, KILL THE TERRORISTS

VENGEANCE FOR PETER

Myles recalled the last words from one of the newspaper articles: "Mr. Newell vowed a Christian revenge for the Toohey killing."

Facing the angry protestors was a much smaller group of about two dozen people, including a few women in hijabs. They stood silently and with little facial expression, hand-in-hand, in front of a doorway beneath a banner that read, "Muslim Educational Centre of Oxford." On either side of them along the sidewalk were supporters holding a very different set of signs:

BLACK & BROWN LIVES MATTER
WE ARE YOUR NEIGHBORS
WE ARE INNOCENT

A phalanx of police stood with hands extended to keep the protestors at bay. Someone threw a bottle toward the people on the steps, and it shattered against a wall to the right. Again, Myles pushed along the sidewalk crowd, his bearings constantly on the left for a turn towards the south and sanity. He used his sleeve to wipe the sweat from his forehead. Meanwhile, whoever had the bullhorn worked up a new chant of "Wogs go home!" The afternoon was heating up in more ways than one. Myles felt increasingly keen to extricate himself.

Finally, he reached Magpie Lane, a narrow, cobble-edged passage meant more typically for cycling students from Oriel and dons walking at a contemplative pace. Neither were to be seen today. He rushed into the open space. He found himself hurrying from the noise and violence, passing Oriel and Merton until he came upon a connecting path that ran along the northern bounds of Christ Church Meadow. That would take him to St. Aldate's Street and, a few blocks south, to Ignatius College.

It was as if he'd been flung out of a Jackson Pollock maelstrom and landed in a Monet garden. The familiar and nostalgic sights, sounds and scents of this bucolic sanctuary washed over him. Finally free to walk at a brisk pace, he breathed deeply, imbibing the cool fragrance of moist grass overlain with buttery daffodils and parti-colored wildflowers. It was surreal. As far as the eye could see spread a lush panorama of blossoming fruit trees, majestic oaks, elms and willows, rows of poplars and manicured shrubs, all dotted with flitting, chirping birds.

Amidst the momentary synesthetic immersion in an idyllic Oxford he once called home, Myles felt the dread and doubt that dogged this entire journey. He replayed Jeremy's email in his head:

Myles, I think I found it—the chalice. You remember the Cuxham legend. I know this all sounds barmy, but I have an idea where it is…or where it might be. Approximately. I also think others know what I know or are close to knowing, and I fear I'm in danger for it. Please don't think me mad, but if you do get news of my death in the coming weeks, contact Eva Bashir here at college. She'll know enough. Always your friend, JS, sj.

Quite possibly the rantings of an old friend on the edge. Jeremy had made no direct request, but how could Myles ignore the threat of danger hanging over a man who had been a brother to him in his previous life? His own pain and awkwardness at returning to this place shouldn't matter.

From a long-hidden corner of his memory he heard the oft-yelled exhortation from basic training, "Time to man up!" and picked up his pace toward Ignatius College.

11

3

Myles found the room on his own. He knew where it was, a some-time guestroom for visiting retreat masters to the Jesuit community at Ignatius College. He figured he'd been assigned the room because it was in a sort of no-man's land in the college, between standard guestrooms and the cloister of the Jesuit community. He tossed his duffel and jacket on the bed and took in the detail of the room. Flanking the narrow bed with a sagging mattress was a careworn, mustard-colored armchair against one wall and a cruci-fix—the room's only "artwork"—on the other. The air itself seemed purposed for the space—a remnant brew of cigarette smoke, mothballs, and perspiration. Painful as it was for Myles to admit, he recognized an undeniable familiarity with the shabby dignity of it all. "Priestliness," he said aloud.

He walked to a set of three windows that looked out onto the main quad and opened the middle one, grateful for the momentary breeze. It was then that he noticed the box on the desk. About the size of a briefcase, it looked familiar but had been long forgotten. Someone had printed in block letters "Rev'd Myles Dunn, SJ" on the top of the box. At some judicious point between then and now, another hand had obliterated the "Rev'd" and "SJ" with a Sharpie. Likely Felix Ilbert at work, the Jesuit Master of Ignatius College. Even when Myles was in the Society of Jesus, Ilbert made no secret of how little he regarded the American. Then it was out of envy; now it was likely out of malice. The slashed "Rev'd" Myles couldn't care less about; he'd never been comfortable with priestly titles and Roman collars that set elegant wedges between clergy and the people they were meant to serve. But the "SJ" for the "Society of Jesus" had been harder to let go of: sixteen years of life and learning, much of it in religious formation and seminaries; friendships with men like Jeremy formed in so many places, and that sense of being connected with thousands of other Jesuits across the globe. And not only that, but also back in time, across four and a half centuries.

Just as he began to feel the riptide tug of memory, Myles sternly pulled himself back to the present and the reasons he'd returned to this place.

He pulled open the cardboard flaps. The brittle, two-year-old tape broke easily. Inside were two books, an old Oxford sweatshirt and a bulging Manila folder bound with two rubber bands. Myles lifted the books out. One was a volume of Sanskrit stories an old tutor had given him when Myles studied Hindu several years back. He tossed it back into the box and picked up the second book. It was a compact leatherbound copy of *The Spiritual Exercises* of St. Ignatius of Loyola, a sort of spiritual training manual for any seeker of God, but especially for Jesuits. They were to know the four weeks of exercises inside and out. As he paged through the worn text, he glanced at familiar biblical references, prayers, and meditations—all prelude to the four weeks of exercises themselves. Famous among those were meditations on different callings in life, a general examination of conscience, and the meditation on the "Two Standards." Ignatius, a former soldier, wanted his spiritual fighting men to choose which standard, which military banner they would fight under—God's or Satan's. Darkness or light: everyone must choose. For Myles years ago, it was an easy choice. Perhaps too easy, as his decision to live under the banner of Christ seemed to him now naive.

He closed the book and tossed it back into the box along with the remembrance of all that faith in God, organized religion, and himself. As he did so, his eye caught the corner of a small picture frame, resting between the bursting Manila folder that held a copy of his doctoral dissertation and the college sweatshirt. He'd forgotten he put it in there two years ago and took a deep breath before pulling the frame out of the box. It showed the very quad outside his window now centered with three bright faces, all laughing in front of the fountain. On the left and pointing to the other two people in the photo was Jeremy, fastidiously groomed as always, but here sporting a rainbow tee shirt, a droll grin, and a goatee. Myles had long regarded Jeremy's out-and-celibate status in his Jesuit community as brave and deserving of great respect. Seated on the edge of the fountain, orange and red leaves around their feet, were Myles and a young woman, both smiling broadly. Myles had his arm around her, and their heads were tilted toward each other so that they touched. She wore a mid-length dress and a leather jacket and had sandy-colored hair pulled up into a loose bun. His sister, Jeremy used to tease, got all the looks in the family, though the photo showed their resemblance.

Myles closed his eyes and allowed himself to be pulled into the photo—and memory. Pippa had mischievous green eyes and an infectious exuberance. Plucky and impudent and game for anything, she was irresistible to the restless adrenaline-seeker in Myles. For all this, what most drew him to her was the expression on her face and in those eyes when she wasn't being playful or laughing or even smiling, but merely listening or reading or taking in a Cotswold sunset. She was possessed of a quiet, calm self-assurance that he wanted to be part of, an internal compass that until knowing her he didn't even realize he'd lost. He could feel her arms around his torso, holding him from behind, their bodies one as they leaned together into the sharp turn. It felt right. Until suddenly he heard the truck's tires screeching along the slick pavement and felt himself losing control of the motorcycle. "Hang on!" he'd yelled, but in that moment he felt her arms slip loose and heard her cry out.

A shout and an eruption of voices from the quad outside broke his inner fall and startled his eyes open. He had stopped breathing. Still holding the photo, he walked to the open window. Looking down at the college fountain three stories below, he saw a group of students huddled around a young woman who lay face-up on the cobbled ground. He hadn't noticed them earlier, and based on the placards and signs strewn around them he surmised that they'd come from the protests. One of them shouted, "She fainted!" Just then he noticed that the black-suited college porter who had admitted him and given him a key to his room darted from the lodge and knelt beside the young woman, feeling her pulse before helping her sit up and sip from a water bottle one of the students handed him. He said something to the same student, who nodded and ran in the direction of the administration building. The porter appeared to have the situation calmly in hand.

Myles took in a deep breath of the rain-washed air and tried to exhale the memory of moments before. Gazing across the western gables offered a view of Tom Tower, the iconic entrance to Christ Church College—and beyond it a receding forest of spires, finials and Radcliffe Camera's anomalous Italianate dome rising next to the Bodleian Library. The mingled scent of lilac and rose came from somewhere just beyond the quad. Low clouds sailed eastward as a swarming band of swallows swooped and dove somewhere over St. Aldate's. It hardly seemed an hour ago that he was caught in a mob on High Street.

He returned the photo to the box and set it on the floor beside the desk. He needed to wash the dust of the day off his travel-weary face. At the small sink, he switched on the light above the mirror and leaned his hands on either side of the old white basin. To his fresh dismay, what looked back from the mirror was not the smiling and enthusiastic young priest in that photograph with the Strands, but a jaded and disoriented traveler marked with his share of time's impious abrasion accrued along life's more circuitous roads. His full head of dark brown hair hadn't seen a barber in weeks and was flecked with unruly streaks of gray. Lines had begun to crease the margins of his eyes and mouth. Probably the effect of this college's notoriously poor lighting, he kidded himself. He ran his index finger along the three-inch white scar beneath his right jawline and exhaled slowly, reminded of a line from his favorite Eliot poem. *To be redeemed from fire by fire.*

He splashed water on his face and braced himself for his impending reunion with Jeremy, his one-time fellow Jesuit and best mate. He hastily put his clothes in the built-in wardrobe and emptied out his few toiletries at the sink, with the exception of the Zoloft prescription he'd filled before leaving Colorado. Reaching into his pocket for his phone to see if Jeremy had yet replied to his text, he realized that he must have left it at the porter's lodge. He'd set it down while retrieving his passport, which the politely efficient porter had required him to produce "in keeping with our policy, Dr. Dunn."

Myles retraced his steps from the musty guestroom to the porter's lodge. A narrow set of stairs led him back to the main wing of the Jesuit Residence, from which he traversed a long hall leading to the broad, elaborately carved central staircase. He took the stairs two at a time, not pausing to admire the familiar fluted pattern of the tall leaded windows on the landing, nor to dwell on the wave of nostalgia that flooded his senses. That wave was harder to ignore upon pushing through the enormous oak double-doors that led to the Great Hall. The soaring collegiate space drew the eye upward to the coffered ceiling and echoed with an indifferent formality as students and dons rushed across the scuffed parquet floor to lecture halls and tutorials. A massive portrait of St. Ignatius of Loyola added to the indifference, showing him kneeling and looking not at the people passing below but to some mysterious light from above.

Past the entrance and into the quad, Myles saw that the young woman who had fallen was now seated on a bench beneath the sheltering branches of the college's signature gnarled oak, rumored to be the oldest tree in Oxford. She was being attended to by the college nurse.

As Myles approached the entrance, the porter emerged from the lodge, his arm extended, holding Myles' phone in his open palm. "Thank you, Mr. Brooke," said Myles, reading the nametag and noticing that his title was "Sub-bursar" rather than porter. Probably a decade younger than Myles, he appeared to be in his mid-30s with perfect posture and intense features bordering on peevish: a narrow, pinched nose, cheerful blue eyes and a traditional schoolboy haircut of sandy hair that belied his age, all brought together in a look of reliability and helpfulness.

"Careful of that one!" boomed a slightly raspy voice from behind. A grinning old man dressed in a graying black clerical suit and Roman collar stepped out of the entrance to the Great Hall and approached the lodge.

"Tock!" Myles exclaimed, turning to meet the open arms of his old mentor, Nigel "Tock" Forrestal, SJ.

Without hesitation they embraced warmly, then parted and gave each other quick, appraising looks. Tock was eighty-four, but the hands that gripped Myles' arms were strong. A beaked nose and thick white hair swept back from his forehead gave him the look of an ancient eagle, wise from long soaring and searching, but bearing plenty of scars, as well.

As they stood, Tock exchanged greetings with several passing students.

"You haven't lost it, Tock."

"I'm glad you think so, but believe me, son, at my age you lose a little bit of something every day. But as Wordsworth put it, 'for such loss, I would believe, abundant recompense.'"

They stepped more deeply into the quad and its early May gardens, the sounds from the lodge and the shouting movements of students receding.

"Tock, I...About your emails. I wanted to reply. I just—"

The old man shook his head. "I'm just happy you're alive and well. Until you replied to Jeremy's recent note, no one had heard anything."

"I can try to explain…"

"Oh, you will," he said with a stern expression and twinkling eyes. "But for the moment, other things take precedence."

Myles figured the old man meant Jeremy, but it was hard to tell in Oxford's current upheaval.

"What's going on, Tock—I mean, with the city and this horrific murder?" He lowered his voice. "And with Jeremy. This is all crazy." Myles ran through a description of the near riot on the High and the student hitting the ground near the fountain.

Tock bit his lower lip and looked down at the gravel path.

"I wish I could tell you, Myles. Part of this unfolding tragedy, of course, is how little we know—about young Peter's murder and the fear that's gripped much of Oxford. I'm sorry you had to land here in the midst of all this. And for reasons unknown we've had a visitor from the Vatican these past few weeks to boot, a furtive and strange man called Moretti. All of which has tended to put everyone on edge." He shook his head. "As for Jeremy, that's a longer story. I've been concerned about him for months, his increasingly clandestine comings and goings, his obsession with this Hopkins manuscript." Tock looked up at Myles with a sorrowful expression. "And I've told the Master as much."

"That sounds like it's going nowhere, assuming Ilbert is still Master." Myles had long been impatient with the Oxbridge hierarchies of masters and minions, but Ilbert belonged in a category of his own.

Tock gave Myles a sidelong look. "It's not, and I'm afraid he is."

"Tock, you look like you're heading out for a walk and I'd really like to see Jeremy now. He's here, I presume."

"Well, he both is and isn't. Jeremy had some sort of panic attack in the library this morning and the college nurse, who's been exceedingly busy today, gave him something to calm him down. Let him rest for a while. Meanwhile, why don't you join me. The Isis and the Meadow may be one's only refuge from the tumult."

"I'd like that, Tock, but I need to check in with Cora, and I want to see Jeremy as soon as possible, even just to look in on him."

"Of course. Anyway, you must be exhausted. What time is it in Colorado? And where have they put you?"

"The old retreat master's room." In response to Tock's grimace, Myles continued, "It's fine. I don't mind being off the beaten path."

"'Twas ever thus," Tock said through a grin. "But Myles, Jeremy will be a challenge. He's damn lucky to have you as a friend. But I know, too, that it can't be easy for you to come back here after... everything that happened." He paused and gave Myles a look he'd often seen in spiritual direction sessions with the old man. "We'll have that talk soon. For the moment, the focus is Jeremy." The old man patted Myles on the shoulder and walked through the familiar Tudor archway.

4

Monsignor Giacomo Moretti sat by his window, tapping cigarette ashes into one of the few remaining ashtrays left in Ignatius College. Charcoal scarrings had nearly blotted out the college coat of arms etched into the heart of the dark glass tray. This was his fourth cigarette in fifteen minutes, though they weren't *his* cigarettes, strictly speaking. He hadn't puffed a single one, just lit them and let the tobacco burn while watching that bewitching smoke curl and uncurl out the open window as if in search of someone worthy of its spell.

Since his heart attack ten months previous, Moretti had been ordered off smoking, and he complied, not merely because he shared a physician with the Holy Father, but because failing hearts and early deaths were hallmarks of the family Moretti. When he turned fifty-nine, the Vatican Undersecretary for Relations with States thought he'd broken the curse. But one month later genetics, too many dinners at La Pergola and unfiltered *Nazionali*s had finally caught up with him. Sitting here now, contemplating the burnt ashes that teetered on the end of his cigarette, he allowed himself the thought that it was a shame that a virile man long accused of breaking the hearts of womankind for becoming a priest should succumb to the ravages of time.

He tapped again and continued to look beyond the open curtains to the American one floor up and across the quad, staring out his window. Moretti shook his head. The man's arrival was both unanticipated and inconvenient. From what he was able to elicit from the Master—and it took embarrassingly little effort to pry information from him—Dr. Myles Dunn was an intimate of Father Strand and here "to assist him," whatever that could mean. Dunn had evidently achieved great things at Oxford as a rising scholar of comparative religion and was *uno favorito* in the Jesuit Order, but in an act of "singular failure" (the Master's words), he

19

had left Oxford and the Jesuits precipitously. Moretti had known hundreds of priests who rose and fell, saints and sinners. This one was of little interest to him save for the fact that he was here now. What kind of assistance would he be rendering Strand? Might it have anything to do with the chalice? That concerned Moretti, who wanted Strand left alone completely: undistracted, unimpeded.

The Italian looked at his watch. 3:45 p.m. In fifteen minutes, he'd receive his daily phone call from the Vatican. He'd add one more item to the agenda: background on Myles Dunn and learning far more than that *buffone* Ilbert could tell him.

5

Myles grabbed some dinner leftovers from the college kitchen and nearly fell asleep in the abandoned dining hall. But he pushed against the jet lag, thinking of Jeremy and his need to see him before calling it one long day. A part of Myles didn't want to do this, didn't want to face whatever demons his friend had been entertaining. Myles had enough demons of his own rumbling through his psyche. He'd come a long way, though, and if anything motivated a journey he couldn't afford to a place he wanted to forget, it had to be his friendship with Jeremy.

The Jesuit Wing was on the top floor of Campion House, the oldest part of the college and named for the Reformation martyr, Edmund Campion, SJ. Myles had lived there for four years, so he knew his way down the dark corridor. It was just after 9:00. All the doors of Jesuit rooms on either side of the hall were shut. A few showed thin lines of light at the threshold but most were dark and silent. As he approached the last door on the left, he heard the low sounds of a piano piece. More oddly, he caught the scent of fresh wood and varnish.

Myles knocked three times and waited before the door opened a few inches and a voice said, "Who's there?"

Myles could make out the left eye and cheek of his friend but was obviously himself invisible to Jeremy.

"Amazon delivery. Who the hell do you think it is?"

"Oh, Myles! You've come."

Jeremy slid the chain lock and opened the door wide revealing a person who looked faintly like Jeremy Strand. This version of him, however, seemed a pale contrast to the smiling man in the photograph. Jeremy had lost weight, far more than he needed. He was dressed in stained blue jeans and a gray long-sleeve tee. His hair was long and stringy and the goatee he had always favored had morphed into an uneven, untended beard.

"Myles, please—come in! I told Tock you were coming, and he said he'd make the arrangements. I seem to have lost track of the days…I had…this morning, something of a…"

"Yeah, Tock told me. And look, I don't want to keep you up long. I just wanted to duck in and say hi and see when we can get together."

"Right. Well, then, have a seat." Jeremy pushed a pile of folders and papers off a chair and gestured Myles to it. Without a word he turned the music down, then walked to the sink in the corner of the room, grabbing a water glass out of the cabinet.

"Did you get my text earlier?"

"I turned off my phone this afternoon and never turned it back on."

While Jeremy was at the sink, Myles scanned the wreck of a room. There had to be more clothes on the bed and floor than in the green wardrobe beside a cold fireplace. Papers and journals were scattered on desk and floor, the wastebasket overrun with detritus. Books, however—and there were dozens—were piled respectfully on the floor, forming a small literary Stonehenge minus the cap-stones. Myles noticed at the top of one of the book-piles a title, *Secret Societies and Mysterious Enclaves of Great Britain*. Supporting it was a thicker volume, a journal called *Midlands Archaeology*. Jeremy's desk was the epicenter of the disaster: more papers in disarray, marked with wild pen-strokes and teacup rings; an open laptop, hemmed with a dozen scribbled-on post-its, pulsed with a weak light; and a tall green bottle, doubtlessly the source of whatever liquid Jeremy had in the glass perched on the edge of the desk.

"I like what you've done to the place."

"Oh, pay it no mind, Myles," Jeremy said, nodding about the room as navigated back to his desk chair. "Here, this'll take some of the edge off your jet lag. When did you arrive?"

"Early afternoon, just in time for the riot. What happened this morning?"

"The protest, you mean?"

"No—what happened to *you*? Tock seemed concerned and—"

"Oh, I'm fine. Everyone seems to be fussing over me, afraid I'm about to step off some abysmal edge. I had a…moment. I've been having a few moments of late." He trailed off, looking as tired as

22

Myles felt. "But I'm glad you're here. It's been awhile," he smiled, sipping at his scotch.

Myles decided not to argue the point and shifted direction.

"God, Jeremy, where to begin? I want to know what you mean by having a 'moment,' but do we need to clear the air first? I mean, two years of a ghosted friendship, my leaving the priesthood, your looking like, well—" Myles gestured toward Jeremy as if his worries should be obvious. "And Pippa..."

Jeremy stared at his glass. "I think about her all the time, as I'm sure you do." His voice sounded weary, but he took a deep breath and waved his free hand with something between resignation and resolve. "I agree there's loads to discuss, and I'm grateful that you came all this way. Truly. But can we save all of that for another day?" Then, more urgently. "How long are you here?"

Myles was beginning to regret the absurdly expensive open-ended ticket he'd purchased a few days before.

"At least a week, maybe more. I didn't know how I'd find you... or what you needed."

"What I need...God, Myles, I don't know myself, except some confident bearing on sanity again. I've been so fixed on this manuscript and the chalice. I know it's more than it seems and yet I'm lost in its blind turns and dead ends." He looked up at Myles, tears welling in his eyes. "I need someone with your mind, Myles, someone who knows how to cut through the non-essentials, how to take things apart and get to what matters. That's why I reached out, that's why I'm so incredibly glad that you're here."

Quiet passed between the two friends as Myles sipped from his glass and winced. "Okay. Let's start tonight—but with the short version. I know I'll be fresher tomorrow and then you can have the full brunt of my cynicism. Now, you mentioned a manuscript and a chalice..."

Jeremy sat there for a moment and stared at Myles silently, calculating his next words.

"All right, old boy, here goes. In my email I mentioned the Cuxham Chalice."

"We're talking about the Oxford legend, right, the one that draws the occasional treasure hunter to the dreaming spires?"

"True, Cuxham is an old Oxford canard, but you have to ask

yourself, why? Why one more legend in this excessively legendary place? Haven't we enough? Who's to say?" Jeremy's eyes flashed with a strange brightness. "I'll come back to the chalice in a moment. The manuscript is even more intriguing." Jeremy put his drink down on the desk loudly and shifted in his seat to get closer to Myles. "It's in the Hopkins miscellanea—"

"—you mean Gerard Manley Hopkins."

"Right. I've been studying it for nearly four months. Actually, credit where due. Eva found it." Myles raised a querulous eyebrow. "Eva Bashir, our librarian. New since your time, and thank God she's here. The college is hosting a Hopkins anniversary exhibition next year, and Eva was going through his miscellanea to recheck cataloging and all that. She didn't know what to make of it—I mean, who would?—and showed it to me. It's a scrap of a thing, misread by anyone who's handled it over the past century plus. I mean, it's a mess. I'll show it to you tomorrow. It's incomplete, awkward, strange poetry, even for Hopkins. But it's not what it appears to be, Myles." Jeremy was wide-eyed and rubbing his hands.

"And what does it appear to be?"

Jeremy spent the next fifteen minutes going on about past archivists at Ignatius College, the assumption that the Hopkins fragment was a sketch of a poem about the Holy Grail and contemporary Oxford theologians on nineteenth-century Eucharistic piety. Myles did everything he could to keep jet lag from dropping him into a coma.

"Now," his friend continued, "the link between the Cuxham Chalice as a legend and this Hopkins poetic fragment is…well, I think that's what the poem's about." He waited a beat for Myles to register the outlandish statement. "And not only that, Myles…" Again that calculating silence. "My contention is that Hopkins isn't simply writing about the chalice but is writing about having actually *seen* it—in the flesh. Not a legend, Myles, but an actual medieval artifact, there, with Gerard Manley Hopkins! Isn't that fantastic?"

It was Myles' turn to be silent, but it was an act of will. His impulse was to dismiss the whole thing out of hand and yank his friend back to *terra firma*. He was beginning to see how Tock's concerns about Jeremy were sadly well-placed.

"Um, Jeremy, this is fascinating, as you say." Myles did his best to sound buoyant. "Have you tried your ideas out here in college or around the university?"

Jeremy leaned in closer.

"What you're really asking, Myles, is if anyone who's sane has given my hypothesis the time of day." Jeremy's grin struck Myles as almost manic. "I know, this sounds potty and I'm taking huge leaps with it all. But again, this blasted poem, like so much of Hopkins, is anything but straightforward. Yes—to answer your question, I have talked with others about the fragment. That was precisely the point of a literature seminar I gave this past February—across the street at Pembroke. The seminar was an occasion to float a theory: the eminent Jesuit poet Gerard Manley Hopkins, a likely last poem and a mythical chalice from the Middle Ages."

Jeremy laughed nervously while Myles remained quiet, listening attentively and with mounting alarm.

"The seminar was poorly attended—I blame it on February—but there were a few locals there who seemed passingly interested in what I was saying. And afterwards, two or three devotees—of Hopkins or the chalice, I guess, certainly not me—lingered with questions. But no one in that group has stuck out for me as anyone who would be all that interested, or interested to the point of..." He trailed off, his voice diminishing with anxiety.

"Jeremy, I have no idea whether this has anything to do with you, the manuscript, the chalice, but who's the Vatican visitor Tock mentioned today?"

Jeremy looked away from Myles and seemed to weigh his response carefully.

"Oh, right. Moretti. He's from the Secretariat of State, a minor bureaucrat, here on a short sabbatical. He's an odd duck, if that isn't a case of the pot calling the kettle. More of a mild nuisance than anything, really. He has an antiquarian interest."

"I ask because you're obviously worried about someone. Any idea who broke into your room?"

Jeremy stared. "How did you know?"

"You don't have to be Inspector Morse to smell varnish and fresh oak. And the deadbolt and chain lock are new. I figure you had them installed as an extra security measure."

Reaching down to retrieve his glass, Jeremy gulped the scotch and coughed sharply into his sleeve. "Someone's more interested in all of this than I'd like. Whenever I step out of college to go to a library or a pub, I swear I'm being watched, followed." He punched his right thigh and in a lower voice said, "I think someone else might have the sonnet."

"Someone stole the fragment?"

"Heavens, no! Not the original, at least. Had that been the case, you'd have found me at my grave, Myles, rightly put there by one Dr. Eva Bashir. No, she was furious enough when she learned I'd even had the manuscript in my room, so I returned it to the archives at once."

"Well, Jeremy, if you put the poem back quickly, why do you think someone else has it? I don't get it." Myles relented and took another swig of the third-rate scotch.

"Because I'd placed it in this book on Hopkins' poetic techniques"—Jeremy lifted a chunky tome from the pile closest to his desk—"and one day two weeks ago, I found it here on my desk."

Myles nodded, deciding to accept what his friend was saying rather than explore the possibilities of forgetfulness and paranoia. "So, you're thinking someone broke in and then...what? Copied the poem or took a photo and then purposely placed it where it hadn't been in order to...?"

"Who knows why the sonnet was moved. I just know I didn't do it." Jeremy's voice trailed off to a whisper. He sighed and shook his head. "I'm not going mad, truly. I need you to trust me. I have a hunch here about the fragment and its contents. Of course, I can't defend every turn of my thesis, but you know what I mean about *sensing* something before it's as plain as a fact."

Jeremy looked at his friend with pleading eyes. "Would you do me a favor and look at the sonnet? Study it for a little while and then tell me that there's nothing there." He hesitated a moment. "If you don't see anything to it, any possibility that it might be more than simply an unfinished sonnet, I'll leave the entire thing aside and become the obedient, docile religious I'm celebrated for." He smiled painfully, and Myles could see a "last hope" look in his eyes.

"Of course I will, Jeremy. Just tell me the time and place."

"Excellent. Actually, I've already arranged for it. Tomorrow morning, ten o'clock sharp in the D'Arcy Archives Room, ground floor of the library. Eva has agreed to spend part of her Saturday running us through the paces of the poem."

"Sounds like a plan," Myles said with a forced trace of enthusiasm. Both men stood up.

Jeremy leaned forward and embraced Myles, the same gesture Tock had used earlier that day. But where the old man's hug was an unself-conscious act of deep friendship, Jeremy's grip felt like that of a drowning man.

6

The sharp blare of a truck horn pierced Eva's troubled trance and made her jump. Now noticing that the traffic light had turned green, she glanced in the rearview mirror and saw the grill of a truck and its driver shaking a fist at her. Her blood pressure, already high from replaying yesterday's argument with Sam, now spiked even higher. Everyone was on edge and lashing out. There seemed no refuge. *Even in my own home*, she thought. She shook her head and let out a long sigh, realizing only now that she had been holding her breath.

A block later a second glance in the mirror revealed that the truck had mercifully turned, but she noticed that her eyes and creased forehead were involuntarily stuck in a worried scowl. *Deep breath*, she told herself in an attempt to defuse the tension coursing through her body as she made her way from work as Ignatius College Librarian to her home in Summertown, north of Oxford. Normally she left work promptly at 4:30 in order to make dinner and spend the evening with her sixteen-year-old daughter. But she'd had to catch up on paperwork, the protests had diverted traffic, and now she was running more than two hours late. Sam's school had let out early the past few days because of the protests, and Eva had wanted to be home with her daughter, not three hours late. Especially today, after their argument last night. She cursed under her breath.

"Don't you trust me?!" was the question Sam kept hurling at her mother last night. But of course, trust wasn't the issue. Or was it?

"You're being ridiculous!" Sam insisted. "I know what I'm doing. I'm not talking about marrying the guy; we're just hanging out. And I like him."

"I know that, Sam. My concern is how little you have in common with him."

"Oh my God! When are you going to admit, Mum, that you're prejudiced?"

"Sam, that's absurd. I'm—"

"Anti-religion. Especially anti-Islam." Sam glared accusingly at her mother. "You're anti-Islam. You're against me seeing Rabi just because I met him at the Muslim Education Center and he's a practicing Muslim."

"Sam, you're reading into it. My concern is for your education. You're preparing for A-levels, and Rabi is a half-hearted student who works in a pub. Where's the future in that? For that matter, where's the present?"

"You're the one who's reading into things! I'm dating a boy you've met twice, and you want to control my social life. And don't you think it's more than a little hypocritical of you to try to stop me from seeing Rabi because he's Muslim? I mean, look who you married!"

That one had hurt, and not because Sam was wrong.

"That's none of your business!" Eva heard herself blurt out.

She immediately regretted her outburst and said so, but Sam was already storming to her room in tears. Of course, her daughter had felt attacked. Only later, lying awake all night and sitting at her desk this morning, had Eva realized that Sam felt the same thing from her mother that Muslims in Oxford were feeling acutely in recent days: intolerance, suspicion and existential threat. Eva shook her head in chagrin at her outburst and her failure to strike a balance in her mothering. She had always prided herself on granting her daughter the kind of freedom she herself had never known as a girl or as a young wife. Now she was finding it wasn't so easy.

She glanced again in the rearview mirror and rubbed her hand over her forehead trying to smooth out the worry lines.

Keen to avoid knotted traffic caused by the protests still going strong into the evening, Eva took a roundabout route well to the southwest of Oxford, then north on the A34 and east on the A40, and finally south again through Summertown. She was dismayed at how long the drive had taken but nevertheless relieved to have averted the angry crowds. After turning off Banbury Road she began rehearsing again the delicate but important conversation with Sam. She planned to take a conciliatory approach today.

CRACK! Eva slammed on the brakes. Something had hit the front passenger window, which had completely splintered. Her heart rate already soaring, Eva instinctively put the car in Park. Before she could decide what was happening and what to do next, her car was surrounded. Four or five young men—all white—began pounding the hood, sides and trunk of her car with their fists. Three others holding beer cans in one hand and rocks in another cheered them on.

After a thrashing that seemed to last several minutes, they all joined in rocking the car back and forth. Eva was sure it would tip over. She felt paralyzed in fear. She didn't dare try to appeal to them. Nor did she dare try to drive away for fear of killing someone or of inciting them even further.

One of them put his face an inch away from the driver's window and screamed: "Get the bloody hell out of England!" The entire group shouted a stream of insults at the tops of their voices.

Before she could think to lock her door, the one nearest her grabbed the driver's side handle. He flung the door open and thrust his head toward her, his bloodshot eyes inflamed and piercing.

"Where's your burka?!"

A wave of alcohol breath overtook her. She shrank back, petrified. "What do you want? Leave me alone—go away!"

"NO!" he shouted. She now saw that he was clenching a brick in one hand. "Go back home, Arab cow!" He stood up again and cocked the arm holding the brick.

Cowering but not taking her eyes off him, she grabbed her cell phone. With shaking hands, she pressed 999.

The man threw the brick at the ground directly outside Eva's door, sending pieces of it flying up and into her car. She closed her eyes and turned away but could feel tiny shards on her hands and face.

After another minute, the men were laughing and pointing at Eva. They picked up the signs and placards they had tossed aside before. Several of them spit on her car until her windshield was nearly covered with their saliva. As they began drifting away, they continued to scream insults, some of which Eva could read on the placards they left behind: GO BACK TO THE DESERT! AN EYE FOR AN EYE!

As soon as it was clear, Eva slammed her door and sped away, her hands still trembling and her heart palpitating. She practically screamed when a police dispatcher's voice came through the phone. Eva described in a shaky voice what had just happened, aware even as she did so that nothing was likely to come of it. The police had their hands full with threats, assaults and property damage, from the High to Welton Leys. But this occurrence in North Oxford served as graphic evidence of just how widespread and volatile—and dire—the vitriol had become.

7

Grisholm Dunn, dressed in his Denver Police Department uniform, backed his Chevy Suburban across the sun-washed driveway, smiling and waving at Myles as he drove casually over the red bicycle. Myles stood aside, holding Cora's hand, watching the whole thing unfold slowly, the oversize tires of the SUV rolling with dreadful inevitability. Myles raised his right hand to shield his eyes against the sun, but to his father it looked like a damned good salute and the old man saluted back, beaming. There was nothing Myles could do to stop his ears from the shrill crack of crunching metal and the low, hollow popping the Suburban's tires against the bike's plastic headlight.

Myles bolted upright in bed, slightly out of breath and unsure where he was. Sounds of glass breaking echoed in his mind. He looked around blankly. Were his neighbors fighting again? Was this a trash collection day? Kids breaking car windows? None of it made sense. The room wasn't right, the windows all wrong—they should be smaller and on the north wall—and the bed was tiny, almost coffin-like. The camphor scent of the bed linens, like smelling salts, brought him back to where he was.

He picked up his phone on the bed stand. 3:19 a.m. England, not Colorado. Oxford, Ignatius College, Jeremy, the Cuxham Chalice, Pippa. The last image hung about and Myles shook his head to loosen its hold. He breathed deeply, exhaling slowly, wanting to slow down his heart rate. He knew something else was wrong. Something far from the receding world of dream. Something very present. And nearby.

He looked at the windows again. None was broken. The water glass was still on the desk. He remembered that the northern wall in the retreat master's room, the one to his left, abutted the upper story of the chapel. He also remembered Jeremy's concerns about a break-in.

He stood up immediately.

He slipped into jeans and pulled a tee shirt on quickly. Barefoot, he could better judge the floorboards and steps. He slipped out of the room noiselessly, then turned a sharp left toward the staircase. He descended silently into the dark. He felt the cold stone under his feet and ran his fingertips along both walls. He opened the narrow wooden door at the bottom of the stairway and was on the second floor. The chapel doors lay to his right. Hallways east, west and south diverged from the chapel into gloom.

He moved to the entrance. As had happened yesterday, he was suddenly awash in memories of the place: prayer with other priests, old breviaries with tattered ribbons marking the pages and prayers, the Mass, incense and candle wax, "This is my Body." He pulled hard away from the impulse to remember.

Opposite the chapel doors was a darkened parlor, its door wide-open. A grandfather clock towered in the shadows of the far wall, ticking softly. To his immediate left was a long range of narrow Gothic windows looking out onto the main quad. Little light came from the cloudy and moonless sky. Myles tried to register murky distinctions for some clue as to the source of the noises he had heard. Nothing.

The robustly elegant, Lutyens-designed chapel door emitted its familiar creak as Myles pushed through slowly. He quickly checked his right and left, sensing nothing in the small vestibule. He stepped forward lightly on the cold tile floor. He smelled incense, wood polish and old, cold stone as he stood in the nave just past the main arch. Two dark ranks of pews processed on either side up the center aisle. On the left and right of the altar were the stalls where the Jesuits prayed. A small red glow came from the sanctuary lamp hanging from the ceiling to the altar's right.

He swept his right foot lightly over the floor, then did the same with his left as he moved soundlessly up the center aisle, checking for broken glass along the way. Moving past a pillar, he could make out a thin line of light at the base of the sacristy doorway to the right of the high altar. It was now clear to Myles that whatever glass shattered a few minutes ago wasn't in the chapel. It was in the sacristy. Was there an intruder behind the door? Was it some zealous brother setting up the day's liturgy at a ridiculous hour?

As he moved to the door, he stumbled into a chair someone had set in front of the first pew on the right. Though slight, the sound was enough to alert whoever was in the sacristy. The thin line of light at the threshold disappeared. Obviously, no sacristan was at work.

We both realize the other is here, Myles thought as he now moved determinedly toward the door. He bounded the two steps from the chapel floor to the sacristy. He pushed open the door. Knowing that the light switch for the room was on his right, he quickly extended his hand in that direction. Before he could reach the switch, someone grabbed his right wrist. Myles felt himself yanked into the room. He was spun around in nearly a full circle before feeling a leg behind his own. He tumbled to the floor. The sacristy door slammed shut.

Confused by the twist and fall, Myles tried to orient himself in the pitch-dark room. He got up and stumbled toward the door. He turned on the light, then tried opening the door, but it was jammed. Using both hands, he twisted until it snapped and gave. He ran through the transept and down the nave to the chapel doors, which had also been closed. He threw them open and looked in the three directions of unlit hallways leading from the chapel. He could see no one. He heard only the clock in the parlor chiming the half-hour.

His heart pounding and adrenaline pumping—and ego more than a tad wounded—Myles walked back to the sacristy to check out broken glass and a possible theft. He squinted at the harshness of the overheads and looked around the long and narrow room. The window at the far end was intact. None of the framed images on the walls had fallen to the floor. In the wastebasket he found a few pieces of broken glass, possibly a cruet that had been bumped off its perch near the sink. The intruder was oddly conscientious or else didn't want any suspicions quickly raised by leaving broken glass on the sacristy floor.

To the left of the sink and above the vestment case was an oak cabinet with a metal latch. The cabinet door was opened an inch. Myles knew what was, or should be, inside the cabinet. In case there was a theft, he didn't want to obscure fingerprints, so he put a knuckle at the bottom of the cabinet door and drew it open. Within were three ornate chalices glinting in the light.

Myles remained in the chapel, seated in a hard pew near the back, until daybreak. He was too pumped up to go back to sleep and it was still a few hours before the college administration would be up and running. He thought to report the incident as a break-in and encourage the college to bring in the police, but he hesitated for a few reasons. The Master, Felix Ilbert, would be the obvious go-to person for this, and Myles had no interest in seeing Ilbert unless he absolutely had to. Secondly, he didn't know that any crime had actually been committed other than a broken cruet and his being tossed onto the sacristy floor. The three chalices in the cabinet above the vestment case were locally famous, Jesuit treasures used on special occasions, such as the visitation of a bishop, college Masses, or a Jesuit funeral. All three were there, so no theft had taken place. But what gave Myles the most pause is how deftly and, when it comes to fighting, how gently he'd been treated. Rather than being harmed, he was put out of the way. Still, he would mention all of this to Tock, if only to record the incident and get it off his personal agenda.

He'd wait until the kitchens opened at 6:00 and grab some coffee. He had slept maybe four hours, enough to provide a burst of energy and then leave him in a jet-lag fog. In the faint pre-dawn light, he looked around the familiar space. Closing his eyes and mouth, he inhaled slowly and deeply. His body and spirit alike were infused with the remnants of incense and candle wax, the must of old hymnals, even the scent of the old stones that held the small chapel in elegant place. He opened his eyes to see the main altar and the starched white cloth that covered it, beginning to glow in the waxing light.

Myles couldn't remember the last time he'd been at Mass—it must have been Gris' funeral—and he was tired enough, less resistant now, to miss it. He remembered the many masses he'd offered here in this chapel, preaching earnestly about some gospel passage, believing it all, believing it then, that he, the priesthood, the Church, all made a difference in the world.

The last time he'd stood at that altar was not to preside but to assist Jeremy at a memorial Mass for Pippa. On crutches and fresh out of two weeks' rehab for a broken femur suffered in the crash, he could hardly bring himself to look into the faces of her friends and relatives who'd come up from London or his fellow Jesuits who had gathered to support Jeremy. Myles barely remembered his hobbled movements at Mass that day, the muttered words of the Consecration and, afterwards, painfully long minutes of sympathetic conversation with the Strands. He did remember fleeing the reception room with a purloined bottle of scotch and staying cooped up in his room for two days. Jeremy, as only he could, left food at Myles' door, but it sat there untouched. A week later he left Oxford, the priesthood, the Jesuits, life as he knew it.

He rubbed his eyes again as if to change channels in the cinematic roll of his mind. He wondered if prayer would help, decided it wouldn't, and made his way back to his room.

8

Jesuit House, Dublin, Ireland

A single ember flickers atop a small, smoky mound of ash smoldering in the grate. Its paltry gift of warmth is useless as the man's body is already cold with death. His close-cropped hair is matted and unkempt, his black cassock rumpled and worn. A chamber pot teeters precariously atop a stack of books on the floor next to his bed. On a bedside table are strewn several medicine bottles and a cool, damp towel. His left foot, a pale, waxy blue, sticks out from the bed linens at an awkward angle. An odor of death permeates the room's heavy evening air, while from outside, intermittent waves of steel-gray rain pelt the window panes.

A diminutive priest, Father Timothy Wheeler, SJ, Rector of the Jesuit community, hesitates in the doorway. Beside him stands another Jesuit twice his size, Father Rodger Hughes, the dead man's spiritual director. Despite the oppressive air, Hughes unconsciously rubs his arms as if to ward off the chill of mortality. He sniffs and lets out a long series of coughs.

"The chamber pot," Wheeler says, scrunching up his face and pointing, "hasn't been emptied in at least two days."

"Such disarray," says Hughes, more shocked by the visual than the olfactory impression. "Odd for a man of such exacting personal habits to have let it all go so completely." Bedclothes a mess, pillow on the floor, desk drawers and wardrobe wide open, odd bits of clothing strewn haphazardly, and books and papers in heaps and piles on a nearby desk.

"Can you imagine, only a week ago this man begged me to let him travel to England!" Wheeler shakes his head in dismay. "And he was adamant. I told him he could hardly convey himself from bed to pew, much less Dublin to Oxford."

"It was after Lady Carrick's visit, wasn't it? Seemed he was content to die before she called—and then this wild turnabout. I hesitated to intercede on his behalf with you."

"Well, of course, his dementia was an ill effect of the typhoid, wasn't it? Nothing the poor man said in his final days could be taken very seriously, Rodger. Pens and paper for his scribbling was the least I could do."

"He hadn't written a line for years, and then this final outpouring."

Though having visited the declining Father Gerard Hopkins several times these past weeks, Hughes takes in the features of the room as if seeing them for the first time. The walls reflect its occupant's love of nature and acute awareness of detail: a half-dozen miniature sketches of wild birds in various stages of flight and rest; watercolors of flowers, trees, and especially water. Above the desk hangs an oil painting of a young man standing beside a stream.

The two priests step to either side of the bed and stand over the body. Only now do they see the piece of paper folded up and held in the dead man's fingers. Hughes tugs the white square out of the man's grasp, stands up and unfolds the paper. He glances at the wavering script, the lines and the odd pen-strokes scratched on the front of the page. "I never much understood his verse, God bless him." He turns the paper over and reads "For an Oxford Jesuit."

They both stand quiet for another moment, wanting neither to linger nor to leave.

Finally, Hughes says, "Did you know, just this past January, during his retreat, Gerard says to me, 'All my undertakings miscarry,' or some such thing. 'What is my wretched life?' he blurts out. He was very up-set—shaken, disturbed. When I asked what was bothering him, he said he couldn't discuss it. He simply shook his head and repeated over and over again that a man's bond is sacred. Poor lad."

"Mind if I hold onto this, Tim?"

The rector nods as Father Hughes refolds the paper and slips it into his cassock sleeve. "He certainly was a mysterious creature, God love him."

Saturday, May 6

9

Myles took a pass on coffee in the refectory and, instead spent fifteen minutes with Tock, describing the incident in the chapel earlier that morning. Since the whole thing was oddly ambiguous, he thought it best to put it into the hands of his old friend who could report it to Ilbert, who, in turn, would likely dismiss it as something amounting to little. Myles decided that a run would be a more salubrious way to clear the multi-layered cobwebs of the past 24 hours, and since the images and sounds of yesterday's protest had left a strong impression, he had an idea where he would go.

Before leaving his room, Myles had spotted the newspaper he'd been reading on the bus the day before. The headline made him decide that instead of running in the direction of Port Meadow, his old favorite route, he'd head south toward Wilton Leys. Details from the accounts of Peter Toohey's death and the murder tableau still simmered restlessly in his mind.

Twenty minutes into his jog he'd moved from the Gothic charms of university buildings to characterless concrete tenements and bleak parking lots. Everywhere along the way were signs of the protests and marches that had nearly paralyzed Oxford the past few days: barricades, shop windows boarded up, and underfoot an inordinate amount of broken glass, debris and litter. Obviously the Toohey murder had thrown fuel on a fire that had already been a slow burn. Long-held implicit hatreds becoming explicit, and to those voices shouting *They Don't Belong Here!* came an equally resounding *Yes We Do!*

Because the sun wasn't quite up yet and it was Saturday morning, the streets and sidewalks were nearly empty of people. Decidedly less humid than yesterday, it was also less cool, and Myles appreciated the fresh air through his lightweight running clothes.

As he entered the Wilton Leys neighborhood, he slowed to a walk, the better to take in his surroundings. Streets were lined with empty cars, many of them parked at odd angles as if having been abandoned under duress the previous day. Most of the streetlights had been shattered by well-aimed rocks or bits of rubble from too many dilapidated buildings. Myles imagined that, if yesterday was any guide, in a few hours these streets could be teeming with a fresh wave of protestors: on one side, those infuriated by a terroristic Islamist murder and "Muslim immigrants;" on the other, those decrying the widespread violence and mistreatment based on profiling, stereotyping and willful misinformation.

A pair of bearded men stood outside a 24-hour convenience mart, talking quietly. They glared at him as he approached. He couldn't blame them for being suspicious after what had been happening in recent days. Noting that both wore kufis, Myles placed a hand on his chest as a Muslim sign of respect and slowly passed by. They returned to their conversation.

He knew that a right turn would bring him to St. Clare's, a Catholic convent, school and community center where in years past he had occasionally presided at Mass for the nuns and a small local congregation. A block further east he could just make out the single minaret of a mosque. On his right and a half-block down the street was the old Wilton Leys council housing area. Half its buildings had been leveled to a low pile of broken concrete and tangled rebar waiting to be cleared. The other half of the buildings, also delayed for demolition, stood as a three-story shell.

Myles didn't need to look long for the murder site. He knew two things would likely point the way. The first he saw from a distance of about a city block: the bright yellow Thames Valley Police crime tape that indicated a restricted area and, as long as the tape was up, the site for an ongoing investigation. The second clue was far sadder: piles of floral bouquets wrapped in plastic and tied in ribbons placed along the perimeter of the site. Other mementos were fixed to falling-down fences nearby: photos of the Toohey boy with family and friends, a Manchester United cap and hand-written messages from schoolmates, their bright colors weeping from the rain. The early morning dimness did nothing to soften the harshness of the general setting: ruined walls and buckled floors, broken glass, beer cans and bottles tossed indiscriminately from the sidewalk, McDonald's wrappers and pages from newspapers, rained-on and dried.

Myles stepped back and looked down the street. The smokers outside the market had gone back in and there was no one, at least that he could see, in the opposite direction. Scanning a bit higher, he also noted that there were no CCTV cameras. In one swift motion, he ducked under the tape without touching it and stepped into the crime scene. From the street, it would look like he disappeared.

In the pre-dawn obscurity, he was just able to follow another line of police tape that led further into the site. After a few minutes' careful walking he found himself less than ten feet from the elevator shaft. Myles could see, despite yesterday's rain, dark and persistent bloodstains in the pavement near the shaft where Peter Toohey had been found. He approached, careful not to disturb much underfoot, and squatted down beneath the level of the yellow tape. He peered over the edge into the well—four feet deep and about eight by eight feet. The elevator workings had been removed, and Myles assumed that forensic investigators had already examined what he saw: two irregular shapes of spatter in the shaft and darker stains on the floor, no doubt from pooling blood after the body had been deposited there. Better than half the floor was relatively clean, indicating where the lower part of Peter's body was placed.

He stood up and scanned the immediate area of the shaft again. He saw that most of the blood spatter was on the surface of the pavement and on a section of still-standing cinder block wall adjacent to the shaft. There, the shell of the building would have offered the killer visual shelter from anyone on the street. It seemed clear to Myles that, having lured the boy to the site, as the newspapers claimed, the killer would have performed the initial, bloodiest part here, likely behind one of those walls.

Myles stared at the scene and imagined what it might have looked like in the immediate aftermath of the killing. He'd studied religious violence in depth and witnessed it firsthand. To his mind, the whole thing—a so-called act of Islamic terror—made no sense, at least in the ways it was being spun by the press, the public, maybe even the police. The effect made sense because it worked. Whoever butchered an innocent child had succeeded in terrorizing and dividing the community and, increasingly, the entire country.

But where was the rest of the nearly predictable terrorist ritual, particularly the spectacle? Where was the cell-phone footage of an impossible-to-identify setting, knife-brandishing cowards in hoods, the captive sitting cross-legged in the center or kneeling, waiting? The film was, for most of these fanatical groups, an essential element of the terror. None of that existed in this case, or at least it hadn't yet come to light. And though the murder had taken place nearly a week before, no one had claimed responsibility. Could that anonymity, Myles wondered, be a new twist on terror?

Just then he heard the noise, a hissing sound coming from the right. He moved slowly in its direction until he was standing with the wall-edge closest to the sidewalk and elevator shaft. Before him, across the distance of the shell from one wall to its opposite, was a cleared area that had been the building's first floor. Myles figured he could move to the opposite wall without being heard, then turn and see the origin of the sound.

He hastened across the worksite as fast and nimbly as he could. Navigating the chunks of broken concrete and rebar was trickier than he'd guessed. One misstep and he'd sprain an ankle or be impaled on some metal spike. He managed to reach the opposite wall and turn in time to see a figure wearing a gray hoodie. A young man. He slipped through a low window in the wall, leaped to the sidewalk and sprinted down the very street Myles had jogged up. Within a matter of seconds, the figure was gone.

"Damn!" Myles said under his breath. Breathing heavily, he pushed himself from the wall and walked over to the area where the young man had been tagging. In a script legible enough for Myles to read were the Arabic words:

نحن ابرياء.

"Nahnu abriyaa'," he said aloud. "We are innocent."

At that moment, from the direction of the nearby mosque,

Myles heard the chant of morning call to prayer reverberating from a loudspeaker through the broken dawn.

10

Morning bells. The man had heard them through open Oxford windows thousands of times, from this college...and the next... and the next, and never grew tired of their summons to prayer. Choir and choristers; the light that passed through stained-glass windows and mottled the tiled sanctuary; the few faithful, albeit fewer by the day. The man delighted in it all, but only aesthetically; he was devout in never darkening the door of any church. The trappings were compelling, but theological substance was a different matter. Long ago he had set aside the Christian myth, with all its stultifying enchantments, and in its place found a better altar: Great Britain, her economy and social traditions, her mission in the world, her pride of place among the nations restored. Purity, nobility, hierarchy and order.

For a moment, a slight cacophony between Oxford bells and a BBC voice, Radio 4's Alan Philpott with the 10:00 a.m. news.

"Listen to this," the man said to four undergraduates sitting around the book-lined room. "Listen to change happening in changeless Oxford." He leaned to the left of the desk where he was seated and pulled shut the window against the bells to give Philpott his due:

"Meanwhile, in Oxford, tensions are mounting over the recent murder of twelve-year-old Peter Toohey. While police investigate this horrific killing, a number of Oxford citizens have taken the law into their own hands. Apparent reprisals of property damage and assaults in Welton Leys, Oxford's predominantly Muslim neighborhood, have increased in the last few days, prompting backlashes from local residents. Oxford imam Kaleed Faraman has called for peace while the police investigate, but Britain Now's Conrad Newell rebuffed talks of peace with calls for Parliament to take this tragic incident as impetus finally to address the country's growing immigrant problem..."

"Oh, Conrad, you perfect pawn," the man said with a low laugh, arranging the objects on the desk. "Do your work up and down the country. Preach that gospel of racial purity!" The man nodded toward the undergraduates. "And you're his secret evangelists, not that he would appreciate—or use—you as pointedly as I do."

On the left side of the desk and lined up perfectly with the thin leather-bound blotter lay a glossy 8x10 photo of Peter Toohey. The child was dressed in a bright red Manchester United football jersey, hands clasped military-style behind his back. It had been easy to find at the boy's school website and with a few clicks Photoshop it out of a comically solemn line-up of other twelve-year-old footballers. Staring at the image, the man slowly drew an index finger across the boy's throat, tapped it twice and sighed deeply. "For England's sake, dear child. For England's sake." Suppressing a slow swell of guilt from deep within, he turned the boy's picture over and said to no one in particular, "Now, who's our number two?"

Moving to the right-hand side of the desk blotter, the man lifted a heavy crescent-shaped dagger off a short stack of other photos and placed it at the top-center of the desk, as if everything on the polished oak table now lay under the sword of justice. The dagger was a brilliant find, an eighteenth-century ceremonial piece but also most serviceable. He ran his finger across the slight arc of the sheathed dagger and wondered what its own history of blood had been before he found it in a Cairo market stall. He left the dagger to examine more carefully the photo at the top of the stack. It depicted an elderly woman standing in front of a Tesco Supermarket in her Sunday best, smiling at the camera and wincing a little in the midday sunlight.

"Well done, lads. She'll do fine," the man said to the students.

The man studied the college calendar held in the desk blotter, opened the middle drawer and with a pen drew a circle around an upcoming date. Then, with Alan Philpott working another part of a troubled world, the man reassembled the photos and placed them, dagger on top as paperweight, in a side-drawer with a lock.

11

Myles walked through Ignatius College library's expansive Reading Room a few minutes before ten. The place had opened at eight, but given that it was Saturday, most of the college was sleeping in or lingering over breakfast tables. Only a few students were browsing the stacks or sitting in study carrels with insulated cups of coffee. As had happened earlier that morning in the chapel, smells loosened a flood of memories: that library bouquet of oil soap and polished wood, ancient book leather, and even older tobacco smoke that had clung to pages, walls and wood for a century.

His senses transported him like it was yesterday to myriad mundane and meaningful chunks of his life spent within these walls. Incalculable hours immersed in work at that desk to the right of the fireplace, the one next to a carrel Jeremy had occupied just as constantly. Dessert and port for Guest Nights when the library was appropriated for the overflow, tables rearranged to accommodate the swarms in black academic gowns chattering at tables like overfed crows. A nearly all-night conversation with Tock on that couch near the garden doors when he gave Myles the news that his father had died.

Light through high painted windows dappled the walls and for a moment cheered the somber faces in nineteenth-century Jesuit portraits. The towering old pendulum clock, whose large and intricate case was rumored still to hold a rare bottle of a long-dead Librarian's claret, ticked softly and chimed the hour as Myles walked by. Beyond the central part of the library and down a short hall on the right was the D'Arcy Manuscript Room, a modest-sized archive space for the college's rarer literary treasures. The door was wide-open and Myles stepped into the space where he saw Jeremy seated at a long table, head down and scribbling on a notepad. At the end of the room, facing a large open window, was a woman talking on a cell phone.

"Yes, love, you can have soda in the library. Just make sure it all goes in you and not on tables or books." She turned from the window to see Myles at the door. "Have to run. See you in an hour." The woman put her phone on the table and Jeremy looked up. "Oh, Myles. Morning! Please, meet Dr. Eva Bashir. Eva, this is my old friend Myles Dunn."

Eva Bashir looked to be in her late thirties and maybe even younger were it not for the faint worry-lines in the corners of her eyes. Her jet-black hair was stylishly cropped in a way that loosely framed her caramel-colored face. She wore a white blouse with navy ankle pants that highlighted her sleek form. Her eyes were at once dark and iridescent—and, Myles thought, somewhat sad. Eva took her chair at the head of the table where she had laid out a few pages and file folders. Jeremy sat at her right and Myles took the chair opposite, at Eva's left.

"Happy to meet you, Dr. Dunn. Jeremy told me we had a Hopkins expert visiting us."

Myles couldn't quite detect the librarian's tone—flat enough to be a slight reproach or a simple misunderstanding.

"Pleased to meet you, as well, Dr. Bashir. No, I'm hardly a Hopkins expert. That, of course, would be Jeremy. I'm just here to make him look good."

The humor went nowhere, causing Jeremy to shake his head. "I'm sorry, Eva, Myles. I should've set this up better. Myles is here only…well, Myles is here because I trust him, as I do you, Eva. Myles is a man who knows language and story and a thousand other things I don't have time to relay. I'm hoping that the two of you together can help unlock a clue or three from this blasted poem."

"No, Jeremy, Dr. Dunn," Eva chimed in quickly. "It's I who should apologize." She hesitated for a moment, looking at both men in turn. "Something happened last night. A group of kids—really, they were no more than that: big, stupid, violent kids—surrounded my car at an intersection not far from my home and threatened me. Holdovers from yesterday's counter-protest. They did some light damage to the car but more, I guess, to my sense of safety. I've reported it, the car's getting repaired today, but the whole experience is just showing up in my morning." Jeremy moved to take Eva's

47

hand, but she slowly drew it back to straighten the documents on the table.

"I'm sorry that happened to you, Dr. Bashir," Myles said. He thought to mention that he'd been at Peter Toohey's murder site earlier that morning, but this was clearly not the time.

Eva nodded quickly as if to suggest it was time to move onto tamer things. "Please, it's Eva. Now, can we discuss the Hopkins manuscript?" She patted the top of a black leather folder bearing the arms of Ignatius College. "But before we get into its mystifying language, I think a bit of context would help."

She nudged her chair an inch closer to the table and opened the folder. Carefully extracting an acetate sleeve, she placed it at the center of the table and turned it toward Myles. Eva described how the fragment had come to light, how every artifact in the Hopkins collection had been reviewed and updated in the archives catalog, and every scrap of original poetry from the famous Jesuit had been digitized for easier research access and preservation purposes. Because Hopkins Fragment 24 was in such derelict condition, was incomplete and of such apparent minor status in a collection of some of the most beautiful poetry of the nineteenth century, it had been understandably overlooked for many decades. Eva further described the forensics of the piece: that it was undoubtedly written by Hopkins, that the paper stock had been identified as Irish-produced and sold in the Dublin of Hopkins' time and that its provenance was easily traced from Dublin, where Hopkins spent his last years, to Oxford in the early twentieth century.

Myles noticed a few things in Eva's description, more about the woman than the poem. One was the absence of any academic self-serving. Absent, too, was the nearly manic enthusiasm for the discovery that Jeremy exhibited the night before. It was as if she could take or leave the Hopkins piece, that she was here on a Saturday morning not out of duty or for academic glory, but because Jeremy was dear to her. That endeared Myles to Eva at once. He noticed, too, her facility of expression; her English, though a second language, was idiomatic and confident. There was a fluidity to her words conveyed in the patient, thoughtful way she described the discovery of the manuscript. The cadence of her voice, the occasional pause to find the right word—all invited any listener to pay close attention. And Myles did.

When he turned that attention more fully to the manuscript page, he noticed a few features simultaneously. There was the expected spidery script prevalent in nineteenth-century English cursive, centered on a foolscap page that had obviously been folded twice vertically and twice again horizontally. But the fold lines were not torn, even at the paper edges. This suggested to Myles that once the poem had been folded, it was rarely opened and re-folded.

On the right and left sides of the page were vertical pen-strokes of regular thickness, hinting at pen-tests the author made to put his quill in good working order. The page was hardly a presentation copy, but a work in progress. In addition to the pen-strokes, there were other forms and figures, nonsensical in placement and shape, most appearing at the foot of the page, including three different sized rectangles and a spiral. The number 14 appeared between the last line of the poem and the busy tangle of these figures at the bottom. A prominent design at the lower left corner of the sheet seemed to be a longish X lying on its side with stains or marks at the two open ends. The poetic lines themselves crowded closer together in the center of the page in two uneven sets: the octet or first eight lines typical of the sonnet form and, after a stanza break, the completing sestet or six lines, two of which showed only the initial words.

"And that brings us to here and now and what's to be made of this," Eva concluded, nodding toward the manuscript before them. Both she and Jeremy looked at Myles expectantly.

"It's a hard enough slog as it is, Myles," Jeremy said through a smile. "Read it out loud and see if it makes more sense to the ear than the eye."

Myles lifted the acetate sheet carefully and began to read:

Slake not my thirst with thy brooding blood, spired frail;
Anchor my soul self — acolyte, virgin, priest — fore the mortal foe.
Tongue-slips, slype to the bound-for, longed-for grave,
Into the pitch-black deep, wherein the myst'ry lies:
Numen luminous and, alas, nameless; immured and imbrued.
I now crawl — falling, failing, spirit-chasing flesh — toward
Resurrection undeserved, unsought, but O fought for!
Time-ebbing and trouble-gorged do I, wretch, cry . . .

Unbaptise th'anointed twelve; in boldness fly! He
Cowers not who rights, but routs the fiendish jackdaws, gets
Holy justice alight: guilt-in-gilt unscroll.
Whet . . .
Ah my brother . . .
Embrace thereby the truth 'tween hell and heav'n

14

Slake not my thirst with thy brooding blood, 'spired Grail;
Anchor my soul self—acolyte, virgin, priest—'fore the mortal foe.
Tongue-slip, slype to the bound-fore, longed-for grave,
Into the pitch-black deep, wherein the myst'ry lies:
Numen luminous and, alas, nameless; immured and imbrued.
I now crawl—falling, failing, spirit-chasing flesh—toward
Resurrection undeserved, unsought, but O fought for!
Time-ebbing and trouble-gorged do I, wretch, cry...

Unbaptise th'nointed twelve; in boldness fly! He
Cowers not who rights, but routs the fiendish jackdaws, sets
Holy justice alight: guilt-in-gilt unscroll.
Whet...
Ah, my brother...
Embrace thereby the truth 'tween hell and heav'n.

All three remained silent for a moment. Myles wore a blank expression and looked through the open window of the manuscript room as if hoping for some revelation to beam in.

"As for a meaning," he began, "maybe something about the Holy Grail? There's a good bit of fear, anxiety, though where it's directed, I don't know. As for form, it's obviously incomplete, but strangely so." Jeremy leaned forward as Myles continued. "Words begin lines that are never worked through, at least in the lower part of the sonnet. The sestet, the final six lines, are supposed to resolve whatever dilemma or mystery the first eight, the octet, presents. It's as if Hopkins has an idea of some problem he's facing, but only guessing at the solution. And maybe that's the reason for the 14 scrawled on the foot of the page: the number of lines in a sonnet. As if he feels the need to remind himself."

Jeremy simply raised his eyebrows as if to agree with Myles' sense of the poem's mystery. "It's all over the place, isn't it Myles? Like a madwoman's breakfast."

"Let's try another approach," Myles said, turning the sheet at varying angles. "It's a working copy but I'm wondering, is there any way to know if this is the first or second stage of a poem that Hopkins may have completed but for which we have no extant copy?"

"I'm not sure what you mean," said Jeremy.

"Well, again, look at the sestet. It's as if Hopkins was building a poem around a few, carefully chosen words in those lower six lines. Especially 12 and 13: 'Whet'—that's all we've got for an entire line and the next one isn't much more revealing, 'Ah my brother.' But the last line is oddly complete, as if finally he's landed on something solid."

"Meaning?" asked Eva.

Myles pushed back from the table and shook his head. "I wish I knew. This all seems an odd collection of words, even for Hopkins. You could've told me Lewis Carroll wrote it, and I'd believe you." The frustration in his voice was unmistakable. He looked at Jeremy who simply nodded in agreement, a slight hunch in his shoulders. "I guess he was entitled to that," Myles continued, "given the supposed late stage at which he wrote this. And he died in Dublin of typhoid, didn't he?" Jeremy nodded again. "One symptom of late-stage typhoid is delirium. If this *is* one of his last works, it may be the product of…a deluded mind. For instance, look at the word 'lumenous'—an obvious misspelling of 'luminous.' But, then, it's Hopkins and who knows what he's doing with words?"

Jeremy turned to gaze out the window, a strange look on his face. "Could be, Myles. But, as you imply, it seems clear that he's deliberately *constructing* something here. To your previous point, Robert Bridges, his first editor and the man to whom Hopkins left practically everything he wrote, says nothing of this poem."

Eva gently turned the acetate sleeve over. "Not that we need another puzzle, but here on the obverse of the page is something more."

Myles read the single line on the page. "*For an Oxford Jesuit.*" He looked up at Eva. "Were there any Jesuits at Oxford in the 1880s?"

She laughed. "I wouldn't know," she said, and turned to Jeremy.

"Of course I noticed that," said Jeremy. No Jesuits are mentioned in the official records of the time, though that doesn't mean they weren't here. As you'll remember, Myles, the Society doesn't formally refer to Jesuits here until the turn of the twentieth century, just a bit before Ignatius College was founded in 1912. But there's another oddity in the poem: no reference to Jesuits or even Oxford, for that matter. So we haven't a clue as to what 'For an

Oxford Jesuit' might mean. And, as you suggested, if this page is a worksheet then one side needn't belong to the other, especially for the fact that a dedication usually comes when the work is finished." The last word drifted off into silence.

All three sat at the table for a moment, none of them looking at the poem.

"Jeremy," Myles nearly whispered. "You're the Hopkins scholar. You've spent more time with the man than anyone I know. Surely, you must have some ideas about the poem and all these walls we're hitting."

"This may or may not help." Jeremy nodded to Eva who opened the black folder again and extracted a yellowed catalog form about the size of a small index card. "Someone named Father Paget-Ross, the college librarian who first cataloged the poem over a century ago, describes it as 'an incomplete sonnet, undated and in the Poet's own hand on the theme of the Holy Grail and Man's struggle for salvation…it may have been one of the Terrible Sonnets…received at Ignatius College from Dublin on the death of Revd. Rodger Hughes, SJ, in April 1913 in sound condition.'"

"Interesting, those Grail references," said Myles. "But when he says 'terrible,' does he mean—?"

"Fearsome, dark," Jeremy nodded. "You might remember them as the 'Dark Sonnets,' Myles, with a sort of nod to St. John of the Cross 'Dark Night of the Soul.' This kind of writing describes the pain, hardship and fearsome leave-taking that the believer experiences on the journey from worldly attachments to oneness with God. I think Paget-Ross was correct to classify it as one of the Dark Sonnets. After all, Hopkins wrote them all in Dublin where he was chronically depressed. We know this one also was written there, so it sort of adds up."

"Remind me of the Dark Sonnets," said Myles.

"All right. These are the first lines of 'Carrion Comfort':

I wake and feel the fell of dark, not day.
What hours, O what black hours we have spent
This night!"

Myles shook his head slightly and Eva looked away, as if thinking of another time and place.

"But to be fair to Hopkins," Jeremy continued, "he never used the term 'dark sonnet,' and I don't really believe he thought them dark. His way always seemed to be shadow seeking light." He smiled faintly, as if he were talking about the manners of a long-departed friend. "But, typhoid or not, I agree with you, Myles. There *is* fear and anxiety in these lines. Some elemental urgency. Hopkins isn't simply playing with words, he's trying to communicate something here"—Jeremy tapped the acetate sleeve. "And unless I'm mistaken, it has nothing to do with the Holy Grail and the derring-do of knights." He paused and held eye contact with Myles. "These were quite possibly the last words he ever wrote. The last coherent, if cryptic, thoughts of a brilliant, troubled mind. I believe," he continued, now in an intense whisper, "those final thoughts were, of all things, about the Cuxham Chalice."

The last two words were like a hypnotic suggestion, and Jeremy suddenly looked at his watch. "Good God! I need to leave for a moment. Let's take a break now and return here in, say, twenty minutes?" Without waiting for his colleagues' approval, Jeremy got up and bolted from the room.

Myles looked at Eva as if to say, "What just happened?" And Eva, sensing the question in the look, said, "He's done this sort of thing before."

Eva stood up to leave, saying she had someone to look after. As she was headed to the door, Myles asked if there was coffee available.

"Certainly. I'll show you." Outside the archive room and in the expanse of the Reading Room, Eva pointed Myles toward a corner of the room where a small group of people hovered around a table. As he turned to thank her, he looked up at the mezzanine and saw Jeremy walking with another cleric, dapper and self-possessed.

"Eva. That man up there with Jeremy. Is that Moretti?"

"I've only seen him once or twice myself, but, yes, I think that's him."

Myles, still looking at Moretti, nodded and then asked Eva if she wanted a cup of coffee.

"Sure, just black. But before you go, do you want a peek into Oxford's glorious future? That's my daughter over there."

When they reached the table, the girl looked up, immediately made eye contact and smiled, peeling earbuds away. "Sam, I'd like you to meet Dr. Dunn."

Myles went through the routine of "It's just Myles, please" again and extended his hand to Sam. "Is that Sam for Samira?"

The girl beamed. "Yes! Most people assume it's Samantha and don't give me a chance to set them straight."

Though her skin was a shade lighter than Eva's, Myles saw that Sam had her mother's high cheekbones, strong chin and compact frame. Her lustrous, obsidian hair was also like her mother's, though Sam's fell in long, loose waves well below her shoulders. Both mother and daughter conveyed an intense inquisitiveness, but whereas Eva held her focus and exuded calm—her movements, like her speaking style, deliberate and controlled—Sam's words came in relatively rapid bursts and her eyes shifted restlessly, as if constantly re-assessing her surroundings.

They chatted for a few minutes before Myles excused himself to fetch coffee. He had to maneuver around a team of students rearranging tables for Sunday's Guest Night celebration. He nodded to the sub-bursar he'd met the day before, John Brooke, who kept library silence as best he could by stage-whispering requests to the student workers. Once at the coffee bar Myles poured two cups, and as he turned to find Eva, he saw that she had followed. Handing her a cup, he asked if she wanted to walk in the garden for a few minutes before rejoining Jeremy.

They walked through the open French doors into the May morning, inhaling lilac and jasmine and notes of freshly mown grass. Myles was grateful to clear his head, so much had transpired in the last day, a mountain of things to process.

Eva broke the silence. "So, I'm impressed. How did you guess Sam's proper name is Samira?"

"Three lifetimes ago, I was in the military, deployed to Iraq and Afghanistan. Picked up some Arabic and traveled where I could on leave: Israel, Syria, Lebanon. I came across the name often back then. And you being Bashir, a Syrian version of a common Arabic name, I took a guess about Sam. Is that what you prefer to call her?"

"Yes. Her father and I are both from Damascus originally. He named her Samira for his mother, who never liked me much. After the divorce, I so wanted everything dealing with family to be different. I guess Samira's name went into the mix. Anyway, she used to like being called Sam, but at sixteen she's becoming more and more interested in her extended family, her father, her ancestry... his religion."

Myles nodded thoughtfully, noting what sounded like Eva's self-exclusion from Islam. "Oxford seems a tale of two religions these days, doesn't it?"

"The entire country does. This has been going on for years; Brexit only made it worse, and now with this...murder. I've heard it referred to as an execution, a martyrdom." She shook her head. "The ignorance is...disheartening."

Marveling at her restraint, Myles agreed whole-heartedly. He offered his take on Friday's protest and near riot, wondering openly how it could all possibly be resolved. "In the midst of all this, here we are parsing an indecipherable poem from the nineteenth century while the real world spins madly around us! This could only happen in Oxford."

Eva smiled sadly. "I'm worried about Jeremy, and despite my earlier snap about you being an intruding expert, I'm glad you're here. He's been lost for months and I'm doing my best to support him." She didn't say she was at the end of her tether, but Myles had the sense that Eva was doing all she could to hold it together.

"Well, as you can already tell, Eva, I'm not at all sure what insight I can lend to this puzzle of a poem. But I'm glad that we're both at least giving Jeremy our moral support."

Eva nodded and smiled, then looked at her watch. "Speaking of which, maybe we should get back to D'Arcy."

Jeremy and Moretti entered a study carrel in the library mezzanine. He'd tried to apologize to the Italian for being ten minutes late to a meeting they'd arranged two days before. He felt like a lower sixth-form student who'd been caught out by the schoolmaster and hated himself for feeling that way.

Jeremy leaned on a chair by the table while Moretti took his place at a tall window overlooking the garden and people strolling through its May blossoms. Moretti looked from the window to Jeremy and shook his head slowly. He glanced at an iPad he was holding as if checking off something and then put it on the table. Taller than Jeremy, he stepped closer to the Jesuit to emphasize his advantage. The physical contrast of the two men was nearly laughable: while Jeremy was at best an unmade bed, the Vatican prelate wore a tailored Italian suit. He oozed with the confidence of an accomplished athlete or opera star whose ascendancy had rendered him impervious to the reality that the years had taken their toll. His well-combed hair was the color of steel and his anachronistic black-framed glasses gave him the look of a CEO accustomed to getting his way. The eyes behind them looked sternly at Jeremy, who shifted awkwardly. As Jeremy opened his mouth to speak, Moretti seized the upper hand. He alone would set the tone of their meeting.

"Please sit, Father Strand. Am I to understand that Dr. Dunn is here at your request?" His ariose tone and almost preternatural composure, rather than disguising or mitigating his manifest displeasure, made it more palpable.

Jeremy looked nonplussed. "Um…well, in a roundabout way, I guess he is. He's really here at the invitation of Father Forrestal, which I seconded. A bit of a reunion, I suppose." His voice hardly rang with conviction and Moretti heard as much.

"That your friend is here is one thing, Father Strand. That you have spent the last hour discussing this…this poem and the chalice is quite another. We had an agreement."

"But please try to understand, Monsignor. Myles Dunn could be of immense help to me—to us—regarding the chalice."

"And how might that be?"

"Well, for one thing he's brilliant. And he's a useful ally to have under…adversarial circumstances."

"Adversarial." Moretti repeated the word slowly. "We have talked about this, no?"

Jeremy nodded vigorously. "There may be others, even now, who seek the chalice."

"Precisely, Father, which is why all of this should be *sub rosa*, a matter of complete confidentiality. Involving the librarian—this I understand. After all, she originally found the manuscript. But Dr. Dunn—how well do you know him?"

"He's like a brother to me...or was."

"And you trust him?"

"With my life."

"And did you trust him with your sister's life?"

Stunned, Jeremy stared at Moretti. "How did you...? That was an accident. He loved her as much as I did, if not more. How dare you—?"

"Calm yourself, Father Strand. This is part of what I do. What I must do. The Cuxham Chalice is far more important than wounded egos, yours or mine...or your American friend."

"What do you mean?"

"Father Strand." Moretti took a deep breath as if to regain composure and steady his voice. "I do not mean to insult your friend or you, but this man has fallen to greater depths than you may know. He has little money, no social standing or patronage, and..." Moretti hesitated. "Who is to say he would not benefit personally from the discovery of the chalice?"

Jeremy nearly laughed, the thought of Myles absconding with a treasure was so fantastic. "Monsignor, you don't know him. Again, he could be of benefit. Without him, I don't know what next steps I can take." He felt a surge of anxiety and a wavering sense that he could trust no one, certainly not this Vatican prelate. And perhaps, against his insistence to the contrary, even Myles.

Moretti seemed to detect Jeremy's slow retreat and offered a smile and a light nod. "*Certamente, dottore.* I apologize. But you must realize that the fewer people who even suspect that the chalice exists, the better off you are. If it does exist and if this poem holds a clue to its location, you are likelier to find it alone." Moretti placed his hand on Jeremy's shoulder and looked intently at him. "Keep your sight on the prize, *Pater*. You must not let personal ambition or sentiment cloud your judgment. What you are doing calls for the utmost discretion. Tell your colleagues as little as possible, at least for the time being. Are we clear?"

Jeremy shook his head, as if trying to absorb all that he'd heard but not exactly wanting to. "I understand," he finally said. "But please understand that if I'm to decipher this sonnet and perhaps discover more about the Cuxham Chalice, I will require the help of trusted colleagues. That will mean sharing information, insight, ideas. If I'm withholding, they'll figure it out."

"Not withholding, Strand. Think of it as...uh...judicious intercourse, if you will pardon the word choice. My English...Keep your own counsel." He flashed that smile again, then narrowed his eyes, as if admonishing from on high. "Be cautious."

12

May 1866

Candlelight and shadow dapple the stone-cold crypt. Eight candles of different shapes and sizes offer Hopkins barely enough light to draw by. He sits at a rickety table in the largest of the rooms—if rooms they can be called—a small maze of burial chambers in the long-abandoned crypt. To his left is a single set of stairs that lead up to the bright Oxfordshire daylight. Seeing with any detail here is a challenge, but he senses the lines, recessions and reliefs from memory; he can hear the contours in the scratching sounds of the occasional mole and—

"Gerard!" His friend calls him from beyond the wall to his right. Thomas Carrick has been busy in a small chamber adjacent to the crypt.

"Be silent, Tom. You'll wake the dead," Hopkins states in a less urgent, distracted voice. He continues his sketching.

"Gerard, come here. I've something to show you."

"In a moment." Hopkins guides his hand across the paper, hastily sketching three recesses, tomb-spaces in vertical array: long-empty, their bones, jeweled rings and crosiers, beads and miters all scattered by dour Puritans and grave-robbers. Eying the triangular pile of rubble that long ago swallowed the northeastern corner of the crypt, Hopkins hits the paper with short nubs of the graphite, guessing at the features of the rubble: pieces of medieval carved stonework that fell from the ceiling in tides of plunder and fire; the cold, gritty-golden Cotswold earth that spilled in when the upper eastern wall collapsed who-knows-when; and irregular shapes of rock and twisting tendrils of tree-root from some caved-in grove. He sees a few of the roots spiking out of the rubble like accusing fingers pointing at the intruder.

Hopkins had stumbled upon the crypt months before on one of his frequent rambles into Binsey and Godstow. Had he been searching for it, he'd never have discovered the boarded-over entrance, the earth and grass obscuring the old planks. And he returned many times before confiding its whereabouts to his closest and most eccentric friend. Since that time both men have guarded its secrets and treasured their flights from Oxford pomposities to this rustic lair. With every subsequent visit over the months, they have steadily conveyed from the university candles and books, a few errant chairs and the small toss-away table where Hopkins now sits.

He puts down the pencil and blows warm air into his cupped, numbing hands, hunching his shoulders to bring the purple and black Balliol scarf closer to his ears. A distant and low muffle of thunder from somewhere above ground pulses through the stone vault. He turns to his right and sees a smiling Carrick peering through the passage in the wall. The candles on the table are not the only ones in the crypt; the few that Carrick has taken into the ossuary flicker from behind and his tall shadow shifts spasmodically on the wall.

"Tom, don't stand there," Hopkins says, his voice sharp with concern. "You know that's dangerous."

"All right, but come here. I want to show you something." Carrick turns to descend into the ossuary and picks up a bottle standing on a narrow bit of floor that divides the ossuary from the crypt.

Hopkins steps through the opening in the wall and moves cautiously along the rugged steps that descend into the old bone-room. It's not the first time Hopkins has been in the ossuary, but he has never seen it so clearly. Carrick has organized the place, pushing pieces of vaulting away that have fallen over the centuries. Amid the faded medieval murals of the eastern wall, Hopkins can now see the holes, some of them carved by monks who reached through them to drop fraternal bones into a space below. But Nature has created her own recesses so that the wall looks as if it's suffered cannon fire. Still, Hopkins marvels at the reds and blues that endure, of chevron shields, a local bishop's coat of arms—a Robert Crowley by name, faint crenellations of a ghostly castle, pennants waving in a dead breeze and knights brandishing swords stilled forever.

Carrick extends his arms in the small room, nearly touching the walls on either side. "What do you think?"

"I think it's bloody disrespectful. It's an ossuary, not a pantry."

Carrick wears an exaggerated look of disappointment. "Who's to toast these poor bones if not we? And who's to toast my recent admission to Lumen if not you?"

Hopkins has been quietly supporting his friend's singular achievement in his induction to Oxford's most prestigious and secret society. He half-wonders if his friend will lose his soul; Carrick takes Gerard's quiet for collegiate jealousy. Grinning through the worry they share in that moment, Carrick leans against the muraled wall.

"Then, m'lord Viscount," Hopkins announces solemnly, "I toast your very good health and prosperity amid these ancient bones!"

Carrick offers a quick half-bow and turns abruptly. In the corner between the two bannered murals, he places one foot in a small niche in the hardened dirt wall. Steadying himself with his right hand against the adjacent wall, he shoots his left into a dark opening to retrieve what he'd placed there moments before.

"You do realize, Tom, one of these days you're going to extract your hand from that cubby and find a pestiferous rodent gleefully attached to one of your fingers."

Carrick chuckles shortly, pulling out a bottle that flashes a glint of candlelight. He steps down agilely and twists the cork out in a few short squeals.

"Please, Gerard, it's not a cubby—get the Greek right, man. It's a zeta. It has to be if it's holding something as valuable as this '51 claret."

Hopkins feigns a pensive look. "Well, I'm not entirely sure. A zeta is a small keep in a church, and I suppose we're in a church, by degree, but to be a proper zeta, it should have a door and a lock."

"I'll complain to the Crowleys next time mother entertains. For now, concede the point and you may toast my success." Carrick extends the dusty bottle to his friend who begins to raise it to his lips.

"Truly, here's to you, dear Thomas. And here's to Lumen, blessedly lucky to have you!" Hopkins gestures with the bottle to the walls in the narrow bone-room. "And here's to this house of the dead."

13

Jeremy was already back at the table when Myles and Eva walked into the room. Myles noticed that his friend's mood had shifted from mild and alert to anxious and distracted. He would have given anything to know what Moretti wanted from Jeremy, but now was not the time to get into that. He decided it might be best to accentuate the positive.

"Jeremy, I think you've got something here. I'm not sure what it is other than an incomplete poem by Hopkins that posits a mystery as to its nature and purpose."

Jeremy looked at Myles and Eva with a faint hope.

Myles continued, "I mean, if you try to paraphrase it, remove yourself from the strange, poetic words and imagine what it could be saying, paraphrase it." He shifted in his chair and looked at the poem again. "Maybe it's a kind of portrait, another version of Hamlet holding up and speaking to Yorick's skull." He extended his right hand into an up-raised claw, as if he were holding something aloft and reciting a soliloquy. "Do not satisfy my thirst with your contents, 'spired (or maybe inspired) chalice. As an acolyte, virgin and priest, I beg you to be my anchor before Satan. Speechless, I slip toward my death, where the answers to all the questions lie. The true Spirit is trapped within mortal flesh. My dying body and anguished spirit crawl toward the eternal life that I do not deserve but for which I yearn. Dying and woeful, my wretched soul cries…"

Eva looked impressed.

"Okay, good so far, but what about the final sestet?" said Jeremy.

"Well, those lines are more problematic. Who's Hopkins addressing these lines to? Himself? A particular brother Jesuit? The tone is completely different from the first eight lines. These final six feel anxious, pleading, exhorting. And 'unbaptise.' What the heck is that? To unname? Unsanctify? Expose?"

Jeremy nodded, as if to encourage Myles to go on. "What do you make of 'th'nointed twelve'?"

"The Twelve Apostles come to mind. But, then, why should they flee?"

"I don't think it's the Apostles," Jeremy stated emphatically. In response to quizzical, expectant looks from Myles and Eva, he continued. "I mean, that feels too simple for Hopkins, no? What's even more interesting are these jackdaws—black birds known for stealing."

"That ties in with the 'guilt,' though what kind of guilt would one unscroll in or from gilt, or gold?"

"Gold-covered shame?" asked Eva.

Myles nodded. "Yeah, he's working on a metaphor that's either brilliant or tortured."

"To 'whet,' obviously, is to sharpen, though it can be used more imaginatively—kindle, arouse, spark, stir, fuel, tempt."

"Right," said Myles, "as if he's spurring the 'brother' of the last line to be strong...."

"Or to act," added Eva.

"Now, that's very Jesuit," said Myles too quickly and in spite of himself.

"How's that?"

Myles looked at Eva and then at Jeremy. "Well, action is fundamental to the *Spiritual Exercises of St. Ignatius*. It's the follow-through of discernment, lest what's discovered in that process remain simply a good idea." Myles was quiet for a moment and looked as if he'd gone elsewhere. He shook his head to come back and pointed once again at a line in the sonnet. "So, the action here may be to embrace some truth that lies between heaven and hell."

"Well-done, you two!" exclaimed Jeremy, who had been following excitedly. "If it weren't for the sestet, the sonnet would simply be designated an incomplete, lesser version of a 'dark sonnet,' with all the self-flagellation and self-doubt of those great poems but with only hints of their sublime refinement. Because of the sestet, however, this becomes an entirely different kind of 'dark' sonnet. 'Dark' not only because of the speaker's troubled soul, but for the way the lines point to a more than spiritual source of his angst."

"That seems about right," said Myles. "It's all pretty grim. And it's a hell of a vocabulary challenge. What on earth does 'slype' mean?"

"Yes, I had to look that one up, as well. It's an architectural term, a sort of covered passageway," Jeremy said. "There are a couple in Oxford. Here in the poem it could be a metaphor regarding Hopkins' passage from life to death."

Myles looked toward the window, his brow furrowed. "Wait a minute. What about the rhyme scheme? Didn't all Hopkins' sonnets have some sort of reliable pattern? There's none here at all."

Jeremy smiled strangely. "Point taken. It may have been simply weariness and illness at the end of his life. Or," he raised his index finger and leaned forward, "he departed from the expected rhyme sequence precisely to raise that question in the reader's mind— why? Why is the author doing something different with the sonnet form? Paget-Ross missed it and so have the two or three others who ever bothered to look at the piece. I'm glad you spotted it. Eva asked the same question a few weeks ago and we've both been puzzling over answers. But do you get the possible Cuxham reference?"

"'spired Grail,' I presume," said Myles.

Jeremy looked at Eva as if this were her cue. Eva glanced again at Myles with that same friendly, pleading look, as if to say, "I'm doing this because he's my friend." She stood up and walked across the small room to a pile of folio-sized books on the table under the eastern windows. She hefted a particular volume and brought it to the conference table, opening it up to a page marked with a post-it. "This is from Isaac Whittaker's *Compendium Oxoniensis*, a reference catalog to Oxford University college treasures published in 1782. You know, every college and private hall around here has its own legacy of plate, chapel vessels, vestments—the whole works. Whittaker associates the Cuxham Chalice—as everyone else did for a long while—with the city of Lincoln and then later, though vaguely, with St. Frideswide's Abbey, here in Oxford."

"Interesting," said Myles. "The original monastic foundation that eventually became Christ Church College," Myles recalled.

"That's right, at least eventually—but let me read Whittaker's own words: 'The fabled Cuxham Chalice is said to have emerged from a London goldsmith's workshop between 1260 and 1270. Based upon manuscript illustrations, the chalice, fashioned for

Stephen, the abbot of Cuxham Abbey and later bishop of Lincoln, was decorated with twelve semi-precious stones, four on the cup, four around the node and the last four on the octagonal base of the chalice in alternating facets. In addition, within all eight facets descending from node to base were incised eight small spires, from the ancient minsters of Britain. It is said to have come into the possession of St. Frideswide's in the sixteenth century. Long after the Cuxham Chalice disappeared, it is still called the Spired Grail.'"

Myles was clearly intrigued and grinned at the neatness of the connection. "So, the St. Frideswide association may, in fact, be a link with Christ Church College, right?"

"Right," nodded Jeremy, "formerly Wolsey's Cardinal College. The connection is imprecise, but it's a simple matter of bridging narrow gaps, especially given what Whittaker writes."

"Okay," said Myles, "let's assume, for the sake of argument, that Hopkins is referring to the Cuxham Chalice in the fragment. He's addressing the cup in the first line: he calls it 'spired with an apostrophe, implying 'inspired,' attributing a spiritual identity that riffs on the chalice's original monicker, 'Spired,' that describes its unique design features. This line—'acolyte, virgin, priest'—had me confused when I first read it, but it must be another self-reference, that Hopkins was all three—an acolyte, an altar server, as is every future priest. I guess he's a 'virgin' through the vow of celibacy and, obviously, a priest."

Jeremy nodded.

"So," continued Myles, "maybe he did write this poem shortly before his death. But it's curious: he's addressing the chalice from what vantage point—Oxford, where he might have seen it, as you suggest, Jeremy, or Dublin, where he's dying twenty-some years later?"

Jeremy tapped the table with both hands for emphasis. "I tend to think it's both, Myles. If he's writing the poem in Dublin, close to his death, that means he's writing with a certain urgency. He needs to say something here. Cryptic, yes, and there must be a reason for that. Secondly, he's recalling a very vivid moment in his life when he *did* look upon the Cuxham Chalice, the "spired grail.' Again, what that opportunity was is beyond me."

Jeremy turned the manuscript more directly toward Myles.

"Notice the shift in address, from the chalice to 'Ah, my brother.' His brother, whoever it is, needs to right some wrong. The same for the twelve here that should be 'unbaptised'—what a horrific curse! They're surely not the Knights of the Grail, as Paget-Ross thought. 'He/Cowers not who rights, but routs the fiendish jackdaws.' The twelve are compared with jackdaws, the thieving crow. It's also an allusion to witchcraft and the demonic, the jackdaw often being associated with the devil. Certainly, whoever's being addressed in the unfinished sestet—'ah Brother'—needs to be doing something, some clear action, as you suggest, Myles. But what that is, I haven't the foggiest."

With that, Jeremy suddenly got up and started pacing about the room.

"Well, then, that's it," said Myles, watching Jeremy move back and forth. "We know that a sonnet often sets up a problem in the octet and resolves it in the concluding sestet. So, let's go along with the Strand Thesis and say the octet is about a chalice that's been 'immured and imbrued'—walled in, buried. Hopkins wants the last six lines to resolve that wrong, which means, I guess, un-burying the chalice, no?"

Myles watched Eva's brow furrow before she spoke. "But the fact that this sestet is so tantalizingly unfinished makes it all the more frustrating. And the 'scroll' very likely points to those jackdaws, but how?" She spoke for the threesome, after which she and Myles sat in silence and Jeremy stood leaning against the table near the windows, staring at the ceiling.

After several moments of pensive silence, Myles finally spoke while staring at the poem.

"Well, this may not help in any obvious way, but I think I finally concede your point, Jeremy."

"Which one is that, old friend?" Jeremy asked as he walked slowly toward Myles.

"The one that says this poem is more than a poem."

"Yes?"

"The octet—it's a reverse acrostic." Myles pointed to the manuscript. "The first letter of the first eight lines, from bottom to top reads TRINITAS, Latin for the Trinity."

Myles leaned back and grinned as if he'd just played the winning hand in a poker game. Eva beamed at Myles and then at Jeremy who met her smile with one of his own.

14

Moretti once again let the lighted cigarette rest in its ashtray and picked up the tablet to review the encrypted report he'd received from the Vatican regarding Myles Dunn. To say that the profile held a bit of mystery was an understatement. He was impressed by two things: Dunn had accomplished much before entering the Society of Jesus, but he rose meteorically through his eighteen years as a Jesuit. Moretti scrolled down the file, studying the string of victories and accolades for the American:

1978, February 4: born, Highlands, CO, USA

2000, May: graduated Colorado State University (ROTC, Engineering)

2000 - 2004: U.S. Army; Fort Huachuca, AZ; deployed Iraq, Afghanistan

2004, August: entered Society of Jesus, Missouri Province

2006 - 2008: philosophy studies, Loyola University, Chicago

2008 - 2010: Jesuit Mission, Nepal

2010 - 2013: theology studies, Jesuit School, Berkeley, CA

2013, June 12: ordained priest, Oakland, CA

2013-2015: Curate, St. Monica's Parish, Denver, CO

2015, September: matriculated at Oxford University, Ignatius College, for DPhil, comparative religions

2020, June: awarded doctorate, with high honors

2020, September: departed the Society of Jesus; laicized 22 April, 2021

Current employment: Arapahoe County Community College (Adjunct); Highlands Hardware, Highlands, Colorado

Moretti flicked an ash, leaned back in the squeaking leather chair and shook his head. "*Che discesa fantastica!*" he muttered. What an amazing descent! Against all established trends in the man's life, Dunn had attained a singular achievement—ordination as a Jesuit priest and then a doctorate from Oxford University—after which he abruptly left the Society of Jesus and the priesthood altogether and was now teaching in a vocational school and sorting nuts and bolts in a hardware store. Had he used the Jesuits to grab an expensive doctorate and then teach in a lucrative placement, Moretti could understand it. But this path made little sense to the Vatican official.

Moretti had presumed that his secretary in Rome had ended his report with Dunn's current employment, but he scrolled even further to find this final note: *Precipitating event to departure from the Jesuits: death of Pippa Strand, sister of Rev. Jeremy Strand, SJ.*

And yet the man comes back here, Moretti thought. *Perché?* He didn't ask Strand why during their meeting in the library earlier that day. But he did emphasize the importance of keeping anything about the Cuxham Chalice quiet, from both the librarian and the American. He assured Strand of his help—of the Vatican's assistance in this cause—but secrecy was of the utmost importance. *This American demands watching.*

As far as anyone in the college knew, Moretti was an Italian art lover traveling abroad, discovering and doting over English *objects d'art*. Thus convinced that the Monsignor's interests were purely antiquarian, Strand had even shown Moretti the impossible-to-understand poem by Gerard Manley Hopkins. For his part, Moretti hoped to discover if the aimless Jesuit scholar might actually have new evidence about the long-lost Cuxham Chalice, something Moretti and his office at the Vatican had been interested in for quite some time. After a little coaxing and a half-bottle of scotch in Moretti's room one night, Strand had been more than happy to share what he knew, or thought he knew, about the chalice.

Moretti lifted the cigarette and fought mightily against the desire to put it between his lips and pull deeply on the burning tobacco. Instead, ruefully regarding his paunch and shaking his head in a wistful remembrance of his lost athletic form, he exhaled heavily, stabbed out the *Nazionali* and checked the time. 3:52 p.m.

He turned toward the stack of books, notes, photographs and photocopies on his desk, pushed a few of them aside and found the picture he was looking for. It was a high-grade reproduction from a page Strand had shown him in a book titled *Compendium Oxoniensis*. Even as an artist's imagined version of the Cuxham Chalice, it was exquisite. Moretti studied the image for several minutes, marveling at the craftsmanship and wondering if such a treasure still existed and, if so, whether he would ever exhume it. At that moment the ringtone sounded.

"Father Slater. *Si, si...grazie per la comunicazione...*but let us have our conversation this afternoon in English, Ian. I shall put you on speaker." Ian Slater, a Dominican priest from Sydney, was adept and punctual, performing his duties in the only way Moretti—and his clandestine office—would tolerate: thoroughly and discreetly. His English was hard for Moretti to understand, but his Italian was impossible. Since communication for Moretti was more important than courtesy, he pushed his secretary to speak in his mother tongue.

"Now, Ian, the material on the American I referred you to last night is most enlightening, but I have questions. What do you know of his military service and how did he make a connection with the Jesuits?"

Slater did have some context for several of the bullets on Dunn's timeline. He explained that the American had an earlier career trajectory in the U. S. Army, served in Army engineering, military intelligence and communications, was a bit of a linguist with an impressive facility in Arabic, and that he was discharged honorably at the rank of Major.

"But I keep hitting security walls," Slater continued, "when I try to find out more about his military service. One obvious feature, of course, is that he was in the Army when 9/11 occurred. That may have altered his trajectory a bit."

"*Si, grazie.* Ian, what do we know about his early connections with the Jesuits? Colorado?"

"Actually, Monsignor, he made those connections while he was in the Middle East. He managed to get the right visas and visited a Jesuit house in Beirut regularly. Once discharged from the Army, Dunn made his way to the Jesuits in his home territory."

"Excellent, Ian. But keep trying to find out more about his military service. And you might check that Jesuit house in Beirut. We have a little more authority over them than the United States military. Now, what further report do you have on the chalice?"

"Monsignor, I've run a trio of sequencing series on existing documentation and sampled all of our databases for references to 'Cuxham,' 'chalice,' 'Cuxham Abbey' and now 'Cardinal Wolsey' and 'monastic properties.' I ran those through the central database, cross-referencing any documentation from the Secretariat of State, the Vatican Library, the British Museum, the Ashmolean in Oxford, and the Vatican Secret Archives. Oh, and I've added the term 'votive chalice,' as you suggested. The oddness of the term helped narrow down the results considerably."

Moretti nodded as if his assistant could see him. "*Bene.* Votive chalices, as I have discovered, belong mostly to England. I was looking for one in the college sacristy earlier this morning, when this Dunn decided to investigate. Ian, did you find any clues as to location?"

Slater set the cryptic reference to Dunn aside and continued. "As to the chalice's location, it's consistent in all extant records, Monsignor. It has always been in England, or at least the records never show its appearance elsewhere. And unless it's been destroyed or simply disappeared along with any record of its whereabouts, it's still where it last was…wherever that is."

"And this is a help?"

"Not entirely, Monsignor. But I conflated all medieval references to the chalice, even oblique ones, and merged them with the single image we think depicts the chalice—that antiquarian account from the seventeenth century *Compendium Oxoniensis* that you referred me to. I checked the Vatican Library's copy and included in my searches anything bearing on the abbot of Cuxham who became bishop of Lincoln, the first recipient of the chalice. The bishop obviously favored his old abbey, because in his will he left the chalice to Cuxham. Hence the name that has continued to this day. Lastly, I entered pertinent phraseology from Fragment 24, Ignatius College Library, thanks to your transcription. To that, I calculated estimates of structure, dimension, metallurgy, density, weight, decoration—mainly the precious and semi-precious stones on the chalice—and have come up with the following."

Slater went quiet for a moment, as if combing through notes.

"I estimate that the chalice was, or is, about 25 centimeters high, 12.5 centimeters wide at the base, and weighs over seven pounds."

"*Dio buono!*"

"As for the value, it's inestimable, in two ways."

"Priceless, yes, I know." Moretti pondered the possibilities, not merely for the staggering wealth the chalice represented, but the kind of people who would stop at nothing to possess it. "What is the second form of value?"

"That goes to the point of origin, Monsignor. My research indicates that a chalice of this quality, the kind and abundance of gold and silver that went into making it, means that it was likely produced by the Guild of London Goldsmiths—"

"*Ebrai?*"

"Correct, Monsignor. It was a Jewish guild, famous for its superlative workmanship. And the timing of the chalice's creation seems to be just a few years before the last great pogrom in England in the late 1260s. About twenty years later, King Edward I would order the expulsion of all Jews from England. And if I may deduce one last thing, Monsignor?"

"Do so."

"Well, I've been thinking: why the bishop of Lincoln, the former abbot of Cuxham, of all people? As a churchman, he was a rather minor figure. I mean, why not the archbishop of Canterbury, or the bishop of Winchester who was the royal treasurer?"

Moretti shrugged. "Perhaps it was payment against some sort of debt. Perhaps the abbot had been friendly to the goldsmiths," Moretti reasoned. "Do you have a theory, Father Slater?"

"I think it's more local. Oxford, like Cuxham, was in the medieval diocese of Lincoln, and the bishop would have had considerable authority over various communities in his see, including the Jews. Given the persecutions Jews had to contend with in England at this time, perhaps the chalice was created with a hope that further reprisals would end. Again, locally, the bishop of Lincoln, at least for that moment in Jewish history, could have become a protector."

Moretti was silent again and then sighed deeply. "*Grazie*, Ian. *A domani.*"

He hit the end-call button, slid the phone into his black Armani slacks and left for tea.

15

For the past hour Myles had been sitting on his bed, leaning against the wall. He cradled his laptop while grading term papers for a night course he had been teaching at Arapahoe County Community College. His phone dinged. A text from Tock: *Join me for a pre-prandial semi-spiritual meander?* Myles smiled at the term that Tock used for a walk along the Thames towpath, something they had often done together in years past. *Sure*, he replied. *Meet you at the Porter's Lodge in five.*

After traveling a short distance south along Abingdon Road, just before Folly Bridge they passed the Head of the River pub, where the dining patio teemed with laughter and clinking glasses and silverware from students eagerly imbibing the mild temperatures by the pint.

The sidewalk veered off to the left just before the bridge and led past a dozen boathouses. The one immediately below the bridge housed a fleet of punts for hire, and in this part of the Isis—Oxford's nickname for its stretch of the Thames—was a near logjam of would-be punters at all angles, bumping awkwardly into the shore and one another. Further along, where the paved path gave way to gravel, were the university boathouses, each festooned in the colors of its particular college and housing sculls of various lengths.

In no time, Myles and Tock were enveloped in the canopy of mature oaks and tangled willows whose wispy extremities seemed to reach lazily for the river's steady, primordial current. The traffic was soon a distant memory eclipsed by the sound of their own steps on the gravelly dirt. Sun had finally broken through the stubborn gray mantle and streamed through the budding trees, casting long, whimsical shadows at their feet.

Any ambivalence Myles had felt about seeing his old friend and former spiritual mentor melted away in the tranquil setting and the presence of Tock's all-embracing mien. The old man had

75

a way of unobtrusively and often wordlessly comprehending one's heart. When Myles had decided to leave the priesthood, Tock was the hardest person to tell—and, besides Pippa, the least surprised. Unlike some of Myles' other fellow Jesuits, Tock didn't take the departure personally. "'In my end is my beginning,'" he had said with characteristic pith, squeezing Myles' hands in his own while quoting from *Four Quartets*.

Nigel Forrestal, his given name, was thoroughly and simply a Jesuit. Though the list of his degrees and accomplishments during his Oxford career was long—including a fellowship in the Royal Historical Society, distinguished teaching awards and a handful of celebrated debating triumphs at the Oxford Union—he was best known for his understated wit and humble manner. To venerable Oxford dons and the greenest undergraduate alike, he was simply "Tock." The moniker had come about decades earlier, a shorthand for tick-tock in homage to his clockwork punctuality and adherence to routine, and it remained accurate more than a half-century on.

"Now that you've had a chance to spend some time with Jeremy, what's your impression?"

"I'm not sure, Tock. Based on his fevered email, I came here expecting to find him huddled in a corner or banging down the doors of the constabulary. I can understand why you'd be concerned about him; he seems distant, preoccupied, hard to read. From a guy who was always an open book, this all feels a bit off. And when he said he thought someone may have broken into his room…I must admit, I honestly can't say I'm sure it wasn't paranoia. On the other hand, it's great that he's fired up about work again."

"This manuscript, you mean. Anything there?"

"I was skeptical, but after digging into it a bit this morning with him and Eva Bashir, Jeremy may be onto something. I don't know if it merits paranoia on his part, but there does seem to be something intentionally elliptical about it."

"Yes, I'm afraid I'm with you regarding his anxious suspicions of an intruder. Still, with all that's happening around this city, one can't fault him for assuming the worst." He was silent for a few moments. "So, aside from the travails of our mutual friend, you've certainly come at a difficult time. What happened to that boy… absolutely horrible. And the ongoing violence."

"The response to the murder misses the mark," Myles said, considering whether to tell Tock about his visit to Wilton Leys.

"The truth will out, whatever it is. In the meantime, it comforts me that you're here, and not only for Jeremy. I was so relieved that he wrote to you. I urged him to do so, and I'm glad that you made the trip."

Hearing the old man's mild, melodious voice, Myles realized how much he'd missed Tock. They hadn't spoken or corresponded in two years, but Myles felt that he could—and in many ways needed to—pick up where they left off.

"Tock, I appreciated your emails. I'm sorry I haven't been in touch."

"It stung for half a year or so, but I finally realized that distance was what you needed. How long can you be with us here?"

"A week. Maybe two. I bought an open-ended ticket."

"Tell me, how have you been keeping busy back on the home front?"

"Believe it or not, helping my mother run the hardware store."

"Resurrecting the engineer in you, eh? Those strong hands of yours were always uncommonly handy: fixing the boiler on Christmas Eve, retooling the antediluvian dishwasher in the kitchen, restoring that old motorcycle…" He stopped and put his hand on Myles' arm. "Forgive me. I shouldn't have—"

"Not at all," said Myles with a vague smile meant to reassure.

"Aside from helping your mother," said Tock, as they resumed walking, "how has the time helped you re-situate yourself in the world? When you left here, you left…everything. As a self-professed adrenaline junky—your term, not mine—who happens to be a polyglot with an advanced degree in world religions"—he grinned and shook his head—"are you on the path you want to be on?"

"Depends on your definition of 'path.' And don't underestimate the complexity of a three-quarter inch hex-head bolt, Tock."

The old priest's smiling face turned pensive as they watched a rower speed by in a single scull. "Amidst all those bolts, surely you've been mulling the scope of your life, past and future alike."

"I taught a course this past semester. Just this morning I was grading their final exams online."

"Tell me more."

"It's an interdisciplinary course in the Liberal Studies program. I call it 'The Birth and Borderlands of Belief.'"

"Sounds intriguing—and right up your alley, if I may say so. What is its premise?"

"We explore the ways in which individuals and cultures have formed their belief systems, along with the ways those systems falter and fail. It's part religious studies, part anthropology and part psychology. The how and the why of belief, I guess you could say."

"Solving the mystery of Mystery?"

"More like unpacking than solving, but yes."

"That process—that's as much for you as for your students, I presume. What grade do you give yourself?"

Looking over at Tock, Myles saw in his face not judgment or glib curiosity, but a broad avenue of friendship, sincerity and wisdom.

"Ask me again in a few years," Myles said.

"Fair enough, and I appreciate what you mean. Still, forgive the cliché, but life is short. And you're so talented with so much to offer. 'Unpacking,' as you call it, is another word for living, and I hope you're not waiting until the baggage is empty before you re-engage with life. Because it never is. Never will be."

"That was some transition, Tock." His casual grin looked to Tock like a camouflaged plea for help, and his playful tone sounded more like a supplication—for exactly what he had yet to discover.

"The last time we spoke, after the funeral and on the eve of your departure, you told me you were done. With the Jesuits. With priesthood. With everything you'd been working toward. You said you'd lost your faith. Although we'd spoken for several months about questions and doubts you were experiencing, your leaving struck me as abrupt. Was it?"

"Yes and no. Pippa's death was a wake-up call. It made me realize that in my mind I'd already moved on. I'd lost that uncontainable desire to serve God. Hell, I no longer even knew what 'God' meant to me." He heard the world-weariness in his voice and felt ashamed of it. He wanted nothing to do with this—talking about himself, his failed vocation, Pippa's death—but at the same time he thirsted for it. "You're right about being back here. It's painful. I had to come back for Jeremy, but I guess I also hoped that it would be a chance to face the demons I'd left behind, unresolved questions I could barely formulate, let alone confront, in Colorado."

They exchanged hellos with a vivacious couple sunbathing atop a narrowboat that was moored at the water's edge. After walking in silence for a few minutes, they turned off the towpath toward Christ Church Meadow. Leaving the river behind, the vista opened up into majestic trees overlooking attractive fields of swaying grasses that led back to the limestone of Christ Church and Merton.

"What happened with Pippa," resumed Tock, "was horrific, life-changing, and I know you felt some responsibility and bear the scars"—he pointed to Myles' chin—"but it was an accident."

"Life-*ending*," corrected Myles, and "I *was* responsible. We both loved the thrill, but I pushed it too far on a slick road. I was caught up in the moment, showing off." He paused. "The decision to leave was right. I don't doubt that."

"But…?"

"But I don't know how to move forward without betraying Pippa's memory, along with an essential part of myself."

"I never fathomed just how important she was to you."

Myles nodded slowly. "In the months leading up to finishing the DPhil, I stopped being able to see myself growing old in the life I had imagined for so many years. Those feelings weren't because of Pippa. She didn't pull me away from the Jesuits or my faith. But something—maybe it was God, I don't know—lit a fire that I could see burning ahead of me, lighting the way to a journey I wanted to take—with her."

"And that fire died with her?"

Myles let several seconds pass before replying. "Yes," he said quietly but firmly.

"Is it possible, Myles, that the fire still burns ahead of you and within you? That she was part of it, fueled it, shared it with you, but wasn't its source?"

"It's not that simple."

"Of course it's not. I was in love once. Oh yes, strange but true. As a young Jesuit in graduate school, I fell in love with a fellow-student. We were friends, mostly. This was back in the riotous 1970s. After getting her DPhil, she landed an academic position in Toronto, and that was that. For the better part of a year, I wept and prayed and wallowed and dreaded my lonely future and prayed some more. And one day I realized that I was in love again—with this." He made a broad sweeping gesture with his hands. "With my life as a Jesuit: scholarship, teaching, writing, saying Mass, living my vows, mentoring students. Not all of it perfect, God knows, but all of it, I genuinely believe, *ad majorem Dei gloriam.*"

"I had no idea, Tock."

"One rarely does." He let out a small chuckle. "But life does go on, like it or not. You successfully rehabilitated your shattered leg and, I noticed early this morning, are back to your running. The question isn't so much 'What's next?' as 'Am I where I want to be *now*, where I need to be *at this moment?*'"

A pair of goldfinches swooped down and in front of them, and both men stopped to watch them swirl around and among the budding limbs of two ancient oaks before flying out of sight. The distant whoop of a siren from an emergency vehicle speeding up St. Aldate's Street punctured the idyllic image.

"Shall we?" Tock motioned toward a wooden bench beside the wide, speckled trunk of a sycamore, and the two men sat. From here they had an expansive postcard-perfect view across the Meadow toward the Oxford skyline.

Myles leaned forward, resting his elbows on his knees, and staring at the ground. "The truth is, I feel stuck."

Tock lightly placed his hand on his younger friend's back. "The cloud of unknowing is a grim and arduous place to be, but it is also rife with possibility." He removed his hand and knocked his knuckles twice against the wood. "You came here across great distances because you want to help Jeremy. But perhaps you've also come here to forgive yourself."

Myles sat back and pivoted to face Tock. "For what happened to Pippa or for losing my faith?"

"Perhaps both. And for surviving."

Never taking his eyes off his younger friend's face, Tock lifted one hand in a calming gesture, as if holding it over the Blessed Sacrament at Mass. "Think back over your life, Myles. You've done it before—changed direction, gotten new bearings—and I don't mean the kind you sell at your hardware store." He smiled wanly. "Your life before entering the Society, your life as a Jesuit, your life in the past two years—as long as you're living in response to God's grace, you *are* moving forward, wherever that leads. When you're with people you love, people who need you—whether here or Colorado or anywhere else—you never stop the journey. And God knows, you're a traveler on life's road."

Myles felt a welter of emotion swelling deep in his chest, forcing its way to his throat. He rubbed his hand across his unshaven face, swallowed hard and took a deep breath.

"But that's just it, Tock. I don't know about God anymore, or grace, or that clockwork of life that was my vocation, as a priest and as a Jesuit. That life ended, and before I'd had a chance to start a new life, it was over, too."

Quiet passed between the two men, Myles staring across the field of green at the skyward profiles of Christ Church, Radcliffe Camera, All Saints, and Magdalen College. A pleasant breeze blew Tock's white mane into chaos; he took no notice.

"I won't pretend to know what you've dealt with internally," said the old priest, "the psychologically dark places you've been in the past two years, the grief and regret and self-doubt. But you still have choices."

"When I turned sixteen, my old man, Gris—"

"I remember many stories about Gris," interjected Tock fondly.

"He gave me a compass, because he knew how much I liked getting lost in the backcountry. He told me, 'Never lose your bearings. If you lose your bearings, you die.' I had them as a young man, and in the Jesuits, and I had them in the life I imagined going forward with Pippa. And now...the compass is broken."

"You know, Myles, in keeping with what brought you here—Jeremy and his manuscript—Gerard Manley Hopkins said it best. Beauty is pied. That's a good, old-fashioned English word we don't use much these days: pied. Mottled. Imperfect." He gestured toward his body. "Look at me. Wounded up and down. Hobbled. Decrepit. And yet this old thing is beautiful in God's eyes. I fail most of the time to live up to my calling, but there it is. I'm damaged goods. A mixed bag." He paused. "We're all broken. We're all 'pied beauty,' as Hopkins said. 'Glory be to God for dappled things.'"

Myles, knowing the poem to which Tock referred, recalled what he could of Hopkins' imagery and themes. "I hardly know what 'God' means these days, let alone glorifying whatever God is. And as for all things dappled, stippled or pied, I wish I could see the beauty in them—I really do, Tock—but I feel directionless. Purposeless. Wherever that next thing is, I can't seem to get there."

Tock listened in silence, his face a canvas deeply creased with age and weathered with understanding, an earthy counterpoint to the sky's serene cerulean.

"Maybe you're already there, Myles. 'In between' is a place. Obscurity contains its own beauty. You knew that when designing your course: the borderlands of belief are a kind of belief."

Myles met Tock's eyes like one probing the sky for a shooting star on a foggy night.

"I don't know," Tock continued, his tone now solemn and soft-spoken, "what's right for you. Truly. But I urge you not to avoid or decry the unknowing but to embrace it, throw yourself into it, for in the very depths of unmooring and darkness and incomprehension one often encounters a numinous light. Be receptive to it."

Chiming bells from Tom Tower tolled six.

"To be continued," said Tock. "I must head back. Evening Mass at St. Clare's with the Benedictine sisters." Assisted by his hands and a grunt, he rose. "If it weren't such an insufferable mixed metaphor, I'd say those women are at once the salt of the earth and a treasure." He shook his head in admiration as they resumed the path that would circle back.

"And Sister Pax—she's still leading the way?"

"As unflinchingly as ever."

"Jostled in that mad crowd on the High yesterday, I could swear I spotted her among the throngs of peaceful marchers."

"Wouldn't surprise me a bit. You'll be able to ask her yourself at Guest Night."

Myles shot Tock a glance, but the old man kept his gaze straight ahead. "That's right, my unsuspecting friend, you've arrived just in time for our final Guest Night of the academic year."

"Lucky me," said Myles wryly. Tock knew all too well that Myles had never much enjoyed the once-per-term elaborate formal evening and found that Guest Nights brought out the worst in everyone.

"In all seriousness, I highly recommend that you be there at Jeremy's side."

Myles nodded. "I'll be there, though I didn't pack for a Guest Night so I may be underdressed."

"'Twas ever thus," quipped Tock as two joggers ran past and disappeared beyond the massive oaks in the direction of the river and towpath. "Just don't wear your running togs."

After a few minutes of silence, they turned onto Poplar Walk, so named for the mature trees that lined the wide gravel path. The late afternoon sun against the poplars streaked their path in light and shadow.

16

Miss Florence Ballard carefully lowered the freshly iced Victoria sponge onto the center of the doily, which she had placed in the center of her best cake stand. She stood back and assessed the arrangement.

"There," she said to Miss Minnie, "I think we're ready."

She glanced up at the antique Thomas Tompion clock at the very moment it chimed eight, smiling with satisfaction at its familiar tone. Not for the first time in her eighty-one years, she wondered if the pride she took at her generosity in sharing her baking skills with her fellow parishioners would be held against her on Judgment Day. She thought not, but the matter bore further prayer.

Untying her rose linen apron and hanging it on its hook—after first brushing off a few crumbs into the sink—she adjusted her ivory and pink shawl before the cheval mirror that sat on the sideboard just below the ivory crucifix. She couldn't decide whether to watch a rerun of *Grand Designs* or *Gardeners' World*. If she'd had a child, she would have wanted him to be just like Kevin McLeod and Monte Don—so likable and clever!

Awakened by the familiar squeak of the floorboard, Miss Minnie languidly arched her back and glanced in the direction of the kitchen, contemplating a slurp of cream and, if the spirit moved her, a nibble of kibble.

Florence had just reached the snug when she stopped. What was that sound? She listened. There it was again. A soft knock. At the kitchen door, of all places.

"How odd," she said, frowning as she once again glanced involuntarily at the clock. "On a Saturday night?"

Miss Minnie couldn't have agreed more. This never happened—and such atrocious timing. With uncharacteristic alacrity she leapt off the settee and hid on the windowsill behind the velvet drapes.

Florence made her way slowly back to the kitchen. With an arthritic index finger, she flicked on the outside light and gently pushed aside the lace curtains from the small window on the back door. Her face lit up, and she opened the door.

"It's you," she beamed with undisguised pleasure and surprise. "How lovely to see you—oh, do come in, my dear." She stepped back to let him inside, imagining how delightful it would be to share her programs with him in the snug. "I didn't expect to see you until tomorrow morning. Can I get you a c—?"

She never had a chance to finish her question. Once past the threshold the visitor shut the door with an ominous combination of speed and silence before hooking a gloved hand around Florence's head and covering her mouth. The force of the movement sent her shawl flying. He spun her body around and tightened his grip from behind.

"You'll be avenged, Miss Ballard. You do us a great service," he said in his usual calm, clear voice.

Oh, dear God! thought Florence. She tried screaming but was too stupefied to draw breath. She felt sure her heart would explode through her chest. Instinctively, she reached up at the arms that held her, but instead of trying to pry him off she hysterically squeezed his jacket sleeves to no effect.

"You will join the martyrs you've always venerated," he said, nodding with his head toward the religious images in the hall and parlor.

The pain and her inability to breathe so overwhelmed her that the final words she would ever hear were little more than a rush of sound. "We will make you a righteous sacrifice for the good of England. For the good of Christendom."

The last thing she saw was a glimpse of her grotesquely contorted face in the silver steel edge of a nine-inch blade, poised before her eyes. *Such a clean and shiny blade,* she mused absurdly, simultaneously aware and uncomprehending of her fast-fading cognition. *Meticulously maintained. So like him. But why is he bringing it so close to my—?*

Then a series of agonizing, shooting pains in her forehead, followed immediately by a warm, sticky wetness in her eyes and then mouth. Then blackness. No longer sure if her eyes were open or shut, or whether she was alive or dead, the last thing she heard was the disembodied sound of her own choking.

She went limp. The thin, white, wrinkled skin of her throat offered little resistance. Spurting blood instantly covered her ancient neck and hands, her vintage dress, her pristine carpet.

Peering at the carnage from behind the drapes, Miss Minnie blinked nonchalantly and decided that the kibble could wait.

17

June 5, 1867

The frenzied rapping on his door startles Hopkins out of a deep sleep. He fumbles for his glasses on the bedside table, hastily lights the portable oil lamp and glances at his watch. "Half past 3:00," he mutters to himself, shaking his head and rubbing his eyes as he shuffles out of his bedroom and across his sitting room to the door.

He no more than turns the knob when in tumbles Carrick.

"Good God, Tom! What the devil are you—"

Before he can finish Carrick presses his palm firmly over Hopkins' mouth, his face just inches away. His wild, bloodshot eyes frantically dart around the room.

After several seconds he removes his hand. He rushes to the open window, careful not to stand in front of it. He shuts it and yanks the curtains closed. His face is flush and his hair, normally fastidiously neat, is disheveled. Despite the mild, muggy night, Carrick is wearing a full-length overcoat.

"Time is short. You must listen," Carrick says in a staccato whisper.

"What are you talking about, Tom?" Hopkins insists.

When he puts a hand on his friend's shoulder and tries to urge him to the chair in which he has so often relaxed, Carrick jumps back. "No!" he hisses, his tone and expression panicky and uncharacteristically defiant.

"This isn't like you," says Hopkins, furrowing his brow. "What's go—?"

"I'm not the person...you think I am."

Hopkins notices that Carrick has been clutching his coat, or rather clutching something beneath his coat.

"I need you...to listen. Say nothing." He reaches over to where Hopkins has set the lamp on a butler's table and turns down its flame so that the room is in near darkness. He swallows hard before continuing breathlessly. "Horrible things I've seen...am privy to. I may not have

thrust the bla—that is, committed the deed—but I am not blameless. I've been blind, Gerard. I've chosen not to object, given tacit approval." He leans forward close to Hopkins, who sees in the dim glow the haunted face of despair. "I am…complicit!"

Hopkins opens his mouth to speak, to insist on an explanation and offer consolation. Before he can utter a word, his friend shoots an index finger in the air and violently shakes his head.

"Lives taken can never be reclaimed…but I may yet redeem myself, if only in some small degree." He lunges forward and with his one free hand grabs Hopkins by the front of his nightshirt. "But for that to happen, you must play a vital role!"

Hopkins is shaken by the combination of desperation and sorrow in Carrick's face and voice. "You know I would do anything to help you, Tom. What are you asking?"

The hand that has been holding something inside his coat slowly appears. In it is a burgundy-colored velvet pouch, cinched at the top with silver twine and embroidered with a gold insignia. His hands shaking, Carrick opens the pouch, reaches in, and extracts an elaborately adorned chalice. The room immediately seems twice as bright. The angulated chalice shimmers as if by magic, its countless facets catching and reflecting the lamp's dancing flame.

Momentarily transfixed, Hopkins finally looks from the chalice up to his friend's near-crazed eyes. "How did you come to possess this?"

"As the treasurer, I have access. But never mind that. I must leave forthwith for London." Carrick places the chalice back into the pouch, cinches it closed and holds it out to Hopkins. "Take it."

Hopkins' expression turns from perplexity to incredulity. The bag is touching his chest, and his hands slowly open and remain poised inches away from its velvet folds. "What? Why?"

"I implore you, Gerard!" urges Carrick.

"Why the hurry? Convocation is in three days. There's so much to be done."

"I can't worry about any of that. I must leave Oxford immediately. It's no longer safe for me! They're looking for me. In the name of friendship, take it! In the name of all that's holy…Take it to our place. Secure it in the zeta. *No one can find it there." He pauses until Hopkins' fingers slowly encircle the pouch, touching but not holding it. "It must be done before you leave Oxford. And make sure you're not followed.*

88

Lives depend upon it—including mine." He sees the incomprehension on Hopkins' face. "It holds evidence of horrendous crimes."

Hopkins' eyes move to the coffee table. He walks to it and picks up a newspaper, pointing to a headline that reads, "Third Murder in Three Weeks Intensifies Backlash against Irish."

He meets his friend's eyes. "Lumen? My God, is this the work of Lumen?" Eyes glistening with emotion, Carrick stares mutely at his friend. Hopkins jabs at the article with his finger. "Are you involved in this?"

He shakes his head. "I never should have—I should have followed my better angel. For the devil himself has seized my very soul." He falls silent for several seconds. "But you must trust me, Gerard. I have a plan, worked out to the very detail, a plan in which you are instrumental."

After a full minute, Hopkins slowly drops the newspaper back onto the table. Tentatively he reaches toward the pouch, cradled in Carrick's extended hands, and takes hold of it. Instantly he is staggered by its weight.

Carrick's breathing is deep as he continues to stare into Hopkins' eyes. "I'm going down to London to plead with my father. I leave at once." He opens his watch and glances at it. "In a few hours' time I will have told him everything. He will be appalled, of course, but he'll know what to do, find some way to end the madness...I will make it right. You must trust me. Can I trust you?" He squeezes Hopkins by the shoulders. "Do not forget: secrecy is paramount. Promise me! Take it to the zeta and leave it for me. And, for God's sake, don't return. We can't take that chance."

Carrick stands up and Hopkins follows. "Gerard, dear friend, I'll be back within a matter of days. I'll see that the chalice and, God forgive me, what it contains will be placed in the safest hands. Please do what I ask."

"I will do it," says Hopkins, as much out of fear as friendship, though even as he forms the words he wonders what he is committing to.

Carrick heaves a sigh, nods in appreciation and a moment later is gone.

After he leaves, Hopkins bolts the door. He then collapses in the chair, trying to absorb what has just transpired. He turns the flame higher on the lamp and glances down at the newspaper headline, recalling Carrick's words. "Lives taken...I may yet redeem myself...I am complicit...end the madness...lives depend upon it...the devil himself...it holds evidence of horrendous crimes..."

How can he follow through with his promise to Tom?

How can he not?

*He removes the chalice from its velvet sack and places it on the but-
ler's table in front of him. It is the most beautiful thing outside of nature
that Hopkins has ever seen. It stands about ten inches tall; its etched
lines and precious stones seem to draw the candlelight towards it. He is
torn between studying every aspect of the fabled treasure and hiding it
in darkness once again. He cannot take his eyes from it, the small but
stately minster towers etched in its Gothic, angular base. The node, the
size of a small apple, joins the base with the large half-globe of the cup
and, incised around it in three roundels, images of the Virgin Mary, a
priest saying Mass, and a youth holding a candle.*

*Hopkins lifts it carefully from the table and feels a moment of trep-
idation, a would-be priest daring to raise the holy cup. He lowers it
again but sees as he does the Latin words at the base:* HIC CALIX
ABBATIAE CUXHAMENSIS EST, *"This is the chalice of the
Abbey of Cuxham."*

*Hopkins meticulously examines the treasure from all possible van-
tage points in hopes of discovering what evidence of horrendous crimes
Carrick had referenced. Flummoxed after half an hour, he opens the
velvet pouch, now recognizing its gold insignia as a stylized image of
its contents, and begins to slip the chalice back into it. As he does so, he
notices something for the first time and frowns. Moments later, hearing
nothing but his pulse beating in his ears, he gapes in amazement.*

*He leans closer to the lamp. As he reads, hands trembling, his mouth
slowly opens and his face drains of blood.*

Sunday, May 7

18

Celia Frick rolled her eyes and, from her usual position hidden in the middle of the pack, indifferently surveyed the faces of her co-workers, who stood in a semicircle around the Master. Most of them looked as bored and bleary-eyed as she felt, though most likely not so hung-over. How much longer could the old windbag twaddle on? She knew all too well the answer to that question. And she needed a cigarette.

Packed into the staff break room, on the lower level, just off the kitchen, was the Critical Event Team, the Master's turgid designation for a dozen or so domestic staff members tasked with orchestrating Guest Night. Essentially a walk-in closet whose sole decor consisted of a small corner table with two chairs and employee timecards alphabetically arranged in slots on the wall beside a punch clock, the windowless room was redolent of floor wax and body odor.

"...cannot emphasize enough the importance of tonight's Guest Night—above all other Guest Nights."

As head of the kitchen staff, Celia had seen and heard it before, but to be specially summoned this bloody early—and on a Sunday morning, no less—to hear this knobhead's drivel?! Who ever heard of a Guest Night on Sunday, anyway? Shaking her head in contempt, she shifted her weight from one disinterested tapping foot to another and sighed. *Might as well settle in*, she told herself. The Master was building steam as his face went from its usual chalky pallor to a clammy crimson sheen while his improbably high-pitched voice grew louder and more tremulous. Like some sort of lunatic sermon.

"Blah blah blah," she muttered under her breath in response to Father Ilbert's so-called pep talk. It must not have been completely *under*, based on the reproving look shot at her by Mrs. Cassidy, the Head Maid and fixture of the college since the 1980s, who stood at attention in front. The usual description of her was "long-suffering;" Celia merely thought her insufferable.

Celia dug her elbow into the tall young man next to her, partly to enlist a co-conspirator in misery and partly as an excuse to feel his hunky torso. Trevor Baptiste, assistant chef, glanced down at Celia's heavily made-up face with a look of beseeching panic, as if to say, *please don't get me in trouble!* The poor sod, she thought. Constantly worried that he'll be sent back to Haiti. He's no fun. *Still,* she thought with a lascivious grin, *I wouldn't kick him out of bed for eating biscuits.* Sure, she may be twice his age, but he'd not soon forget a roll with her. She pulled a hairpin from the pocket of her smock, gave her long grayish-blond hair a good shake and gathered it into a loose bun, the better to accentuate her girlish neck and cheekbones.

The sermon droned on.

Felix Ilbert, S.J., Master of Ignatius College, stood at a portable lectern that he'd had specially made for just such occasions. "Occasion" was loosely defined, as it included anytime he needed to address students or staff. It was more a matter of status than stature, he told himself. Everyone associated with the college constituted his flock, after all, and as such it behooved him to declaim from a proper perch. Indeed, known in equal measure for his appetite, his asperity and his bombast, he seemed to the soapbox born. Any covert sniggering with respect to his likeness to a penguin he had long attributed to his steadfast attire of black suit, black shirt and Roman collar. Or envy. To all appearances, he carried his jowelly girth as a visible manifestation of his considerable power as Master of an Oxford college, not to mention priest of God. If in his decades in community life he had availed himself of a few mere alimentary privileges of his rank and station, well then it spoke volumes of the countless truly iniquitous indulgences of which he so admirably deprived himself.

The Master paused in his speech, reached his fingers an inch or two into his left cuff and pulled out what appeared to be a stiff rag of a vaguely grayish-green color. *Blimey, no! Not the hankie from hell!* thought Celia, averting her eyes in disgust. He gave the wadded-up and brittle mass a single emphatic shake, upon which Celia, her eyes tightly shut, swore she could hear dislodged particles hit the floor. He brought the now slightly less stiff cloth to his nose with one hand, blew into it with a jarring two-part honk, examined it briefly at close distance, removed his glasses with his free hand and wiped the lenses with the rag, and finally, with practiced swiftness, replaced the petrified cloth just inside his cuff.

"Now, where was I? Ah yes, security. I don't need to tell you that all of Oxford—nay, the entire nation—is perched on tenterhooks. And with good reason. Violence has been done unto us all. And the innocent are most vulnerable..."

In that case, I'm safe, murmured Celia with a smirk and another elbow to Trevor.

Another Cassidy glare.

"...as we have seen most gruesomely. The perpetrators call themselves religious! These...these...one hesitates to call them people... have committed unspeakable crimes against civilization. Against humanity. And no one is safe. Not even in this college. This holy place! This blessed plot! This realm! This..." His voice trailed off until he panted to a stop. Fat beads of sweat teetered on his brow and upper lip like threats to each of his listeners. As they rolled slowly southward, he reached instinctively into his cuff.

Celia grimaced. *Bloody hell!*

Even Mrs. Cassidy's unflinchingly dutiful expression gave way to a cringe as Ilbert swept the hankie across his forehead and mouth.

As the rag was returned to its burrow, Ilbert tried to compose himself, an undertaking which involved much blinking and patting of pockets, as if feeling for a clue. "Oh dear. I seem to have..."

John Brooke gently cleared his throat. "Security, Master." The sub-bursar stood next to Mrs. Cassidy, hands clasped behind him, and spoke in a low monotone.

"Yes, of course. Quite so, Brooke. I have taken unprecedented security measures, hiring off-duty constables to monitor all points of entry. I will take no chances with the safety of college members and our guests. Why, just the other night an intruder somehow made his way into the chapel and gave our American visitor quite a fright. Nothing was taken and no one was hurt. Thanks be to God, I was awake and reciting matins when I heard a suspicious sound. I emerged from my quarters posthaste, which no doubt helped ward off the culprit."

"My sweet arse it did," muttered Celia between gritted teeth as Ilbert gave a vainglorious wag of his index finger.

"Nothing can be allowed to taint this college's reputation for consistently delivering the university's finest Guest Nights. To that end, let me reiterate, I expect each of you—and your underlings—to perform at the highest level. Let no detail be amiss."

Celia gave Trevor a few beckoning taps with her foot. "Did he say underthings?" she whispered into his ear after he made the mistake of leaning closer. "He ain't gettin' within a mile of mine!" Trevor wished he could distance himself from her impish grin, which was sure to get him fired—or worse—but he couldn't help chuckling ever so slightly.

"Mr. Baptiste, as you seem to think this is all very amusing, then I'm sure you can be relied upon to scrub the kitchen floors and walls before going home this evening—or, more likely, in the wee hours of tomorrow morning. Mr. Brooke will make certain that you do." He glanced at Brooke, more reliable than the rest of them put together, though he'd been there only two short months. The sub-bursar merely nodded.

"Very well, then," concluded Ilbert with a clap of his hands. "Be at your conscientious and solicitous best, and you shall earn the greatest reward: my approbation."

As Ilbert was shuffling out, Mrs. Cassidy close behind, he continued gesticulating and instructing poor Brooke, who carried the precious lectern.

"Sorry 'bout that, love," said Celia to Trevor. "I won't say I'll stay and help you, but I know how I can make it up to you."

19

Entering the college's Senior Common Room was like stepping into the gilded drawing room of a once-wealthy family lately fallen on hard times. Its name was standard Oxford collegiate to distinguish itself from the Junior Common Room where lesser beings sipped tea and read newspapers. Typically, only dons were allowed in the SCR. Faded glory reigned languorously in the air. Splendid from the doorway, appointments revealed their warts upon closer inspection. Overstuffed chairs with apparently antique upholstery felt, upon sitting, more original than one would have liked. Leather wingbacks gave one the feeling of being grasped in a vintage catcher's mitt. The Persian rug, in tones of faded burgundy and black that may have been museum quality in generations past, now gave the distinct impression of having absorbed more spills than character.

The coffered oak ceiling and windowless walls, intermittently paneled in mahogany and canvas, gave one the sense of being entombed. On Guest Nights and when the college fellows congregated there for an after-dinner drink on occasion, stale and musty opinions poured forth as unreservedly as the booze. All in all, the room engendered a feeling somewhere between timelessness and torpor.

As was the Sunday morning custom after community Mass, Jesuits and college dons who weren't home with their own families ventured in for coffee, scones and conversation. After a full night of sleep, Myles had finished up final grades for his course back at Arapaho and emailed them to the department, phoned his mother and, not finding Jeremy in his room, decided to try the SCR. It was fair to say he knew what he was getting into.

Upon entering the room, he could see that Father Ilbert had cornered Monsignor Moretti in a chair near a painting of the Jesuit martyr, St. Edmund Campion. As Myles scanned the room for Jeremy, he felt a lively slap on the seat of his pants. Pivoting to his left, he was greeted by a compact, wiry woman in her fifties wearing a domestic staff uniform and a saucy grin. One hand rested on the handle of a trolley strewn with used glasses and coffee cups and the other was now planted on her hip, a gesture that Myles recognized all too well.

Leaning close enough for Myles to note her prodigal application of lipstick and the blurred haze in her baggy blue eyes, she murmured in her characteristic gravelly purr, "I hear you're available."

After a half-step back and a few seconds of speechless bemusement, Myles smiled. "Celia Frick," he said in a voice louder than he'd intended. "I'm...happy to see you, too."

"You chucked the collar, eh?"

Half-embarrassed, wholly amused and hoping to salvage a semblance of decorum, Myles glanced around him to see if anyone had taken heed of Celia's latest irregularity. Over the course of his five years as a doctoral student, they had developed a spirited rapport which for Myles had been nothing more than verbal capering but for the frisky Celia had bordered on brazen flirtation.

"I have, indeed, left the priesthood. But," he added, with a furtive wink, "I'm afraid I'm still unworthy of your charms, Celia. You deserve someone far less dull and dreary, though I can't say I'm not flattered."

She shook her head in mock dismay. "Modesty don't suit you, Father Dunn. And I'm still calling you that 'til you come 'round to the sad truth: you're a heartbreaker."

With that, she let out a cackle, turned and wheeled the trolley out the door.

Hoping Jeremy would appear at some point, Myles decided he could use some caffeine. As he approached the coffee urn along the wall, Father Ilbert was gesticulating vigorously and decrying "the shrinking hegemony of Christian ideology in the present era," while the Vatican official raised his eyebrows and appeared bemused by the bloviating Master.

Myles was now able to get a better view of Moretti, Jeremy's nemesis, best friend or merely pain in the ass. He decided to wander into the orbit of their conversation.

"...needless to say, I find the backlash regrettable insofar as it affects the university. But I daresay the greater tragedy is the boy's murder—Toomey, O'Toole, something like that. And besides, those people—"

"You mean Oxford's Muslim citizens, Father Ilbert?" said Moretti, leaning slightly forward in his chair.

"Precisely. With their mosques and imams and burkas, or what have you—they're courting attention, and it doesn't take much to see that they're spoiling for a fight." Ilbert paused long enough to slurp his heavily sweetened coffee and glance peripherally at the newcomer.

Moretti's coal-black eyes smiled through his black-rimmed glasses as he gestured to an empty armchair next to him. "It's Dr. Dunn, isn't it? Please join us. May I introduce myself. Giacomo Moretti." He extended his hand.

"Pleased to meet you," said Myles, attempting to grasp the Italian's hand but being instantaneously suffocated by its iron grip.

Myles sat down and nodded to Ilbert who returned the gesture. Was it a signal of truce from the Master or mere indifference?

"Father Ilbert is plumbing the depths of the current crisis," Moretti said with what seemed to Myles barely disguised irony. "I am sure he would welcome your unique perspective as a scholar of religion. Do continue, Father Master. You were saying…?"

How the hell does he know so much about me? Myles wondered, taking an adjacent chair while discreetly regarding the Italian as Ilbert droned on. Well-manicured and clean shaven, his gray hair was short and distinctly parted on the left. His skin had a burnished quality, like some Vatican altarpiece depicting a swarthy Mediterranean saint. He wore his pressed black suit and Roman collar as comfortably as most men wear old jeans and a tee shirt. Though definitely on the wrong side of late middle age, Myles reckoned that the man was at one time a formidable athlete.

"…and the solution," continued the Master, his oily face shiny with perspiration, "is not—is *not*, I repeat—to placate. The slippery slope, Monsignor. The slippery slope!"

A slippery slope, indeed, thought Myles as he watched Ilbert's bulbous jowls waggle back and forth with each shake of his head. His faded, dandruff-flecked navy-blue suit embroidered with the college crest strained to contain his over-indulged girth. He looked to Myles like a sloppily manufactured, overstuffed teddy bear that has been discarded for being reprehensibly uncuddly.

"I share many of your concerns, Father Ilbert," interjected Moretti in a voice at once calm and commanding. "Still, Christ welcomed the sinner. And it seems the crowds have convicted an entire community of Muslims when the police have not identified the culprit, Muslim or otherwise. Is this not an opportunity, Master, for Oxford Catholics—starting with your college—to lead by example?"

Ilbert waved his hand dismissively and once again shook his head emphatically, generating further fleshy horizontal waggling.

"The problem, Monsignor, is that the one true faith is under threat of dilution, and I don't just mean from without. You of all people should appreciate this! Priests"—Ilbert shot a judgmental glance at Myles—"today ought to emulate the purity and fortitude, not to mention the courage, of their forebears." He took another slurp of coffee before resting the cup on his belly.

"Ah, yes," said Moretti, "what you might call 'the good old days.'"

Ilbert nodded, instigating a vertical jiggle, then pointed to without looking at the portrait of the martyr on the wall behind him. "There was a day when priests were priests! When being a priest meant something, required sacrifice unheard of today!" He shot Myles a second admonitory glare, but Myles looked instead at the portrait of Edmund Campion. "Take the Elizabethan age. Many a priest put his life at risk by covertly saying Mass for loyal Elizabethan Catholics. Yes, yes." He nodded and scooted laboriously to the very edge of his seat. "Many were apprehended, tortured and killed. We in our day of sybaritic overindulgence"—another incognizant slurp—"know nothing of such sacrifice, such courage." He raised a finger, narrowed his eyes and lowered his voice. "The cagey few escaped via priest-holes."

Moretti knitted his brow. "*Veramente*? Tell us more about priest-holes, Father Ilbert."

"Surely you've at least read about them, Monsignor. Built into the chapels of great homes belonging to Catholic gentry, priest-holes were hidden escape passages that allowed ingress and egress far from the house. Priests came and went with the sacraments, protected completely from prying Elizabethan eyes."

"You seem quite taken with these priest-holes," said Moretti with what Myles could swear was suppressed glee.

"Oh, I've seen more than a few," Ilbert continued. "Museums, homes on the historic registry and the like. The most one can hope for is sliding aside some hidden panel, as it were, perhaps poking one's head in, sometimes into the very bowels of the old house. They're rare these days, most having been destroyed in the renovations of great estates or converted to wine cellars or simply blocked up with the centuries."

Just then a familiar voice interjected, "What have I told you about speaking of one's bowels in public, Father Ilbert?" A grinning Tock Forrestal had suddenly appeared—as suddenly as an octogenarian can.

Myles stood up and gave Tock his chair before grabbing an unused one from a nearby chess table for himself.

"Thank you, Myles. Good morning, Monsignor, Felix." Tock gently tapped Ilbert's blue serge shoulder with his hand. "Forgive my adolescent jab, Felix. You can take the boy out of the sixth form..." He chuckled. "I suppose I've been taking lessons from Strand, our resident prankster. Speaking of whom, I expected to find him here with you, Myles."

"I thought I might find him here, too." Myles gave the room another glance.

"I understand you are here as his guest, Dr. Dunn," said Moretti.

"Jeremy is a dear friend from my doctoral days."

"But," said Moretti, his fingertips joined under his chin, "I think someone told me you were here to help with Father Strand's project. The Hopkins manuscript, I believe."

"I'm not sure who would have mentioned that to you, Monsignor. I'm here on a very informal basis and find myself happily assisting both Jeremy Strand and the college librarian, Dr. Bashir, in several interesting discussions."

"But Father Strand is the scholar of English literature, not you, correct?"

Tock saw something flash in Myles' eyes and leaned in. "Myles, you're too modest," the old Jesuit said. He then looked at Moretti. "Myles has an affinity for language, religion, figuring out how things are put together—and, well, for just about everything he tries."

"So you are an expert in literary analysis?" asked Moretti, though it sounded like more of a statement, and he continued without awaiting a reply. "Your Hopkins—he was, I believe, a student of Roman literature—what you call the classics, no?" Myles nodded. "But this poem—it is in English?" Myles nodded again. "So why, Dr. Dunn, does it present such a challenge that a scholar of English literature needs the assistance of an expert in world religion?"

Moretti had hardly moved in his chair, sitting straight-backed while seeming perfectly at ease. At the moment he seemed like a dog that wouldn't let go of a bone, making Myles all the more intrigued about the man's motives.

"Actually, Monsignor," interjected Tock, "along with being a superb classicist, Hopkins was—and few people really know this—quite a puzzle-master."

"É vero?" Moretti asked with genuine interest, taking another sip of coffee.

"Hopkins was a master philologist, but he had a sense of humor, as well. It's not surprising that Jeremy is drawn to him, being a sort of puzzle-master himself. One never knows what Hopkins was up to, just as we seldom know what our slippery Strand is up to."

Ilbert rolled his eyes while Myles furrowed his brow imperceptibly and looked intently at his old friend.

"In all my years as a Jesuit," burst out Ilbert skeptically, "I've never heard anything about Hopkins as a lover of puzzles."

"It makes sense, doesn't it?" said Tock. "Every poet has to be a word-master, selecting, working, weaving and patterning to create. Of course, Hopkins' artistry was...*sui generis*." He waved a hand in the air.

Moretti smiled inscrutably. "Perhaps you might offer an example, Father Forrestal."

Tock gazed thoughtfully at the floor. "Take 'The Windhover,'" he said after a few moments. Resting both hands on the arms of his chair, he closed his eyes:

"I caught this morning morning's minion, king-
dom of daylight's dauphin, dapple-dawn-drawn Falcon...
Of the rolling level underneath him steady air, and striding
High there, how he rung upon the rein of a wimpling wing
In his ecstasy!"

The group remained silently spellbound as Tock stopped, his eyes still shut. After a few seconds he opened them slowly and smiled. "That poem is about Our Lord, Monsignor. It's about the kestrel and what Hopkins saw in the flight of that marvelous bird: the swift and deft and utterly unpredictable movement of God's grace. And it's also unmistakably Ignatian: seeking God in all things!"

"Elegantly recited, Father Forrestal. The true poet is a puzzler—and a sleuth, of sorts—milling words to finest, most mysterious grain. I am reminded of Dante's *terza rima* in *La Commedia*, such a masterwork of interlocking rhymes and linguistic architecture."

Tock nodded. "It's interesting that you should speak of Dante's threefold rhyme scheme. The number three and puzzles—have you ever noticed how often that occurs? Three doors to choose from, three wishes from the genie out of his lamp, three Persons in the Blessed Trinity. Hopkins enjoyed all forms of wordplay, and in so doing he was really breathing the air of his own age. Nineteenth-century Englishmen loved word-puzzles: crosswords, anagrams, cryptograms, rebuses, acrostics, syllacrostics. Queen Victoria herself spent hours wandering through word-mazes, even commissioned crosswords and the like for her own amusement."

As the conversation continued in this vein, Myles sipped his coffee, ruminating alternately over the sphinxlike Italian and Jeremy's increasingly worrisome absence.

20

With a tedious Guest Night looming later in the evening, Myles decided to skip the dining hall and grab a late lunch outside of college. The streets and sidewalks teemed with activity, not least of which were bobbies on every corner, wearing custodian helmets and conspicuously brandishing truncheons. Moreover, the Chief Constable of the Thames Valley Police had banned indefinitely any individual gatherings larger than ten people. Likely encouraged by this development, passels of tourists along Broad and High Streets gawped at history-haunted spires while crapulous undergraduates and bookish dons moved in and out of college archways.

Morning gray had given way to sunshine, and after half an hour of meandering in the invigorating warmth, Myles stopped at one of the eateries on Cornmarket, a shop-lined pedestrian mall just north of Oxford's city center. He bought a veggie wrap and a fruit smoothie and made his way to a group of tables and chairs at the northern end of the mall.

Halfway through his lunch, Myles' attention was drawn to an eruption of voices at one of the mall entrances. When it got louder, he stood up and took a few steps for a closer look. Across the crowded market he saw three twenty-something men in a circle, gesticulating, taunting and shoving. As Myles approached, he could hear a smattering of insults—"bitches…Arab wog…back to your own country"—and saw at the center of the skirmish a sturdy-looking young man with dense, close-cropped black hair and wearing a gray hoodie that had seen better days. Behind the young man stood Eva with her arm around Sam. Both wore horrified looks. The young man seemed to pay no heed to the fact that he was seriously outnumbered.

Myles set down the wrap and smoothie on an empty table and began to approach more determinedly now. As he weaved his way through the lunchtime crowd, he got the sense that something had been said to escalate the scuffle. The yelling turned to a brawl, tables and chairs were knocked over, and onlookers were scrambling to get out of the way. Someone had shouted for the police.

Myles now moved rapidly, and by the time he reached the fracas two of the men had hold of the gray-hoodied teen while the other threw punches at him. Eva and Sam stood on the perimeter, looking on in horror. Just as Myles reached them, one of the men, a beefy fellow wearing a tight white tee shirt, shoved Eva hard, nearly knocking her down. "Back off, bit—"

Before he finished the insult, he was flat on his back. Myles had grabbed his collar from behind, wrenched it backward and slammed him against the concrete. The gray hoodie, held by the other two, glanced up at Myles with a look of confusion. At that moment one of the men kicked the teen in the groin. A split second later the kicker reeled backward as Myles landed a hard right to his jaw. Myles pulled the kid out of the grasp of the remaining thug with one hand and held up the other toward the attackers.

"It's time you turn tail and leave." His voice and demeanor were distinctly calm.

"Who the hell are you?" shouted the gormless yobbo with the white tee shirt, getting slowly to his feet before reaching into his back pocket.

"Just move on" said Myles. "We don't want any trouble. And neither do you."

White tee shirt now held something in his hand. "I said, who the hell are you?!"

"I'm the one giving you a chance to leave before I get angry."

The crowd of rapt onlookers watched silently at a safe distance. They seemed intrigued by the contrast between the physically intense confrontation and the American's remarkably composed disposition.

"What are you," said white tee shirt as he flipped open a switch-blade, "some kinda Muslim bitch lover?! I bet you—"

In a flash Myles' right foot connected with the man's mouth, which immediately gushed blood. He lunged at Myles with the knife, knocking the American onto his back. The two struggled for several seconds before someone yelled, "Cops are coming!"

The other two men seemed relieved to break free from Rabi,

who had been more than they could handle. They grabbed their bleeding mate and fled.

Eva and Sam had stepped back several feet, clutching one another, watching in shock, along with a dozen other onlookers.

A trio of policemen pushed through the crowd just as the four men scattered. The tallest of the three approached Rabi, grabbed hold of his hoodie just below the neck and yanked hard. Still holding Rabi, he looked at Myles. "What's the trouble?" he asked accusingly.

"Those assholes attacked us!" exclaimed Rabi truculently as he pointed at the fleeing men.

"The Yank just scared off them three," chimed in one of the onlookers.

Thanks, thought Myles. He turned to the man holding Rabi, a broad-shouldered, pock-marked fellow who thrust his chest out. "These two women and their young friend here were being bullied and assailed by three men. One of them was wielding this." He handed the closed switchblade to the cop. "I helped this young man stop them." After glancing at the policeman's name tag, he gestured toward the exits. "The bad guys are getting away, Constable Thornton. These people are the victims."

"It's Sergeant," he barked, aiming an index finger at Myles. Thornton adjusted his cap and peered at the women, then at the young man and Myles. "In this country we don't allow citizens to take the law into their own hands. I'll need your name and address."

Myles considered a few trenchant rejoinders but decided that forbearance was the better part of valor and showed the man his passport and said he was residing at Ignatius College. Thornton hardly looked at the passport. Before turning to walk away, he pointed that same finger at Myles and the young man. "Watch yourselves."

Myles said nothing, and the young man muttered, "Are you kidding me?!"

As the crowd dispersed, the girl ran up and threw her arms around the young man. "Rabi! Are you all right?"

At the same time, Eva walked over to Myles and put her hand on his arm. He winced slightly.

"Are you—?"

"I'm fine," he said. "It's been a long time since I did anything like that. What about you? Did they hurt you?"

She shook her head, clearly upset. "What is happening to this town, Myles? Innocent people attacked, and dozens of others simply gawk." She pointed at his upper right arm. "You're bleeding."

He glanced at the left upper arm of his jacket and saw that it was somewhat damp and red. "It doesn't feel too serious—just grazed by the tip of his blade, I think. I'll clean and bandage it back at Ignatius." He took a breath, hesitated as if not sure what to say. "Listen, I'm sorry about all that. I—"

"Sorry? You've nothing to be sorry about. We're grateful."

"I mean, I'm sorry you had to hear all that...venom those idiots were spewing." He looked at Eva as if wanting to say something else. "We're just grateful you and Rabi were here. By the way, Rabi, this is Myles Dunn, visiting from the States. Myles, you know Sam, and this is her friend, Rabi."

"Pleased to meet you," said Myles. Myles had his hand extended for a full three seconds before the young man reciprocated. When he did, the grip was firm but cursory. The skin of his hand felt rough and calloused. He wore a thin beard that traced his strong jawline, and his clay-colored face and deep-set eyes gave the impression of crumbling stone: hard but brittle.

"Myles, you looked like you used to do martial arts or something," said Sam, smiling with relief that the whole thing was over.

Myles grinned. "The operative phrase is 'used to.' My dad taught me not to suffer fools gladly, and I learned a few tricks in the Army. But your friend Rabi here is the one to be commended. I'm glad he was on my side. He was fearless—and a bruiser."

Meeting Myles' eyes only momentarily, Rabi said nothing.

Sam chuckled. "Are you sure you used to be a priest?"

Myles smiled. Before he could reply, Eva spoke up. "Well, we should get back home, and you should get back to your studies," she said to Sam.

"You want me to walk with you?" asked Rabi, holding Sam's hand while addressing Eva.

"No thanks, Rabi," said Eva. "The car's only two blocks."

"I guess I'll see you tonight at Guest Night," said Myles to Eva, who nodded and smiled.

As Eva and Sam walked away, arm in arm, Myles and Rabi watched them exit the Covered Market and turn onto St. Aldate's. As Rabi started walking in the other direction, Myles called after him.

"Got a minute?"

"What for?"

"I wonder if you've gotten yourself into some kind of trouble."

Rabi shot Myles a defensive look. "You saw what happened. Those yobs started the whole thing."

"I'm not talking about today, here. I'm talking about early yesterday morning."

Rabi's expression turned to confusion mixed with fear.

"At the old council housing. The spray paint."

Dawning awareness swept over Rabi's face. "That was you?"

Myles nodded.

"I did not do anything!"

"I never said you did," replied Myles. "*Nahnu abriyaa'*. You *are* innocent, of everything but tagging. But I think we both know that that can change in a heartbeat. There's innocence, and then there's foolishness. A boy doesn't know the difference. Do you?"

Rabi stood, dumbstruck, his fists clenched inside the pouch of his hoodie.

"You're caught between two cultures. Those borderlands are a difficult, complicated place to be. I get it. I just hope you realize that you're not alone in believing your people are innocent of this crime," said Myles. "Think about it."

With only a fleeting glance into the older man's eyes, Rabi turned and disappeared into the crowd of shoppers.

21

After an hour's worth of sherry and posturing in the Great Hall, Guest Night attendees—some 64 in all, including forty members of Ignatius College and twenty-four of their guests—found their way to assigned seats in the dimly lit formal dining hall. After the library, the dining hall was Ignatius College's next best architectural gem: a black and white marble tile floor, rich oak paneling between graceful oriel windows that rose to a hammer-beamed ceiling. Edwardian wall sconces and silver candelabra at each of the eight tables glowed under the imposing portraits of former Jesuit masters, who seemed to frown upon the Epicurean profligacy transpiring below, though whether with opprobrium or envy no one could say.

By the time Myles found the table Jeremy had reserved, introductions were under way. Jeremy, who was already laying into his second glass of wine, was seated at Myles' right. Joining them at table were Eva; Cyril Jacoby, holder of the prestigious University Chair in Modern History and Fellow of All Souls College; Monsignor Moretti; Sarah Penrose, principal of Christ Church College, a formidable scholar in economics and political philosophy who had made no secret of her aspirations to be the first female Chancellor of the university; her protégé, Simon Cole, a plainly dressed and doe-eyed young tutor in economics whom she had asked Jeremy's permission to bring. Bringing up the table for eight was one of Myles' favorite people, Sister Evelyn Paxson, director of St. Clare's Convent and School and a longtime friend of the college. She was affectionately known around Oxford simply and appropriately as Pax.

On arriving at the table, Myles smiled widely at Pax, and they exchanged a hug. He leaned toward her and said in a lowered voice, "What do you say we leave all this foolery and go to some pub?"

"If we do," replied Pax in a conspiratorial tone as she squeezed

Eva's hand, "we're not going without this dear thing." Pax had known Eva for over twenty years and was a sort of second mother from their time together at the convent school.

Like most of the professors in attendance, Penrose and Jacoby were dressed in formal academic attire: billowy black gowns with rich brocade running down the front panels. Moretti wore his monsignor's black cassock with purple piping. Pax wore a dowdy navy polyester skirt, blazer, and a simple chained cross. Jeremy's suit looked as if he'd slept in it, but his black doctoral gown hid most of the wrinkles. Myles wore a coat and tie that Tock had quietly provided—he ignored the doctoral gown the Master had sent to his room—and Eva wore a flattering long, slender black skirt with a boldly striped black and yellow blouse.

After Father Ilbert's protracted and braying benediction, and just as relieved guests were half-way into their chairs, he raised his hand and launched into an oratorical declaration: "In this college on this night you shall find an island of timeless civility and culture amidst the raging seas of madness and chaos around us." He stopped for a moment, as if awaiting awed applause. Finding instead bemused faces and awkward silence—and keen to conceal his growing discomfiture—he hastily gestured for everyone to sit.

After introductions and polite conversation for fifteen minutes, Sarah Penrose stepped immediately into the current Oxford troubles. She decried the recent violence and anti-Muslim sentiment, to which Simon Cole added with a pained expression, "Even in the highest reaches of the university, I've heard lamentably prejudiced cant." While everyone was shaking their heads in dismay, Cole asked Eva if any of the backlash had been directed at her.

Eva smiled politely. "As it happens, I'm not Muslim. I only look like some people's image of one."

Cole was wiry with a cleft chin and wore tortoise shell glasses beneath his high forehead and stringy light brown hair. He apologized, and as Myles watched Eva coolly deflect the misconception, Jeremy leaned over to him. "I heard about your display of heroics in the Covered Market this afternoon. It's good to know you've still got the firepower when you need it." He grinned, and Myles shook his head.

As servers cleared away the hors d'oeuvres plates, the table had fallen into smaller conversations. Penrose whispered something to Cole, who blushed. Eva and Myles were both catching up with Pax when Jeremy suddenly blurted out, "Well, it was rather more sparsely attended than one would have liked."

Myles could see that Jeremy had begun to feel the effects of sherry and a few glasses of wine. Eva looked at him, slightly cocking her head and raising her eyebrows.

Jeremy scanned the blank faces at table. "I mean, my lecture in February, just before the end of Hilary Term. Professor Jacoby was just asking about it."

"Oh, dear Jeremy, I'm sorry to hear that," Penrose chimed in. The Principal of Christ Church looked glamorous with her sandy blonde hair wound neatly into a French updo, her specially tailored academic gown with its laced, low-cut neckline string, and her lithe hands punctuated by crimson fingernails that stood out against her double strand pearl necklace that she would occasionally fondle.

Myles found it curious that she was on a first-name basis with Jeremy. Obviously, there was some history between them.

Penrose laid her hand familiarly on Cole's. "Anytime I'm scheduled to speak, I press Mr. Cole into service, just so I know there'll be someone in attendance. And intelligence and loyalty are by no means his only virtues. He's an admirable humanitarian, as well."

"What sort of humanitarian work, Mr. Cole?" asked Pax energetically.

"Principal Penrose is too generous with her words," said Cole with a humility that was almost painful to watch. "I manage to do some volunteer work when I'm not tutoring—Oxfam, Meals on Wheels, that sort of thing."

Myles, realizing that he'd rather be having a root canal, took a moment to look around the room, mainly to see how things were being orchestrated. He was especially interested to see if Ilbert had indeed bolstered security for the evening. He noticed a few tough-looking young men in blazers and ties standing at doorways and figured they'd do in a pinch. The sub-bursar, John Brooke, was managing the student workers with impressive precision. They moved deftly around and in-between tight tables while carrying large trays for the entrée and bottles of wine. Myles observed Brooke cast a stern glance at Celia Frick, who, oblivious to the sub-bursar's displeasure, leaned insouciantly against the kitchen doorway while attempting to chat up one of the blazer-wearing security men. Across the dining room, Tock appeared to be engrossed in conversation with an effervescent young woman whom he had earlier introduced to Myles as one of his doctoral students.

Myles suddenly felt a nudge at his foot and his attention pulled back to the table to see Pax, ever the grade school teacher, giving him a wink and a smile.

"In any event, Father Strand," said Jacoby, "you were saying the topic of your lecture was a bit of verse penned by your Jesuit forebear, Gerard Manley Hopkins. A 'dark sonnet,' I believe you called it. I wonder if that's because it has never seen the light of day," he added with a chuckle. Tall with receding graying-brown hair, Jacoby wore his illustrious reputation easily and somehow managed to make grandiosity appear utterly relaxed. His dark eyes sparkled as he looked about the table and stroked his closely groomed beard.

"If I may," said Pax, her tone calm and confident, "'dark' in Hopkins' case refers to his spiritual struggle, no? As in one of his famous poems, '*No worst, there is none. Pitched past pitch of grief.*'" Pax's manner and speech were as utterly devoid of pretension as her wardrobe was of fashion. In that moment, Myles saw her as an island of sincerity in a sea of pomp.

A server came round with more wine, and Jeremy held up his glass for a refill. As if from a broken tango, Ivy Cassidy spun out of nowhere with a basket of rolls.

"Quite right, Sister," Jacoby stated and then turned back to Jeremy as he'd forgotten his original prey. "But, really, old man—buck up!" Jacoby said with a coy grin. "Things can't be all that bad."

"That's just it, Professor Jacoby," said Jeremy excitedly. "Things *can* be that bad."

"*Signor Professore,*" Moretti added, giving Jacoby a calculating look, "for the one who struggles in faith, there are times when relief, confidence, joy seem forever gone."

If Jacoby felt a slight reprimand from the Vatican prelate, he showed no indication of it, but simply nodded respectfully.

Jeremy drank half his glass of wine and continued. "The sonnet in question came to light shortly after Dr. Bashir began digitizing our Hopkins collection. Not a very accomplished piece and, quite frankly, oddly underwhelming, especially for Hopkins. But beneath its devotional surface it holds one of those sensational Oxford secrets we all love." He took a drink and raised his eyebrows.

"Come now, Jeremy," said Penrose, as Ivy speedily refilled the table's breadbaskets, "how sensational could it be, considering the source?"

"How about the Cuxham Chalice?" Jeremy said as if issuing an impish challenge.

Myles and Eva exchanged quick glances. Moretti smiled tightly while studying everyone with his eyes.

"In a Hopkins poem?" exclaimed Jacoby. "What *about* the Cuxham Chalice?"

"That it exists," said Jeremy dramatically.

Jacoby and Penrose frowned, then let out simultaneous puffs of laughter.

"You mean that Hopkins believed it was more than mere legend?" asked Jacoby. He didn't wait for an answer. "Many people did hold to that idea, though not as late as the Victorian era or any time in the nineteenth century, for that matter."

"No. I mean yes," said Jeremy, polishing off another glass and leaning forward. Clearly, he was relishing everyone's curiosity. "The poem doesn't merely imply Hopkins' belief that the mythical cup was historically real. It implies the existence of the chalice *in his day*."

An awkward, awestruck silence fell momentarily upon the table. Myles noticed that Moretti's expression went from watchful to anxious, though he wondered why.

A flock of servers descended upon the table with plates of beef tournedos, a potato and leek galette, and pan-roasted white asparagus. Eva had chosen an alternate entrée, a white bean risotto instead of the beef. A server placed a bottle of Rhone at each end of the table, and Jeremy wasted no time in reaching for the one closest to him.

"It all seems rather fanciful, don't you think—that the chalice would appear in your Hopkins' sonnet?" Penrose said by way of a judgment dressed up as a question.

Before Jeremy could respond, Jacoby leaned forward with a skeptical grin. "One hardly knows how to respond, I must say.

If the Cuxham Chalice ever did exist—and that is not an insignificant *if*—it disappeared from any historical reference after the Great Reform. Or at least some fabled chalice did. And, Sister Pax, this should interest you: Cuxham was a Benedictine house. But, alas, any residual history to the cup fled and hysteria replaced it, as I'm afraid often happens in human affairs." He smiled as he sipped his wine. "Well, the point is, the Cuxham Chalice became as chimerical as the Holy Grail."

"Some people, unlike Professor Jacoby here," chimed in Penrose, "do believe the chalice was real. And not only that, but that it came into the possession of Cardinal Wolsey, founder of my own college. He then willed it to Christ Church upon his death." She picked up her glass of wine as if to toast the long-dead cardinal.

Moretti tilted his head back slightly before addressing Penrose. "If I may make a slight but important correction. I believe your phrase, 'came into the possession of' is what you call a euphemism. The way Wolsey, and others like him, 'came into possession' of valuable and sacred objects was to...um...apprehend them from churches and monasteries, *non è vero?*"

Myles noted Moretti's careful turn of phrase—and the pleasure that Jacoby seemed to take in seeing Penrose corrected.

"Quite so, Monsignor," said Jacoby. "The fact is, the so-called Cuxham Chalice came to be a deeply meaningful symbol of Oxford's medieval heritage. I say *symbol* because, as I've shown in my second volume on the history of the university, no objective evidence exists. The fact is, no serious mention has been made of evidence having existed regarding a chalice under the monastic name of Cuxham since sometime in the seventeenth century." He glanced at Penrose. "It was described as pure gold lavishly adorned with gems of all kinds. Mind you," he added with a slight chuckle, "if it did exist it would be fantastically valuable. It would be like—"

"Finding the Holy Grail," said Pax, in a delighted tone.

"Well, there it is," said Penrose abruptly, as if it were time to get on with other talk.

"And just as implausible," asserted Jacoby definitively. "I'm sorry to burst your—or rather Hopkins'—bubble, Father Strand."

"The manuscript leaves *me* in little doubt," asserted Jeremy, rather too loudly. "Moreover, the Cuxham Chalice may not even be the most noteworthy implication Hopkins makes." He paused for dramatic effect, as he could see that he had everyone's attention. "I believe the poem is also very much about Lumen, the self-proclaimed 'keepers of the Grail.'"

If Jeremy had planned on provoking his listeners, his hopes were fully realized. Expressions of bewilderment and disbelief seized every face.

22

As she walked up the sidewalk to 39 Carrington Lane, past a group of anxious neighbors huddled around an elderly woman who was weeping, Chief Inspector Hilary Stratham observed a young Thames Valley constable standing in a bed of periwinkle and heaving up the last bits of his lunch. *Well, this is going to be jolly,* she thought as she scaled the three steps to the door and entered the crime scene.

Four Thames Valley personnel moved deftly about the body lying under an archway between the living and dining rooms. Two arcs of blood, one larger and longer than the other, painted the living room wall closest to the body. A pool of drying blood had settled into the pink braided rug beneath the body. One officer was looking through papers piled neatly on a small side-table, another was jotting down notes on a TVP stock issued pad, while a third was photographing the body from every possible angle, the camera flashes followed by soft, high-pitched whines. On the floor next to the body, slowly pulling off latex gloves, was the medical examiner. All four glanced at the Chief Inspector and nodded silently as she stepped into the room.

"So, Watkins, what have we got?" she asked as she stepped past the settee and stood next to the body.

The officer with the notepad read. "Deceased is Florence Ballard, 78 years old, pensioner, never married, no local family, has a nephew in Surrey, retired schoolteacher, head of the Women's Guild at Mary Mags."

"That's St. Mary Magdalene, Officer Watkins," Stratham said in a mock matronly tone. "This must be the same Florence Ballard my mother volunteered with for years in the Vestry, poor dear. What else?"

"No sign of forced entry. Neighbor phoned it in an hour ago. A Mrs. Powers just across the street who often had tea with Miss

Ballard here. Knocked at the front door, and when the old lady didn't answer, came around back, found the door opened and... well, this." He pointed to the body. "Forensics will dust for prints and look for any blood clean-up the killer or killers might've attempted, but there's nothing obvious at first glance. A pretty clean job—well, except for all the blood, that is."

"Miss Ballard lived alone?"

"Yes ma'am, except for a furry feline. It's under the settee and isn't happy that any of us are here, includin' the old lady, I'd guess."

Stratham snapped on a pair of blue latex gloves and bent down to the body. She could now appreciate the plight of the junior officer leaning on the front garden wall. The old woman was lying on a lace tablecloth likely torn from the dining table. Between her chin and the delicate fingers pointing toward it was a ragged, gaping wound that stretched from her left clavicle to just under the right corner of her jaw. The cut was so savagely deep that Stratham wondered how the head could still be attached to the body. The woman's forehead was scored in several deliberate strokes. In a grotesque juxtaposition, her eyes were wide-open with shock, while her arms were folded gently over her breasts as if ready for her own wake.

Stratham sighed, looking up at the Medical Examiner. "Terry, what do we know so far?"

"Well, cause of death was exsanguination resulting from a deep laceration at the neck and the severing of the carotid artery. The neck wound was caused by a large, brutally sharp blade, but the tearing of the skin is the result of the blade worked back and forth in a sawing fashion. Looks like left-to-right from behind—first strike—and then two more, right-left, left-right again. Killer was right-handed. In spite of the obviously staged position of the body, I'm guessing she was killed in close proximity to where she lays. The blood says as much. Considering what was done to her, the killer was damned efficient about it."

Everyone in the room knew where this was going.

"Any sign of sexual assault?"

"Not from my preliminary exam, Chief Inspector. Clearly, there was a tussle and she was dragged, probably from the dining to the living room, given the single shoe-groove in that Persian and the fact that the other shoe is under the red armchair. And there's the spatter here on this wall. My guess is that it all happened fairly quickly."

"Watkins and Harrison—any signs of theft?"They reported that the victim's purse was in the kitchen, undisturbed, as was a small cash box in the upstairs bedroom. "Right, then. Let's wrap this up, lads. And Terry," she said, turning to the ME, "the markings on the forehead?"

"As you can see, there are three, maybe four deep strokes, likely made by the same blade that caused the neck wound. Whereas the neck wound is ragged and brutal, these cuts on the forehead are very precise. Seems the murderer staunched the wound so that the markings would be more visible. Of course, I'll need to do a full autopsy to be sure—about everything." The ME was silent for a moment, staring down at the body.

"What's bothering you, Terry?"

"Two things, Inspector. The markings are nearly identical to those we found on Peter Toohey a week ago—"

"Jesus," Watkins whispered hoarsely.

"Steady on, Watkins," Stratham said. "All right everyone, listen up. We could have a serial killer here. Could be a copycat, but the MO is similar and the forehead wounds look a little too similar to the ones on the Toohey lad. For obvious reasons, TVP will release this information very carefully to the press. I'll ask PR down at the station house to deal with that. Watkins, you breathe a word of this to *anyone* in the next forty-eight hours and you'll be walking a beat in Jericho. *No one* mentions serial killer, not until Terry closes the autopsy and does the necessary comps with the Toohey kid. We'll have a full forensics report within the same forty-eight. And you all know the drill when it comes to the media. Let poor Finley out there know that he's to keep his mouth shut as well. That is, when he's finished spewing what looked to have been a perfectly respectable chicken curry. The last thing we need is more fuel for riots."

She turned to the ME once again. "Terry, you said *two* things bothered you about those markings on Miss Ballard's forehead. What's the second?"

"Whoever did this to her made those cuts on her forehead before she was killed. This poor woman was tortured."

23

"Lumen? The twelve-fold light?" Penrose's incredulous tone and quizzical eyes stung Jeremy with their skepticism.

Jeremy nodded enigmatically. "Lumen!" he affirmed, loudly enough to turn the heads of several diners at nearby tables. Like the faces of everyone else at his own table, Myles saw that they, too, registered disbelief.

Myles burst in, "Say, Jeremy, don't you think you should—?"

"No, Myles, I'm fine." His words slightly slurred, he waved Myles away. "Barely even squiffy. Never better."

"Surely, Father Strand," Penrose broke in with a pitying smile, "this must be wishful thinking, isn't it? Poetic license or mystical imagination on Hopkins' part—call it what you will. One quasi-historical legend, the Cuxham Chalice, being merged with a true but equally mysterious one, Lumen?"

While her tone suggested confident but kind dismissal, Myles observed that her hands were tightly clenched around her knife and fork like a surgeon determined not to lose her grip.

While she continued, Jeremy leaned into Myles and whispered, "Myles, it's there. It's all there—trust me." Jeremy turned to the other guest and opened his mouth to say something, but it was Jacoby who spoke.

"I can tell you, there remains much of this great university's story that we've yet to learn. It keeps people like me in business. Almost nothing surprises me any longer. There are many stories—bodies, as it were—buried at Oxford, and I don't mean those old monks in college crypts." He grinned, but no one else acknowledged the humor.

Moretti filled the uncomfortable silence that followed. "Perhaps someone might enlighten me—please pardon the pun—as to who or what is Lumen."

Penrose spoke up. "Lumen was founded in the 1520s by Cardinal

Wolsey as a collection of twelve clerks or scholars expressly dedicated to king and pope. The name, Lumen, was inspired by the university's motto, *Dominus illuminatio mea*, 'the Lord is my light,' from Psalm 26. The group was based at Christ Church—then called Cardinal College—and soon became and remained the most exclusive, illustrious and prestigious undergraduate society at Oxford." As she spoke, Penrose's expression and voice reflected tremendous pride, but her eyes suggested that her mind was calculating something. "Little more is known of it, though it is reliably chronicled that its members—the university's most brilliant and charismatic—went on to the highest-ranking positions in church and government, industry, medicine, academia and who knows what else."

"Ah," interjected Jacoby with the aid of a wagging index finger, "who knows, indeed! My dear Sarah, you omitted the most important element: the shroud of secrecy surrounding Lumen."

"Secret it may have been," said Penrose, refusing to let her counterpart from All Souls steal her thunder, "but dining societies are as old as the university itself and almost universally confidential. Lumen happened to be the oldest and most distinguished of those clubs."

"You've written about Lumen, haven't you, Professor Jacoby?" asked Cole in an apparent attempt to defuse the tension between his mentor and the esteemed historian.

"Passingly, and quite some time ago," replied Jacoby in a self-deprecatory tone. "And Sarah's quite right about the group's early dedication to king and pope—they were all Catholic priests, of course. After the Reformation, they maintained their ecclesial loyalty, but to the Anglican Church. In time, as the university became more secularized, so, too, did Lumen and its members. But in spite of Sarah's…shall we say, modesty, Lumen was no ordinary dining club. It remained far more sinister and controversial to its very core. And," he added with a melodramatic gesture and emphasis, "to its mysterious dissolution."

"Sounds positively Dan Brown!" interjected Pax with a glance around the table.

"Oh, make no mistake, Sister," said Penrose emphatically. "This is no fiction. I assure you it is quite real, though Cyril exaggerates and extrapolates, as is his wont."

Jacoby raised his hands in mock self-defense. "I'm merely recounting what has been gleaned from the scant historical records that survive. Lumen's reputation was, as Principal Penrose asserts, sterling. They augmented their image by making countless donations to worthy causes and charitable organizations over the centuries, a drop in the bucket of its reputed wealth and scads of art and antiquities. But through it all the group's activities were surreptitious and its true purpose regarded with vague suspicion. Deserved or not, Lumen always remained encircled by insinuations of danger and the taint of foul deeds."

"Ah, but let us return to that 'mysterious dissolution' you referred to," said Moretti, cradling his wine glass by its stem while gently swirling its contents.

Jacoby continued. "For such a group—the most heralded in the history of the world's most celebrated university—some would characterize its dissolution as more ignominious than mysterious." Myles glanced at Penrose, who clenched and bristled but remained silent. "Nothing official appears in the historical record. The university never disavowed the group, but then most dining societies neither sought nor received official sanction by the university to begin with. Written references and records, along with the dark rumors, continued until the latter decades of the nineteenth century, then simply faded away. While the group survived until the Second World War, it was at best a shadow of its former self."

"And no one knows the event which precipitated its decline and eventual demise?" asked Moretti pensively.

"Hopkins did," Jeremy declared with a boozy, glassy-eyed grin.

Again, dumbfounded looks on every face.

"What, then, Father Strand," asked Cole after half a minute, "is the connection between the poem—"

"Incomplete sonnet," corrected Jeremy with a wagging fork.

Myles could see that his friend's inebriation had entered the territory of embarrassment. He and Eva exchanged looks of concern and incredulity.

"Forgive me," Cole said congenially, "but what in the sonnet leads you to connect the Cuxham Chalice to Lumen?"

"Well," he smiled broadly, unconvincingly, "the precise answer to that question is yet to be deciphered. But I have Drs. Bashir and Dunn lending their formidable acumen." Jeremy's smile disappeared as he studied the dregs of his wine glass as if peering into a distant galaxy.

All eyes were on him. Myles studied his friend discreetly, wondering if he should intervene.

Jeremy raised his head only to stare into the distance, like one transfixed by some mirage, and spoke as if in a trance. "Hopkins was brilliant...tortured...haunted. They laid his typhoid-consumed corpse in a Dublin grave." He slowly made eye contact with everyone at the table, his eyes wild and his tone overwrought. "But his private torment and much more were buried in this...dark sonnet!"

24

Half an hour later, after a dessert course during which Jacoby and Penrose continued trading thinly veiled barbs and Jeremy, Cole and Moretti conversed volubly about Anglo-Catholic relations in the modern era, Eva and Pax had a quieter chat between themselves. Myles found himself checking his watch and preparing for his friend's next bombshell when the bell marking dinner's end mercifully sounded. As guests were filing into the Senior Common Room, Great Hall and D'Arcy Library for chocolates, port and spirits, Myles made an inconspicuous departure from the chatty crowd to the quiet of a dimly lit college parking lot behind the library. He surveyed the night sky, from which moonlight filtered through high wispy clouds and cast muted shadows on the pavement and stone. He felt relieved and grateful to breathe fresh spring air, so stifling and bizarre had Guest Night been. Hearing a gentle clacking of shoes on pavement, he turned to see Eva walking toward him, carrying a bag over each shoulder and a parcel in her hands.

"What on earth just happened?" she said, setting her bags on the ground next to her car.

"I have no idea," replied Myles. "I was hoping to snag you before you left and compare notes. I could tell by your expression at dinner that you were as shocked as I was."

"Absolutely. And, frankly, annoyed. I've been working with him on the Hopkins manuscript for weeks, and he hasn't mentioned anything about this Lumen business. You even pointed out the word 'lumenous' in the poem as a misspelling yesterday and Jeremy just let it go by."

"Clearly, he knows more about the poem than he let on," said Myles in an irritated voice. "And what happened to the need for secrecy? Do you have any idea why he would withhold this from us?"

"Not at all," replied Eva. "I've seen him in his cups, but tonight felt different. I know it makes no sense, but he seemed almost euphoric."

"Or desperate," added Myles.

Myles leaned his back against the car and faced her. "Eva, do you have any reason to believe Jeremy's in trouble?"

"He's behaved somewhat erratically in the past couple of months—more than usual, I should say. Missing lectures, tutorials, meals. That sort of thing."

Myles nodded slowly, thinking.

Eva studied his expression. "But you mean a different sort of trouble, don't you?"

"He told me that someone broke into his room and that it had to do with the sonnet. I thought he was being melodramatic."

"And after tonight?"

"Well, we're at an entirely different level now, aren't we?" Myles stepped away from Eva's car and rubbed the back of his neck. "Yesterday, I thought this was all about a friend's obsession with a poem that was going nowhere. Now, it's about a fabled Oxford treasure and a secret society, long gone but of vast power. You saw how people reacted. It was the usual academic banter, but tinged with—"

Eva finished his sentence. "Fear."

"And God knows how many people from neighboring tables heard Jeremy carry on. Right now, he's in the SCR probably going over the same story. I myself feel a combination of alarm and anger. Again, I don't know why he didn't tell us about Lumen before."

"Maybe," said Eva, "he thought the chalice by itself was wild enough. In any event, we deserve some sort of explanation. I'm planning on working from home tomorrow, but I'll be here on Tuesday. If you haven't talked to him by then, I'd be happy to join you for a care-frontation."

Myles shot her an amused grin. "A what?"

Eva laughed lightly. "It's a term I picked up from Sister Pax. It's a confrontation motivated by loving concern, which I think describes our current feelings toward Jeremy. Let me know if you want to meet with him together in the next couple of days. Meanwhile, text or ring me if you want to talk about any of this."

"Sounds like a plan," said Myles as Eva reached down for her bags. "May I?"

"Ta," she said as she handed him a shoulder bag filled with books. "So, aren't you eager to get back inside and rub elbows with more of Oxford's snobs? Or is that a redundancy?"

"Not really my cup of tea," replied Myles.

"I gathered from Jeremy that you rather enjoyed Oxford when you lived here."

"The intellectual life and conversation and the international, multicultural mix, yes. Very much. The social trappings, not so much. How about you?"

"I normally enjoy Guest Night," she said.

Myles raised his eyebrows in surprise. "What's your secret?"

"Well, beneath my cutting-edge facade, I'm a conservative snob." She raised her eyebrows playfully. "The truth is," she added more seriously, "despite the inevitable pretense and self-importance at Guest Night, I always learn something."

"You manage to find the diamond in the rough." He looked at her intently, nodding and smiling. "Kind of like you amidst this college."

She returned the smile and opened her trunk. "That's very kind."

As he set the bag down Myles glanced at the books at the top. "*The Origins of the Qur'an* by Weber; *The Varieties of Religious Experience* by William James; *The God Delusion* by Richard Dawkins; *Tao Te Ching*; *Siddhartha*. Just some light bedtime reading?"

Eva grinned. "Sam is worried that because of my agnosticism, or secularism, or whatever, I'm going to hell and threatening to drag her down with me." She sighed. "Actually, she's expressed an interest in religion, and I figure instead of simply fighting her about it I can at least help her be informed."

"You've chosen some heavy-hitting classics."

"Well, I think she's being unduly influenced by her infatuation with her boyfriend, whom you met this afternoon." She shuddered at the memory of the assault.

Myles nodded. "Rabi."

"Right. He's a pretty devout Muslim, smart, and probably a good kid, but I think he's a bit misguided and carries a chip on his shoulder. I can't blame him—he had a hellish childhood in Iraq, made his way here on his own three years ago and now lives with an aunt who's not around much. Sam thinks I'm being over-protective."

Myles paused momentarily before replying. "I don't have kids—obviously—but it sounds stickier than your average parent-teenage daughter-boyfriend dynamic. Even without that, Oxford's current climate has got to be a nearly impossible situation for you, Sam, Rabi. Maybe especially Rabi."

"Yeah, he's a bit...lost. Trying to find his way."

"That I can relate to," Myles said.

Hearing a weariness in his voice, Eva looked at him for a moment after he spoke. She flashed a smile, thought of several things to say and ask, then glanced at her watch. "Forgive me for unloading all that. I should go. After leaving the library yesterday morning, Sam spent the rest of the weekend with her father in London. She'll be home by now, and I want to catch her before bed."

Myles opened the driver's door for her.

She got in and Myles pushed her door shut. She started the engine, lowered the electric window and looked up at Myles. He leaned down and rested both hands on the door.

"You know," she said pensively, "Jeremy shared with me his concerns about a possible break-in and someone looking for the sonnet. I followed up with him a few days later, and he said he had spoken to the Master. He never mentioned it again, so I let it go."

Myles shrugged. "He wasn't sure. Or maybe it's more accurate to say that *I* wasn't sure, given his jittery, erratic state of mind. I mean, you've seen how he lives and his high tolerance for chaos. He probably left his room more of a mess than usual and then his imagination got the better of him."

She nodded slowly and said goodnight, but her expression did not seem reassured.

As he watched her drive away, neither was Myles.

25

June 6, 1867

The medieval tower clock strikes 9:00 p.m. as Hopkins dashes through the downpour across the Garden Quadrangle of Balliol College, his mind preoccupied with the task that awaits him. He is returning from a college ceremony at which his mentor Benjamin Jowett presented him with an award for his First-Class examination results in Classics, or "Greats." In presenting the award, Jowett called him the "Star of Balliol," a moniker Hopkins is sure will elicit japes and jibes from his mates. The all-day rain, coupled with pre-convocation commitments—and an indefinable though palpable tinge of qualm and misgiving—have kept him from doing what he promised Carrick. "I must do it now," he tells himself, as he bounds up his stairwell. He curses his powerlessness over the anxiety that has made his heart race and his entire body tense and jittery since Carrick's disquieting, ominous visit last night. Despite the rain and the long walk that awaits him, he plans to grab the pouch, which he has hidden in his portmanteau, and leave immediately.

Without even bothering to shake off his dripping hair and clothes, he throws open his door. Lost in a welter of worry and wavering resolve, he has taken three swift steps into his sitting room before stopping suddenly. He raises his eyes to find himself encircled by grim and determined faces. Behind him he hears the door softly shut and the lock click into place. For the first time all day he is no longer aware of the portentous thump of his heart, though whether because its rate has multiplied or because it has stopped altogether, he cannot say. He tries to swallow but his mouth is so dry he nearly gags.

The uninvited guests stand motionless and all in black, hands at their sides, except one who wears a form-fitting tan suit and is half a head taller than the rest. His arms are folded across his chest imperiously. Instinctively, Hopkins' attention settles upon this man, who slowly raises one hand to stroke his chin. In addition to his height, he is distinguished from the others by his aggressively angular face, accentuated by his sharply honed Van Dyke, and, perched half-way down the bridge of his nose, pince-nez through which he scrutinizes Hopkins as if from Mount Olympus.

"Hopkins, we haven't time for niceties or sobriquets. We do, however, require your cooperation. *One is tempted to say capitulation, but I trust that the 'Star of Balliol'"*—ironically emphasizing the last phrase, he parades a condescending smile around the circle—"will, no doubt, find the good sense to enlighten us with his astral knowledge."

The boggling question of how this stranger has already ascertained Hopkins' newly bestowed honorific is overshadowed by the man's disconcerting and commanding calm. He speaks rapidly in a voice disarmingly deep and soft, creating the unsettling impression of relaxed intensity. Each word and phrase is steeped in self-assurance. The effortless yet forceful weight of his speech—indeed, of his very presence—awes Hopkins. He fights back a debilitating sensation of weakness and insignificance, as if standing before the torrent of a waterfall at once elegant and implacable.

Moncrieff, he thinks. Though nearly light-headed with exhaustion and nerves, he steadies himself and quickly counts the faces. Eleven.

Twelve minus Carrick.

Lumen.

Hopkins forces himself not to glance at his portmanteau, visible through the doorway to his bedroom. It sits like a tinderbox at the foot of his bed.

"We seek our comrade, Thomas Carrick, and have reason to believe that you are privy to his whereabouts. You see, he seems to have erroneously appropriated something which is not his. No doubt you can understand our keen interest in apprehending our wayward brother. And our missing...possession." *He pauses, staring intently at Hopkins.* "Bear in mind, our intentions are pure and righteous, unadulterated by sentiment or cupidity, and so shall our determination to restore what is ours be unyielding and indefatigable." *His message as peremptory as his manner is self-possessed, Moncrieff regards his involuntary host from within placid, unblinking gray eyes.*

"I have no idea where Tom is," *Hopkins says as convincingly as he can.*

"Ah, it speaks," *remarks Moncrieff with tacit condescension, looking around the room to his intimates, a few laughing softly.*

Even as he feels increasingly intimidated by the scene and panicked by its possible outcomes, Hopkins' brain tells him to steel himself, remain composed and display only resolute defiance. "If he wishes to be found," he declares, addressing Moncrieff with all the bravado he can muster, "I'm sure he will inform you in time." In response to Moncrieff's raised eyebrow, he continues. "You had no right to enter my rooms, and I must ask you to leave. Now."

Belying his internal terror and praying that his trembling does not show, Hopkins unflinchingly meets Moncrieff's steady, penetrating glower.

"One last chance," says Moncrieff. "Tell us what you know, and we shall leave you in peace. The alternative may be unpleasant. History has shown us to be unwavering hunters and pitiless adversaries." Without breaking his stare, he takes two steps forward until he stands inches from Hopkins, towering over him, and declares, as apodictically as if it were scientific fact, "We are indomitable." With his index finger jabbing Hopkins' chest, he whispers, "Do…not…test…Lumen."

A moment later the door shuts and Hopkins finds himself alone. Mind racing and heart hammering, he takes several deep breaths to begin to steady his wobbly limbs. God, where is Carrick?, he wonders. Has he made it to London? Has he yet confided in his father, confessed his crimes? Would that he were here, now! As he is imagining what he will say to his friend when they next meet, Hopkins is overcome with an indefinable and alarming sensation: Will I see Carrick again?

He tries to shake the feeling as he stands at his window, peering from behind a barely drawn curtain into the June gloaming. Heart full, pulse hammering and mind calculating, he watches. His eyes scan, alert to every movement. Front Quad and the porter's lodge leading to Broad Street. Salvin Tower. The archway leading to the Fellows Garden and toward the Master's Garden.

Twilight turns to full dark. Activity ebbs as studious and carousing students alike retire to their digs. Still he surveils.

Sometime after belltowers near and far have struck midnight, he turns from the window. He retrieves the burgundy velvet pouch from within the depths of his portmanteau and stows it in his satchel. He steps from his door into the stairwell. Nothing. The collar of his frock coat turned up, he stealths across the quad. Moments later, with watchful paranoia, trembling hands and darting eyes, he sets out with a purposeful gait into the lamplit night.

26

His bicycle safely hidden in a thicket well beyond the path to the ruins, Jeremy aimed the flashlight at the ground ahead and behind. Anxious, out of breath, adrenaline pumping, he hoped against all hope that this would be the night when he would redeem himself. But he couldn't quite shake the creeping doubts about this whole reckless misadventure. He should have waited until morning, convinced Myles to come along. His head buzzed from too much wine, port, and scotch mingled with exhaustion from a long and wobbly bike ride. He didn't actually smoke that cigar in the SCR, did he? Whenever he closed his eyes, he saw the arched eyebrows and patronizing smirks of all the skeptical and disparaging naysayers.

"Damn!" he exclaimed, startling himself with the sound of his own voice. Anger at himself for being impetuous did battle with disappointment in his self-doubt.

A breeze rustled through the treetops as if to shake him from his misgivings. With a deep breath he pushed them all down. This was his project and he would see it through.

The map he had tucked into his blazer was certainly no help now, for what he sought appeared on no cartographer's charts. He racked his brain to recall details from his previous visit here. That had been on a sunny morning earlier in the spring, when the grass and weeds weren't so overgrown. Now nothing looked familiar, and for the past hour he'd been tripping and stumbling through uneven ground and over stones buried in knee-high weeds and grass.

As he scanned the ground with his light, he replayed his conversation with Goodall: "Slypes are a slippery notion, Strand... not necessarily a covered passage...can be the narrowest of spaces between walls..." *How could I have missed it last time? I must have seen it, perhaps walked right past it.*

Choosing his steps carefully, he squeezed his way between two crumbling and irregular rows of stone. He nearly tripped over one of the sides when he heard a rustling sound from a copse thirty feet to his left. A shiver of fear ran through him. He cast the torchlight in the direction of the sound only to see a raccoon lumbering along the copse's edge away from Jeremy and deeper into the undergrowth.

After several minutes he arrived at an impasse in the form of a concentrated mass of branches and brambles wedged tightly between the collapsed walls. It looked like a thorn bush that had been growing unimpeded for decades. About to turn around and retrace his steps, he stopped. *This has got to be the place. Press on, Strand. You can't quit now!*

He turned his face away from the prickly mass, then drove his whole body against it. To his surprise, the whole thing moved. Its roots must've detached years ago, leaving the tangle of branches and dead leaves a momentary inconvenience. Taking a step back, he took hold of a branch with each hand and yanked. Nearly the whole mass came at once. He tossed it aside and continued forward through the narrow space. Before long his foot stepped on something hard. It wasn't stone and made a slightly hollow sound. He aimed his flashlight on the sunken ground. Squatting down, he brushed aside the overgrown grass and weeds until he saw a partially rotten board. The smells of earth and old wood in the cool spring night began to clear his head.

There were three boards, all roughly thirty inches long and ten inches wide. He tried pulling them up but they were sunken below ground level. After digging frenetically with the base of his flashlight, he managed to wedge the fingers of both hands beneath the edge of a board and pull upward with all his strength. On the second try it lifted. He did the same with the other two, leaning all three boards against the adjacent stone walls.

Sweating, pulse thumping in his head, Jeremy aimed his flashlight downward. He peered into the hole where stone-strewn steps descended into blackness.

Monday, May 8

27

Myles awoke at 7:45 feeling frustrated from little sleep. After his conversation with Eva in the carpark, he had lain awake for hours replaying the Guest Night histrionics, asking himself what more exactly he thought he could accomplish here and ruminating over his recent conversation with Tock.

He reached over to the small bedside table, grabbed his phone and checked for a text he was sure he'd find from Jeremy apologizing for his behavior. A text would be only the beginning of a much-owed explanation to Myles and Eva as to why he had withheld so much information, even guesswork, regarding the poem. Announcing it for all to hear was another matter entirely.

But then, Myles wondered why he cared. If Jeremy wanted to embarrass himself, that was his choice. Maybe Myles was feeling more concern for Eva and her long-patient work with Jeremy on the Hopkins fragment, filling in details, chasing down references, and offering incisive ideas about the poem's odd-angled lines.

There was no text from Jeremy, who was probably still sleeping it off. An email from Eva, however, gave Myles a pleasant lift. The subject line read simply, *It isn't stopping*, and the brief text that followed was all business: *Check out this article. As I mentioned last night, I'm out for the day but I'll look for you in the library tomorrow.* That was it.

Myles tapped the link to an article from *The Guardian*, front page, about the murder of an elderly woman in North Oxford named Florence Ballard. Another Oxford killing had made national news. The story was sketchy, most likely, Myles inferred, because the police were parceling out information in calculated doses. The basic circumstances were there: location of the murder, likely time of death, method employed, and a standard appeal for anyone who knew the victim or was in the neighborhood Sunday to notify the police.

It was "method employed" that caught Myles' attention: another knife-slaying, sawing the head from the body, though in this case the beheading was incomplete. Police suspected the woman had been killed in one part of her flat and her body subsequently moved to the living room and arranged "in a macabre display." The article didn't elaborate on that unsettling phrase. Myles scanned the remainder of the piece for any mention of Islam or Muslim rituals of death and burial and was relieved to find none. But although *The Guardian* resisted using the phrase "act of terror," Myles figured the public would quickly connect the old woman's murder with that of Peter Toohey and the assailed immigrant neighborhood of Wilton Leys.

He pulled on a pair of jeans and a polo shirt, splashed water on his face and made his way to the Jesuit Residence wing, one floor below his guestroom. Many of the doors were open, broadcasting dust-filled rays of sun through book-lined rooms and into the hall. First tutorials were about to begin, and most dons and students were in the dining hall slurping down coffee and kippers. Jeremy's door, of course, was closed. Myles knocked forcefully. No answer. He knocked again, feeling a small inner tug-of-war between venting anger and showing scientific curiosity about his friend's bizarre behavior. After half a minute he tried the door, which was unlocked.

The room was empty. Clearly, Ivy Cassidy and her biohazard waste disposal team hadn't made it into the room yet. Jeremy's bed hadn't been slept in, and the Oxford academic gown he'd worn for Guest Night was tossed onto the smoothed bedding. Myles walked to the closed bathroom door and tapped abruptly.

"JS, you in there?"

Silence. The door was unlocked and the bathroom empty. Myles turned back to the bedroom, looked around, and felt a sudden shimmer of fear for his friend. Myles knew it was a gut reaction, and he waited for that calmer, inner voice that called for steadiness and reason. The likeliest explanation was that Jeremy was stretched out on some overstuffed Edwardian couch in the Senior Common Room, an empty bottle of single malt by his side. But then there was the gown: Jeremy had to have come up to his room, toss the thing on the bed and then...?

He called Jeremy's cell and it went immediately to voicemail. "Where are you?" Myles said into his phone. "Ring me when you get this." He typed the same text message and sent it.

As he stood in the doorway about to leave, he scanned the room for a full minute. It appeared much the same as it looked the night he and Jeremy had first discussed the Cuxham Chalice and Hopkins' sonnet. But something was missing. There had been a picture or some graphic tacked to the wall on the other side of the open door. Whatever it was had been pulled down in haste because small torn corners at two points were still stuck under thumbtacks. Myles tried in vain to recall what it was. The only other significant difference from the earlier visit was a short stack of 5x7 photos on a corner of the desk. Myles quickly flipped them: a hedge above a stone wall, some scattered rocks bedded down in high grass and weeds, maybe medieval stonework long fallen into disrepair. The images could be from anywhere and of anything. He tossed the photos back on the desk.

The wastebasket at the side of the desk overflowed with torn index cards, a couple of news magazines and wads of Ignatius College stationery. Myles dumped the entire contents and picked his way through, seeing nothing out of the ordinary except for one piece of paper. It was torn from a notebook and had a single word printed in Jeremy's hand in uppercase letters:

COLLINGTON

The word might mean anything: a favorite restaurant, a Hopkins authority, a place name, somebody's dog, a newly discovered brand of cheap scotch.

Myles stood up. Instinct told him not to ignore that shimmer of fear. It was time to search Ignatius College, and perhaps beyond, for the missing Jeremy Strand.

28

"You look as if you've been playing in the metaphorical dirt, dear boy."
The priest leans forward and pours tea. "And this," he nods his head
in the direction of his guest seated on the couch across the table, "from
one of Oxford's most distinguished recent baccalaureates." He sees that
the young man's agitated look isn't changed by humor or compliment.
"Gerard, what havoc is this?"

"Oh, Father Newman, I'm sorry." Hopkins has the desperate and
depleted look of a world-weary man three times his age. He glances
down at his clothing and moves his hands lightly and ineffectually about
his chest. He sees now what he hadn't an hour before, when he was in
the crypt: the dust of centuries on his vest and sleeves. He knows whence
it comes and imagines the tiny fragments of bone and medieval rock
that must be in his cuffs, pockets and hair. He has carried death into this
room.

"I was fetching luggage from one of the basements in Balliol and fell."
Fell indeed, he thinks. Here he is, in confession to John Henry Newman,
his spiritual director, and he lies about the smeared grime and the toil
that made it. How many sins, he wonders, did he carry in the chalice?

"If you've fallen, then we must raise you up. What burdens you, son?"
Hopkins trusts Newman with his life. The priest whose conversion
to Rome has helped light Hopkins' own way to Roman Catholicism and
priesthood is a treasured confidant. How many times has he sat here,
on this couch, sipping Newman's teas and speaking of his soul's journey,
the Society of Jesus, books and Christ and love. And still he cannot
speak of what he's done, where he's gone and what awesome duty he has
performed. He wants to say, "I have buried one of the great treasures of
Oxford and medieval Christendom." But he cannot. He will not.

Hopkins gently places the teacup and saucer on the table before him.
"Father, may I posit a moral dilemma?"

The priest nods.

"If a man makes a vow, a promise to a friend, under what circumstances may he break it?"

Newman arches his eyebrows, sips his tea and rests saucer and cup against his black cassock. He ponders the young man's question and searches the high dark oak wall of books that towers behind his guest's head. Afternoon birdsong from the college gardens wafts in with a breeze that billows the oriel sheer. He looks directly at Hopkins.

"This is serious business, Gerard, and I should think that the circumstances under which a man may break a promise are rare, indeed. Let us take this...individual. First, to what has he sworn?"

Hopkins looks down to the patterned intricacies of the Persian rug. "That I cannot say. I've given my word."

"Ah, then the nature of the bond is something that should be kept hidden. Is that correct?"

Hopkins nods, looks up and then adds: "The thing hidden, that is, the secret kept, is only part of the bond—though, dear God, it is a mighty one." Hopkins shakes his head in a combination of wonder and fear. He wishes he were rid of this knowledge and the action behind it: hiding the Cuxham Chalice. Waiting on Carrick...hoping. He falls silent, and both men wait. The tick of a captain's clock on the Tudor-style stone mantle is louder than Hopkins remembers.

Quietly, almost at a whisper, the priest asks: "You said that the thing hidden is only part of the bond. Are there others?"

"Trust. Friendship."

The young man stands up and walks to the window. Gazing at the college gardens, a glorious efflorescence of color, he sees nothing but the terror in Carrick's eyes, the stone-dark walls of the crypt, the place where he has hidden the chalice. The clock ticks the minutes and hours, the days that Hopkins must wait and hope that Carrick is true to his word.

Hopkins is suddenly aware of the priest standing just behind him and to the right. He, too, looks out into the garden. A black-gowned don of Oriel College walks by, a raven with books tucked under a wing.

"Gerard." The priest puts his hand on Hopkins' shoulder. "Are you willing to trust your friend?"

"I am," says Hopkins. "I must."

"Then do it, Gerard, in peace. Trust your friend with all your heart. Believe what he has told you until you learn otherwise."

Hopkins turns and looks at his confessor. The sad, gray eyes have known trusts held and broken, secrets kept and honored. "Until I learn otherwise."

Suddenly, it all feels possible to Hopkins. He can carry this burden lightened by trust, carry it away from Oxford tomorrow to Newman's Oratory School at Edgbaston, where he will teach until summer's end. He can carry it into the Society of Jesus when he enters in the fall. All of this until he hears otherwise from Carrick. His friend will come for the chalice and for the dark revelations it holds. His friend will do the right thing, as he promised.

29

Monsignor Moretti slammed his breviary on the desk and sat forward in his chair, head in his hands. He suddenly repented the act, wishing he'd been able to vent his frustration without bruising the scriptures. He drew an apologetic sigh and pushed himself up and out of the chair. A *Nazionali* burned indifferently in an ashtray near the desk lamp. For the fifth time in the past hour, he was pacing his room at Ignatius College. He checked his watch; only noon and he had hours before his scheduled phone call to the Vatican. It was possible that Slater had more information for him on Myles Dunn and, more importantly, the Cuxham Chalice. Furthermore, he wondered whether his initial assessment of Jeremy Strand needed revision, including background material that might have been missed months before, when planning this operation.

Moretti couldn't understand the Guest Night performance. Was Strand so unhinged that a fragile ego and a few glasses of mediocre wine could undo what the two of them had built during their month-long collaboration? What could he possibly gain from those public guesses about the chalice and—what was it called? —Lumen?

"Why did the man not heed my admonition to minimize discussion of the chalice?" Moretti bellowed in Italian to no one in particular as he paced. Given the range of personalities at that table, their colleges and connections, the Cuxham Chalice was likely on the risible lips of every Oxford don this morning. "Let them laugh," he muttered, "but do not let them get involved." His work, he knew, would now require more agility and misdirection than he had either the energy or desire for. And now, of all things, Strand had vanished.

"If he is anywhere nearer the chalice without telling me… Oh, to hell with schedules and Vatican protocol," he said as he speed-dialed his Vatican office. "Slater works for me."

"*Pronto.* Slater *qui.*"

"Ian, this is Moretti," he sighed.

"Monsignor—!"

"Yes, yes, I know. I did not want to wait for the call." Moretti rode past Slater's quick pleasantries. "Look, Ian, we have suffered..." Moretti was shaking slightly and he winced as a bolt of pain ran through his chest. Sweat broke out on his forehead and he lowered himself gingerly into the desk chair.

"Monsignor? *Que così?*" With the exception of a slight whisper of static, the phone was silent.

Moretti, against the intensifying pain in his left shoulder, gently put the phone on the desk and fumbled in his black suit pocket for a small prescription bottle. He took a deep breath to steady himself and quickly placed a tiny white pill under his tongue.

"Monsignor? *Sono li? Non ti sento...*"

The pain and pressure quickly receded. Moretti felt steadier, picked up the phone again and whispered hoarsely. "*In inglese,* Ian. *In inglese.*"

"Sorry, Monsignor. I thought I'd lost you there for a moment," the priest chuckled.

Moretti knew his secretary meant a dropped call, but he was contemplating a much more comprehensive, existential loss.

"Ian, I was saying we have suffered a setback here. Father Strand has—well, there is no other way to put it—disappeared."

"Surely, one doesn't just lose a Jesuit, Monsignor."

"Well, you do not know this Jesuit, Ian. Look, I want you to review his personnel file and see if our systems show any pattern of departures from Oxford, say, in the last two years. That sort of thing may well be under our radar, but see what you find." Moretti could hear his assistant tapping keys. "And have you found out anything more about this Dr. Dunn, anything that can be useful to me here?"

"I don't know that there's a lot more to find, Monsignor. We're figuring, of course, some type of covert military operations or national security work during his service. But apart from that, his bio seems unsurprising."

"Very well," Moretti sighed with disappointment, "though see if you can use our contacts with the NSA to find out more about those military years. And one last thing: it is a common Latin word, so you will have to use a number of data filters, but see what you can find out about an Oxford University private club called 'Lumen.' It or they may have had something to do with the chalice—well, at least as far as our missing Jesuit thinks." With that, Moretti offered a quick *grazie* and ended the call.

30

Eva had just finished a late lunch at Sweet Dreams, a bistro tucked behind the Ashmolean Museum. Morning clouds had given way to intermittent sun, so she had chosen a sunny outdoor table alongside the cobbled sidewalk on Pusey Lane. Tourists, shoppers and students in sub-fusc walked past in twos and threes, some pushing bicycles, and the occasional scholar strode by in a lecturer's gown. Every few minutes a vigilant, grave-eyed bobby walked by, part of the ongoing police presence in Oxford.

After the waiter cleared away her plate and she had ordered coffee, she looked up to find Myles walking toward her. She smiled and cocked her head as if to say, "What are you doing here?"

"Hey, I'm sorry if it looks like I'm stalking you—and on your day off—but I needed to see you."

Eva removed her sunglasses and set them on the table. "How did you know where to find me?"

"Well, let's see…it's a beautiful day and I'm guessing you're not the stay-at-home type. Last night at dinner you picked the non-meat option, so I figured you might be vegetarian. I noticed a magazine sticking out of your bag the day we met—*Vegan Journal*. So, I narrowed it down to vegetarian places with outdoor seating. This one is near the Ashmolean and across from Oxford's best antiquarian bookshop, two places I imagine you might frequent. So, what can I say? Sweet Dreams came to mind when I thought of you." Myles was suddenly aware of how flirtatious his words had just sounded and hoped he wasn't blushing.

Eva didn't say anything for a moment. "That's some impressive deduction. Oddly impressive, in fact." She frowned lightheartedly before inviting him to join her. He flagged down a waiter and ordered a coffee, then removed his rumpled blazer and took a seat.

Eva gestured toward the bandage on his arm. "How's the cut?"

"A little tender, but not bad. I put some antibiotic on it, and I think that'll keep it in check. Thanks for asking. Actually, Eva, I want to talk with you about Jeremy. He's gone, and I mean from-early-hours gone. And if there's anything Jeremy hates, it's early hours. Any guess where he might be?"

She shook her head. "No. I imagine you've already looked in all the usual places?"

"I think so…" Myles voice trailed off. "Eva, what's that store over there, the one with the window-shoppers?"

"Kesselman's. It's a map store, from Roman Britain to the latest road atlases. Why?"

He snapped his fingers. "That's what was on Jeremy's wall."

"What?"

"A map, an old one of Oxford. Not the tourist kind you see everywhere in the city. This was a reproduction of an engraved map, maybe from the eighteenth or nineteenth century. It was on his wall last Friday when I first talked with him. This morning it was gone."

"I suppose it's possible he took the map this morning, I mean, after the Guest Night revelries. But he could've taken it down for other purposes over the weekend, right?"

Myles said nothing in response. It was true, Jeremy might have taken down the map for any reason. But if he needed a map of the university and city just now, why take something that's been out of date for a century or two? Myles looked at Eva and shrugged. "Anyway, all of this seems a little too coincidental."

"Well, if it's any consolation, Jeremy has stood me up a few times for meetings—and important ones—and for days. He always crawls back, sweetly apologetic with an armful of flowers but little explanation. What do I know? I thought his disappearing acts might be a British affect or a Jesuit one or a combination of both. But, let me tell you, that kind of behavior wouldn't have been tolerated where I come from," she laughed.

Myles decided to take a chance at switching gears. "And how does a woman from Damascus end up in a Jesuit college at Oxford?"

"In my case, circuitously. I'm an only child from a traditional middle-class Muslim family. When I was five, my parents were both at a Saturday market three suicide bombers just happened to target that day. I was sent here to Oxford to live with my aunt. Of course, at first, I hated it all—the accents, the clothing, the blasted chilly weather. But my aunt was a gem. I swear, every shilling she earned she put toward my education. She'd been a nurse in Syria but the only work she could find here in the UK was as a domestic. So, she tended to be gone most days and I ended up spending a lot of my non-school hours with the sisters at St. Clare's, mostly Pax. It was great seeing her last night." Eva laughed. "Here's this little Muslim girl surrounded by Catholic nuns, but I had no sense of religion and such differences. It was like having eight more aunts. They were lovely..."

The waiter delivered Myles' coffee and topped off Eva's.

"The sisters sent me home with books every day and I read a lot. I grew up learning about the library tunnels running like rabbit warrens underneath the Radcliffe Camera, with connecting chambers of old volumes and medieval manuscripts under the Bodleian. It was like some buried treasure trove I knew I had to explore!"

She sipped her coffee and glanced nonchalantly at a group of American tourists noisily passing by along the sidewalk, unabashedly discussing how to find the spot where Peter Toohey's mutilated body was found. Myles looked at Eva with an apologetic expression as if to say, *My country, but not my people.* The single subtly raised eyebrow and ephemeral grin that he got in reply made him realize that he was more than a little smitten—and not by the tourists.

"Anyway, one year turned to five, public school locally, university in London, books, books, books. Seventeen years ago, I married a Syrian man named Azeem—a successful London businessman. But I quickly discovered that our notions of marriage clashed pretty starkly. The traditional, conservative religious family that I thought would make me feel safe and secure instead made me feel suffocated. Five exhausting years later we divorced, and Sam has been with me ever since. Her father sees her a few times a month, though. I took various jobs in Oxford, and when the position came up at Ignatius I applied, thinking it was an impossible reach. But it wasn't!" She raised her cup of coffee toward Myles in the gesture of a toast. "And, as you well know, I was following a long and distinguished line of Muslim women at the Jesuit college."

Myles rose to her whimsical irony. "I hope they included combat pay in your salary package." As they exchanged a knowing smile, Myles felt increasingly drawn to her directness and understated humor, subtly conveyed in her expressive eyes and silky voice. "I can only imagine how things have been for any real or perceived Muslim in this city these days. The protests have been ugly and the tension is, as you know from your experience the other morning, literally palpable."

"I'd never personally been confronted with that kind of hate before," she said with a sigh.

Myles nodded empathetically and recalled how stalwartly she handled the attack on her car and set it aside the next morning to focus on what must have seemed by comparison the trivial matter of the Hopkins sonnet. And yesterday in the Cornmarket she showed more equanimity than he did. She possessed what his mother lovingly called, in reference to her late husband, "Gris's other two g's": guts and gumption.

"I'm really sorry you had to go through that," he said, "and of course it wasn't an isolated incident. The confounding part is how wrong it all is, starting with the fact that these murders can't be Muslim crimes. None of it makes sense that way."

Eva looked at him in surprise. "You sound…confident."

Myles hesitated. "I am. I just hope the police figure that out soon—and publicize it." He sensed she didn't want to go further on the matter of religion, so he remained quiet.

"But you, Myles, what brought *you* here?"

Myles was touched by the sincerity in her voice and eyes. "You probably know from Jeremy that we were students together here, that I was a Jesuit at the time but left the Society two years ago. I decided to spend some time back in my hometown, near Denver, be with my family and try to figure out what's next. My dad was a cop who took early retirement and sunk his savings into a hardware store. He loved it. Since his death five years ago, my mom has been running it. When I went back, I realized *it* was running *her*—into the ground, and vice versa. She can't bear to sell it because of its connection with Gris—that was my dad's nickname. So, that's where I've been for a while." Myles laughed. "You know, as I review the path, it must sound crazy. Still, it has a certain kind of logic. What word did you use—circuitous?"

"More loving than logical, I'd say." She gave him an assessing look. He was leaning forward, elbows on the table, chin resting on his folded hands, looking like someone desperately in search of his lost idealism as much as his missing friend. In his demeanor, his bearing, even his appearance, he defied the polished image of a man with an Oxford doctorate. It was hard to believe he used to be a Jesuit priest. Rugged and slightly rough around the edges, in some ways he was very American, but that wasn't all bad. She was sorry she'd misjudged him at first. "It sounds courageous. Believe me, I understand the unexpected turns that one's life can take."

Myles heard nothing of judgment in Eva's voice, but rather openness, warmth and a wisdom hard-earned. While he'd done some dating since leaving the Jesuits, he couldn't remember the last time he found himself in a meaningful conversation with such a direct and thoroughly compelling woman. He was so taken with her that he had to catch himself from being obvious about it.

"I should get home," Eva said with a hint of regret in her voice. "Sam and I are cooking together this afternoon."

"Driving or walking home?"

"I'm parked around the corner." She gestured to the left.

"Great. I'll walk you as far as the Bodleian," said Myles as he stood up.

"You do realize," Eva said, "that the Bodleian is several blocks in the opposite direction from my car."

"Oh, really?" said Myles with an impish grin. "I haven't been here in so long I sort of forgot. Besides, it occurs to me that I won't be allowed into the Bodleian without some letter of reference, and I'm hoping you might vouch for me with a fellow librarian."

"The only other way would be to use one's charm and good looks." She mock-frowned before donning her sunglasses. "So, I guess you'll be needing my help."

"Touché. And thanks."

"Since I'm putting my reputation on the line to secure you a pass," said Eva as they crossed St. Giles, "may I ask what it is you'll be researching at the Bod?"

"Given last night's odd movements, I think I'll spend a few hours finding out what I can about Lumen."

"Good idea," she replied.

A minute later, chatting as they walked, Eva gave a friendly wave to someone across the street. Following her eyes, Myles saw the smiling face of sub-bursar Brooke, jogging down Parks Road with a group of students, all clad in running gear. No doubt they were coming from University Parks and headed in the direction of the river and towpath. More noteworthy for Myles, though, was how his picture of Eva Bashir was starting to fill out: pulling strings for him at the Bodleian one moment, waving naturally to a member of the domestic staff whom she barely knew the next. There was a lot to admire in this woman.

31

A sound in Jeremy's head told him to wake. But a clanging chorus of smaller, distraught voices told him to stay in the gray shallows. *Waking isn't in your best interest,* they yelled. But instinct urged him through the heaviness and his eyes opened slowly. Nothing. He blinked and still nothing but a stagnant, cool air against his eyes. A sound, a low-pitched buzz: his cell phone was ringing, but it sounded like it was coming from a separate place, a short distance but not nearby. He closed his eyes tight and hoped when he opened them to see his cluttered room and the May light spilling through the windows on the east wall.

Still, only blackness and the feel of grit and stone against his left cheek. He tried to turn his head in the opposite direction, but pain shivered through his skull and he let his face fall against the cool earthen floor. He tried to raise his right hand but it wouldn't move; neither would his left. The buzzing phone persisted. He realized that he was on his left side and his hands and feet had been immobilized by some sort of coarse stricture binding wrists and ankles.

An ungainly attempt to raise himself only intensified the searing pain at the back of his skull, and in the effort he nearly lost consciousness again. To fight it, he instinctively attempted a deep breath but could not inhale. Something covered and sealed his mouth shut. Panicking, gagging, he heard more than felt his heart pounding in his chest. Rapid, shallow breaths through his nostrils were all he could manage. Besides the acrid reek of his own stale perspiration and the adhesive of whatever tape covered his mouth, his heightened olfactory sense detected dank, thickly musty air and what he could only describe as old, stony decay. *Where in Christ's name am I?* The buzzing stopped and was followed by the chirping sound that a message had been left.

Irrationally, he tried to shout in alarm, producing only a guttural grunt and its bizarrely suffocated echo, which in turn induced further frantic panting. Beads of sweat formed at his forehead and dripped into his eyes. He blinked rapidly, which in turn exacerbated the splintering sense of unreality that possessed him. A wave of claustrophobic horror heaved within and, against all logic, he strained with every muscle to move, run, escape his condition. Again the scorching pain at the back of his skull.

His swirling mind struggled to distinguish consciousness from unconsciousness in the fathomless black. In a fleeting moment of lucidity, he recalled the Old Testament verse—was it Jeremiah? Joel? *Their fate is the utter darkness of darkness for eternity.* He shivered, both from a chill rising up through his aching limbs and from a soul-clenching sense of isolation.

Everything around him felt sepulchral. He felt buried, his senses infused with and paralyzed by cold earth and stone. At the same time—and this, he knew, saved his mind—he *felt* space all about him, felt dank air moving through that space. He knew he wasn't entombed, not exactly. Somehow, somewhere, the slightest bit of air was breaking through fissures in the earth above. He heard from somewhere ten feet to his left—or a thousand feet away, he couldn't tell—a soft plunking sound of water dripping from a height into a puddle. Or was he imagining it?

Steady, old boy, Jeremy counseled himself as if calming an unidentified trauma victim. *Get hold of yourself.* But every erratic surge of consciousness signaled a welling terror that he could scarcely contain. He struggled to remember the boozy steps that brought him to this moment: last night, guests, tables, food, too much drink, way too much talk. *Damn it, Jeremy!* That look of disappointment and surprise on Myles' face, then his departure while Jeremy continued the party in the SCR. The conversation with Barry Goodall, and later, deep in the night, the wobbly bike ride. He'd hidden it in the brambles, then found the slype just as Goodall had described it. He pried loose the planks revealing the opening to…where? Here? And what was here? It had to be subterranean. As if to confirm his dread, the earth pushed little bits of stone into his left cheek. Had whatever chair he was bound to been pushed over? Did he cause the fall himself out of rocking panic?

If I'm where I think I am, then I may be close to the chalice. For a moment, he began to weep, the juxtaposition of discovery and dread having their way with him. *Maybe. But someone else knows it now...Am I as good as dead?* The mounting panic again. *Steady... steady. Listen.* He thought he heard the distant sound of wind, but it was likely the blood rushing through his brain. Seconds passed... or minutes...or hours. Over the wheezing repetition of his shallow nasal breaths, small stitching sounds ahead of him and to the left, maybe a dozen feet or so.

In the effort to focus his mind, he felt a rapidly rising nausea and a crushing light-headedness. Depleted, striving to summon non-existent energy to remain conscious despite his horror and his throbbing head, he heard the low, short squeaks drawing nearer to his face. A moment later he felt a furry touch along his chin. He shook violently until the thing, whatever it was, scampered off amid the stones. For now.

The terror that Jeremy had been scarcely holding in check tore free, and the blackness of an endless night echoed and pulsated with his muffled screams.

32

Thomas Carrick has but one purpose in returning to the crypt. To that end, he walks determinedly past the familiar table and chairs, but before he can reach the far end of the burial chamber he hears a scuffing sound behind him. He wheels around and, framed in the vaulted archway, sees the menacing smile of Alec Moncrieff.

"How are you here?" he utters in undisguised disbelief.

"Dear Carrick," says Moncrieff, both hands resting on his walking stick, "how imprudent of you to have sent a note to the Balliol bursar regarding your things. Have you forgotten how far Lumen's tendrils reach? And once you returned to college from wherever it is you've been, you were as easy to follow as a broken-down hansom. The question is, why are you here?" Without waiting for an answer, he casts his eyes around the room. "Bravo, brother. Most atmospheric. One of my colleagues said you had gone to ground, and so you have. Literally."

As Moncrieff's deep, susurrant voice resonates in the crypt, Carrick feels it penetrate his being and shake him to the core. Moncrieff approaches the table where sits the lantern that Carrick has just lit, along with several books, two glasses and a half-empty bottle.

Moncrieff picks up the bottle and reads its label by the light of the lantern. "A fine claret, Thomas. Not easily acquired. I see that you've been enjoying it with someone. Have you been bringing women here?" He grins menacingly. "Never mind. On to the business at hand—the pressing and," he looks about the grim chamber, "not to put too fine a point on it, grave business of your late thievery."

Carrick stands stock still, feverishly reviewing and rethinking his plan. Did Hopkins place the chalice as he promised? How much does Moncrieff know? Has he gotten anything out of Hopkins? Has he harmed him?

"Where is the chalice, Carrick? Good God, man, you haven't put it anywhere in this frightful place, I hope!" Moncrieff chuckles and walks a few steps, ducks his head into an adjacent chamber, his voice echoing back to Carrick. "The chalice deserves better. Lumen deserved better." The last words are meant for Carrick.

"The chalice is safely in London," says Carrick with as much calm as he can muster, "where I've been this past fortnight. You can be sure that the authorities will hunt you down and bring you and the rest of Lumen to justice...once they find out what's in the chalice."

Moncrieff's eyes flash angrily.

"Carrick, you're merely weak. It was my mistake thinking otherwise. I had hopes for you that went far beyond Oxford: that your family connection and your predictably lofty future would put you in a position to continue the work we've begun these past weeks, the purification Britain needs of this Irish vermin. That, as I say, was my mistake. This"—Moncrieff gestures with his stick to the crypt surrounding them—"was yours."

Moncrieff presses a button on the silver handle of his walking stick. A six-inch blade springs out at the tip. "Sit down, Carrick. In that chair. SIT DOWN!" Carrick submits. "Are you so naïve to think these 'authorities' are beyond Lumen's sway? Can you imagine the Cuxham Chalice remaining hidden in some London bureaucracy?" Moncrieff's laugh throws receding echoes through the vault. "You know me, Carrick," he says through gritted teeth. "I will find the chalice." As he speaks the last word, he thrusts his arm across the table and buries the blade in the center of Carrick's chest. "And if I fail," he jeers, pulling out the blade, while Carrick chokes and gags and looks down at the blood spouting from his chest, "then Lumen will continue this mission until the chalice is found. For you see, unlike you and your puling labors, Lumen is inexorable!"

With the last word he once again lunges across the table, this time driving the blade deep into the center of Carrick's throat.

Tuesday, May 9

33

Ignatius College was hardly large by Oxford standards, but after a restless night Myles rose early and spent the better part of an hour searching every corner for Jeremy. He asked a couple of Jesuits if they'd bumped into him and they hadn't. Ivy Cassidy, still cleaning up from Guest Night, said she'd keep an eye out for him and send him "to your room straightaway, Father Dunn." Myles gave up correcting her—he hadn't the time. All the likely places, including the Edwardian couch in the SCR, were empty on a quiet Tuesday morning.

One place remained, and that was the college chapel. Maybe Jeremy was sufficiently penitent to force him to the sanctuary. Myles walked in and saw bright morning light pouring through the higher windows, coloring the walls with blues, reds and yellows. A solitary figure sat in the first pew just to the left of the sanctuary and altar, and it wasn't Jeremy.

Myles walked quietly down the center aisle to where Tock was sitting, hands folded in his lap, head bowed. With an awkward nod toward the tabernacle, Myles slid into the pew and put a hand gently on Tock's shoulder. He left it there for a few moments without saying a word. As Myles sat looking intently at his spiritual father, the old priest seemed to come slowly back from a faraway place. He looked at Myles and smiled wearily.

"Tock, I'm sorry to bother you, but I'm looking for Jeremy. I don't think he slept in his room either of the last two nights. And I've checked every place in college."

Tock stared at Myles for some moments, his mind working in the ways that thinking about Jeremy often required: *Should I worry or smile the worry away?* Tock seemed to settle somewhere in-between.

"Haven't seen him, Myles. And someone mentioned that his bicycle is missing. But if he's hidden himself away somewhere, I shouldn't be surprised, after his performance the other night."

"Oh, you heard about that, did you?"

"Myles, word gets around, especially in a house full of Jesuits. Even the Master has had enough, or so he claims. But slipping away has been Jeremy's manner over the last few months. These flights have gotten so familiar one of the lay tutors has come to call them 'errant Strands.'" Tock passed a hand lightly through his white hair to illustrate.

"Tell me, Tock, did those flights have any particular pattern? Any guess where he might be?"

"No place that I know of. You remember—Jeremy's always been tight-lipped about where he's going and where he's been. The fact is most of his 'errant Strands' have been entirely legitimate. He'll take off to do weekend ministries in some London parish without so much as a by-your-leave to the Master. He spirits small groups of students off for a three-day retreat. Who knows? I imagine he does all of this just to get away, and any annoyance or inconvenience to the Master is simply icing on the cake." He grinned mildly, but then his face grew pensive.

One of the chapel doors opened with a fleeting screech. Myles glanced up to watch a student genuflect and take a seat in a pew at the back. Tock leaned further into Myles and whispered.

"But I don't think Jeremy's shepherding some London flock this morning, Myles."

"What do you mean?"

"I'm not sure what I mean. I've only feelings to go by, Jesuit paternal anxieties. Maybe it's the havoc in the city, the violence hanging about these old stones, and all those Muslim kids pushed to the wall. Is there a murderer among them? I don't know…but Jeremy has me concerned in a number of ways. And I'm likely to stay that way until he's safely back in college keeping his odd hours and his wrecked room."

Both men sat in silence for several minutes before Myles spoke again.

"I take it you've heard about the second murder."

"Sadly, yes." Tock's eyes registered a combination of sorrow and foreboding that Myles had never seen before. "The Toohey boy's killing seems now only the beginning of a violence that preys upon the most vulnerable. That's true terrorism, isn't it? But from which quarter? Now that this looks like a second Muslim anti-Christian murder, those hateful people from 'Britain Now' will soon be here by the trainload." Tock leaned back into the pew and sighed, rubbing his eyes with one hand. "Myles, who could be committing these crimes?"

Myles shook his head absently. "I haven't a clue."

"Of course you don't, my boy. But what kind of person does this sort of thing? How is it possible to slaughter a child and an old woman and find *meaning* in such cruelty?"

Myles sensed that Tock's question had to do with the kind of violence the younger man had been witness to in Iraq and Afghanistan, a topic Myles had broached on more than one occasion while in spiritual direction with Tock. "I can't believe this has *anything* to do with Islam, Tock, other than to stoke an anti-immigrant fire that's already out of control. It feels too calculated, too well-timed. It's someone who's smart enough to plan and execute both murders without apparently leaving any trail." He turned to the old man and again put his hand on a cardiganed shoulder.

"Don't worry. I'll find Jeremy." Hearing his own words made him feel at once more determined and less certain than he would have liked.

"Worry, Myles?" Tock chuckled lightly, shifted in the pew and looked at the younger man. "Worry not for tomorrow; it has itself to take care of. The old man in me will likely worry in any case, but I hope the Christian in me"—Tock turned from Myles to look in the direction of the sanctuary and tabernacle—"will trust that Jeremy is somehow safe. He's come too close to living again, with this odd snippet from Hopkins. I've not seen him this excited and purpose-driven since the two of you were hammering away on your dissertations years ago. God will see Jeremy through." The old man fought tears in his eyes and looked again at Myles. "And, I think now, this may be the real reason why you came."

34

Eva had gotten the call at 8:25 a.m. from the Thames Valley Police Station on St. Aldate's and immediately felt apprehensive. The morning papers were full of news and speculation about the second grisly murder, along with accounts of a second wave of violence that had erupted overnight. A detective had politely asked her to come in as an "area expert" on something having to do with "a current police investigation." Eva wanted to decline but knew that she couldn't, not with a second murder, not with the mounting tensions. She agreed to meet with an investigator, wanting the ordeal finished as soon as possible.

She walked through the front doors of the TVP Station at 10:00 a.m. to find a waiting room packed with visitors representative of international Oxford: people of all sorts of hues and ethnic dress, from baggy blue-jeaned chavs to ties and tweeds, at least three women in hijabs and more than a dozen young men in kufis. Most of the men were Rabi's age, in their teens and early twenties, brought in for questioning, either as potential witnesses or part of some yet-to-be-named plot. Moreover, countless relatives of these were milling about, talking in Arabic, some in English, all of them looking fearful or dejected.

One of the ties-and-tweeds that Eva saw leaving the station as she entered was Pamuk Serash, Regent Professor of Semitic Languages at Merton College. He wore an expression of dismay crossed with anger or fear—Eva couldn't tell which.

While negotiating her way through the crowd and in a momentary break in the human chaos, she spotted Rabi across the room. He was being roughly escorted to an interview room with two other young men. She forced an uneasy, encouraging smile as their eyes met before he was yanked in the opposite direction.

Once past the crowds, she found her way to the Southeast Counter-Terrorism Unit, an oblong room with a number of desks, most of them manned by a police officer either speaking on the phone or tapping away at computer keys. A woman sitting at one of the desks looked up at Eva and smiled. She closed a folder and swung around the desk, her hand extended.

"Dr. Bashir, thanks so much for coming down here, especially on such short notice." Chief Inspector Hillary Stratham was fifty-something, with shortish blond hair tucked behind her ears. She was dressed in a gray twin jacket and skirt and might easily disappear into a crowd of barristers on Chancery Lane were it not for the badge dangling from a lanyard around her neck and the shoulder holster showing through her jacket. After a polite handshake, Stratham gestured toward a steel-framed chair next to the desk.

"Would you mind if we taped this?" asked Stratham, pressing the button as Eva sat down.

Eva calmly extended her right hand and pressed the stop button. "Taped what?" She was only half-surprised by her boldness. While she was hardly the type to resist authority, including and especially the police, she was also shaken from the unwanted tour of the Thames Valley Police Department and the vague nature of the request that brought her there.

Stratham smiled wearily.

"Sorry, Dr. Bashir. Let me offer some context." She leaned back in her chair. "You're the third of twelve people we hope to interview today. We've searched our files for…um, resources here in the community. We've also made our own best guesses as to who here in Oxford might help us in our investigation."

"And what particular resource do I provide to"—she turned to read again the sign at the door—"the Southeast Counter-Terrorism Unit?"

"Dr. Bashir, I'm actually a homicide investigator for Thames Valley, but recent events have pushed our investigation into the anti-terrorist division. We think there are serious overlaps between two recent homicides in Oxford and terror cells here and elsewhere in Britain. As you probably know from news reports, no extremist group has claimed responsibility, Islamist or otherwise."

Stratham immediately picked up on Eva's anxiety. "Dr. Bashir, I have serious reservations that the murders have anything to do with terrorism, at least officially. Unfortunately, much of Britain thinks otherwise. The evidence gathered from the murder scenes of Peter Toohey and Florence Ballard suggest the possibility of... well, symbols that may be associated with Islam. We've run them through the Yard's data banks and have come up with nothing." Eva now placed Pamuk Serash in the mix. "Based on your work in Muslim iconography, we were hoping you might have some idea..." Stratham let the sentence trail off, trusting that Eva would get the gist.

Eva had done a master's thesis at the University of London on marginalia in late medieval Persian manuscripts. Had she not been so tense in this setting, she would have been amused at the reference to work done fourteen years earlier and nearly forgotten. Fully appreciating Stratham's stern sense of urgency, however, Eva knew that to cooperate would mean getting this all behind her more quickly.

"Of course, Chief Inspector. I'd be glad to help in any way I can."

With that, the senior officer cleared her throat and pushed the record button on the machine. "Dr. Bashir, I'm going to show you two of these photos. They're details, so we'll spare you the more gruesome aspects of the murder scenes. Even so, these images are unpleasant."

Stratham opened the folder and spread out two glossy medical examiner photographs on the table between the recorder and Eva.

Eva instinctively gasped. She closed her eyes for several seconds and took a deep breath before reopening them.

Slightly pixelated from enlargement, both images showed thin, clean, red-brown lines crossed over a pallid background which might have remained ambiguous were it not for the wet, blond strands at the top of the left image: Peter Toohey's hair. The photo on the right bore similar hash marks, though the parchment-thin skin had separated and pulled away, thereby showing broader versions of what appeared on the boy's forehead. The dull sheen of bone on the right image made Eva look up.

"These lines, Dr. Bashir, were made with a knife, a very particular kind of knife that our analysts suggest is a kirpan, a ceremonial dag—"

"Yes, I know what a kirpan is," Eva said in a shaky voice.

"Dagger. Right. I merely wanted you to know what you're looking at. These weren't by any means fatal wounds on either victim."

"Were they done while the victims were alive?" Eva asked in revulsion.

Stratham hesitated. "We don't know that for certain." She took a yellow pencil out of her jacket pocket and began tracing lightly the lines of the wounds on both photographs. "Although the images aren't precisely the same, they're close enough to suggest a pattern. Notice these major cuts." She pointed to the right side of the child's forehead. "We count three: the first is a downward cut from the hairline here at the top of the forehead to just above the inside of the right eyebrow, above the bridge of the nose. The second starts above where the first one ended and follows in the opposite direction, just above the outside of the right eye. So, we have what looks to be an uneven X, the right arm and base smaller than the left. The third cut seems to connect the left arm and base of the X so that it might be a Roman numeral IX. Lastly," she added, pushing the tip of the pencil to a place between the right arm and base of the X, "this point, or dot, here seems to have been made by the dagger tip. It's strangely precise."

Stratham sat back in her chair but kept a keen eye on Eva as she studied the patterns on both images. "Can you tell us anything about these marks?"

Eva looked up and saw the pleading look on the detective's face. "I'm sorry, but at first sight, I haven't a clue." Eva paused, running through the myriad images she'd ever come across in her manuscript studies. "The straightness of the cuts makes it hard to see anything Arabic here, as I'm sure you know. But the dot in the right side of the vertical and the x-shaped cuts might be an Arabic diacritic mark." Her tone was more questioning than confident.

Stratham tucked the pencil back into her pocket. "You're sure you don't see anything...It needn't be grammatical. Is there any symbol in these cuts, these lines, from an Islamic point of view?"

Eva looked at her, then back at the grizzly photographs and shook her head. "I'm sorry, I don't recognize this as anything."

Stratham turned off the recorder and both women stood. "Well, if anything should come to you on reflection, please let us know.

We don't want to see this carved on anyone else's forehead. And please take care, Dr. Bashir. After this second murder hit the news yesterday, we're seeing scattered assaults on non-whites."

Eva nodded. Glancing a final time at the ME's photos, she turned and walked out of the office.

35

Darkness still engulfed Jeremy upon his second awakening, but it had been transformed into a kind of ethereal obscurity. The first thing he realized was a slightly gratifying sense of uprightness. No longer on the floor, it was clear now that he was bound to a chair, his wrists and ankles tied firmly to thick, coarse wood. Instinctively, he strained against them, to no avail. Whatever gag had been placed over his mouth was gone. His impulse was to shout for help, which he did, over and over again until he was hoarse, but nothing came back to him. He strained to hear anything that might suggest movement or change, some cause for hope. The plink of water was still there. He wondered if his phone's battery had died by now, whatever time or day it was.

He blinked, but without his glasses could only make out in the dark the faintest shape of things: a few feet before him were the vague and uneven lines of a low wall, and to the right, where the rat sounds had come from and perhaps in some corner, the faint, surreal hint of statuary. As he tried to look deeper into right or left, a blazing pain bolted through the back of his skull.

He allowed the pain to recede and became hazily aware of something else in the dark space, something not of rotting wood or broken stone.

A presence.

Immediately behind him.

Breathing.

"Who's there?" he said in a panicky whimper. Nothing. "Please, where am I?" And then more calmly: "Who are you and what do you want?" He tried to turn his head but once again the paralyzing pain.

"My, my, but Father is full of questions, isn't he?" came a barely audible whisper from above and behind.

"Please! I don't know what you want or why you've put me here, but I beg you, let me go! I've a few quid in my wallet—take it and let me go. I promise, I won't tell a soul." The surge of energy and the exertion of speaking sent a ripple of lightheadedness through his throbbing skull.

"Oh, dear. You think *this* is a crime, Father Strand," whispered the voice, "this minor inconvenience you're suffering? If you could see anything in this pit, you would find that you have a perfectly serviceable roof over your head, a table, chairs, all the comforts of…a tomb. And that is precisely what it will become if you attempt to loosen your bonds and topple your chair again. I hardly think your aching head needed that fall."

The hoarseness of the voice made it impossible to determine its tone or detect any familiarity in it. The man—at least it seemed like a man—knew his name and that he was a priest. Jeremy's mind raced. *Who the hell could this possibly be?* "Tell me, what do you want from me? How can I help?" he said, struggling to change his tone from fear to compliance.

"Well, that's marginally better. Now, let's see…what do I want? Only the Cuxham Chalice."

"What?!" Jeremy was stunned to hear a reference to the chalice. Were he not fearing for his life, he'd have thanked his captor for giving his work some credit. He tried forcing his foggy brain to race through every mention he'd made of the chalice in public. Was this person at the failed seminar? Did someone overhear talk of the chalice in the college library? And then the thought came: is this the person who broke into my room? He felt an inner swell of fear and recalled—was it last night? two nights ago?—Guest Night and his boozy chatter at dinner about the chalice and Lumen, then again to a greater audience in the Senior Common Room. "For Christ's sake! I don't *know* where it is. I don't even know *if* it is!"

Electric shockwaves suddenly sent his body into a freakish spasm. All sensory awareness left him except for the jackhammer pummeling of the taser on every nerve. The stings of a thousand hornets simultaneously and repeatedly.

The convulsions suddenly stopped and Jeremy swam unsteadily beneath the surface of consciousness. He felt something at his lips. Unable to register what it was let alone resist, he next felt a cool, sweet liquid pass through his mouth. The first swallows were involuntary and not unwelcome. Stirred back to a semblance of apprehension and volition, he thrust his head forward in frantic gasps for more of the energy drink, only to have the plastic bottle withdrawn.

Then came once again the chilling whisper in his ear. "Ah, but you were so certain the other night. Just showing off, were you? Everyone could hear. We won't be providing anything like the viands and wine at Guest Night, but we must keep you *compos mentis*. But only just. Your reply to my question lacked the ring of truth. Think carefully before you next speak. Apply yourself, man. Unless, that is, you enjoyed that little taser treat."

Jeremy felt fingers grasp his hair and abruptly yank his head backward. The words that followed had lost all pretense of gentility and seemed to issue through a clenched jaw. "We haven't much time. More accurately, *you* haven't much time. Now, let's take this logically. You're in a subterranean chamber—a crypt, though there's nothing here but a set of tombs long-plundered, three chambers, rubble and rats. You found it, Strand, so why don't you tell *me* where we are?"

Jeremy's guess that he'd found the crypt was confirmed. He'd explored the terrain above three weeks before, but that was guesswork based on a few things he drew from the poem. *Hopkins showed it without naming it.* Even in his stupor, Jeremy realized some profound sense of kinship with his nineteenth-century Jesuit brother. "This is Hopkins' crypt," he said slowly. "Not that he's buried here, of course, but one he wrote about…"

"You're following the logical course, Strand, so my next question should be obvious. Where is the chalice?" The voice, its hoarseness somehow softened, seemed nearly tender, eerily intimate.

"Oh, but I've no idea," pleaded Jeremy. "I didn't even know *this* place existed, much less the chalice. I can't imagine—" The blow was immediate, a powerful swing that struck the back of his skull hard enough to rock the heavy chair. Jeremy's body radiated with a pain that sent his entire being into a stuporous nausea. A cold undertow took him for a moment into deeper darkness, but something else, some instinct for survival, sent him back mercilessly to the surface where all was ache and terror.

He felt and smelled the warm breath now inches from his ear as it whispered. "All right, Father Pansy, let's concede for the moment that you *don't* know where the chalice is. Yet. Think through that sonnet of yours, the one written by that other Jesuit fairy, and find a clue. At the very least, you'll live a little longer. Longer than your friend here across the table from you."

Jeremy felt a jerk as he and the chair were pivoted ninety degrees to the right. He could feel more than see the table before him. His senses were suddenly alert. What "friend" was the man referring to? Had his captor done something to Myles? Eva? Was it possible that one of them lay dead within this very space?

Panic rising within his agony, Jeremy heard sounds of movement behind him: riffling in a bag, the sound of tearing and a snap. A soft light began to wax in the crypt.

"This glow-stick should last about an hour, allowing you time to meditate on your listless counterpart." A hand moved smoothly and quickly from behind Jeremy, placing the chemical luminescence stick on the rough wooden table. A sickly light washed the crypt.

Across the table, seated in a chair similar to Jeremy's, was a desiccated human corpse. Dusty, stone-flecked hair sat atop an eyeless skull whose skin had been nearly eaten away, and what remained stretched in small gray patches over pitted ivory bone. The Victorian waistcoat the skeleton wore was stiff and shiny with age.

A ravening anxiety welled up from within and rapidly inundated Jeremy, and he heard a howl of startled terror that he quickly realized was his own as the voice from behind joined along in mocking laughter.

36

As much as she tried, Eva couldn't shake from her memory the police photos. The glisten of dead bone through sliced skin, the old woman's forehead like torn parchment, the child's like a scored chicken thigh.

The thought of children took her immediately to Sam and then to Rabi, who tried to look so brave while in custody. It was all getting worse. Eva was angry—at the killer terrorizing Oxford and at the police for their own kind of terror, especially towards children, notwithstanding their principled efforts to nab the killer. Rabi was a kid, for heaven's sake, misguided and quick-tempered, yes, but flaunting more teenage bravado than menace. She had spent nearly her entire life trying to fit into British society, trying to disappear into it. But all of that was forgotten in how the authorities saw her—as Arab, Muslim and a near collaborator with whomever was terrorizing the community.

Her heels clicking her exasperation along the flagstones, she walked past the college porters with an abrupt "Morning." She wanted nothing more than the quiet refuge of her office, the silent company of books and time to think, time to repair. She bounded up the library steps, pulled open the heavy oak door and felt the cool shade of the old building, the musty smell of its leather and paper trove. Gratefully, there was hardly anyone in the main room, just someone searching the books in the reference section. He looked up at her. It was Myles.

In the minutes it took to get from the Reading Room through the administrative wing, Myles had updated Eva on the events of the morning. He'd had an unscheduled meeting with the Master in which he asked whether a missing person's report had been filed yet with the Thames Valley Police. Ilbert had been shocked at the very idea, insisting that Jeremy had done this sort of thing before and would be showing up to college any hour now. It wasn't in the college's best interest, or for that matter Jeremy's, to bring official Oxford into a private Jesuit matter. Ilbert's tone was a warning to Myles to leave this one alone.

With a jangle of keys from her purse, Eva unlocked the office, flicked on lights and gestured to Myles to take a seat in the chair in front of her desk. As they both sat, Eva said, "Funny you should mention Thames Valley and a missing person's report for Jeremy. I was just in that zoo. The place was packed; it looked like an immigration desk at Heathrow. Sam's friend Rabi was in the whole sordid mix, and I was helpless to do anything."

Myles thought of the young man in the gray hoodie and their recent encounter, wondering what had landed him at central booking this time.

Eva described the conversation with Stratham, the grizzly post-mortem photographs and the inscrutable markings on the victims' foreheads. She pushed her chair back from the desk, opened a drawer and took out a notepad. With a few quick strokes she reproduced the pattern and showed Myles.

"These are the markings—sort of—on the forehead of Peter Toohey and Florence Ballard. They meant nothing to me at the station, but there's something about them that's nagging at me. In both cases, they look like an uneven X lying on its side, the lower strokes much more abbreviated than the upper. And there's a point or dot in the middle of the lower part of the X. See?"

"Can I have that pencil?" Myles asked without looking up. He studied the image for a few moments as Eva studied Myles, his mind working as he drummed the pencil's eraser end against the notepad. He erased something on the notepad and then emphasized a couple of lines with the pencil. "It could be a stylized X or maybe an upper-case V sitting on a point or a less-than symbol— < —preceded by a dot or point."

He was silent again, as if pulling something up from memory, then worked the pencil in a clear area on the page next to Eva's sketch. "Do you have the Hopkins manuscript handy?"

"The original's in the manuscript room where we left it," Eva replied, "but I've got a photocopy here."

She got up and went to a filing cabinet on the other side of the office, pulled open the drawer and drew out a dark green folder. She opened it as she walked back to the chairs and pulled out the copy. Myles placed it next to the notepad and pointed at the bottom of the photocopied poem.

"Interesting. Look here at these marks at the foot of the page—what we thought a few days ago were doodles from the hand of a bored or demented poet. Does this look anything like those images the cops showed you?"

Eva looked at the photocopy and then back to Myles' amended image of the penciled figure. "I suppose it could be similar...In both cases the image is a matter of three strokes—"

"Or cuts," Myles added. "And that single dot."

Eva shivered to think that it had to be made on the foreheads of the victim with a knife-point pushed into the skin and then twisted back and forth for a drilled, circular effect. Then her eyes widened. "But, if they're the same image, what possible connection could there be between what Hopkins drew a hundred and thirty years ago in Dublin on a sheet of foolscap and murders that have taken place in Oxford in the past week?"

Myles got up from the chair and began pacing around Eva's office. "I'm not sure, but there are a couple of possibilities. First off, Eva, who else has seen this manuscript, I mean besides you, Jeremy and me?"

"Well, Tock certainly has, only because Jeremy showed it to him early on in his investigations into the fragment. And Jeremy has to have shown it to Monsignor Moretti, as well, shortly after he arrived. But Myles, you couldn't possibly—"

"Tock is no more involved in these killings than you or I. Moretti strikes me as guarded, even enigmatic; not warm, but courteous in a Mediterranean, courtly kind of way."

Eva nodded in agreement. "Jeremy had the manuscript in his room for a little while around the time of his seminar—I scolded him endlessly for it—but he'd never have taken it out of college. And if he didn't show it to someone, it's practically impossible that they would've seen it any other way. I've got the keys to the archives, and I'd have a record of anyone who's used D'Arcy in the last months since I pulled the fragment from that miscellaneous box." She stared again at the manuscript copy. "Myles...I'm thinking about Jeremy's concerns of a break-in a couple of weeks ago. It seems that few people—including Father Ilbert—took him seriously, despite his insistence that he wasn't imagining it." She paused. "Perhaps someone saw the manuscript and took an image of it."

"I was thinking the same thing," Myles said. "But why that mark and what does it mean? Why connect a symbol from Hopkins' own hand to victims of what are meant to be Islamic acts of terror?" He returned to his chair and sat down in it heavily. "Unless…"

Eva stared at him. Myles finally spoke. "Try this on: whoever murdered the Toohey kid and Miss Ballard knew about this image, this symbol—whatever it is—but not from the Hopkins manuscript."

"Well, I suppose that's feasible," Eva said, looking again at both her notepad and the photocopy, "but why would you say so? I mean, what do you take the symbol to mean? How common could it be?"

"I bet if Jeremy were here, we'd piece this together pretty quickly. I think it's all related, including and especially his disappearance. Think about it: Jeremy claims—wildly, according to most listeners—that the Hopkins fragment is about the legendary Cuxham Chalice. Anyone in Oxford paying attention, including me, laughs it off." He felt a blushing current of regret pass through him. "And then at Guest Night two nights ago, he further associates the poem *and* the chalice with Lumen." He waited for the light to go on in Eva's eyes.

"My God," Eva said, dropping the notepad on the table and putting her hand to her mouth. "The symbol carved into the victims' heads isn't simply from the poem. Its primary association is with Lumen, not with Hopkins!"

Myles nodded slowly. "It may be. What's more, Lumen may still be around Oxford, in spite of what Jacoby and Penrose were saying the other night. What we know for certain is that there's a missing link between the murders and the manuscript. And depending on what that link is, Jeremy may have been right about the Cuxham Chalice."

Myles picked up the notepad once again, studied it for a minute, then shifted the angle so that the uneven X was vertical with the point centering the lower opening. "Try looking at it this way. Could this be a representation of a chalice?"

"I suppose it could." She sounded dubious. "I think I can see it in the main lines, but that tiny circle in what would be the base of a chalice—that doesn't make much sense, does it?"

"Not really. Not yet. But excluding that small circle, we might still have a connection between Lumen, the sonnet, and the murders of Peter Toohey and Florence Ballard."

Myles stood up and headed for the office door.

"Where are you going?"

"We've got to show this to the police," he said. "The whole Lumen-Cuxham Chalice thing isn't an Oxford joke anymore, and Jeremy isn't out on a bender. In fact, he may be in the gravest possible danger and we've got to find him!"

37

"I just love this place, Rabi," exclaimed Sam, glowing as she gazed up in awe at the imposing leaded dome of Radcliffe Camera. She felt exhilarated by the after-lunch hum and bustle of university students walking and cycling past, some carrying books and lost in thought, others laughing and carousing. "Can't you just *feel* the energy?" She took a sip from her coffee mug and seemed to inhale her surroundings with a broad grin and unalloyed delight. Her long black hair was pulled to one side so that it draped the front of her right shoulder.

Though Sam's question had been rhetorical, Rabi couldn't help but reply. "I guess," he said begrudgingly. He studied the faces of a row of gargoyles perched along the roofline of the Old Bodleian Library. Like most of the other faces in Oxford, their grotesque, mocking expressions seemed to look down upon him and regard him with aloof disdain.

The couple sat at an outdoor table at King's Lane Coffee House, dating to the sixteenth century and situated at the end of a narrow lane bordered by high walls of medieval stone. They were sipping coffee and waiting for their lunch order.

Rabi felt self-conscious and claustrophobic. He'd grown very fond of Sam but didn't share her attraction to the ancient university and its timeless, pulsing life. Sam knew this about him but had insisted on coming. Not only did she find it exciting to imagine herself as a student here, but she also hoped to distract her boyfriend from the troubles that had come to consume him in recent days.

She reached across the table and took his hand. "I'm worried about you. Do you know that?"

"I think you have mentioned it once or twice or a hundred times," he said with a sidelong grin.

She pointed to the purple-green bruise under his left eye. "You've been detained by the police twice in a week. With everything that's happening, don't you think you should keep a low profile?"

He shrugged as the waiter delivered sandwiches and salads.

"I'm not sure what you want out of this...this acting out, this anger," she said. "More than anything, you seem so sad."

Before he could shrug again or respond, a group of passing students bumped into his chair, muttering, "Sorry." Rabi abruptly stood up and faced them aggressively. One of them raised his hands in placating mock surrender while slowly backing away. "Whoa, Saddam. Chill out. I said I was sorry." They all laughed and continued on their way.

"Rabi, it's fine," said Sam soothingly as she gripped his sleeve. "It was an accident. Try to enjoy our time together."

It was not fine, Rabi thought as he sat back down and seethed, his adrenaline pumping. Such insults were all too familiar to him, especially from privileged, heedless Oxford students. They knew nothing about him and nothing about life. The things he had seen, been forced to endure, including his father's bloody death. He had tried to fit in, wanted to fit in, plan a bright future and forget his past. Now violence had re-entered his life and haunted his fitful sleep—in the form of the butchered boy, the protests, the assaults on his identity, his religion, his girlfriend, and even the strange white disk he still had in his possession.

He drew a deep breath and let it out slowly. "This is not how it was supposed to be."

"I couldn't agree more," Sam intoned as calmly as she could manage while studying Rabi's despondent expression. "I've been reading about Islam, and I've been reading the Qur'an. And I think I know why you feel so passionately about it." She paused, but he still did not meet her eye. "It's because of love. It's all based on love." He looked at her now. "I don't want to see you descend further into violence and hatred. I want you to be happy."

He leaned forward and said in a hoarse whisper, "Someone started a fire outside the mosque last night! Luckily, neighbors saw and put it out before anyone was hurt or the building was damaged. But what if fighting violence with violence is the only way to shatter the ignorance and make people listen? What then? Do we continue to accept their insults? Their blame? I sometimes wonder why I want to fit in with such people."

"I don't have all the answers, Rabi. But not everyone is like those ignorant ones. You know that. And not everyone is against you. That American working with my mum—you can't say he's against you. You saw that the other day. And my mum, where exactly does she 'fit in'?"

"Everyone—the police, the community—is convinced that one of us committed the murders. One of *us*, Samira!" He was nearly breathless, his tone a combination of insistent and distraught. "You say you are interested in joining us. Then you pull away." He shook his head, sadly. "You do not have to be one of them. Yes, you were born here in this country, but you have more in common with us. With me."

"Rabi, why must it be 'us' and 'them'? Things aren't so black and white. Why not fight prejudice and ignorance by fulfilling your dreams? You're so smart and talented. Don't give up on yourself… And, by the way, I'm not 'one of them.' I'm just…me. And all this hostility scares me."

"Well, get used to it," he said ominously.

"What's that supposed to mean?"

"The police are threatening to close the mosque and bring armed troops into the neighborhood."

"Oh God. You have to stay out of their way, Rabi."

He hardly seemed to hear her. "Last night while I was in custody the police kept saying that we would have to learn the hard way to control our tempers. I asked them what they meant. In response they gave me this." He lifted his shirt to reveal a swollen and shiny black-and-blue bruise on his rib cage.

In response to Sam's gasp, Rabi shook his head and once again took her hands in his. "Maybe I should go away," he said, staring at Sam intently.

Sam frowned and tilted her head in confusion. "What do you mean?"

He shook his head and looked away. "I want to make a difference. I know one place where I can learn how to do that."

Sam's expression turned from puzzlement to horror. "No. Don't tell me you're thinking of"—she leaned closer to him, glanced around and lowered her voice—"not back to Iraq or one of those training camps."

Rabi's blank expression seemed to answer her question. "I have not made a decision."

"You cannot"—she grabbed his hand in both of hers and gently squeezed, speaking in an urgent, emphatic whisper—"*you cannot do this!* You don't want this. It's not you. And it's wrong. Wrong for you. Wrong for anyone!"

As she continued to stare pleadingly at Rabi and squeeze his hand, Sam became aware of the sounds of low music wafting from an open window in Brasenose College just beyond the stone wall. It all seemed so absurdly insignificant—music, idle chit-chat, drinking a coffee or a beer—compared to this. Compared to a young man contemplating committing himself to extremism, throwing his life away in the name of some warped distortion of a beautiful religion.

But it did matter; it all mattered.

A bell from distant Magdalen Tower chimed the hour.

"I should go," said Rabi, standing. Sam remained seated and their hands parted. The earlier exhilaration had been deflated. And when she looked up into his eyes, her worry turned to dread.

38

Before grabbing her car keys, Eva had tucked the Hopkins photocopy back into its folder and handed it to Myles. There was no way she'd bring the original to show the police. "If they want to verify the scribbles at the foot of the page, they can come to college," she told Myles as they climbed the stairs into the station.

Upon entering the lobby, they observed the same chaos Eva had witnessed earlier. As they maneuvered through the crowd, she grabbed Myles' sleeve and pulled him toward the intake desk near the back. A small group of middle-aged women in black hijabs were slowly walking away from the desk. A tall desk sergeant with thinning blond hair and a sallow, pock-marked complexion was busy looking through office forms fanned out before him.

"Yes, can I help you?" the sergeant growled hurriedly without looking up. Myles now recognized him as the officer named Thornton who had broken up the Cornmarket fight.

Eva leaned on the counter. "Yes, doctors Bashir and Dunn, of Ignatius College. We'd like to see Chief Inspector Hilary Stratham, please."

Maybe it was the official titles that woke up the sergeant, or maybe it was the honeyed sound of Eva's voice. He looked up at her, then glanced at Myles and gave him a long look of recognition. Turning to Eva, he asked brusquely, "Do you have an appointment?"

"No, but I was here earlier and—"

"Sorry, Miss," said the sergeant, returning his attention to his desk, "but the inspector's in interrogation all day."

"It's Doctor, not Miss," Myles snapped. He looked squarely at the sergeant, who met his glare with a distracted frown. "Dr. Bashir met with C.I. Stratham this morning. We have new information bearing on the recent murders in Oxford, and we'd like to see someone in authority." Myles drew out the last three words with their implicit judgment regarding the competence of the desk sergeant.

Thornton directed a protracted glare at Myles. "Can't you hear, Yank? I said the inspector is busy. Can't you see that every bloody one of us is busy? Thanks to this lot," he added in undisguised disgust as he nodded toward a group of Muslim men waiting to be interrogated.

Summoning every ounce of self-control, Myles made his voice cooperative. "Sergeant, Dr. Bashir has discovered some significant material which we're sure can help advance your investigation. In fact, it's the very reason she was summoned here this morning."

"The markings on the victims' foreheads," Eva interjected.

She took the file folder out of her valise, found the photocopy and handed it to the sergeant. Thornton glanced at it, looked back at Eva and shrugged.

Eva stretched her hand, pointing to the page. "It's the marking at the foot of the page. See? At about center, near all those oblique lines." She quickly explained the Hopkins lines, pointing out their similarity to the cuts on Peter Toohey and Florence Ballard, but refrained from any mention of the Cuxham Chalice or Lumen.

"I'll grant you a similarity, Dr. Basher"—Myles and Eva both resisted correcting his pronunciation—"but this business of the forehead cuts has all been cleared up. Happened late this morning, perhaps around the time you were here."

Myles and Eva shared the same stupefied expression. "But how's that possible, Sergeant? You can see that these marks from a hundred-year-old page are similar to an image carved by a madman on two innocent people this past week!"

"Dr. Basher, someone from the university passed the information our way a little while ago. Seems it's a—what did the Chief Inspector call it?—a pictogram connected with some tribe in Yemen or thereabouts."

"Which 'someone in the university' told you this?" Myles asked.

"All police information regarding this investigation is confidential," Thornton fumed at Myles, clearly approaching the end of his tether. He handed the page back to Eva.

"But that's not possible, Sergeant," Eva said, her voice stern and insistent. "There's much more to this than a combination of lines, here on this page and again on the bodies of the dead. In fact, we've every reason to believe that this mark, the contents of this poem and the disappearance of a don at Ignatius College—a

Jesuit priest—are all connected." As she spoke, Eva realized how desperate and crazy she must have sounded.

Another officer approached Thornton, handed him a stack of files and pointed to the group of detained men.

Shaking his head and looking even more overwhelmed than before, Thornton stood up and sighed loudly. "We haven't heard about any missing dons or priests. Now please, ma'am, leave the police work to us. God knows, there's more than enough of it at the moment." He nodded toward the crowd being processed slowly in the foyer. "This mess is bigger than Oxford. We're getting requests for information, even help, if you can imagine, from places like Birmingham, Newcastle and London, where things are almost as tense with your lot. So," he added with finality as he shook the stack of papers in his hand, signaling the conversation was ending, "we thank you for your civic interest and your willingness to comply with our request."

"What request would that be?" asked Myles.

"To bloody well keep out of police matters."

39

"I hate to say it," Myles said with grim resolve, "but I've become increasingly convinced that Jeremy was right about being in danger, maybe more than he knew."

It was forty-five minutes since leaving the constabulary, and Myles leaned back in a chair across from Eva's library desk. She was still fuming from the dismissal they'd been handed by the TVP sergeant.

"If the police have found their so-called Islamic symbol, then what else can we do?" Eva studied Myles, who had crossed his legs and was softly drumming his right shoe with a pencil he'd grabbed from her desk. "What are you thinking?"

He looked up at her. "A lot of things. I'm thinking that if the symbols aren't the same, then I must be seeing things—but I believe they are. I'm also thinking, fearing that Jeremy's lost, maybe injured, or..."

"Or what?"

"Or someone's gotten to him. We have a person missing in a city that's being rocked by all kinds of danger and crime, from property damage to murder. Who's to say Jeremy hasn't been detained in some way? Drugged. Abducted. I don't know." Myles trailed off to a place of pulsing worry. He then thought of what Tock had said that morning about worry being overrated. He looked up at Eva with a look of fresh determination. "We've just got to find him."

Eva hesitated to speak. "Myles, after the last couple of hours, I'd be the last to go to the police for anything right now, but should we tell them about this? At least they could begin some kind of search, put out alerts, that sort of thing?"

"I understand why you'd say that, Eva, but you saw the chaos at the station. They have their hands full, and Jeremy apparently has something of a reputation with the cops for unsubstantiated claims of break-ins and theft. And I doubt Ilbert will file a missing person's report until he's absolutely sure Jeremy has disappeared and is in undeniable danger. I don't want to chance waiting that long. What's more, I'm not sure we can trust the police at this point."

"What do you mean?"

Myles hesitated a moment to get his thoughts in order. "I don't mean crooked cops or anything like that. But they obviously have some source, some Oxford authority with pull who's managed to get ahead of us about those markings on the victims' foreheads. You saw how quickly they shot us down. And isn't it a little curious that just as we make the connection between the markings on the bodies and the symbol Hopkins scratched on a page that's a hundred and fifty years old, someone else jumps the queue and persuades the police to believe them and not us? And the timing's curious—it's almost as if they knew what we were going to do."

Eva stared with growing alarm. "But how could they know?"

"If I'm right about this, whoever we're talking about either has a copy of the poem—"

"Jeremy's break-in," Eva gasped.

Myles nodded. "—or he or she is extracting information from the only other person who knows anything about the last sonnet of Gerard Manley Hopkins."

She felt a chill. They both knew exactly who that was. "All right, then, where do we start?"

"With what we know. Jeremy's been gone just shy of forty-eight hours. Who knows, he could still show up here for dinner tonight, though somehow I don't think so. We think that wherever he's gone has something to do with chasing down clues from the Hopkins sonnet, clues he didn't share with us. We think now that there's a connection between the sonnet and the markings that have shown up on the foreheads of murder victims here in Oxford. And that it may have something to do with Lumen and that blasted Cuxham Chalice."

"Though truth be told," said Eva, "we know that Jeremy is real. I can't say as much about the chalice."

Myles liked her way of thinking. "You're right. We need to forget about the chalice for now and just try to retrace Jeremy's steps. For that, we need to mine the poem the same way he did." Myles paused and turned his head toward the open office door. "I keep saying 'we,' Eva, but if Jeremy's in danger—and my gut tells me that he is—then whoever follows his trail is likely to be in the same danger. I don't want you to risk—"

"Myles, we don't know each other that well and I do appreciate your concern. But Jeremy Strand is my friend, too. And if you haven't noticed in the past few days of our acquaintance, I'm stubborn. How do you think I've survived in this bastion of male power? I want Jeremy back and safe as much as you do. I'm heartsick that my finding the sonnet months ago was the beginning of all this, so I'll look for Jeremy with or without your help." Myles looked at Eva with admiration and respect as she continued, "So, you're the copper's son. Where do we start?"

"Obviously, a major part of what we know has to do with timing: Jeremy went missing immediately after Guest Night, so it's reasonable to think that something happened during or after dinner that sent him out of college to God-knows-where."

"Something at our table?"

"Maybe. Jeremy dropped a couple of bombs into the conversation, and you saw how it rankled most of the table. But then, anyone within earshot of Jeremy could easily have found themselves in possession of new information about Hopkins, the manuscript in this library, a long-lost chalice, and a shadowy Oxford club from centuries past. That's just the people moving around our table—student workers, staff, guests. Remember, the last time either of us saw Jeremy, he was heading to the Senior Common Room in search of scotch and a new spate of listeners for his odd theories."

"True enough, but let's start with our table. Who was particularly interested in what Jeremy was saying? Was anyone upset, I mean besides the two of us?"

"Moretti, for certain. The man has a lot of pull and is used to having people do his bidding, but I don't get a sense that he's a personal danger to Jeremy. Shadowy and enigmatic, yes, but he showed that same mix of alarm and dismay over what Jeremy was saying that we had."

"So, it must be Pax who's behind this caper," Eva said to lighten the heaviness of the conversation.

Myles played along. "Top of my list. She could have used a dozen rosaries to shackle Jeremy in some convent dungeon."

"Well, then, that leaves us with Jacoby, Penrose, and her facto-tum—what was his name?"

"Simon Cole. He struck me as the docile, obliging type, though I wonder if that's an act. Clearly, if Penrose told him to jump off Tom Tower, he'd ask her what time. He's obviously devoted to her."

"And maybe a little more than devoted. You saw them at Guest Night—whispering, touching, blushing. She was quite the cougar, wedding ring notwithstanding. By all accounts, she seems to rule with a delicate hand that hides a stinger. And she had a vested interest in ruling out Lumen as having anything to do with the sonnet." Eva pulled a water bottle from her desk drawer and took a drink.

"You're right, Eva. Jacoby showed his own interest in the question of the chalice as well as Lumen's presence at the university, historically and even now. What I can't quite get is that both Penrose and Jacoby were Jeremy's guests, and Simon Cole by way of Penrose. Jeremy knows them, though Jacoby seemed more interested in pontificating than graciously accepting Jeremy's hospitality. Also, at times that night, Penrose was practically doting on Jeremy as if he were a wounded bird."

"It's almost as if they were an intended audience for Jeremy's revelations."

"More like an exhibition or even a broadcast, the way he carried on," Myles said, shaking his head. "But wait a minute—so were we!"

"We were what?"

"An intended audience. Who put the table together? Jeremy did. So, maybe he wanted us to hear what he was going to hear from Jacoby and Penrose once his theories were out there. Moretti was meant to be a witness, too. Jeremy knew at least something, if not a great deal, about Penrose's and Jacoby's unique and intimate familiarity with Oxford history, in general, and with Lumen and the chalice, in particular. He wanted to gauge their reaction to what he knew. That's why he invited them."

"With dear Pax as the only disinterested party. But Myles, if we were there as witnesses, could Jeremy have planned on confirming to us the next day what we all heard at table, only there was no next day? Could this have been part of an elaborate plan on his part to get closer to the chalice by better understanding the cryptic references in the poem?"

Myles didn't answer. He stared at the floor for nearly a minute.

"What, Myles? What is it?"

"Jeremy said something to me at table. I don't know if you or anyone else noticed, but while Jacoby, I think, was droning on, Jeremy whispered to me, 'It's there, Myles. It's all there.' And then he asked me to trust him." A swell of regret rose in Myles, but he shook it off, knowing this moment wasn't about him, but about Jeremy. He looked up, his eyes shining brightly. "Eva, the poem—can you bring it out again?"

She opened the green folder on the desk and slid the copy between them.

"Okay," said Myles, "how would you describe this sonnet?"

"Are you kidding?"

"No, just look at it, don't try to figure it out. What do you see?"

"Besides a writing mess," Eva said, shaking her head, "I see something that's obviously incomplete, unfinished."

"Precisely," said Myles, grinning.

"I'm still flummoxed. What are you saying?"

"I'm saying that the sonnet is incomplete, but in a complete way. In other words, why does Hopkins begin some lines in the sestet with clearly chosen words, while leaving the rest of the line unfinished?"

"Well, we assume he was ill, maybe even dying. He wasn't able to complete it."

"Yes, but just maybe he was able to put the necessary elements on the page. In fact, he clearly prioritized the words that are here. He just didn't have time to complete the lines in sonnet form. Jeremy was right: it's all here—Lumen, the Cuxham Chalice, Hopkins—but not in a way that's obvious. There's a reason for that, though I can't figure out what that is. So, when you ask, Eva, where we start, it's here," he said, tapping the acetate sleeve, "here with the poem. Not just the words, but everything on this page. Right now, the only clear clue we have is the acrostic, *trinitas*. I know it's a big word around here, in Latin and English, but maybe it was meant to be the first clue, the most obvious one. Just maybe it has to do not with doctrine, but with a place."

"Well, for Oxford, that moves Trinity College to the top of the list," said Eva, staring at the poem. "I know one of the librarians there who might be of some help." She swiveled to her computer and typed a quick series of words. "There's also Trinity Day Care, a company called Trinity Software, and a Trinity Bed & Breakfast... Oh, dear, this could be impossible."

"True, Eva, it's going to be a commonplace, but we also have an endpoint to this reference. We look at nothing with Trinity or Trinitas that appears *after* Hopkins wrote this poem, 1888 at the latest." Myles continued to jot down some words on the notepad. "Then we're back to what an acrostic is—a word puzzle. And we've got a *reverse* acrostic which may extend the clue to some particular place. Having an acrostic in this poem suggests there may be other, less obvious word puzzles here."

"We've got our work cut out for us." She glanced at her watch.

Myles noticed the look of worry pass over her face. "How are you doing—I mean, since the incident the other day in your car?"

"I'm fine, thanks. It's just, well, Sam." She shook her head. "I know her and I trust her. And yet...There are so many influences coming at her these days. So much out of her control, not to mention mine."

"I can only imagine," Myles said quietly. "If there's anything I can do..."

Eva smiled. "Thanks. It's good to have another ally. Anyway, I should be getting home, but I'll try to find as many pre-nineteenth century references to 'trinity' in Oxford and environs."

"Perfect. And I'll get an appointment with Jacoby. He seemed less high-strung than Penrose about Lumen. Maybe he's willing to share more about the group. We'll also need to end up at Christ Church College sooner than later because that's where so much of the story buried in this sonnet takes place. So we need to keep Penrose and Cole in the frame, as well: they may know something that can help us find Jeremy."

"But what if any one of them is behind all of this—that's possible, too, right?"

"Yeah, Eva, it's a knife-edge we're walking, no grim pun intended. Right now, we focus on the sonnet. Dig out of it anything clearer we can garner from Jacoby and Penrose. We can confirm for ourselves whether any of them—and I'm including Cole here—knows anything about where Jeremy is without tipping our hand. Giving anything away might further endanger Jeremy."

"Understood, Myles. Thanks. I'm on this trinity thing and I'll let you know what I find. Tomorrow?"

"First thing in the morning." Myles returned the notepad and pencil to Eva's desk, headed to the door and turned around. "You know, until a couple of days ago, I couldn't imagine anyone orchestrating Jeremy's disappearance other than Jeremy himself. Or maybe a local pub owner. I know we're both still hoping he shows up soon, in which case, we kick his butt for acting like a damn fool and worrying us. If so, all this speculation will be moot. But in the meantime…"

"We've work to do," said Eva with a worried smile. She caught something in Myles' expression that gave her hope, the look of an explorer who's just found his map.

40

Jeremy pushed heavily to the surface from hallucinatory depths haunted by skeletal figures rattling through fields of overgrown grass and weeds. Somewhere in the shallows, hammering pain and the blurred feeling of a body beginning to fail made him aware that he'd been dreaming. Bones fell away in vague ivory fragments. He was aware of the smell of urine and the cold wet of his pants, the chair, the stony floor. Tears began to well, but sadness gave way to dread. His captor was back. Sounds from some adjoining chamber. The bony figure across the table seemed to lean its head back and slightly to the right as if straining to listen with Jeremy.

The hard sound of metal against stone clanging in a frantic cadence. People at work in a room beyond. Stones being pushed from piled heights. The grunts and groans of obsession. The work sounded methodical, as if progressing from one space, one chamber, gradually toward another. One voice louder and commanding, a few—was there a woman's voice?—speaking lower. Confused, Jeremy thought for the briefest moment that this might be a rescue team come to liberate him. But no. The dominant voice was unmistakable and its now-familiar threat merely augmented by the presence of others doing his bidding.

In the dwindling glow of chemical luminescence, Jeremy surveyed with stupefaction and sadness the remains of the person who sat across the table. How had he—the remnant clothing made Jeremy conclude it was male—met his end? Who or what had brought him to this subterranean place? Were they circumstances similar to the ones Jeremy found himself in? Most baffling, if Hopkins had wanted the reader of the sonnet to find this place, had he any idea that it was an active burial perhaps near his own time?

The longer he considered, the more he became filled with pity and melancholy. He uttered a quiet prayer for the man and a family who likely never knew their beloved's fate.

Guessing he had little time before his captor returned to resume his brutal interrogation, Jeremy took quick advantage of what he could see of his surroundings. This must be a central chamber because someone had placed a table and chairs here, though for what reason in a crypt, Jeremy could hardly surmise. The room was squarish and about fifteen feet on each side. To his left a narrow archway led into darkness. Before him, to the right of the corpse, lay a heap of rubble the size of a small car, stonework that had fallen from the vaulted ceiling and upper walls over the centuries. To the right of the rubble stood a broken statue, perhaps of a medieval knight. On the floor immediately to his right sat a round container with "Luggable Loo" printed cheerily on its side. A port-a-potty. He found it almost impossible to turn his head any further because of the excruciating ache that still thrummed at the back of his skull. But from what he could see through the arch, there was a bas-relief on the far wall. A seated figure, perhaps the ruins of a tomb.

He let his head fall forward in exhaustion.

A clanging sound resonated from the adjoining chamber. A pick or shovel tossed to the stone-paved floor. Then the sound of steps. Jeremy put his mind to counting the steps, if only to get a sense of the dimensions of his prison. The footfalls were neither heavy nor light, casual but with obvious purpose. He counted ten or eleven of them before sensing, unaided by his glasses, a shadow pass from the archway on the right and assume its position behind Jeremy's chair.

The figure snapped a second glow stick and placed it on the table between the man long dead and the one well on his way. In spite of the alarm he felt at the return of the voice behind him and the sharper eeriness of the skeleton, Jeremy was heartened by the light, a reminder of day and fire and heat.

"Please, what day is it? What time?"

There was no response, only the sound of a simple movement. Jeremy braced himself for another blow to the back of the head or a taser strike to his side. He nearly fainted with surprise when a hand reached from behind holding a bottle of lime-green liquid, a straw protruding from the narrow top.

He leaned forward to grasp the straw with his cracked lips. He hardly cared what was in the bottle and pulled on the straw furiously, to the point of coughing out Gatorade from his windpipe.

He caught his breath with a frenzied intake of air. A small piece of old cheese was pushed into his mouth. It seemed the finest thing he had tasted in his life.

"What time is it?" echoed the voice, barely above a whisper. "I'd say it's time you learned some basic lessons in hygiene, Father Fetid. You've stunk up the place more than the old-timer across the table."

Reboant laughter thundered through the small chamber, then the adjacent ones, gradually subsiding. All was quiet again except for the quieter sounds of others at work in the crypt.

"You'll be assisted by one or two of my young friends to use that portable loo. You'll do your business, they'll stand guard. I don't think I need to tell you what would happen if you attempted to... decline our hospitality. Meanwhile, does it strike you as curious, Father Strand, that it's you who seems to be asking all the questions? Why do you think you're strapped to that chair—to keep you from scaling Oxford heights of academic glory? *I* ask the questions, and if you provide some answers, well, then I'll do the same for you."

"But I really don't—" The swift slap from behind stung but Jeremy knew it was merely a warning of greater torture to come if he refused to cooperate.

"Wrong answer, Father. Now, we both believe that these two lines from the sonnet indicate that we are presently in proximity of something special, no?

Tongue-slip, slype to the bound-for, longed-for grave,
Into the pitchblack deep, wherein the myst'ry lies.

What further meaning do you garner?"

Fearful and weak, Jeremy summoned whatever mental strength he could. He described to his captor that the lines, at best, merely put them in a subterranean place. That it was true, they were both in a crypt, but he'd racked his brains for weeks trying to figure out more of what Hopkins meant. To give his captor something—and it would be no great revelation—might at least indicate that there was some method to Hopkins' madness. So he revealed that the reverse acrostic, "*trinitas*," in combination with the information Barry Goodall had given him at Guest Night about slypes formed his most recent best guess of location.

"Well, that didn't hurt much, did it, Father? Clever of Hopkins, in a middling sort of way, to employ an acrostic. As you say, it's not a bad beginning. I'm encouraged."

Then his captor said with surreal brightness. "Now, I don't mind answering a few of your questions. What day is it, you ask? It's somewhere between the end of Tuesday and the beginning of Wednesday. It was a lovely springtime day in Oxford, where half the city was utterly self-absorbed in student indulgences and the rest was about to explode in chaos. Your absence, I'm sorry to say, hasn't been much noticed, except for that irritating American and the Muslim wog, Bashir. My friends are scattered about the university, gathering information as I need it. Bright and ambitious undergraduates, minds completely out of your league. They tell me that your two friends harbor some hopes of finding you.

"Oh, and I've convinced the police that the markings on the murder victims' foreheads were, indeed, of purposely obscure but decidedly Muslim origins. Something from ancient Iraq—the authorities love that kind of thing. It all took some doing, but police, especially in academic centers, can be won over with the right assortment of words, figures, and tweeds."

Jeremy felt something cave inside. In these countless dark hours, he had never thought of Peter Toohey or the incendiary plight of the old city. He thought of the chalice, of Hopkins, certainly of himself and his fate. But he hadn't thought of the boy. The fact that this person was somehow part of that crime made Jeremy nearly regurgitate the cheese he'd just swallowed.

"You mentioned murders, plural. What do you mean?"

'Requiescant in Pace, Father Strand. But don't let all your pity run to them. I had to work quickly and efficiently to keep that boy from ruining everything. He put up quite a fight. The old woman was considerably easier but no less a mess. Still, it's all for a good cause. You can't imagine how a twelve-year old bleeds out."

"Mother of Christ," Jeremy said and then began to weep. "Why? For God's sake, why?"

"I'll grant you, it's a good question, Strand, but like most of your work, completely unoriginal. The better part of England has been asking that very question this past week. As per my well-orchestrated plan, most of the country thinks it has something to do with 'radical Islam.'" His derisive tone was discernible even through the hoarse delivery. "It is, however, the work of Lumen."

"You can't be serious!"

"Indeed, I am. Lumen isn't fully restored but is poised to be so. One thing that many of our countrymen will agree on is that this diseased flow of immigrants must be cut out of the body politic. You'd be surprised how easy it is to animate hatred. To distill and purify soft-hearted liberalism into the fury that makes great change. Social media's a marvelous thing.

"And speaking of the media, you've not been getting the morning paper here, have you? I'll need to have a word with that newsboy. Ha! You should read the articles." His chameleon captor altered an Oxbridge accent into something between Cockney and working-class Liverpool. "Them Islams has kilt annuvah victim, they 'as, an old lady name-a Flo-rence Balla'd.' Yes, she'd be number two…with one more to go!"

"Dear God!" Jeremy exerted every bit of strength he had and attempted to turn the chair toward the voice.

He surprised himself by moving nearly a foot in the direction of his captor. Before he could look up, his body jolted into paralyzing spasms from numberless hammering barbs. The taser. Two hands grabbed the back of his chair and pushed him violently into the table. In response, the skeleton opposite shook, as if to scold Jeremy against further protests.

"Do something like that again, Father, and I'll introduce you to a kind of physical torment you've only read about in comfy chairs on the subject of Christian martyrs. What you need to do right now is not preach to me about the deaths of innocents. I know all about it. And I—we—know what glories may be gained by just the right kind of deaths of the right kind of people. And at this moment, there's precious little in our way."

A hand reached from behind Jeremy and deftly snatched the glow stick. The figure could then be heard walking slowly past the dead man's side of the table, his footsteps receding in the darkened crypt.

41

Myles sat alone in the Reading Room long after D'Arcy Library had closed. He'd gotten Eva's approval and assured her that he'd pull the main door shut when finished. Distant bell towers around the venerable city and the stately library clock had just tolled two in the morning, but he was far from ready to leave. He sat bathed in a pool of light emanating from a single table lamp. The rest of the library, cavernous, still and high about him, was shrouded in black.

His mind had been a jumble of emotions, most of them centered on Jeremy's continued absence. He'd checked his friend's room for the umpteenth time that day. Anger and frustration at what happened at the police station fueled a growing sense of resolve to do something. Anything. He decided to return to the Hopkins manuscript, which he had been reading aloud and dissecting for the past hour. There was so much of the poem that was opaque, even considering Hopkins' affinity for sprung rhythm, verbing nouns and nouning verbs.

He pushed the poem aside and rubbed his eyes. He remembered Jeremy suspecting aloud that this perhaps final poetic work of Hopkins was one of his "dark" sonnets, freighted with a kind of fear barely limned with hope. Myles wasn't so sure. There was too much calculation in it. Even its incompleteness seemed a clue he couldn't quite crack no matter how far into that dark he delved.

He leaned forward over the table and looked at the spines of the dozens of books he'd gathered earlier. Among them were tomes about Oxford clubs and organizations through the ages, along with one about Jesuit conspiracies and global political cabals. He had searched the stacks and reference area for anything that might offer clues about the elusive Lumen and, now by association, the equally mysterious Gerard Manley Hopkins. What could *he* possibly have to do with Oxford's prestigious club? Nothing in the Hopkins corpus or biographical data made reference to Lumen or any other secret society.

Myles examined the notes he'd been making for the last few hours. The basic facts about Lumen were clear. The group had been founded by Henry VIII's astute chancellor, Cardinal Wolsey, as a sort of college within a college: twelve clerical scholars housed in an elegant hall. They were to serve as a model of intellectual brilliance and dedicated service for the rest of what was then called Cardinal College. Wolsey obviously didn't have a weak ego. But Lumen's exemplary nature was not merely for the college; it was for Oxford itself, even the kingdom.

After the turbulent decades of the Reformation, the group retained its clerical prerequisite in the Anglican Church until the eighteenth century, when Lumen was opened to lay members. Upon graduation—and this was, without exception, into positions of authority and leadership in church and government—"old boys" were free to reveal their Lumen-ous association, but disclosing anything else about the group was stringently forbidden. It was curious that so few seemed to want to do this, however far up the ladders of power they ascended. In his authoritative history of the university, Professor Jacoby had noted a few cases of celebrated associations—men who publicized their membership in the elite group—but this was usually in connection with some lavish gift of property or other form of wealth to Lumen or the university.

Sizable benefactions came to the group in such a way that it amassed tremendous wealth over the centuries. At the same time, it was carefully generous with its wealth, granting substantial sums that advanced the cause of king and country.

The sitting group itself—Lumen as an Oxford undergraduate club—was bound by strict secrecy: where and when they met, the subject of their meetings, and members' names, at least while they were still at Oxford. Any connection with Hopkins, then, was doubly difficult to clarify.

And then there was the sharp turn of fate that Lumen took in the twentieth century, their disappearance from Oxford without much evidence of a story behind it. It was this detail that most intrigued Myles. What could have happened that would force a group to fade away that had been part of Oxford's elite for four centuries? Was there some scandal that hastened the end? Perhaps some sexual indiscretion that required a secret end to all the secrets? Was it some other act of violence? Was there a murder?

Myles thought he heard the creak of a floorboard from far behind him. He turned in his chair and peered into the darkness. A deathly hush prevailed except for the steady ticking of the pendulum wall clock on the mezzanine. He leaned back in his chair, clasped his hands behind his head and studied the dim reaches of the floors above him.

After nearly a minute, he leaned forward again, turned to his laptop and quickly began typing an email to Jacoby.

He suddenly felt a bony hand grip the back of his neck. He turned quickly.

"Jesus Christ, Tock!" His pulse raced.

"Well, I'm glad to hear that you've returned to prayer, Myles." A grinning Tock shuffled to the other side of the table across from Myles.

"What are you doing lurking about in the middle of the night? I could've beaned you with one of these tomes!"

Tock looked at the open book in front of Myles, appraising its size and weight. "That would've done it, I should think." He then looked at Myles more intently. "At my age, sleep is a fickle mistress, and, alas, not one that violates any of my sacred vows. What are *you* doing up this late? Night belongs to creatures of darkness, not creatures of the light. Check your Saint Paul."

Myles chuckled softly. "As it happens, it's the men of the light that I'm researching. Ever heard of Lumen?"

"Ah, Lumen. Ironic name. I should say they were more men of obscurity than light." The old man pulled out a chair and sat down across from Myles.

"Tock, you know Hopkins—not just the poet, but the man, the Jesuit. What are the chances that he was affiliated with Lumen? Could he have been a member?"

"I dare say, he was certainly sharp enough for it."

"But it sounds so far from who Hopkins was—a group dedicated to church and crown."

Tock rubbed his stubbled chin thoughtfully. "Well, when I think back to the Dark Ages, when I was an undergraduate here, I had no idea I'd find my way to the Society of Jesus and the priesthood. I was imbued with the spirit of this place: Oxford was everything to me." The old man smiled. "You may be looking at Hopkins too much through the lens of his later years. You know, he wasn't a Jesuit all his life."

Myles stared into the library's murky shapes and considered what Tock had just said. "Our fragment was written in Dublin, along with the other dark sonnets. But this piece"—Myles tapped the copy before him with his index finger—"seems both more and less than the others. It's darker in mood but also in origin and meaning. There's a struggle here, but I don't think it's against despair." He frowned and shook his head. "I'm stumped. And more than anything, I'm damn worried about Jeremy."

"I know. Let sleep assist, dear boy. I'm going to bed now, Myles. But I'll say a rosary for you as I drift off—or at least half a Hail Mary." He grinned and lightly tapped Myles' shoulder. "Good night, lad."

Myles watched the old man recede out of the lamplight, his hardy but unsteady frame burdened and bowed with many years.

Wednesday, May 10

42

"Welcome to our humble hunting ground," said Cyril Jacoby, extending a hand to Myles and smiling more with his eyes than his mouth. The venerable scholar was dressed in carefully creased chinos, a casual white shirt and a dark blue blazer with gold buttons sporting All Souls College arms.

The morning was overcast but pleasantly warm, and upon stepping out of college after breakfast Myles quickly shed his sport coat and stuffed it in his canvas briefcase. He had on the same dress shirt he wore at Guest Night, this time untucked, and lightweight pants. Although the police had successfully quashed protests, as he walked up St. Aldate's he noticed a busload of tourists being dropped off near Carfax, so he took a quieter route toward All Souls via Bear Lane and Merton Street. During the ten-minute walk, his thoughts had bounced between what he'd read last night about Lumen and speculation about whether or not Jacoby could know anything about the group or, more importantly, where Jeremy might be.

After passing through the arched entryway, abrupt turns brought them out under a massive yew-tree whose gray-brown limbs uncannily spanned the distance between the iconic Palladian windows of All Souls library. The tree's intricate mass of gray limbs and eruption of gnarled roots reached implacably in every direction, calling to mind the reckless beauty of a mountain and the centuries-long workmanship of a cathedral.

"An ancient yew," said Jacoby casually pointing to the tree. "Symbol of death and life, permanence and change, at the same time. Now there's an irony to provoke cogitation."

"Or depression," offered Myles dryly, to which Jacoby nodded ever-so-slightly in tepid approbation.

Jacoby led Myles through a partially enclosed cobblestone walkway lined with elaborate stonework and a carved oak ceiling that gave way to an impeccably maintained quadrangle overlooked by imposing twin spires and an extraordinary stained-glass window. The topmost dome of Radcliffe Camera loomed in the background. Beginning with the tree and continuing as he entered the heart of this most exclusive and sheltered of Oxford's colleges, Myles was struck by an atmosphere of otherworldliness. The place appeared nearly uninhabited. The lawn, shrubs and ornamental trees were immaculately groomed. Perhaps by virtue of the fact that the buildings of the quad were higher and the towers more numerous than any other Oxford college, not a hint of the city's inescapable traffic noise made its way into this sanctum. The two highest spires soared directly above a magnificent window, which was actually a composite of more than three dozen windows, all of exquisite stained glass.

"The views are spectacular," remarked Myles. "It's a wonder you get any work done."

Jacoby chuckled. "These environs, this ambiance—it *can* exercise a narcotic effect on the scholar, to say nothing of the sybarite."

After pointing out a few finer details of Hawksmoor's designs, Jacoby led Myles up a serpentine stone staircase to his apartment. The historian's rooms were tastefully sumptuous, decorated in rich blues and greens and featuring pressed metal ceilings and plush Persian rugs. Besides being impeccably well kept, what most impressed Myles was the stunning array of art, mostly paintings and small sculptures from the Renaissance and neoclassical periods.

Jacoby gestured Myles into his book-lined study and to one of two large leather chairs set a perfect distance from an expansive bay window. On the table between them was a delicately painted porcelain teapot and a silver serving tray bedecked with assorted brightly-colored sweets.

"Now, Dr. Dunn, how may I help you?" Jacoby nodded and opened his hands, palms out, in a gesture of magnanimity.

"First, thank you for meeting me so early," said Myles, to which Jacoby repeated the gesture. "At dinner the other night, you said that Lumen had disappeared on the eve of the Second World War, but you used the phrase 'mysterious dissolution.' My first question for you is could Lumen be active today in some form?"

Jacoby looked surprised and leaned back in his chair. "We've no record of Lumen after 1943, and its extinguishment was so—shall we say, complete?—that I think I'd know if it were flickering again." There was no disguising the fact that Jacoby savored his play on words nearly as much as he did the silken sound of his own voice. "But at the risk of seeming impertinent, why this query from you rather than from Father Strand?"

Myles had prepared for this and he watched Jacoby carefully. "He was called to London on some Jesuit business and asked me to help Dr. Bashir continue his research while he's away."

Jacoby raised his eyebrows. "It sounds like he considers this a time-sensitive matter. I can't imagine why…" He tapped his finger-tips together expectantly.

Myles noted Jacoby's curiosity and wanted to deflect it, though not in an obvious way. "I volunteered."

"Quite so. Old mates stick together and all that." He smiled and then nodded for Myles to go on.

"So, to my question. Was Lumen's decline widely known, or was the group's very existence some sort of secret?"

"Both and neither." Jacoby's grin struck Myles as enigmatic and forced. "As near as anyone can tell, it was an open secret. You see, once enshrouded in scandal in the latter decades of the nineteenth century, the group lost its cachet. Perhaps the opposite of what would have happened today, when we're all in the thrall of Twitter and Instagram. Back then, however, the group was merely discred-ited and largely forgotten."

"But still continued to exist?" asked Myles.

"Technically. But it became nothing more than a dining society, and a minor one at that. All dusty and tired, I'm afraid, like one of those London clubs where old men nod off reading news of the Royal Court. In the case of late Lumen, it was indolent and wealthy undergraduates. By the time of its demise in the early years of the Second War, it had become as significant as a Rotary Club. But there's something symmetrical, almost poetic about its end."

"How so?"

Jacoby elegantly lifted a petit four from the silver tray and ate half of it before putting the remainder on a small plate. "As I'm sure Dr. Penrose would be loath to tell you," he continued, daintily touching the corners of his mouth with a cloth napkin, "Lumen's beginnings were really quite modest, nearly imperceptible. A small coterie of scholars selected by Cardinal Wolsey and supported by his early rapine grabs at the monasteries. A rather lavish scholarship fund, you might say, but in spite of their comparative wealth and comfort, really just another group of 'clerkes of Oxenford.' By the time they ended some four centuries later, no one in Oxford really paid them much mind at all."

"So, the war pretty much clinched the deal."

Jacoby laughed lightly. "Yes, 'clinched.' As you must know, the war shook everything in England to its foundations, even this sandstone relic of a university. All efforts were devoted to the cause. Even the residual grandeur of Lumen was impossible to rationalize any longer. So, the 'Final Twelve,' as they came to be known briefly, decided in 1939 with surprising perspicacity and courage to dissolve their society. Most of them went down from Oxford and off to war."

"I would imagine that even a group as secretive as Lumen thought highly enough of itself to have kept written records of some kind?"

Jacoby nodded. "The only documents to have survived the group's changes are the founding charter, now at Christ Church, and the Register, which resides behind locked doors in the Duke Humphrey reading room at the Bodleian. The charter's quite a beautiful thing in and of itself, written in a florid sixteenth-century hand with ribbons and seals at the foot. You should try seeing it, in any case, though Sarah Penrose is stingier than Scylla and Charybdis when it comes to allowing anyone past the archives door." Jacoby leaned back and laughed. "No, Sarah's quite a gem, really. She simply labors beneath an overdeveloped sense of territoriality." Jacoby arched his brows as he lifted his teacup to his lips.

"Can you tell me anything about the Register?"

"Tedious content in a splendid form, not unlike Lumen itself, I suppose." Jacoby smiled with self-satisfaction. "Let's see, I looked at it some years ago for my history. The usual contents: organizational statutes, a few pages on rituals, a bit of its own story, Wolsey and whatnot. They weren't the most transparent organization. And lists of names, many names. Do you like reading telephone books, Dr. Dunn?"

"I'm presuming the names are members."

"Yes, that and more. Members, officers and of course the *Praeses*, who ran the show. Future prime ministers and cabinet secretaries, most. I think there's an archbishop or two."

Jacoby stopped for a thoughtful moment, and in the quiet mid-afternoon bells sounded from neighboring St. Anne's College. "Do you have other questions?"

"Just one more. Can you conceive of any basis for a connection between Gerard Manley Hopkins and Lumen?"

Jacoby worked his face into a benignly condescending frown, a visage that Myles suspected was second nature to the man. "Hopkins in Lumen? Surely not. Clearly, Father Strand has a notion that the Jesuit poet had some association with the group, but wholly indirect, I should think. Perhaps a chum or a classmate, that sort of thing. It happened all the time and why wouldn't it? Lumen's twelve had friends, though the ethos of the group was to limit revelations of membership. Anything beyond that for Hopkins would be...most astounding."

Jacoby glanced at his watch. "Well, as I mentioned, I have a lecture to prepare." He grinned and stood up, and Myles followed suit. The two men left the study's oaken floor and crossed the plush carpet of the main sitting room. Before they reached the door, Myles turned.

"If I may, a quick and final question. Does the word Collington mean anything to you?"

Jacoby smiled wearily, as if Myles had asked one too many questions. "Well, of course, it's not an entirely uncommon English placename, including a few villages. But I think, given our luminous context today, you may be referring to Sir Stephen Collington. He is known by the rare few who care about such things—such as myself—as Lumen's 'last light.' And, all things considered, not a bad way for Lumen to go out of existence. A kind man, gentle, well-bred. Beyond ancient, if he's still alive."

"So, you don't know that he's living?"

"I've enough difficulty keeping abreast of my own mortal situation, Dr. Dunn. I'm fairly certain Collington was an old boy of Christ Church. Perhaps the fair Sarah can apprise you of his whereabouts, above or under the ground."

Jacoby opened the door and offered a short, regal bow. After thanking his host once again, Myles was immediately met by a black-suited valet who mutely escorted him from All Souls.

43

Eva's fingers nimbly scrambled over the keys of her office desktop computer. She had brought up several databases and keyed in variations of "trinity," "trinitas," in combination with "Oxford." There were about a thousand hits, but most of them could be ruled out, not least of which was Trinity Autoworks in Banbury. Most of the references related to Oxford's prestigious Trinity College, but the name was so prevalent that she felt at sea with all the catches: offices, dons, buildings in the college itself, its history, alumni, library manuscript references, members of its boat crew.

She narrowed the search by adding to "trinity" and "Oxford" the word "chalice." Eight references appeared, all of them in reference to the college chapel, its plate and what the Reverend Elsa Shaw used in a Communion Service last Christmas.

One other entry caught her attention: under the British Antiquarian Society was reference to Trinity Church in Godstow, a few miles from the outer reaches of the university. If there was any particular association between Hopkins' acrostic and an Oxford "trinity," it was likely to do with the college and maybe its chapel. But she noted the Godstow reference all the same.

She placed a call directly to Ashton Carter, her counterpart over in Trinity's library, and arranged to see him in a half-hour. She hadn't seen Ashton in months, on one of those arcane and stuffy occasions when Oxford's librarians assembled. Eva had come to know him fairly well in London when they were both studying library science. He was Oxford brilliant, whimsically funny and always accessible. They arranged to meet at 10:00; it was now 9:30.

Just as she was about to walk out of her office and into the library stacks, her cell phone chirped.

"Hello."

"Eva, it's Myles."

Eva smiled to hear Myles' voice. "G'morning. I'm here in my

office, avoiding the work I get paid for but having a ripping good time learning about your Trinity." She heard Myles' laugh get drowned out by a passing bus. "Where are you?"

"Catte Street. Just got out of a meeting with Jacoby that was more intriguing than informative. I'm on my way now to the Bodleian to get a pass into Duke Humphrey so I can look at the Lumen register. Any success on your end?"

"Not yet. I've got a bit more to do and then I'll pop over to Trinity College to talk with its librarian. I know it'll sound barmy, but I want to find out if he can make any connection at all between his college and the Cuxham Chalice. It's a shot in the dark, but what hasn't been with that poem? Myles—any sense of Jacoby and Jeremy?"

"Hard to tell in all that aloofness whether he was playing dumb or knew something of Jeremy's whereabouts. But I don't think so. He was notably incurious about Jeremy. Oh, Eva, one more thing before you go?"

"Sure."

"I'd like to track down an Oxford alum named Sir Stephen Collington. Could you find out anything about him: an address, phone, immediate family? I think he might be able to help us in ways no book or library will."

"As if we didn't have enough of the enigmatic these days. But sure, I'll dig up something on the old boy. Meanwhile, say hello to Duke Humphrey for me."

44

Myles climbed the stairs to the upper tier of the old Bodleian, Duke Humphrey's Library and the bookish heart of Oxford University, maybe even of the English-reading world. The eponymous duke, Humphrey of Gloucester, the youngest son of King Henry IV, had given his name along with his books to Oxford in the fifteenth century.

Myles paused at the librarian's desk that sat at the entrance to this ancient wing. He wrote on a cream-colored note card for patrons the title of the manuscript he was searching for. The librarian, a young man with a curly coal-black beard and a nimbus of black frizzy hair, glanced at the title on the card and told Myles that he might take a seat at a reader's table while the book was retrieved.

Myles turned to his left and walked down a broad hallway flanked with tall wooden stacks filled with large, timeworn folios. The stacks alternated with tall lancet windows that flooded the space with morning light, revealing dust motes in its sharp beams. Above the stacks and twice as high was the roof of Duke Humphrey, emblazoned with Oxford's shield and motto repeated scores of times in old but still bright blue, gold and white on oak panels: *Dominus Illuminatio Mea*. Oxford's motto, "The Lord is my light." *Light...Lumen. No escaping it,* thought Myles. He proceeded to the west wing of Duke Humphrey, an elegant two-tiered, book-lined reading room called the Selden End. Tall windows on three sides colored with occasional panels of Jacobean glass enveloped the reading tables and patrons in warm light.

Myles took a seat at a long oak table at the south end. Moments later the hirsute librarian gently lowered onto the table an *Oxford University Archives* box containing a battered volume. He handed Myles a pair of white cotton reader's gloves, standard requirement to keep away oil smudges from manuscript pages with every turn. He smiled and quietly departed. Myles removed the top of the archives box and carefully lifted the book out. Its spine had crumbled long ago, but the folio threads were just managing to hold it together. He laid it on a Styrofoam reading wedge.

It was as nondescript as any accountant's ledger. In spite of the highborn men whose names paraded through this book, it lacked any degree of refinement. That wasn't the only thing that impressed Myles. He was also struck by the irony that a group so obsessed with secrecy and cloaking the identity of its members was here, long past Lumen, accessible and open for all the world to see.

Hammered into the brown leather front cover in faded gold letters were the words:

REGISTRUM FRATRUM LUMINIS

Being the Book of the Brotherhood of the Duodecimal Light

Statutes & Charters

&

The Book of Names

He'd get to the contents in a moment, especially the names, but Myles first wanted to get a general look at the volume. Careful not to loosen the fragile binding, he turned the book in his hands and opened the cover. Nothing on the inside pasteboard but a few penciled library notations from when the Register was admitted into the Bodleian Library's collection. Between the front cover and the title page was a yellowed typed note on Bodleian stationary: "This book along with the financial papers of Lumen Oxon. were appropriated by the Commissioners of the University's Proctors after the society disbanded, Oxford, 1943."

He set the book face down and gently lifted the backboard, hoping to find some identifying imprint.

He was not disappointed.

On the inside of the back cover and hammered into the leather with gold leaf was the Lumen seal, or insignia. It appeared as a somewhat more cursive version of the stylized chalice scrawled on

199

the Hopkins manuscript and, Myles was convinced, gruesomely on the foreheads of Peter Toohey and Florence Ballard. Not just the image of a chalice, but that baffling circle at the base—here it was, as well.

He stared at it for several seconds, then let out a long exhalation. It was now clear that somehow Hopkins had gotten hold of Lumen's symbol and had worked it into the manuscript sonnet. Not verbally, as maybe he had planned, but graphically in the collection of scribbles and strokes that surrounded the poetic text.

The same symbol, clearly a central feature of Lumen, had also made its way to the psychopath who was terrorizing Oxford citizens and inflaming communities, Muslim and non-Muslim alike. But who could be doing this? And had Lumen somehow been revived?

Myles turned the book face-up again and opened it, reading quickly through the Latin dedication. He found the florid hand harder-going than the ancient language it was written in. It was predictably rhetorical, with its deep bows to Church and Crown, both of which supply "light that burns away ignorance and unburdens the soul." He turned the page to find in the same flowery cursive a list of contents, beginning with Statutes and Charters and ending with a "Book of Names."

There were seven chapters covering areas of Lumen life, including a brief and highly self-aggrandizing history. Myles read the opening line of the first chapter:

Twelve clerkes, men ennobled of good birth and bearing, possessed of right reason, and true Faith, shall constitute the Brotherhood of Lumen. They shall, each one, be part of the Twelve and the Twelve together be one. They shall share a common board and be of harmonious philosophie, excellent in the praise of their tutors and without peer in Christ Church College, Oxon.

A line was drawn through the last four words, and in the margin next to them were words written in a different hand: "all colleges and halls of the University of Oxford." Whenever the original text was written, Myles thought, it had to be before Lumen's decision to allow candidates from colleges other than Christ Church.

The next two chapters described in painstaking detail the role of the chief of Lumen, the *Praeses* or the "First Light," and a highly rigid code of ethics called "The Twelvefold Way." This was followed by a paean to "Sophia" and "the excellence of study," the importance of secrecy in all of Lumen's dealings, and a final chapter on "goodly wealth, legacies and benefactions." Paging through the latter, Myles could see that Lumen had been in possession of properties, some for many decades if not centuries. These included Oxfordshire place names and several others—no doubt, estates gifted to Lumen—in counties such as Yorkshire, Surrey and Essex.

Each of these chapters was written in the same billowy eighteenth-century hand, suggesting that whoever the scribe was had copied the whole of the text from earlier pages. Myles moved through these with only mild interest.

His goal was the final part of the register, *The Twelve Perpetual or the Book of Names.* The list began in 1732 and ended in 1942. For some reason, the membership rolls from the group's first two centuries either hadn't survived or weren't copied into this register. Another difference was in the last pages of the register: by the late 1930s, the adherence to twelve names slipped from term to term. Some academic seasons had the full complement of twelve, but others had ten, seven and, in 1942, only four names. How the mighty have fallen, thought Myles.

He leaned back in his chair and scanned the room. He counted only six other patrons in the library, five buried behind stacks of books piled around them, each lost in his or her own literary world. A sixth stood on the mezzanine above, back against the railing and reading.

Myles returned to his own work and penciled some notes on the pad at his right. What he had been reading in the register matched what Penrose had said at Guest Night about Lumen and certainly what Jacoby had just confirmed. The founding members of Lumen belonged to "Cardinal College," the former name of Christ Church College. By the early eighteenth century the group had expanded its membership base from Christ Church to include all of Oxford University. This was hardly a move toward egalitarianism, thought Myles. Rather, it was a growth strategy that involved cherry-picking the best and brightest from all Oxford's colleges, thereby becoming more, not less, exclusive.

The preponderance of the register and Myles' main interest, the Book of Names, was markedly different in appearance from the seven chapters on statutes. The long list of names was busy with many different hands changing over the years. Most of the names repeated from term to term and then dropped off after the eighth or ninth appearance.

Myles took out his phone and checked a file he'd created the night before when working in the library. Hopkins' first year at Oxford was 1863-64, so Myles turned the pages to the mid-nineteenth century. That would be a beginning place to find the names of Lumen's members and possibly some Hopkins association. He paged forward to Trinity term, 1867, when Hopkins left Oxford to teach at Newman's school in Birmingham and begin his life as a Jesuit. Marking that page with a strip of paper, he turned several more pages of the book until he was in the spring or Trinity Term in 1867, after which Hopkins had left the university. He read through the names of Lumen that term. Alec Moncrieff, First Light, a name that had come up frequently in the list from previous terms. Moncrieff was followed by three others, typically: Eden, De Vere and Percy, with their positions in Lumen named respectively as Sub-*Praeses*, Chancellor and Treasurer.

But in the Trinity term of 1867, one of those three, the Steward, had changed, from Bartholomew Percy to a name that Myles couldn't make out immediately because it had been canceled out with a bold, straight line of ink. A member of Lumen stricken from the record—even the boldness of the line indicated anger and hard judgment. One of the twelve had failed somehow, perhaps betrayed the others. Myles could not resist the sardonic self-reference: Where have I seen *that* before?

He studied the canceled-out name and drew on his notepad what upper and lower parts of the letters he could make out. In a minute he had it: one Thomas Viscount Carrick. Myles paged back through the register just to make sure: no other name across two centuries' worth of Luminaries had been canceled out.

Clearly, something had been going on with Lumen in the spring of 1867. While he didn't expect to see Hopkins' name enlisted among these august twelve anywhere in the register, the once-and-future poet had to have some connection with the group.

Otherwise, how could he have seen a fabled chalice associated with Lumen? How could he have written obscure lines about it toward the end of his life?

He spent the next twenty minutes writing out the names of Lumen's members from 1863 to 1867, just to be sure. The apparently disgraced Viscount Carrick appeared in the spring of 1866 and then for the three terms of academic year 1866-1867 when, without benefit of explanation, he disappeared from view. The register, Myles felt, had more to yield. He wanted to read through even the highly rhetorical statutes in case there was something to be found between the lines. He could leave that for another day.

He stood up and stretched, put pencils and notepad into his backpack and then cradled the register safely back into its archives box.

As he carried the box back to the librarian's desk, he was unaware of being watched by the reader standing on the mezzanine, paging absently through a book on medieval monastic furnishings. Monsignor Moretti.

45

Myles walked the short distance from Bodley to Oxford's Covered Market to grab a late lunch and hammer out something of a strategy based on what he'd discovered in the register. The cloud cover had disappeared, and after the ill-lit confines of the Bodleian, he squinted in the brilliant sunlight.

The market was loud with local vendors and customers shouting above their own din, mixed with the noisy bustle of tourists and kids on skateboards zipping down the small alleys between stores that sold anything from Oxford shirts to newspapers, umbrellas, leather goods, phone accessories, tarts, fresh meats and cheeses. The town was enjoying a welcome moment of normalcy.

Georgina's Grill was packed with a lunch crowd of mostly students and dons, so Myles got a sandwich and coffee to go and sat at a small table in one of those shopper-crowded alleys.

He reached into his backpack and opened his notebook on the tabletop. What had he learned? Was there anything from the visit with Jacoby or the Lumen register that might put him in step with Jeremy and help lead him to his friend?

The Lumen insignia had confirmed some kind of Hopkins connection; Thomas Carrick, whoever he was, likely got tossed out of the club. This seemed noteworthy and yet at the same time too little to go by: there was no mention of the Cuxham Chalice on the long list of estates, properties, endowments and trusts. But would there be? If part of the chalice's fame was its apparent non-existence, and if the chalice, as the symbol suggested, was a central feature to the secretive society, might its very existence not also be cloaked in secrecy? He kept returning to the same questions: How much of this does Jeremy know? and Why would he withhold anything from Eva and me?

Myles drained his cup, then glanced at his watch. He figured he had another hour before going back to Ignatius and finding out what Eva had learned about Oxford-area "Trinitas." He left his notes, pencils and backpack on the table—it was all in view of Georgina's take-out stand—and headed over for a second cup. As one of the waitresses poured indolently, Myles glanced back at the table. A herd of tourists wearing *Italia* windbreakers moved between his view and the table. As they exited the area, he saw that everything was on the table as he left it.

He sat back down, placing his coffee mug next to the notebook. What he saw on the open page flabbergasted him. He glanced up from the table and scanned the crowd. No one stood out, no one was walking hurriedly away from the table, and no one without an *Italia* jacket seemed to work into the departing group.

Myles looked down again at the Host on the notebook. He had seen them a thousand times before. Had elevated them in the Eucharist for the congregation to see and reverence. Had broken them over the chalice at the "Lamb of God" and consumed both parts in the priest's reception of the Blessed Sacrament. This Eucharistic Host was of the traditional sort. Nearly the size of the palm of his hand, a classic depiction of the crucified Christ dye-pressed into the circlet by a group of nuns who famously made hosts for nearly every Catholic church in the world. A faint line, the one the priest uses to break the Host, bisected the white disk, which was smudged but otherwise whole.

Along with dozens of questions, any number of feelings coursed through Myles as he stared at the Host. If someone had left a bag of gold doubloons on the table, he would have been less surprised.

He leaned back into his chair and looked up again at the milling shoppers. As he re-scanned the crowd, his eyes locked with those of a young man standing half-behind an "Oxford Mom" tee shirt on a hanger: Sam's boyfriend Rabi. Myles raised his eyebrows in a questioning look and the boy slowly nodded. Then Myles, eyebrows still raised, gestured with a nod of his head to the small empty chair on the other side of the table. To his infinite surprise, Rabi walked from the shirt rack to the chair and sat down.

"We seem to meet in remarkable circumstances, Rabi."

The boy said nothing in response but looked down at the table, his hands pressed nervously between his knees.

Myles tapped softly on the table just next to the wafer. "As far as I know, Rabi, this isn't something often found in the average

Muslim household. Would you mind telling me how you came to have it?"

"I found it. You should have it," he said quickly.

Myles realized he had to play this very carefully. The boy might run, or he could just shut down here at the table and Myles would learn nothing.

"So, why give it to me?" Myles asked.

"Because you are one of their priests. You should have it."

It struck Myles that Rabi might think the Host was some sort of fetish or talisman, the sooner out of his hands, the better.

"A *former* priest, Rabi."

Rabi looked at him incredulously. "But when you are an imam, you cannot be a former imam. You are a leader of your people." He paused. "And you speak Arabic."

Myles figured his demonstrated facility with Rabi's language probably had more to do with this meeting than his position as an ex-imam.

"Okay, Rabi. I'm very familiar with this. It's called a Host, and you're right, priests have these all the time. But how did you get it?" There was nothing edgy or insistent in Myles' voice.

Rabi was silent for a long moment, and Myles thought again he might bolt. He didn't let Rabi see, but his right hand was poised under the table for a sudden grab at the kid's shirt, if necessary. He wasn't about to let him get away.

As if giving up a brief struggle within himself, Rabi's shoulders relaxed and he settled deeper into his chair. After looking quickly all about him, he leaned forward. In a low voice he recounted his May Morning walk from the pub where he worked washing glasses to the demolition site where the two of them had their near encounter. He described the placing of Peter Toohey's body, the blood, the prayer rug and this…this object. He gestured toward the Host with a kind of fearful reverence.

Myles was careful not to mention phrases like "tampering with evidence," "obstruction of justice," or the shitstorm that would descend upon Rabi if the police found out about this "object."

"Rabi, was this the only thing you took from the place?"

The young man nervously pushed the hair from his forehead and nodded.

"And did you touch it?"

Rabi looked up at Myles as if he'd asked him how many fingers he had. "Of course, but in this way." Rabi placed his right thumb and middle finger at the edges of the wafer but did not pick it up. He pointed to the pouch in his hoodie. "I put it in this pocket and then into a book at home. I did not know what to do with it." He turned his head sharply to his left, as if looking at the Host was some sort of indictment. When he looked back at Myles, there were tears in his eyes. "Who would make such a blasphemy, to your people…and to mine?"

Myles quickly filled in for himself Rabi's motives for taking the Host from the site. The discarding of a butchered Christian boy in a fake Muslim execution was inflammatory enough. But adding to that defilement, this primary symbol of Christian worship and identity was mockery to the nth degree. Myles was still stumped by the odd combination of symbols and the care taken with the tableau. But he was gaining a better sense of the young man before him. Just as he had done with the chavs a few days ago—a wiry boy taking on a trio of thugs—Rabi was trying here to confront, if not understand, an enemy that would murder a child and desecrate not one Abrahamic religion, but two.

"I don't know, Rabi, but you're right—whoever did this blasphemed terribly."

Myles studied the image on the Host again. It was without a doubt the single most common image in all of Christian iconography, the Crucifixion. He found himself regarding it now from the perspective of this young and devout Muslim. Rabi didn't believe in the Crucifixion, but he no doubt regarded it in nearly the same way as he saw Peter Toohey's lifeless body, as a senseless slaying of the innocent.

Myles was suddenly aware of a faint memory, more a feeling, again, associated with the Toohey boy's death and the placement of the body. What had triggered it just now, though, was the connection between the killing of young Peter and Jesus. But as soon as it came up in him like a cooler current in a warm tide, it disappeared.

"Look, Rabi, I said the last time we met that 'you *are* innocent,' and I meant not just you, but your community. The murders in Oxford over the last ten days haven't been committed by Muslims,

I'm sure of it. This Christian holy object only adds to my conviction that you, this murder, the whole town—all of it and all of us are part of an elaborate manipulation. Some people would see it as further evidence of a Muslim plot to insult Christianity, and I know that's why you took it from the site."

Rabi leaned forward again and whispered, "But how do you know it was not done by one of my people?"

"Because it just doesn't add up." Myles realized how subjective his words were and likely how unsatisfying they were to this young man who wanted to see the world with black-and-white clarity. With the addition of the Host, he was clearer than before that if there was a plot unfolding in Oxford, it wasn't a Muslim one. "Trust me, Rabi. Just like you've trusted me with this." He pointed to the Host.

Expressionless, Rabi locked eyes with Myles. After an almost imperceptible nod, he got up and walked away. Within moments he had disappeared into the crowd.

Now, thought Myles, staring down at the Host, what the hell am I going to do with evidence snatched from a murder scene?

46

Eva needed to clear her head. She'd spent an hour wandering around Trinity College, followed by lunch back at her desk while trolling through various databases researching the image on the bottom of the Hopkins manuscript and listing all possible "trinities" in and around Oxford. Her efforts had produced little by way of satisfying results, and she was feeling the walls close in. And Jeremy seemed to be on the other side of them.

She stood and opened a window, letting in the sounds of students laughing and bustling about the quad. Hearing a text tone, she turned and pulled her phone from her bag. A text from Sam: *Thinking of you. Hope you're enjoying the beautiful day. I've got a free period and am sitting in the school library wading through the books you brought me the other day. Love you, Mum.* She smiled, savoring her daughter's words and gesture that seemed to make all of the cold, regrettable words they'd lately exchanged melt away.

Afternoon sun had begun to filter through the high windows that overlooked the Reading Room, in which Eva saw only a few patrons. As she approached the hallway that led to the Archive Room, she passed an older man looking through one of the old-fashioned card catalogs. When he glanced up at her and nodded a polite smile, she recognized Monsignor Moretti. She returned the smile, and in her mind wondered how she would possibly survive this place filled with old Catholic priests.

That brought her next, in a chain of priest-thoughts, to the unpleasant conversation she'd had that same morning with Father Ilbert. The Master had phoned her to ask if it was true that she'd spoken to the police. "You represent this college, Dr. Bashir," he fulminated, "and anything you say in public must first be cleared by the college." He had no interest in hearing her explanation of the circumstances. She shook her head, still rankled by his attitude. Eva chafed at any such reminder of the patronizing and patriarchal worldview that formed the backdrop to much of her life—from her upbringing to her marriage to Oxford's old boys network—that she thought she had left behind. All too uncertain of her own position in the college hierarchy, however, Eva would leave the matter alone. At least for the time being.

Rounding the corner to the archive room, Eva nearly bumped into Tock. Now, a trinity of priests for her day. What next? Tock was using a cane and held it up in mock self-defense, but his face was unperturbed.

"Was it something I said?" In response to Eva's look of confusion, he added, "You seemed lost in thought—and by the looks of it, I'd say you were plotting a revolution among the stacks."

Eva appreciated the twinkle in his eye. Even more than that, she marveled at his keen ability to read people. "You're close. Let's just say the Master's charms are an acquired taste."

"Indeed. On a par with jugged hare," Tock said with a wry grin. There was something felicitous about the culinary allusion: one didn't jug a hare, after all, until it was in the first stages of decay. "Don't let me hold you up, Eva—you're obviously on a mission. I just got up to stretch my stiff old legs and coming to the library is like visiting old friends."

Eva looked thoughtful, considering something. "Actually, Father Forrestal, may I ask you something?"

Tock nodded. "Of course—but only if you call me Tock. Step into my 'office.'" He pointed with his cane to the couch in the Reading Room foyer, a favorite spot for reading the Sunday *Guardian.*

After they sat down, Eva looked at the old man. "I've heard on more than one occasion that despite all the Victorian Lit dons ambling about Oxford, you're one of the great experts on Gerard Manley Hopkins. I've read his poetry, and it's technically brilliant, of course. But I've little sense of what he *means.*" She smiled worriedly. "Perhaps you can help?"

"Well, Eva, I'm not really that sure I've got more of a bead on Hopkins than others. Surely, Jeremy knows him more thoroughly and deeply." The priest looked away for a moment and Eva could see that his eyes registered care, love and worry. "But, yes, I've what you might call an earnest friendship with Hopkins. Perhaps you could pare your question down a bit. For instance, which Hopkins are you interested in—the young Oxford undergraduate, the nature poet, the Jesuit priest?"

"The later Hopkins—the years that produced the 'dark sonnets.'"

"Yes, the Dublin years. The end of his foreshortened life." Tock rubbed his wrinkled face and looked down as he began speaking. "Those were unhappy years for him, shrouded in spiritual ennui. He was a man struggling mightily to accept and accede to his—well, to his faith, his vocation and even his God. Here's an example of what he penned in such darkness:

> *Not, I'll not, carrion comfort, Despair, not feast on thee;*
> *Not untwist—slack they may be—these last strands of man*
> *In me or, most weary, cry I can no more. I can;*
> *Can something, hope, wish day come, not choose not to be."*

Tock could see by the look on Eva's face that she was caught in the downward spiral of Hopkins' lines. "It's one of his darker dark sonnets, and they're all well named—certainly this one is. You see, the theme of 'Carrion Comfort' is the soul, Hopkins' deepest self. He churns in turmoil as a result of self-doubt. Not only that, but doubt in the very presence of God, which is a hard thing for a priest to admit. There's also something profoundly *faithful* about this poem. He addresses Despair and says something to the effect that 'I'm human and hence deeply flawed, yet I stubbornly refuse to allow my humanity—my innate tendency to doubt—to defeat me, to own me. I *believe*, even as my faith roils.' So, the Hopkins of those Dublin years was a man who genuinely felt himself a wretch who wrestles with God."

Eva let several seconds pass. "That's a lot to consider and absorb. It's beautiful, actually, if doubt and pain can be beautiful. There's something universal about it. Something triumphant. Redemptive, I guess you'd say."

Tock closed his eyes and nodded emphatically.

"But," Eva continued, "how could this keenly insightful and sensitive man have allowed himself to be caught in such a despairing place. Why didn't he leave Dublin and find something more… life-giving?"

"Ah, Hopkins was a Jesuit, and in those days if you were told to go somewhere by a religious superior, you went. You didn't dare ask any questions, except which train or boat got you there sooner and cheaper!" Tock thumped his cane against the library floor as a judge might strike a gavel.

"What do you think made Hopkins choose the Jesuits?"

"An excellent question, to which you'll receive a different answer from others, but to my mind it had everything to do with the Spiritual Exercises. Hopkins loved his freedom—he would take long rambles into the countryside not far from where we're now sitting, losing himself in the language of nature. But he felt equally drawn to discipline, rigor, method—in his academics, in his drive for spiritual purity, and of course in his poetry. In the *Exercises,* Ignatius lays out a highly structured process of training the heart, mind and soul for spiritual growth. And spiritual battle."

"'Spiritual battle.' With Satan?"

Tock nodded. "But with an even more formidable adversary. Oneself. And that brings us back to the dark sonnets, doesn't it?" Eva leaned forward and rested her chin on her hand meditatively. Tock continued. "The Exercises are a sort of instruction manual, a guide to decision-making or, to use a key Ignatian term, discernment."

"So," said Eva, "if someone's trapped in indecision, these Exercises would show her the way out."

"Show her the way out, yes. Out of herself. And also the way *in*—to her deepest self, where true vision resides. To the core of one's relationship with God. The goal, as Ignatius saw it, is balance and thus freedom to choose rightly."

"To choose rightly," Eva repeated.

"Jesuits believe," Tock continued, "that all things are given to us by God, even that which seems inimical to our growth or happiness. We exist among countless created things over which we have little or no control. They are what they are. The great question—the only question—is how *we* live. How we choose to use our talents, passions, time. How we love."

Eva found herself rapt by the old man's words. She heard them not as an attempt to wrap the messiness of real life in gauzy religious language, but as an authentic effort to engage the messiness of human experience. It put her in mind of Sam's version of all this. It was a refreshing revelation to her that must have shown on her face.

"Have I struck a chord—or more likely a sour note?" Tock flashed a kind smile.

"Not at all. To be honest, I'm not much for religion. After I immigrated, I was raised by an aunt who was nominally Muslim—and of course Sister Pax. And my ex-husband's brand of Islam was, well, enough to turn me off to organized religion. But as you describe it, the spiritual life seems a lot like the psychology of happiness."

"Well," Tock grinned, "if I can convey such a thing, then there's hope for me yet."

"You've been a great help," she said.

"Oh?" Tock cocked his head.

"I mean with respect to the Hopkins fragment. I'm beginning to imagine it less as a religious poem and more in the context of a crisis, a decision."

"Well," Tock said with one hand on the table and the other fingering the unusual scrimshaw handle of his walking stick, "there's one thing Hopkins knew for sure." His voice was gentle yet forceful. "We're all broken." He let out a slight groan and winked again. "Some of us more than others."

His words and his earthy, dignified bearing, at once unassuming and charismatic, had captivated Eva. It took her mind off Jeremy and the struggles with Sam, if only briefly. She studied the lines of the old man's face, which seemed to grow deeper the longer she looked.

Tock shifted in the chair and hauled himself up heavily, letting the cane steady him. "It was a delight speaking with you, Eva."

Eva stood and wanted to hug the old man but refrained from doing so. She watched him amble metronomically across the Reading Room floor and out the open double doors.

She then walked back past the card catalog. Monsignor Moretti had disappeared. She passed a few students working amid piles of books on tables and made her way to the Librarian's office. The day had felt endless and it was only early afternoon.

She sat down at her desk and jiggled the mouse on the Ignatius College pad to wake up her computer. When the desktop lit up, she was surprised to see lines of text moving across the screen at an oblique angle, hit the corner softly and move in the opposite direction. She quickly looked up and around her office. The door was wide-open. No sign of any patrons in the stacks just beyond. She returned to the screensaver, read the words again, then shook her head in confusion and dismay.

47

Eva endured a library staff meeting with far more on her mind than binding repair in the literature section. As soon as she had a free moment, she picked up her phone. "Myles, I think I may have something for us. I've looked through every possible reference to 'trinity' as a place name in and around Oxford. I've got some updates on a few things at the university, but my bet's on Godstow, just a few miles out of town. There's a Trinity Church there that might give us another bearing on all of this. What do you think about driving out there and seeing if it's possibly a place Jeremy would have gone to."

"Sounds promising," said Myles as he dodged a cyclist while crossing Turl Street. "I'm just leaving the Covered Market and I'm free anytime. You?"

"I can get away in about fifteen minutes," she said. "Don't bother coming back. I'll pick you up at Martyrs' Memorial. That'll give you time to grab me a coffee. There's a place right there on Beaumont called Yvette's."

"Sure," he said and hung up.

Twenty minutes later they were driving north on Woodstock Road. "Sorry to be so last-minute about this, but I wanted to check this out together."

"What is it?"

"It's an Anglican parish church named for the Trinity, just a bit north of the city."

Myles furrowed his brow. "In my four years here, I never heard of it."

"Nor have I," said Eva. "Here, I'll trade you." She pulled her iPad from the bag wedged between the seats and handed it to him in exchange for the coffee he had been holding for her. "You can scroll through the results of my 'trinity' research."

"I will in a minute, but first, tell me how your visit went at Trinity College—any possibilities there?"

"I'm not sure. I discovered that Sir Thomas Pope founded the college for twelve fellows and twelve scholars, which may be a connection to the phrase 'th'nointed twelve' from the poem."

Myles nodded slowly. "Of course, that was, what, the sixteenth century? It seems twelve was a proper number to found any religious institution. I think medieval monasteries began with twelve. And we know Wolsey started up his elite group with the same number. In the case of Trinity College, by the time Hopkins wrote his poem, the place had grown to include a lot more than twelve fellows, right?"

"Right. Add to that the fact that if the twelve in the poem refers to Lumen, as Jeremy seems to believe, then it's less likely to have a connection to a college other than Christ Church, where the group was based."

"Good point. Any sort of 'trinity' at Christ Church?"

She began to shake her head and then paused. "Nothing spectacular—I mean, no particular place in the college is associated with trinity. Walk into the cathedral, of course, and you've got all the obvious: Trinitarian symbols in stained glass and architectural details, the triforium tier of pretty much any high church. But all that's commonplace. I guess it depends on how narrowly we interpret 'trinitas.' Hopkins isn't making this easy for us."

Myles nodded and smiled. "If we take it to be any trio, then the domain of possibilities is hopelessly broad. If we take it to refer to some sort of actual 'trinity'—something with that name—then the domain has got to be pretty small. So, tell me more about this trinity in Godstow."

"It's Holy Trinity Parish Church. The present structure was built in 1849, but like a lot of English churches, Trinity has far older foundations. Tock told me about Hopkins' famous 'rambles' around Oxford, so we're going somewhere that the young poet likely saw numerous times." Myles watched Eva drink the last of her coffee and then yawn.

"Not much sleep last night?"

Eva sighed deeply. "The result of some difficult late-night conversations with Sam."

"Did she react badly to those books on religion that you carried home the other night?" asked Myles.

"Actually, she seems to be taking them in. It's just…I worry. And not just about her. Jeremy, too, of course. And now today…"

Myles looked over at her. "What?" he asked with concern.

Eva nodded at the tablet sitting between them on top of the notebooks and an Oxfordshire road atlas. "Pick up the tablet, Myles, click on the docs icon, then 'trinitas.' Scroll down to the end and you'll find what I'm referring to at the bottom." She waited a moment. 'See those lines of verse?'

Myles did as Eva instructed and began reading silently, then aloud:

"To mend him we end him,
When we hew or delve:
After-comers cannot guess the beauty been.
Ten or twelve, only ten or twelve
Strokes of havoc unselve
The sweet especial scene…"

He looked up from the tablet and at Eva. "Where did you get this?"

"The lines were on my office computer screen. I found them marching hither and yon as a screen saver after I stepped away from my office and ran into Tock. I didn't have time to look them up; I just found them weird."

"They're from a Hopkins poem, 'Binsey Poplars,'" said Myles, reading from a quick search on the iPad. "He wrote it as a sort of lamentation for the felling of a row of favorite trees near the village of Binsey back in his Oxford days. But there's a crucial change here, Eva. Hopkins gave the trees a nurturing, feminine identity, so the first line should read, 'To mend *her* we end her.' Why the change in gend—" Myles stopped and stared at Eva. "Pull over."

After a quick glance in the rearview mirror, Eva pulled the car onto a gravel-shoulder with a slowing crunch and stopped. A look of concern swept over her face.

"What's the matter?"

Myles looked up from the tablet screen. "Eva, while you were with Tock, did you notice anyone enter the library who shouldn't have been there?"

"All kinds of people come and go who shouldn't be there. Heck, half the staff…There was a handful of students, a few library workers. But you know the place—anyone who looks Oxonian enough can walk into it and be right at home."

Myles re-read the lines. "'To mend him we end him…when we hew…strokes of havoc unselve…'"

"Oh, my God, Myles—you think it's about Jeremy! But, how—?"

"I don't know. Someone who knows how to access your PC system managed to type these words while you were out of your office. It was chancy, but whoever it was managed to steal in and out without being noticed. And, I know, there's the whole police thing again, but what would we tell them? That someone played a practical joke on you and mistakenly typed some words from a nineteenth-century poem on your screen? They'd lock us both up for being nuisances."

Eva shivered. "Well, it's bold and creepy. And if we're right, then it's Jeremy that someone is threatening to…what was that word, 'unselve'?"

"Think about it. Someone who knows where Jeremy is, someone who has some measure of control over him, has taken a risk in communicating these lines to you. To us. It could be a taunt, something meant to frighten us. But it could also be a warning. The language is present tense but there's a future threat hanging over the poplars. They haven't been hewn or unsolved *yet*, and that gives me hope that Jeremy is still within reach! But damn it!" he pounded the dashboard, "how do we find him?"

Eva steeled herself, put the car in gear and slid off the gravel slowly onto the road. "We do it, Myles, as we're planning to: by finding out more precisely what Jeremy knew and where the clues in the poem took him the night he disappeared. We both know it's a shot in the dark, but it's the only thing we've got now." She already had the car pushing the speed limit for rural roads. A distant steeple came into view over a small berm to the right. "And that church may just give us the first real clue."

48

"You're kidding," Myles said disappointedly as he got out of the car. Expecting a country church from somewhere out of Jane Austen's time, he was standing on macadam that could've been laid last week. There were a few cars in parking slots, most of them with the titles of church offices: rector, verger, gift shop. To the left of the churchyard was a thick copse that formed a western boundary with the church grounds. What looked like a typical English farmer's dry stone wall appeared distantly between dark, thick trunks. The church itself was a hybrid construction: most elements were a nineteenth-century Gothic revival with a southern porch and doors that had suffered some serious modern renovation. Overall, the church's simplicity, in contrast to the grandness of Oxford University buildings, seemed more a matter of the parish's financial limits than any conscious decisions in style.

Between the parking lot and the church was the customary lichgate shaded under a brooding, fragrant hemlock tree. The tree was ancient, the lichgate something hammered together by local and not very skilled carpenters. To the right of the church was a brick two-story rectory, built in the 1950s, with parish offices. To the left lay a cemetery that covered about an acre.

"I'm having a hard time imagining the collegiate Hopkins walking across this car park, Myles."

"I know what you mean." Myles turned 360 degrees to get a sense for where he was. He blurred away the twentieth-century signage, the cars and macadam. One could very well "come upon" Trinity Church without intending to. There were a few scattered neighboring houses, post-war structures that intruded upon what must have been for a very long time a country church. Bounding all sides of the church buildings and cemetery were what seemed neglected woods, green and dark against the bright afternoon sky. A breeze swayed the tops of thickly growing beech, ash, and oak.

"Well, since we're here, we might as well take a look."

Myles and Eva walked through the lichgate to the door of the church. Just as Myles opened it, three elderly women stepped out of the gloomy vestibule. One of them paused, smiled and nodded before proceeding slowly toward the rectory.

The interior was pretty much as Myles had expected: a central aisle, the nave, and one side-aisle on the right. The building was cruciform with two transepts, north and south, with the sanctuary behind a rood screen to the east. A Romanesque font, possibly Norman, stood at the entrance to the main aisle.

"You're the ex-priest," remarked Eva, "what do you think the images in the windows are all about?"

He began to study the glass on the southern side of the aisle, pointing out standard images of saints, apostles and martyrs portrayed in bright reds, yellows and blues. Not surprisingly, each of the twelve windows, six on each side, was surmounted by a trefoil symbolic of the Trinity. One of the window themes Myles didn't know, though he could guess its subject. It depicted a serious-looking bishop, arrayed with miter and crozier, holding in his left hand a model of the church. Standing around him, diminutively drawn, were monks and clergy, apparently from the parish and its environs, including Oxford.

"That image usually represents the founder of the church," Myles said, pointing to the model the bishop was holding. "The clergy at his feet, looking up with such admiration, must be the priests and monks involved in the pastoral care of the church." He turned to Eva. "But I thought you said it was built in 1849. That glass is a lot older."

"That's because it is," chimed in a tiny voice behind them.

They both turned to the elderly woman, who was smiling at them. She was one of the three who had exited the church minutes before.

"Yes, you see, that's Bishop Robert Crowley, founder of Trinity. Late twelfth century. Not the glass, the man," she laughed and extended her hand. "I'm Beverly Green, the parish verger. Are you young people visiting here for the first time?"

It was Eva who spoke first, shaking hands. "Eva Bashir, Ms. Green, librarian of Ignatius College, and this is Dr. Myles Dunn, who's…" Eva went blank, not knowing quite how to describe Myles. He intervened. "A lover of English churches, Ms. Green. And this is one of the finest I've ever seen."

Eva could see that Myles was laying it on thick and trusted that he must have a reason. "Ms. Green, you said that the church is older than 1849. Could you say more?"

"Robert Crowley's family founded this church and a few other religious sites north of Oxford in the twelfth century, when there wasn't much at all of what we'd call a university. This was a chapel belonging to one of the larger churches in Oxford. Most of what you see here is nineteenth-century construction, though the windows are much older, indeed." She gave the bank of windows to her right an open-handed, sweeping gesture she probably used during every tour of the place. "Some of the panels were replaced over the centuries, but the one you see of Bishop Crowley is a rare example of nearly perfect thirteenth-century glazier's work." She turned and smiled admiringly at the window.

"And the grounds of the church—they include the rectory and the cemetery," Myles observed. "Is there anything else here that's part of the church?"

Ms. Green leaned forward toward Myles, as if she hadn't quite heard him. "I'm afraid I don't understand."

"What I meant was, are there any other buildings, plots of land, older structures that are part of the parish?"

"Oh, I think not," Ms. Green tsk-tsked. "While it's a very old place, it's also a rather modest one."

"Is there a crypt?"

Ms. Green looked at Eva with a slightly pained expression. "Indeed there was, but oh, that's long gone now. They removed it for the new construction in the nineteenth century—you'll see that in our guidebook. The bones were placed in the cemetery. There were several tombs here in the church, as well—there often are— up there in the sanctuary. Local lords and ladies, a cleric or three. They, too, reside in the cemetery now. We use the old crypt for our gift shop. Doesn't seem quite appropriate somehow, but when you walk through you'll be pleased with the renovations."

"Can you tell us when those renovations occurred, when the bones were re-interred in the parish cemetery?"

"I should think around 1849, when most of the church was built over the old ruins. It was quite a ceremony transferring the remains."

"You've been very helpful, Ms. Green," said Myles with a quick smile. "I have one more question. I'm looking for an old friend of mine—or ours, actually." He gestured toward Eva. "And we're curious if he's been here lately." Ms. Green smiled and arched her eyebrows. Myles went on. "Father Jeremy Strand, a Jesuit priest from Ignatius College."

"Here? In Trinity?" Ms. Green's hand went to where a broach should have been. "Oh, dear no. At least, I shouldn't think so. Perhaps Reverend Thompson would know. You'll find him in the rectory." She nodded, a bit too vigorously. "A Jesuit? Oh, my."

Myles and Eva thanked the verger and followed her directions to a descending spiral staircase in the southwestern corner of the church, not far from the Norman font. As promised, it looked nothing like a medieval crypt. It had gone through more than one renovation. The old stone walls had been covered with plaster painted a soft beige. Fluorescent lights cast the area and the revolving racks of books and pamphlets in a cold, bluish glow. Display cases carried all sorts of mementos of Trinity Church and one side of the crypt a coffee and tea dispensary had been set up. A few visitors sat at tables chatting quietly.

Myles sighed. "For a minute there, I thought we might be onto something. The timing was on our side—1849 was well in advance of when Hopkins was at Oxford, but look at this place."

Eva nodded. "Knowing Jeremy, if he'd been here he no doubt would have ingratiated himself if he wanted access around here. A bit like what you were doing with those compliments about English church architecture."

"Not very subtle, I know," said Myles. "But I'm also trying to imagine Hopkins' next step. Let's say, for the sake of argument, that this church is the 'trinitas' he meant in the poem. Let's also say he wants the reader of the poem to know that he's been here. Did Jeremy think so, and did he come here? If he had, there's no indication of it."

Myles and Eva climbed the spiral stone staircase to the back of the church. Ms. Green was walking a trio of admiring visitors past the rood screen. As he and Eva stepped into the vestibule, Myles glanced at a small window on the right and stopped. He stared at the image for a long while. Eva followed his eye to the window, then back to Myles. She watched his face change from initial surprise to mounting horror.

"Myles, what is it?"

"I think I know why Peter Toohey was murdered."

49

"Tick-tock, tick-tock…"

Jeremy woke to hear his captor whispering into his right ear. "How is 'Time's Eunuch' this afternoon? I love that phrase of Hopkins, don't you? Fits you to a T. For this eunuch, however, time is expiring and I'm no closer to my chalice." His captor moved away from Jeremy's ear and stood a few feet right of the chair.

Who is he? Again, the voice sounded familiar. Maybe that was just because it was multiform, shifting effortlessly among so many tones, accents and speech patterns, from arch to crass, from Oxbridge High Table to streetwise slang. *Like some sort of verbal shapeshifter,* thought Jeremy. *Still, he seems like someone I know. Hell, he seems like any number of people I know. It could be someone from the pub—The Bear, surely, or perhaps The White Horse. Or it could be someone from The Bodleian. Or a fellow-member of the English Faculty…*

"I have to concede, Strand—and I wish for your sake I didn't have to—the first wave of a search in your new home has brought up nothing but stones, bones and rat shit. Yet this little hole in Oxford can't be for naught, correct? The poem pointed you here, and if you're right—which I think you are—the chalice should be somewhere in these walls or under this floor! Isn't that why old bag-o-bones across the table from you came here once upon a time, as well? Have you gotten anything out of him, by the way? Ha!"

Jeremy kept silent, not just because the man's questions were mocking and rhetorical—and increasingly manic. He simply couldn't muster the strength for banter.

"I have something vital that you don't have, Strand. I mean, besides physical freedom and charisma. I have time. Since you haven't tossed up any insights into that poem in the days I've had you here, except that one about 'trinity,' I'm forced to employ other, less literary measures. So, I'll use as many days and weeks as I need to dismantle this catacomb stone by stone until I've found the Cuxham Chalice. By which time, of course, you'll be long gone."

Jeremy heard a theatrical sigh before the voice continued.

"And that raises a question that weighs heavily on me: Does anyone really care?"

"About what?" Jeremy asked groggily.

"About you."

"I had a dog once—"The shock felt like a barbed sledgehammer to the groin. A level of pain so intense that he nearly blacked out. It lasted only a second. The spasm ended, but the aftershock remained. Delirious, Jeremy felt his head fall forward limply.

"When your body—with or without testicles, it matters not to me—is found in three days' time, will anyone really care?"

From the hazy depths of oblivion, Jeremy surmised that he wouldn't be alive in three days to indulge his captor's love of terror. But something in him wanted the man to be afraid, even a little, so he summoned enough energy to speak. "I wouldn't...underestimate Myles Dunn...or, for that matter, Eva Bashir."

His captor was silent for a long while, as if calculating what to say, how much to say. Jeremy braced himself for another wracking jolt.

"Do you have any idea, Strand, what a mess killing another human being can generate? And here I don't mean the physical mess. One expects to put up with blood, piss and shit for the sake of a...meaningful kill. That was Peter Toohey. That was dear old Miss Ballard. No, Strand, the mess I mean is the careful strategy. The time it takes to plan. How to anticipate movement and location. Imagine doing all of that without paperwork, keeping it all in your head. Do you think I just picked young Peter off the street? Four months went into planning his...sacrifice. And then come the scores of dress rehearsals one stages in one's mind before the event—never predictable on its own. All of this long before opening night. I spent weeks mulling over what kind of weapon, where to find it, how to use it. Whether the chosen victim might put up a fight. Victims' neighbors and what the hell *their* schedule is. Details! Details!"

The voice had risen steadily in volume and intensity. Like verbal venom administered directly into Jeremy's ear, it all added to the painful buzzing in his brain.

"My point, Strand, is you *were not* a plan. No, I hadn't thought of you, though now I can imagine a dozen Jesuits who wouldn't mind me putting you out of their misery. There will soon be a third sacrifice, this one less innocent than the first two. My plan has long called for a priest to crown the slaughtered trio. I had targeted one of those high Anglicans over at Pusey. He would have brought a greater reward in public outrage than a washed-up, middle-aged don from Ignatius College.

"But I've had to make a plan for you. I don't like to do that; it's even messier than the attendant blood and shit. Which reminds me: you're due for a visit to our luggable loo this afternoon. A minion will see to it. You know the drill. But I wander. Now, back to those two friends of yours, the Arab bitch and the rebarbative cowboy. I don't need another mess, but I'll make one. And I'll play in it for weeks after, if need be.

"Father, you're as good as dead—you must realize that by now. In fact, I will tell you: you have three days to live, not that you can measure time here. But I'm willing to grant you some grace in your final hours. If you can proffer a cogent theory of the chalice's location based upon that nonsense sonnet, I shall make your dispatch as painless as possible."

"Three days?" Jeremy said in barely above a whisper. "If you're going to kill me, do it now, here. You've already buried me."

"You're not listening, Father. All of this has been punctiliously plotted for months. You will die when the ritual says you are to die. You should know all about that: form, ceremony…sacrifice. All of that isn't up for debate. What *is* depends on your cooperation now. If you are *not* cooperative in these next three days, I will build into my plan a very drawn-out death for your Bashir and Dunn. Meanwhile, perhaps I can find ways to dissuade them."

50

For the better part of an hour, while the two sat on a bench near the lichgate, shaded from the late afternoon sun by the waxy green leaves and yellow catkins of an overspreading oak, Myles told Eva the story of young Hugh of Lincoln. Hugh had become a local icon for anti-Semitism because of the supposed circumstances surrounding his death. But he hadn't been alone. A half-century before Hugh, there was a story from Norwich of an even younger child. He'd been lured from the safety of his home by local Jews, tortured, and then crucified in a mockery—not only of Norwich Christians, but of all Christendom. Where William had been crucified, Hugh had been stabbed many times and buried in a well. That wasn't the worst of it. Hugh's blood was said to have been used to make matzos in a parody of the Eucharist.

The effect of it all was a wave of anti-Semitism, in Norwich and Lincoln, and all over England wherever there were Jewish communities. In Lincoln, some sources claimed, the Jews responsible for Hugh's torture and murder confessed openly to the crime and welcomed the death that was their due. A pogrom followed that was as violent as it was devastating.

Only later was it discovered that Hugh had been captured, abused, and murdered by local citizens of Lincoln who had nothing to do with the Jewish community there. Pent-up resentments against the Jews made them an easy target. A scapegoat to bear and suffer for the sins of others.

"Blood libel," said Myles, "that centuries-old combination of violence and blame. In Hugh's case, an excuse to persecute Jews, cancel out debts owed them, and abscond with their property."

Eva looked at him with a sad understanding in her eyes. "The parallels line up, don't they? I wonder if young Hugh was an altar boy just as Peter Toohey was. Take the water out, and there's not much of a difference between a *well* and a ruined *elevator shaft*. And both bodies were meant to be discovered, weren't they?"

She stood up, paced a few steps away from Myles, then turned toward him. "Peter Toohey's body was meant to be discovered, just as it was meant to horrify, as the death of any innocent would. And it was all intended to do what it accomplished, Myles. To inflame hostility against Muslims in Oxford. And not just Oxford, but all over England. Even in other parts of the world."

Myles shook his head in agreement. "Look how quickly the public and much of the press have taken it all in. The boy, the old woman—their executions have been assigned to Islamic extremists bent on terror, when in fact the results have been social strife, riots, anti-Muslim hatred. Whoever set it up, it's working perfectly."

Myles thought of Rabi's discovery of the Host at the murder site and now the bizarre parallels with the matzos of Hugh's time. He decided for the moment not to tell Eva about the boy's discovery of the body. He didn't want her even distantly implicated in some possible future charge of withholding evidence or obstructing justice. And he still didn't know how to resolve the same problems for Rabi or himself, for that matter. He stood up and walked toward Eva.

"There are some differences—there would have to be—but the incentive and the results are the same. Whoever's doing this knows their history, at least in a way that serves an ultra-patriotic cause. A hatred for anything not British. We're beginning to make some connections, but there are still more questions than answers. Such as what does the Cuxham Chalice and Hopkins' experience of it have to do with any of this?"

"If there is a hinge somewhere in this machinery, Myles, it's likely to be Lumen. You've talked with Jacoby and looked at the organization's early records. Anything there even distantly related to a chalice?"

"Not that I could see, Eva. But Jacoby did say something about a foundation charter at Christ Church College. I'm not sure something that formal will be of any help to us, but there are bound to be other very early documents that might just shed some light.'

Eva glanced at her watch. "I'm dropping Sam at a student government meeting after dinner. I'll call Sarah Penrose and see if she'll allow us an hour in the college archives this evening."

51

As Jacoby had made Myles aware, a request to search the papers of Cardinal Wolsey was a delicate matter. The Christ Church archives were by no means public; even resident scholars needed to apply for permission. Eva was both amused and perplexed that Principal Penrose had not only quickly consented to the request, but assured them the college's full cooperation.

On the short walk from Ignatius College to neighboring Christ Church, Myles and Eva discussed their strategy for the evening. They had already acquired a bit more understanding about Lumen, courtesy of Jacoby and Myles' research at Bodley. The Cuxham Chalice, however, was even more elusive than the august Oxford men's club. The personal papers of Cardinal Wolsey, founder of the original college, just might have something that would shed further light on their understanding of the Hopkins sonnet and its mystifying references to a "spired grail."

They arrived at the college entrance and Porters' Lodge under Tom Tower just as the bass bell was booming eight o'clock. Two porters in their famous black bowlers were chatting with Simon Cole, who seemed to be instructing them in some matter. All three looked up.

"Ah, Drs. Bashir and Dunn," beamed Simon Cole. "Principal Penrose asked me to meet you here and offer the college's hospitality on her behalf. She's at a fundraiser, reaching into deep pockets." He chuckled and looked past Myles and Eva. "Isn't Father Strand coming?"

Eva was about to use the London story Myles had given Jacoby the day before, but before she could get a word out, Myles stepped in.

"He couldn't make it tonight." This was followed by an awkward silence.

Cole looked slightly off-balance but regained it along with his irrepressible charm. "Well, then, it's to the Wolsey archives, no? Something about Lumen?"

"Well, we're not quite sure what we're looking for," admitted Eva. "We hoped to see if the founder's personal papers hold some reference to your college's most illustrious men's club."

"That's a lovely way of referring to Lumen, Dr. Bashir," Cole effused as he gestured Myles and Eva into the vastness of Tom Quad. They walked along the southern boundary of the open space, passing fabled Christ Church Hall on their right. "And, speaking of Lumen, isn't it wonderful having a bit more light in the skies these May days? We had such a gloomy winter."

Myles said nothing. Clouded by an opaque sense of unease and frustration regarding Jeremy, he had little stomach for small talk with a man he considered a sycophantic toady. Eva, however, was deciding that she liked Simon Cole. He seemed too amiable to harbor ill will toward anyone. As for being Sarah Penrose's occasional trophy date, it was probably a matter of surviving in Oxford's fiendish job environment.

They entered a shadowed portico just east of the hall and descended two short stairways that led onto a long, ill-lit hallway. Offices ran the course of the hall on both sides. Myles noticed that a couple of them had lights on behind closed doors, Christ Church dons at work after hours, he presumed.

"I do apologize for the labyrinthine journey," said Cole lightly, "but the papers you want to see are in a more restricted, seldom-visited part of the college archives. Ah, here we are."

They were standing in front of a formidable steel door marked "CC College Special Archives, Admission by Appointment Only." From his blazer pocket, Cole withdrew a ring with a single key and turned it heavily in the latch. With some effort, he swung the steel door open slowly and held out his hand for them to pass.

He flicked on some switches and the room was washed with ambient light. "I've set up a workstation for you in the back." He guided them past several floor-to-ceiling stacks, wider than usual in order to accommodate oversize volumes and sheaves of large maps, documents and manuscript pages.

As they walked, Myles took in the room, which had a smooth concrete floor, a relatively low ceiling and appeared to cover about the area of a small Oxford dining hall. Cole led them to a rectangular wooden table near the far back corner. In the center of the table, beneath the yellowish glow of two small lamps, lay a long, flat gray box. It bore the ubiquitous, many-tasseled cardinal's red hat of Christ Church College. Lying on either side of the box were two pairs of white cotton reader's gloves.

"It's all here—at least, as much as we have," said Simon, flashing a formal smile and gently touching his palm to the box. "How exciting to consider the possibility that something in our archives might shed light on your Hopkins manuscript. A fascinating project, indeed."

"Thank you, Simon," said Eva, returning the smile. Myles nodded his head, as if agreeing.

"Oh, and the Latin dictionaries and paleographical indices are all over there, should you need them." He pointed in the direction of a tall metal bookcase a few feet from the table. He handed a small card to Eva. "Take as much time as you need. And would you mind texting or ringing me when you've finished? You'll find my mobile number on the card. I think you'll be happier if I leave the archives door open enough to allow some air in here. Right, then—please don't hesitate to contact me if you need anything." Cole bowed slightly, turned once and disappeared through the heavy door, careful to leave it ajar.

"Well, he's certainly conscientious," Eva said as she put her small bag on the table.

Myles nodded again, a calculating look on his face. He turned to the reference bookcase and pulled a squat volume entitled *Dizionario Abbreviatura.* "Good. Cappelli's dictionary of medieval and early modern abbreviations. This'll help with some of the more cryptic forms in these original documents." He tossed the book on the table.

Eva reached into her bag for two small notepads and pencils, and they sat down on opposite sides of the table. Immediately they began poring over every item in the box, a voluminous bulk and range of material. Practically every item was from the sixteenth century, handwritten and in various states of fragility and illegibility. They soon appreciated why Penrose had regarded with skepticism their initial one-hour estimate.

After half an hour, Myles finally came upon a sheet marked, *The Last Will and Testament of Thomas Wolsey, Cardinal of the Catholic Church, Papal Legate to England, Archbishop of York, and Lord Chancellor.* It was a working copy that had probably been rendered into something more coherent and graceful for the courts. Meanwhile, Eva was searching through an equally disorganized pile of land grants, copies of royal writs and some land transfers that carried Wolsey's name and seal.

At just after 9:30, Myles looked up suddenly. He'd heard a small sound, or thought he did, coming from the entranceway. He listened for a moment and heard only the soft, scratching sounds of Eva's pencil, transcribing a tight, sixteenth-century hand. He returned to his work.

Finding nothing specific to Lumen in the land grants, Eva turned to an unmarked folder. It appeared to contain Wolsey's general financial records, including accounts of his earnings, private landholdings, household accounts and payments to assistants and servants covering his entire professional career. A few minutes later she emitted a barely audible "hmm" that broke a long silence at the table.

Without looking up, Myles asked, "Find something?"

"Perhaps part of something. It seems here that the old boy never let go of anything he earned. Evidently, he kept all his offices from minor to major, and their revenues as well. Did you know that he was an exceedingly wealthy man even before he became Chancellor of England?"

Myles looked up from the table and rubbed his eyes. "I'm not overly surprised, but I had no idea of the man's wealth until I read this." He held up the first page of the will.

Eva glanced at it, then back at the page in her hand. "Cardinal Wolsey was regularly paid for services rendered to the king as well as the pope—mostly in kind rather than coin, it seems. Henry VIII was cash-poor toward the beginning of his reign, so the cardinal was sometimes paid in the form of a 'jeweled ring' or furnishings for his new home at Hampton Court—that sort of thing. I'm not finding a chalice listed among the prizes, though. Here's one for a 'fine robe of red and vert'—red and green, right? He must've been Father Christmas that year," she chuckled.

Myles leaned across the table. Eva held up the sheet, pointing to the relevant line. Myles read it, then scanned the entire page before looking at Eva. "Quite a treasure trove. Keep looking for anything that looks like a cup. I guess we have to keep in mind that even if there *is* a precise connection between Wolsey, a chalice and Lumen, it may not be noted anywhere at all."

He returned the document to Eva, leaned back and clasped his hands behind his neck, working the tension that had gathered there. "Even so, it's intriguing, to say the least."

They set to work again. At ten minutes to 10:00, just as they were about to call it a day, Myles slammed his palm on the table, piercing the silence and causing Eva to jump nearly out of her chair. "YES!" he exclaimed. "This is it! This has got to be it!"

He slid the page across the table in front of Eva, then walked around to her side. He pulled up a chair next to hers.

As she read, an excited grin spread across her face. She read aloud: "'...and herewith I bequeath to the twelve clerkes of my college a chalyse of great antiquitie.'"

Eva squeezed Myles' hand in excitement.

"And look here, Eva, four lines below: 'Item to the clerkes of Lumen 800 hectares of lands, farms and estates in Banbury, Oxon.' These are the only references to Lumen in the entirety of Wolsey's will. Clearly, this is the Lumen chalice. Wolsey himself emphasizes the importance of the gift by calling it an antique. And even though it's not stated specifically, here we have four lines later a benefaction of land."

"This is bloody brilliant!" The last word echoed through the shadows of the archives room. Myles, who had never heard Eva let loose in this way, grinned at her in surprise. "I just wish we could tell Jeremy about it," she added. A shadow fluttered briefly in her smile and was gone.

Instinctively Myles put his free hand on her shoulder. "We *will* be telling Jeremy about this, and I hope very soon," he said firmly.

Eva met his eyes tentatively, searchingly. She slowly raised her hand to his cheek and stroked it gently. At first Myles made no movement, closing his eyes and relishing the electricity of her touch. After a few seconds he opened his eyes, which met hers squarely. He leaned closer to her face, then paused. Eva leaned forward just enough to meet his lips with hers. Their faces lingered close even after the brief kiss. Eva drew back slowly.

He gently touched the fingers of his left hand to her cheek and held them there. "Eva, I'm sorry if I mis–"

"You didn't," she said, fixing her eyes on his, "so don't be."

Myles leaned in to kiss her again.

Eva closed her eyes, but instead of his lips, she felt the roughness of his palm pressed over her mouth. She opened her eyes to see Myles' alertly scanning the room. His eyes settled on hers, index finger over his lips. She nodded in understanding. He motioned for her to keep her head down.

After a few seconds of listening, Myles suddenly threw his body over the table and covered Eva. They both heard a succession of muffled thuds followed by sounds of glass shattering and hitting the concrete floor. The room fell into darkness except for a small lamp on the table and two weak overhead lights.

Myles immediately took hold of Eva and, careful to keep his body between her and where he guessed the shots were coming from, eased her further under the table. While doing so, he scanned the dark perimeter around them but could see nothing. He knew two things: the gunman was using a silencer and was repositioning for another shot.

Aware that the two overheads put them under a spotlight making them an easy target, Myles yanked the lamp cord out of its floor socket. He then reached from beneath the table and grabbed the book of abbreviations. He hurled it frisbee-style at the nearest overhead light. With a crash the light fixture shattered and broken glass splintered across the table and floor. As he reached up for another book in order to try to knock out the one remaining light, a bullet hit the tabletop, a little over a foot from his hand, splintering the wood.

He strained his ears for some sense of their attacker's location. He heard the barely discernible sound of feet darting lightly across the floor about thirty feet away. They heard a *pffft* sound from behind them. Small clouds of dust and paper exploded from the thick volumes stacked inches above their heads on the table.

Eva tightly clutched one of Myles' hands with both of hers. A millisecond later they heard the next *pffft* as another volume exploded above and behind them.

A moment of stillness was followed by low scuffling sounds across the room. Then a barely audible metallic *click*.

"Stay here," Myles whispered.

He quickly crawled to the end of the table, lifted his head and peered around the shelves. Silence. In one fluid movement he was on his feet and running toward the door. He used his cell phone flashlight to guide him, weaving agilely between and around stacks. Another shot, once again striking a shelf above and behind Myles. He threw himself to the floor, rolled and waited. He debated whether to move toward the door, where the last shot clearly originated, or return to Eva in case the shooter headed back that way.

He listened and heard nothing. He began moving silently back toward Eva. As he did so he heard another metallic *click*. He stopped. The door again. Or maybe the gun being reloaded. Still crouching, he listened. Had the gunman fled? He crept silently toward their table, pausing every few seconds to listen. He worried that he could no longer hear the gunman but knew he had to get back to Eva.

"Myles?" Eva called in a loud whisper.

By way of an answer, Myles flashed the cell phone light. Having heard the most recent shot, Eva wasn't sure if he'd been hit and was relieved to see him a few feet to her right. She reached under the table and plugged the lamp back in.

"Is it safe?" she mouthed silently.

He held up his hand to indicate that they should wait.

After long seconds of waiting in tense silence, Myles walked the rest of the way to Eva. They both stood at the workstation, glancing about the room, taking in the damage done to books and the table. Surprisingly, the box of Wolsey papers remained untouched by the violence they'd just witnessed.

"I think it's safe now." He helped her to her feet while looking around tensely. "Are you all right?"

"Yeah," she replied. She took a deep breath and exhaled slowly before brushing bits of book-paper and ceiling dust from her jacket.

"Don't do anything. Wait here—I'll be back in a minute." And with that, Myles raced from the room and into the warren of hallways and stairs under Christ Church College.

52

"Did you see anyone?" Eva asked as Myles rushed through the door a few minutes later.

He shook his head, openly frustrated and wiping a few beads of sweat from his forehead. Noting that Eva was shaking and taking shallow breaths, he tenderly wrapped her in his arms and held her, a gesture she welcomed.

"Let's get you out of here and into some fresh air, and then we can talk about it." He smiled soothingly and rubbed her back.

"Where's my mobile? I'll call Principal Penrose, or Simon Cole, and let them know." Her voice was steady, but her hands were shaking as she tried to press the numbers.

Myles gently touched her arm. "We can do that as soon as we get outside." She nodded absently and began slowly walking toward the door. Myles picked up her bag and collected their notepads but left everything else as it was and joined her.

Eva stopped. "Myles, I think we should ring them now. We shouldn't leave the scene."

"Before you make a call, can we talk about what just happened?"

Eva looked at Myles in disbelief. "Are you kidding—what just happened is that we were almost killed!"

"That's what it was meant to look like." Myles looked pensive as he shook his head, trying to piece together the details of what had transpired in a matter of a few minutes. "Someone did fire a gun here, but it was more *near* us than at us."

"What are you talking about?" She was still shaking slightly.

"I'm thinking that whoever fired the gun intended to miss us."

"How do you—?"

"Look, I know something about guns and firing them, and every shot was missed on purpose." Eva was still unconvinced and Myles continued. "The initial shots came from left of the only door in the room. And notice what they fired at: the overheads. That

236

was part of the strategy. To put the shooter in relative darkness while we were left as the only illuminated things in the room." He pointed to three fixtures along the ceiling that had been shattered. "That gave the shooter a chance to move into position for the next shots, taken from right over there." He pointed to a tall library stack filled with books except for a conspicuous gap near eye-level. "From that vantage point, the shooter could have easily hit us since we were sitting ducks in the light. But those next two shots struck the shelf directly behind and above us. The desk shot was close, but at least a foot off. As for the final shot, made when I was heading, probably foolishly, toward the door, it again went well above my head. I'd say that's pretty accurate shooting, especially considering it was probably a Glock 17 9mm semi-automatic."

Eva stared at him in open-mouthed surprise. "How could you possibly—?"

"Eva, that's a long story. But trust me on this. The fire action of the gun and the fact that it's unusually precise for a handgun means it's probably a Glock. But what's important here, I think, is the strong suspicion that we were meant to be frightened, not physically harmed."

"Even if you're right, that doesn't feel quite as reassuring to me as you seem to think it should." She shook her head.

"Don't get me wrong. I'm not saying this was no big deal. It was harrowing, and you're right to be alarmed and feel threatened. Which is why…" He paused, assessing her expression.

"What?"

"I know we discussed this yesterday. But you've got Sam to think about, and maybe it doesn't make sense for you to keep putting yourself in danger. I can proceed and keep you in the loop at every turn."

"Danger?" she snapped. "Myles, I've been in danger since that boy's body was discovered. Look at me. Brown skin. Dark features. The moment I step outside my home I'm subject to leering, accusatory stares and verbal assaults, if not worse. *You know that.* What do you think happened in the Cornmarket the other day? And as much as I appreciate your concern—and I do, truly—let me be clear: Jeremy is my friend, too. And I'm in this until we find him, whatever that means. Are we clear?"

Myles nodded slowly.

"Now," Eva continued with a deep breath, "whatever their intention, who could have done this?"

Myles narrowed his eyes and shook his head. "As for who *could* have done it, we passed a handful of occupied offices on our way down here. And Cole left the door open, though I'm not sure it was related to fresh air. Who had reason to shoot is obviously the more disturbing question. I suspect whoever shot at us had something to do with those Hopkins lines on your computer screen."

"*'To mend him we end him,'*" Eva recalled the eerie lines. "So, if they weren't trying to shoot us, they were—"

"Warning us? Threatening us? I'm not sure. Does it have to do with what we've just found out about the chalice and Lumen? Does it have something to do with getting closer to what Jeremy knows?"

"More questions," Eva sighed. "If they meant to frighten us off, they succeeded where I'm concerned." A look of shocked realization came over her face, and she shuddered. "Let's get out of here."

A quarter of an hour later, Myles and Eva stood outside the Christ Church Porter's Lodge, relaying to Penrose and Cole the details of their ordeal. Penrose expressed equal parts concern over their well-being and distress over the damage done to the archives room.

"I feel terribly about this—that it should have befallen you anywhere, of course, but here, of all places." Penrose looked at Myles and Eva almost furtively. "We will most certainly look into this matter. Gunshots, for God's sake! And I'm responsible for the safety of hundreds of students here in college."

Ending a call and slipping his phone into a pocket, Cole spoke up. "Principal Penrose, with your permission, I've just notified our own security chief, who's en route to the archives at this moment with a team. As you know, they liaise regularly with the Oxford police."

Penrose folded her hands and touched the index fingers to her lips, as if considering her options. After several seconds, she said, "Good counsel, Simon. If you would, accompany security to the archives room and make sure I have a full report by tomorrow morning. I'll have to meet with the college council about this."

As if remembering that the two people whose lives were in

danger were standing next to her, Penrose looked at Myles and Eva. Taking Eva's hand, she said, "We will find out precisely what happened and who was involved and see that justice is done. And rest assured that I'll direct our security team to bring in Thames Valley authorities right away."

"Of course. Thank you," said Eva.

Myles nodded in agreement, then looked at Eva, who intuited a meaning in his look.

"Actually, Principal Penrose, there is one thing you might be able to help us with," she said.

"Name it," said Penrose, spreading her open hands wide.

"There's an alumnus of Christ Church whom we've been trying to locate—a Sir Stephen Collington. As Principal of Christ Church, perhaps you might be able to help...?" Eva didn't remind Penrose of Collington's supposed connection with Lumen or that he was quite possibly their last hope of finding clues as to the missing Jeremy Strand.

Penrose's wanting-to-please tone turned to something like puzzled chagrin. "I know the man—or rather know of him. Sir Stephen is positively prehistoric and in declining health. I'm not sure what I can do personally; you see, his generosity to the college is in part precariously balanced on the understanding that we leave him alone." She thought for a moment, then turned to Cole. "Simon, look into this for me, won't you? Use my name, of course, as further inducement."

Simon gave a slight bow.

"Well, there it is, then," she said to Myles and Eva. "Let's see what young Cole here can do, though you must realize I promise you nothing when it comes to Sir Stephen and your obtaining an appointment. If you do, prepare yourself for him to be less than lucid. And, again, I am dreadfully sorry about what happened tonight."

There were goodnight handshakes all around, and Cole vowed to be in touch as soon as he had news of a possible meeting with Sir Stephen. Even as Penrose watched her guests depart out of hearing range, she addressed her protégé in low tones.

"Well done, Simon. The police have more important matters to attend to, and there's no reason we shouldn't handle matters

239

in-house." She finally turned to face him, placing a hand gently on his arm and speaking in familiar, efficient commands. "After security has done its snooping about, clean up the archives posthaste. Make it look as if this never happened. Nothing to the librarians. Replace the Wolsey documents and then get a list of the damaged or destroyed volumes. Remove them and send them out for repair, replacement or, if need be, they can simply disappear. Tell the librarians I made an executive decision based on a report of rats. Anything to prevent the college from being brought into ill light. If furniture needs replacing, see that it's done—quickly and quietly."

Penrose and Cole parted in different directions, while Myles and Eva made their way slowly along St. Aldate's for the return to college. None of them noticed a man standing and watching from the shadows of the churchyard across the street, flicking the ashes of a cigarette he neglected to smoke.

Thursday, May 11

53

Eva's car pulled into the long driveway of Collington Manor, past shapeless, overgrown shrubs and the overhanging branches of ancient oaks. Through small gaps in the greenery, they could see an expansive and well-trimmed lawn and a moat-like pond that curved around three sides of the house. Beyond the pond lay dense woods.

Eva had gotten a phone call that morning from Simon Cole assuring her that Sir Stephen was able to see them both that very afternoon. But the old man's nurse had insisted that the visit be brief. When Eva hung up the phone, she wondered, Was Penrose being helpful? Was Cole? Did it matter? And more importantly, in the wake of last night's disturbing theatrics, should she reconsider her role in all this? Did Myles have a point—should she throttle back on this search? As she debated, her eyes fell upon a birthday card from Jeremy that she had placed on a corner of her desk. It was, like him, funny and sweet and generous, containing a Strand-made certificate for lunch at a restaurant of her choice. She thought of Sam and the kind of role model she wanted to be for her daughter—a person of courage, integrity and fierce love. Resolved to continue, Eva spent the rest of the morning in her office catching up on work, while Myles took another shot at convincing first Master Ilbert, then the police, to take Jeremy's disappearance seriously—to no avail.

During the two-hour drive, Myles and Eva agreed to stick with the plan. Last night's events, unsettling though they were, strongly confirmed their fears that Jeremy had attracted the attention of a person or persons with the means and motive to harm—or worse. Though neither of them said it aloud, both had begun to wonder not only if they would find their friend, but if they would find him alive. It had already been four long days since his disappearance. Regardless, they still believed—had to believe—that the Hopkins manuscript represented their best chance, and Jeremy's.

The remainder of the drive was taken up with deciding the key questions they wanted to ask Sir Stephen. Due to his ill health, they knew they'd have perhaps half an hour with him, and they needed to make it count. They agreed that a top priority was to obtain some corroboration for the notion that Hopkins might have seen the Cuxham Chalice in the 1860s. How to frame that question wasn't so apparent.

Tires crunched on gravel and acorns as Eva slowed down in front of the sprawling four-story country estate. The façade was mainly Regency with hybrid Jacobean elements in the upper stories. The foundation could have been Elizabethan. A middle-aged man wearing coveralls and pushing a wheelbarrow peered over at them from behind a bubbling baroque fountain before resuming his work.

Though the early morning had been bright and sunny, the day was quickly turning unusually cool and cloudy. Puffy white clouds were giving way to darker cumulus ones.

Eva, wearing a mid-length floral sundress, stepped from the car and regarded the imposing house against the backdrop of a darkening sky. "Quite a place," she commented, rubbing her shoulders as she felt a chilly breeze.

"It's seen better days," replied Myles as the two scanned the grounds and stretched their legs after the two-hour drive from Oxford. "Like a down-on-its-luck Downton," he added while pulling on a light sport coat over his button-down shirt.

Vines covered much of the brown stone exterior, and more than one of the several chimneys appeared to be crumbling and listing visibly. The steps leading up to the portico were in similar disrepair, and Myles and Eva scaled them gingerly. The pair of broad oak doors, bearing an incongruous "WARNING: Cotswold Security System" sticker in the lower right corner, appeared timeless beneath layers of cracking varnish. There was no knocker or bell, and while they decided how best to make their presence known one of the doors was opened from within.

"Good afternoon," said a woman with puffy eyes and a twisted smile. She wore a black frock, wrinkled gray apron and small white cap and appeared to be in her early thirties. "They're expecting you," she said timidly as she pulled the door wider and stepped aside for Eva and Myles to enter.

She led them through the vestibule, down a wide, gloomy hallway on the right, tiled in black and white. It was lined on both sides with portraits, mostly of men in military uniform and women in gowns and long gloves.

At the end of the hallway, standing in a relatively small doorway, stood a stocky woman with a sharp, birdlike face and a helmet of gray hair. She wore a crisp white nurse's uniform and an old-fashioned white cap with a black stripe across it.

"Nurse Spinzel," she announced with a bob of her head, her hand extended to Myles and Eva. Her hands were rough, her grip firm, and her accent German. "Do come in, though as I told your colleague at Christ Church, Sir Stephen cannot tolerate long visits. His hearing is remarkably fine, but he is weaker by the day, and what little energy he has comes and goes, as does his mind." She made a face and pointed to her head. "He is in the drawing room. I will introduce you."

Sir Stephen Collington, exhibiting a tall, thin sprout of flyaway white hair and dressed in a voluminous brown cardigan, sat propped in a high-backed wheelchair, dwarfed by the massive fireplace behind him. The beautifully wood-paneled room was fragrant with mildew and wax, and a faded rug depicting an English foxhunt covered much of the parquet floor. Other than two floor lamps, the only light source was a panoramic bay window that extended the width of the room and before which stood a commanding mahogany desk covered in stacks of paper.

Though apparently dozing when they entered the room, Sir Stephen immediately perked up when Myles and, more particularly, Eva were introduced. Nurse Spinzel motioned for them to sit on a settee angled to Collington's right, while she took a chair immediately to his left. Collington unabashedly stared at Eva until his nurse gently nudged him and reminded him that they had come "all the way from Oxford" to see him.

After several minutes of clarifying where each of his guests was from and opining volubly on the "exotic beauty of certain Levantine women," Collington abruptly asked them why they were interested in Lumen.

"We're researching a recently unearthed nineteenth-century manuscript that may be about Lumen," Eva began. She and Myles had decided to reveal as few details as possible about the poem and their search.

Collington looked at Myles and Eva sharply. "Curious, that," he said, shaking his head. "Not likely it came *from* Lumen. Nothing ever did, save the requisite and seasonal communiqués to the university regarding some benefaction the group had arranged."

He paused and then was gone for a moment. The only sounds in the room were from a ticking mantle clock and Nurse Spinzel gratuitously pressing out her white skirt with her hands.

The old man started, as if awakened. "What part of the nineteenth century did you say?"

"I didn't, but we think the piece was written in the late 1880s, Sir Stephen."

"Late…'twas a pitiful and pitiable time. Lumen's darkest hour. A troubled time…" His voice trailed off and he retreated to some faraway place in his mind.

Eva called him back. "Sir Stephen, do you know anything about the Cuxham Chalice?"

"Of course I do," he snapped, though with a smile. "I'm an Oxford man, Dr. Bashir, and every Oxford man—and woman, I suppose—knows that the chalice is a legend, isn't it now?" He offered a wry smile.

"That's just it, Sir Stephen. We think the poem may refer to the Cuxham Chalice," Eva said. "Not the legend but the chalice itself, suggesting that it was extant at the time the poem was composed. We're also led to believe that the chalice was associated with Lumen, and we thought you might be able to shed some light on the chalice as being, well, more than mere legend."

Eva leaned back into the dusty couch, hoping she hadn't overplayed her hand. She glanced at Myles who kept his eyes on the old man, waiting.

Collington paused again, though this time he was clearly thinking, searching through long, ancient memories, weighing his thoughts. He closed his eyes slowly and then opened them with a tired smile.

"I haven't much longer to live, I suppose." Nurse Spinzel shifted in her chair. "Now, now Helga, you know that's true."

He turned back to Myles and Eva. "Yes, the chalice is real... or, at least it *was* real. And you're not the first to show interest in it. Over the decades a handful of academics and treasure-hunters have come to me seeking information about Lumen and the Cuxham Chalice—most recently within the past year or so, if my fickle memory serves."

Myles and Eva exchanged meaningful glances.

"You see," continued the old man, "the chalice had once been part of Lumen's hoard of riches. But that fortune was squandered and sold off in bits over the centuries. By the Second War when I was part of Lumen, the chalice had been long lost." His voice trailed off and his chin dropped to his chest.

"Sir Stephen," asked Eva after several seconds, "you mentioned sales of Lumen's valuable assets. Do you know, were there any records of the items sold and who bought them?"

Sir Stephen stared wistfully at the hunting party on the floor for several seconds before jumping back to the present. "Records? Oh, good God, no. These sales were private affairs. And by private, I mean secret. Lumen was suffering from what might nowadays be called a downturn in fortunes, and the last thing its leaders wanted to do was to draw further attention to Lumen's liquidation."

He shook his head and motioned to his nurse, who helped him to a sip of water. As she attempted to wipe some drool from his chin, he pushed her away.

"But you asked about the chalice. That was never sold. Some say it was stolen. There was a story that it had been stowed away and forgotten. During my tenure, the search for the chalice had become part of our sworn commitment. And had been so since the dark days."

"'The dark days'—you mean sometime in the nineteenth century?" asked Myles, leaning forward.

"Of course!" he erupted gruffly. "The riots of 1867 and 1868 began the great turn of Lumen, the beginning of its end."

"Did you ever come across the name Thomas Carrick?" asked

Eva, who had discreetly shifted a few inches closer to the old man. The old man slowly opened his eyes and set a cold stare on Eva. It lasted long enough that she looked to Myles for help.

"Yes, of course," he answered finally, almost in a whisper. "Every member of Lumen in the last century has known the name of the Traitor. You ask about the lost Cuxham Chalice? Pity you can't speak with Carrick, though I wonder in which circle of hell you'd find him." The old man pulled himself up in the chair and took a deep, wheezing breath. "Still, he was only half the darkness, Dr. Bashir. The other half was Moncrieff—mad, soulless Moncrieff. By turns brilliant and violent. And from a long line of lunacy. It's hereditary, you know, madness is."

"But who was he?" insisted Myles gently.

"The *Praeses*—the leader—of Lumen during the period in question, the late 1860s." He nodded. "And never a more inspired and misguided *Praeses* there was. His reputation was tarnished, to say the least, because he led Lumen into a malevolent passage—and ultimately dire disfavor with the university."

"In what way did he go astray?" asked Eva.

Collington looked intently at each of them in turn. He then frowned at his nurse and waved his hand toward the door. She appeared confused, and he repeated the gesture more forcefully, upon which she reluctantly rose and left the room.

The old man narrowed his eyes. "How he went astray? I should think murder qualifies, don't you?"

Myles and Eva exchanged a look. After half a minute of silence, during which they could hear thunder rumbling in the distance, Myles finally decided to take a chance. "Did Moncrieff kill Thomas Carrick?"

The old man nodded. "No one outside of Lumen has ever known that—evidently, until now." He leaned back and gave Myles an appraising look, as if to decide whether to say more or less. He went on. "Of course, Moncrieff, in spite of his madness, would never have admitted to murder. He'd have called this just punishment, approved by a jury of twelve…or, eleven, I should say." He appeared to be about to say something more but closed his mouth.

"Sir Stephen," said Myles, "did you ever hear anything about Gerard Manley Hopkins in association with Lumen?"

Collington frowned at Myles. "What? Who?"

"Gerard Manley Hopkins. He wrote poetry."

"What?" he said with undisguised annoyance. "No, no, no. Of course, I've heard of him. I have less use for Catholic poetry than I have for the old chapel in this house. What has Hopkins to do with this! Don't you see? I'm telling you something! Listen, man!"

He appeared short of breath and Myles got up to offer help, but the old man waved him away before continuing.

"Moncrieff was a madman and a murderer. If you want to know about Lumen's darkness look to him—and to the riots. They were Moncrieff's doing!"

His labored breathing gave way to coughing, which soon became uncontrollable.

Myles walked quickly to the door and called Nurse Spinzel, who had been sitting on a chair in the corridor. When they returned, Eva was helping the old man to his water. Pushing away his nurse's attempts to intervene, he slowly lifted his arm and put a hand on Eva's shoulder. She flinched but looking at his expression she determined that his touch, rather than inappropriate, was the reach of a person in despair.

"His twisted brilliance didn't die with him." He tugged at her sleeve and looked pleadingly at her, as if waiting for her to reply.

Eva looked compassionately at the man. "You mean Moncrieff?"

Nurse Spinzel stood behind Sir Stephen in a regimental pose, her hands nearly white from gripping the handles of the wheelchair. "I'm afraid you'll have to go now. I need to get Sir Stephen to his room."

"Yes, dear," said Sir Stephen to Eva. "Moncrieff befouled the world with progeny. He married shortly after he went down from Oxford and had a daughter. She married in turn, though I can't recall whose name she took, the poor bugger."

As the nurse began pushing the old man's wheelchair toward the door, Sir Stephen snarled, "Helga, please! One moment more." The nurse stopped and turned the old man's chair toward Myles and Eva.

"I spoke of dark times. Much like the ones we're living through now, eh?" He smiled wanly. "But look to the Oxford riots of 1867. You may find something there of Moncrieff and his ilk."

"If you think of anything else, please call me at this number." Eva handed Sir Stephen a business card, which Nurse Spinzel promptly reached down and snatched.

"That's why Germany lost the war, you know," grumbled Sir Stephen over his shoulder at her. "Too bloody controlling!" He let out a guffaw before offering what might have been a wave of farewell or a dismissal. His nurse gently turned him in the direction of the door and wheeled him out of the room.

Myles and Eva stared at each other, their silence broken a moment later by the maid's voice. "I'll see you out now."

54

May 15, 1889

Dublin, Ireland

Lady Margaret Carrick looks about the capacious parlor with its dour portraits of Irish Jesuits flanking the nearly life-size crucifixion scene. Somehow, it all seems fitting, a semblance of continuity with her own black attire and this season of mourning she must endure. A clock from somewhere in the drafty hall beyond the parlor chimes eleven. Margaret has been waiting in the Xavier Parlor for the better part of an hour; this too, she ponders, must be part of her world of sorrow.

A man steps out of the hall and through the doorway, a corpulent priest wearing a black soutane and an incongruous smile of great cheer. He claps his hands together three times like a mother summoning children to the table.

"Lady Margaret. We apologize for the delay. I've brought Father Hopkins here, but I must tell you"—he leans closer to the seated woman and whispers—"he endured a terrible night. Father Rector nearly canceled this visit, but Hopkins insisted upon seeing you. I prevail upon you to be brief." He leans in yet further as Margaret, a little alarmed, leans back into the wingback chair. The whisper becomes a hush. "It's typhoid. You're perfectly fine if you do not touch or get too close." He arches his eyebrows to suggest an understanding has been reached.

"Certainly, Father."

Father Hughes disappears around the door and moments later reappears, pushing an elderly man in a wheelchair into the Loyola Parlor. He is gaunt and hollow-eyed. Wisps of dark hair turning gray sway in slight disarray in a humid morning breeze that sighs through the window. His left hand trembles lightly.

Margaret's confusion that this overly cheerful priest has fetched some elder of the community disappears the moment she sees the eyes smile. As from a long distance, Gerard is there. A fresh wave of sorrow swells in her heart as she brings a gloved hand and kerchief to her eyes.

Father Hughes arranges the wheelchair in short, jerking movements until Hopkins is an appropriate distance from his guest but directly in her line of sight.

"Thank you, Father Hughes," Hopkins says in a whisper trying to be heard. The cheerful priest leaves the room.

"Margaret Carrick," Hopkins smiles and exhales heavily. "I should be far better than I am and stand to greet your ladyship, but as you can see…" He looks down at his lap, his twitching hand and around the room. He then acknowledges the middle-aged woman dressed in mourning. "Margaret, you are grieving." They both smile in recognition of the poem. "Who is it, my dear?"

"Lord Carrick died two weeks ago, Ger—Father Hopkins," she corrects herself. She hasn't seen Gerard Hopkins in over twenty years, when he was neither Jesuit nor priest, but a charming, if moody, young man of Oxford who'd come down to London with her brother for Christmas at the Carrick house. It all seems ages ago.

"And Tom," Hopkins asks hopefully. "What news of him?"

Margaret stares at the priest with a long look of astonishment, calculating what he cannot know. "Then you never heard?" She opens a valise that's been sitting on her lap and withdraws a thin sheaf of papers. "Where to start, Father?"

"Margaret, please. Gerard, at least."

"As you may remember, my father was a formal man, a proud man and, clearly from these"—she lifts a sheaf of letters—"a discreet and private man. I found these letters in his desk, where they'd remained for twenty-three years. He had never mentioned their contents to me." She sighs and looks out the single, tall window in the room. "Two of them are from Tom, dated within two days of each other, the early days of June, 1867, and postmarked from London. The stationery is from the Pennington Club. They describe— obliquely, I'm afraid—events which transpired in Oxford the previous weeks, not long before you and Tom graduated."

Hopkins is dreading to hear more, and part of him wants to succumb to the crushing fatigue that envelops him. But he looks at Margaret with compassion and more than a little curiosity. He nods for her to continue.

"Evidently, the letters, along with their half-hidden descriptions of 'crime' and 'recklessness,' also contained requests to come to Carrick House and speak with father directly. And so, he did. I actually remember it and was so delighted to see him. But he gave me little time, and I relished the moments we did see each other. Most of his time was spent with father. There were shouts, I remember, and tears and then great, brooding silences between the two. I remember saying good-bye to him the day he left to return to Oxford. He seemed far better than when he'd arrived, almost light-hearted, as if some resolution had been reached between him and father. That was the last we saw of Tom."

"The last?" Hopkins is alert, fending off the dread that continues to close in.

"He disappeared after that visit. Father received a card from Balliol College on his return, merely saying that he'd arrived and was set on doing whatever he and father agreed was best."

Hopkins allows all of this to sink in, though reluctantly. "But surely, the family searched for him." He immediately regrets his implicit criticism.

"Father engaged certain policemen from Whitehall to go up to Oxford, make inquiries, even search for Tom themselves, but they found nothing, no trace of him. There were rumors around Oxford, and they've not abated over the years, that Tom fled the country. We had one report that found him in San Francisco, another in Melbourne. Father explored each with a desperation I'd never seen in him. Nothing came of those searches."

"So, Tom is gone." Hopkins' face has a faraway look before he then looks up at Margaret and feels a strange clarity. "Margaret, did he ever say anything"—he points to the letters—"about Lumen or Alec Moncrieff?"

"He mentions Lumen in his first letter but offers nothing more than a reference. And nothing of a Mr. Moncrieff, though more of him in a moment." She pulls out a yellowing piece of newsprint from her sheaf of papers. "He also included this article from the 'Oxfordshire News' by a Mr. Franklin Garrett concerning the murders preceding the Oxford riots of 1867. When I first read this material nearly a month ago, none of it made any sense to me. But I needed to learn more and so engaged the employment of a London detective. Here is his report."

She pulls another piece of paper from the thin pile and extends it to

Hopkins. *Margaret watches the paper shaking slightly in his hand as he reads.*

Hopkins scans the paragraphs for five minutes and then, with obvious effort, leans back, closing his eyes as he speaks. "So, the great Oxford club was guilty of the slaughter of three innocents: a boy, a maiden, an Anglican priest. Dear God, their sins were many and unthinkable!" *Hopkins looks again at the detective's report, scanning the paragraphs for a name.* "I see nothing of Alec Moncrieff here."

"No, not in anything printed. I shouldn't think one would ever find much of Lumen in the press, least of all an Oxford daily. But on the matter of Moncrieff: shortly after my father's death, as the family attorney and I were going through father's papers, I came upon his journal. I was hesitant to read it, wanting to honor father's memory, not invade it. But because of Tom, I had to."

Margaret looks at Hopkins pleadingly. He nods.

"Father gave himself over to several pages on this Moncrieff creature and the rest of Lumen. He called them a 'miscreant lot' and 'fiendish jackdaws.' Of course, none of this made any sense to me, so I hired another detective, a Mr. Beddles, to find Moncrieff and ascertain something of his business with my father."

"And Mr. Beddles found him? Moncrieff is still alive, is he?"

"You might call it living: he breathes in Bedlam but does little else. Mr. Beddles inveigled some way into that nightmare of a place—I didn't care to ask him how. He spoke with Moncrieff, but the man gave up nothing. He said nothing of Tom. He merely laughed and spoke only of Lumen in mad, impossible patterns."

"Did this Mr. Beddles also search for Tom?"

"Of course, that was the main reason for engaging the man. He tracked the lines of letters, dates and places, in London and Oxford alike. He found no trace of him, which was a sad validation of my father's efforts years before. All Beddles learned for certain—and, evidently, this is a sort of restricted intelligence at the highest levels of government—was that Lumen's membership—unnamed—were likely responsible for the murders, which were spearheaded by Moncrieff. No justice has been rendered for these crimes. A blanket of official silence has been drawn over the entire affair. And thus any hopes of finding my brother."

Lady Margaret reaches toward the report in Hopkins' hand and indicates a line of text at the bottom of the first page of the report. "This *gives me some hope, Gerard. There is a note that Tom was expelled from Lumen very close to the dates of the crimes, so I want to believe that he was guiltless of striking any of those people."*

She dabs her eyes again with her handkerchief.

Quiet passes between them for several minutes before Margaret says: "This is why I came, Gerard. To see, perhaps, if you knew anything of Tom's last actions, any hint at all of why he would have left Oxford and for where. Perhaps with something more, I can send Mr. Beddles in a fresh direction, yes?" She arches her eyebrows hopefully.

Hopkins recalls those last days in June, 1867, the days of dizzying change and tumult, his conversation with Thomas late that night, his earnest insistence on doing right by his friend, then his consultation with Father Newman that morning at Oriel. For a blessed moment, the vagueness that has been his steady companion for weeks is gone. Hopkins feels a freshness that he hardly knows anymore. He looks directly at Margaret Carrick.

"Margaret," he says with palpable determination, "there is something I must do, but it will not be easy. I mean to go to Oxford and help Thomas set things right. My work now is to prepare for such a trip, to seek the permission of my superiors and to right a wrong. Once I have done this—if I can do it—I'll do my best to visit you. Perhaps then all the mystery that surrounds our beloved Tom from twenty-three years ago can be made clear."

He leans forward, wanting to take Margaret's hands into his own, but repents the action and keeps his distance. "With God's help, we may yet find justice for those who have died at Lumen's hands." Among the latter, Hopkins thinks mostly of Thomas Carrick but will not say as much to grieving Margaret.

55

A sharp crackle of thunder overhead startled Myles and Eva as they paused beneath the portico of Collington Manor. A cool breeze swept across the wide circular driveway, and a few seconds later the skies opened up.

"I should've brought an umbrella," said Myles over the clatter of rain against the roof and gravel.

"I should have brought a sweater," said Eva, rubbing her shoulders.

"Here, take my coat," replied Myles as he draped his jacket over Eva's shoulders. After a few moments' hesitation, he grabbed her hand and gave her a mischievous grin. "Well, there's no time like the present."

She smiled, tightened her grip on his hand, and they ran through the downpour to Eva's car.

Eva started the car to crank up the heat and, while it idled, phoned Sam to see how she was doing, staying over at a friend's house to work on a history project. Ten minutes later, driving through the outskirts of the scenic market town of Chipping Norton, they decided to stop for dinner at a pub called The Goose's Gander.

Myles held his sport coat over her as they ran side-by-side from the car. They immediately gravitated toward a table near a huge Inglenook fireplace, where they kicked off their shoes and set them on the slate hearth. In combination with the late afternoon rain, the low, beamed ceiling, the festive aroma of burning logs and the glow from antique sconces made the room feel cozy and warm. A few other diners were scattered among the dozen or so tables, but for Myles and Eva only a low hint of quiet conversation could be heard over the snapping wood in the fire.

After ordering baked trout, salad and wine, they reviewed what they had gleaned from Sir Stephen.

"The most important thing to note," said Myles, "is that the old guy has the hots for you."

Eva smiled and shook her head. "He has the hots for anything with breasts."

"Except for Nurse Ratched." He chuckled. "I actually felt a bit sorry for her. She seemed solicitous and caring, which can't be easy with that guy. He was a trip. How much of what he said should we consider reliable?"

"He seemed to be giving away more than he wanted, though what he did reveal was—what's the right word?—shaded."

"Agreed," said Myles, setting down his wine glass. "I was somewhat surprised that he admitted to Lumen's 'dark' years. That coincided with Hopkins' final year at Oxford."

Eva picked up his line of thinking. "And while the sonnet was written in Ireland sometime shortly before his death in 1889, it's clear now that it refers to a time in the past. Specifically, his years at Oxford, during which he might have seen the Cuxham Chalice."

Myles nodded thoughtfully. "If there's a relationship between Hopkins' concerns in the poem and the events of 1867, then we need to dig deeper and find out."

"News stories from the time might tell us what we need to know."

"Exactly," said Myles.

"As for zingers from Sir Stephen, the part about Carrick absconding with the chalice and this fellow Moncrieff murdering him is a stunner. Do you remember seeing the name Moncrieff on the register?"

"The only name I remembered was Carrick," said Myles. "But while we were driving here I glanced at my notes and read the list of names I'd copied from the Register. Moncrieff was among them."

"So Collington's not entirely batty. If they're available, it might be worth checking police records from the late 1860s for the name Moncrieff."

"Please tell me that won't require the cooperation of the Oxford police," remarked Myles after the wine arrived. "I think that's a blocked road."

Eva sipped her wine thoughtfully. "We might do better with a local news outlet anyway. I think the *Oxfordshire News* goes back to Hopkins' time. We can research articles covering the riots that Collington talked about."

"Yeah, he seemed adamant about that. Hopkins left Oxford in 1867, which is when Collington said the riots began."

"While there, we can search the name Moncrieff. Some of the old newspapers regularly listed police reports."

"Good idea," said Myles. "One thing the old boy seemed sure of: the Cuxham Chalice did exist in Hopkins' day and was considered the cornerstone of Lumen's identity."

"Right," said Eva. "I thought it was interesting that he accused Carrick of being a traitor and, at the same time, was convinced that Moncrieff went too far."

Myles nodded. "I lost count of his references to Moncrieff as mad."

"The more I learn about it, the more I question how Hopkins could have been connected with Lumen."

"I hear you," said Myles, "and clearly, we need to spend more time with that sonnet. What we're learning about Lumen and its association with intrigue, crime and violence makes me more convinced than ever that the poem conceals some horrible secret."

"Or a host of them," said Eva.

As they were finishing dinner, the heavy rain had turned into a full-blown thunderstorm.

"You'd be wise not to drive in these conditions," said the kind, gray-haired hostess as she topped off their coffee. "Since it's mid-week and off-season—and as you're our only guests—I've made up our best room for you at no extra charge, including a locally-crafted mint on the pillow. And for breakfast I make the best gooseberry muffins in the Cotswolds." She patted her belly and beamed. "But you enjoy the fire as long as you like, and whenever you're ready I'll show you upstairs."

Myles and Eva looked at each other, then to the woman, then to each other again.

"I'm afraid there's been a misunder—"

The hostess smiled and waved her hand. "Oh, I understand, pet. Not to worry. No need to get soaked again." With that she left them.

After a few moments, they both grinned and let out a laugh that felt to Myles like a relief. "Well, that was…interesting. I didn't even realize they had rooms."

"Didn't you?" Eva flashed a puckish grin as she sipped her coffee. Myles tried to read her expression. Gazing at the striking beauty of her face and brown eyes, he felt a thrill and attraction he had resisted since meeting her. But he felt something even more surprising and liberating: trust. He wasn't sure what Eva felt, just as he had been uncertain of so many things for the past two years.

"Did she see something we didn't see?" he said.

"Do you believe in women's intuition?" Eva asked by way of a reply.

Myles shook his head. "I always found that term sexist."

Eva grinned. "Good answer. Wrong, but good answer."

Myles tilted his head slightly. "Are you saying…?"

She looked at him directly. "Why did you leave the priesthood?"

Myles looked slightly taken aback. "Was it to be with women?"

"Partly, yes." He was about to elaborate, but stopped himself. "But I don't exactly jump into bed without first…"

"Overthinking it?"

He smiled. "Yeah, something like that. Occupational hazard."

"I'd bet it's more intrinsic than occupational, especially since I doubt your intellectual skills are strained at the hardware store."

Myles leaned back and spread his arms on the table. "How come I feel like you understand me when you know so little about me?"

"It takes one to know one. We both live in our heads." She paused. "But I've seen you in action, and I know you're not all brains."

As attracted as he was to her physically, he found her voice—quietly self-assured with a disarming tinge of vulnerability—absolutely irresistible.

He leaned forward. "So, what are you saying? What do you want to do?"

"I'm not in any hurry to fight the rainstorm. And Sam's at a sleepover. And we can't get into the Oxfordshire News until tomorrow. Whether I sleep here or in North Oxford, it doesn't much matter, though I'd rather not chance the roads tonight. And," she added with a pensive grin, "I might kick myself for passing up those gooseberry muffins tomorrow morning."

Myles nodded in mock seriousness. "First I'd like to try that mint."

An hour later, they lay intertwined in bed, breathing deeply. Hard rain pelted the roof and window, and a low rumble rolled from the Cotswold skies.

"Not bad for an ex-priest." Eva raised her head and looked at him with smiling eyes.

"Ouch," he said, raising his eyebrows.

They both laughed. The lovemaking, initially tentative, had quickly become passionate, both lovers giving in to the spontaneity of the moment.

Myles broke a short silence during which they lay still, listening to the rain gently pelt the roof. "Pretty much since meeting you, I've imagined what it would be like to hold you, to be with you... like this."

Eva rolled onto her side and faced him. "And...?"

"And imagination is nothing compared with reality." He turned onto his side, leaned closer and they kissed, long and slow.

When they stopped, Myles held up an index finger. He rolled over and reached toward the bedside table, then rolled back so that he felt the warmth of her body as he lay propped on his elbow. He opened the tiny gift box and popped a chocolate-covered mint into his mouth.

"She was right," he said. "It is luscious. Too bad there was only one."

Eva stared, dumbfounded. She lightly hit his chest with the back of her hand. "No fair!"

"I meant only one *each*," he said. He held up a duplicate mint.

She snatched it. "Better to melt in here," she said with a grin, popping it into her mouth, "than in your hand."

Sometime later Eva awoke to darkness, the candle they had lit earlier having melted away. Myles lay asleep on his side next to her, one leg intertwined with hers. The rain had stopped, and all she could hear was the sound of his breathing. Though she felt calm and relaxed, she couldn't quell an excitement deep inside as she watched his bare chest rising and falling steadily.

After her eyes had adjusted to the darkness, she slid out of bed and walked to the window. She pulled back the curtains and tugged at the window, which creaked as it opened.

"If you're planning to flee, I'd advise putting some clothes on first."

A glow from the streetlamp allowed her to see his sleepy smile. He saw only her naked silhouette against the faint glow of a streetlamp.

"Where's the fun in that?"

"Bring it on," he said as he held up the sheet for her to crawl in next to him. He put his arm around her and she snuggled in close as they lay on their backs.

They watched shadows from an old oak outside the window dance on the ceiling as a restless breeze rustled through its branches.

"What are you thinking about?" Myles said after several minutes.

"Jeremy. I'm worried."

"Yeah, I know," said Myles soberly. After a few seconds he smiled. "He'd get a kick out of this, though. Us together. He's very fond of you, you know."

"As soon as I started working at Ignatius he befriended me, gave me the inside scoop on college politics, a.k.a. the Master." They exchanged a knowing grin. "Ilbert's a piece of work."

"He's a piece of something."

Eva laughed aloud. "But Jeremy has become a dear friend. He seems to feel the need to look out for me, and he's constantly on the lookout for eligible men—"

"For you or himself?" quipped Myles.

"Stop." She grinned and shook her head. "If, God forbid, he finds out I've got a date, he'll pepper me with questions about the guy and beg for details afterward. It's annoying but very sweet. I'm like his little sister."

Myles said nothing.

"Did you know his sister?"

"Yes."

"So sad what happened to her."

Myles swallowed. "Yeah."

He continued staring at the dancing branches on the ceiling. Eva turned her head so that she could see his face. "He's told me that she would visit him frequently in Oxford. Since you were so close with Jeremy, you must have known her fairly well."

"I did. I knew her very well."

"I'm sorry—"

"Don't be," said Myles softly, giving her stomach a light caress. "She was very important to him and of course he would tell you."

Eva sensed that there was more to this story but had no interest in prying.

After a full minute Myles said, "I was with her when she died."

"Oh God," said Eva. "At the hospital? Or were you in the car?"

"We were on a motorcycle. I was speeding. We loved that rush, and I loved the feel of her holding me tight through the curves. It was a winding road in the countryside, and a truck pulled out in front of us from a driveway. I swerved and we only grazed the truck, but Pippa was thrown from the bike and slammed into a tree. She had internal injuries and died in my arms before the ambulance arrived."

Eva realized she had been holding her breath and slowly exhaled.

"Oh, Myles, I'm so sorry," she whispered.

When he finally looked at her, his eyes were glossy. "I messed up. I was showing off a little, like a teenage kid trying to impress the cool girl. She loved going fast. We both did. She had boundless energy—but it was real. It came from her...her soul."

"She meant a lot to you."

"When you asked if I left the priesthood to be with women...I left for a number of reasons, but mainly to be with her, with Pippa. The accident happened before I'd left officially, but I had been quietly making plans to leave the Jesuits at the end of term, and mentally I had already gone. I found it hard to say Mass, I wasn't sure what I believed. So, that spring we'd begun making plans—a summer trip to Colorado, which Pippa dreamed about seeing, and I was looking at university jobs in London."

After several seconds Eva said, "I'm so sorry."

Myles turned onto his side. "What about you and Sam's father?"

"When we first met, he was charming, urbane, cosmopolitan. But the change happened as soon as we had Sam. I loved being a mother, but felt stifled and resentful by the lack of a real partnership."

"Was it cultural? Religious?"

"Islam is extremely important to Azeem, and initially this felt familiar to me—my family was old-school Syrian. He wasn't exactly an ideologue or a tyrant, but I felt smothered and stuck. So, the marriage only lasted a few years. I stayed in London, raised Sam basically on my own. Her dad traveled all the time for work, and she saw him maybe once a month. The rest—the divorce, moving to Oxford—you know."

Myles lay on his side, propped on his elbow, listening intently to Eva, who sat with her back leaning against the headboard. "I think I know what you mean," he said. "Things—decisions, life choices—make perfect sense. Until they don't. Cracks begin to appear in that carefully constructed life."

Eva nodded. "And you begin to feel attenuated and alone, a version of yourself that you don't recognize. You can wait for change, or you can make a change, as they say."

He nodded in wonder at her insight and her uncanny ability to describe his own experience. "Ilbert notwithstanding, it seems like you made the right move."

They both laughed.

For the next hour they lay side-by-side, captivated by the shifting shadows overhead. They spoke of childhood and favorite books, of dreams unfulfilled and unforsaken, of journeys yet untaken. For both in different ways, it felt as if something inside was loosening its hold, like taking gulps of fresh air after holding their breath for a very long time.

It was nearly dawn when they finished talking, and fell asleep again, holding each other. Myles awoke to the sound of a truck's horn outside the open window. They showered and dressed and decided to grab the muffins to go.

As Eva was reaching for the doorknob, Myles put his hand on hers and held it.

"One second, Eva." She looked up at him. He touched her face with both hands and kissed her. "I had a fantastic evening—and night. Talking. Listening. Learning about each other. I could get used to this."

She smiled up at him and put her arms around his waist. "Me, too." She looked into his eyes thoughtfully.

"What?" he said.

"It's complicated," she said. "This. Us. Your life, my life."

Myles took a deep breath and let it out slowly. "Believe me, I know."

Eva nodded wistfully. "Good memories are rare." Her expression lightened and she shrugged, tapping his chin with her index finger. "But who knows—this may not be the last opportunity to make a good memory before you leave."

He smiled and they kissed.

Friday, May 12

56

Myles waited in the lobby of the *Oxfordshire News* while Eva went to the desk and engaged in library-speak with a receptionist. The building was a low, two-story brown brick pile with nondescript features. Myles guessed it was from the early 1960s. He'd lived in Oxford for five years but had never seen this building and not much of Cowley Road at this end. A working-class neighborhood had grown up around the building and now populated the road with modest houses, faux Tudor bars, a W.H. Smith newsstand and two Tandoori restaurants. The building had the feel of a place soon to be abandoned. With surviving news publications converting to online environments, the traditional thrum of reporters and writers was absent.

Within a few minutes, Eva returned with a smile on her face.

"I guess you didn't have any trouble charming her," Myles said. "Somehow I'm not surprised."

Eva rolled her eyes. "Never mind. She was delighted we were even interested in searching old newspapers. I guess since so much is accessible on the internet, people rarely come here to examine past issues. They haven't quite gotten to the nineteenth-century material for digitization, so let's do it the old-fashioned way. The news morgue is downstairs."

They descended a set of stairs midway on the first-floor hall and found the morgue several doors down a short hallway. The space was about the size of an average classroom, with several long tables and chairs. The room was windowless and the rheostat kept the light low, giving the room a somber cast. Myles thought how appropriate the slang for news archives was: a morgue.

A half-dozen people sat scattered about the tables, slowly turning newspaper pages or writing in notebooks. Four microfilm readers were positioned against one wall; only one of them was occupied—by an elderly woman who looked like the *ancestry.com* type.

While Eva went to the archives desk to submit a request for films from the summer months of 1868, Myles walked over to one of the unoccupied readers and pulled two chairs together.

She brought one roll back to the reader, snapped it in place on the upper right, and then threaded the film leader through two round lenses just beneath the reader light at the top center of the machine. She slid the leader onto the opposite spool, flicked the light on and sat down.

"Myles, give that lever on the left a turn or two and let's see where we are on the film."

Myles gave her a comic deadpan as if she just explained to him how to open a door.

"All right, wiseguy. I guess you *are* old enough to have used one of these contraptions." She dug into her bag and pulled out a yellow notepad and pen.

"Do we know exactly when the riots occurred in the summer of 1867?" Myles asked.

"The clerk at the desk had to look it up. Said it was 28 July that the havoc ended, so let's see what's reported for that day."

Myles cranked the lever and moved the film from the right spool to the left. Print of various sizes and photographs blurred past with intermittent stops to see where they were. When he was past mid-July, 1868, he started to slow down. They imagined the riots would have been front-page material for the local paper, and when they reached July 28 they weren't disappointed. A full-spread headline read, "Squatter Crisis at Peak: Forty-Three Dead."

The article font was small, so Eva stood up and adjusted the magnification:

—Oxford. For the third straight day, rioting erupted again in the University city between local citizens and the Irish squatters. The Hibernians have been living in ramshackle dwellings illegally for the past six months Thames-side in the city's northwest quarter. They were also reported to have commandeered two narrow boats whose owners have fled under threat. In the wake of the recent melee, forty-three people are reported dead, most of them Irish immigrants, but seven Oxford men lost their lives as well. The local constabulary, with assistance from the Oxfordshire 52nd Regiment of Foot, scattered the encampment and burned the remaining huts to the ground.

Myles and Eva scanned the remainder of the article. The fighting had lasted a full three days and two nights. While it was mainly a town affair, gown had gotten in the mix in small numbers. Whose side the university students took was hard to determine, but an Oxford Assize would sort things out in the arraignment of the sixty-some people being detained in the county jail. The last line of the article read, "the Bishop of Lincoln, the Rt. Revd. Samuel Kingston-Pell, has requested prayers for the dead and pleaded for calm."

A second Irish-related article on the same page described the incendiary nature of what was happening in Oxford. Its author, Franklin Garrett, reported that nine other cities in England suffered incidents of varying intensity directed against Irish immigrant neighborhoods. Some strident politicians were calling for the deportation of the Irish, while parrying the counter-arguments coming from mainly Catholic circles. In any case, the Oxford murders and subsequent riots had stirred up anti-Irish and anti-Catholic fervor nationwide.

Eva turned toward Myles. "I don't see in either of these articles any obvious connection with Lumen. But then, I guess one wouldn't, given the group's secrecy."

"True," Myles nodded, staring at the projected page. "What makes this especially difficult is that it's like learning the plot structure of a story by starting at the end. The riots were going for three days, so let's move slowly in reverse from the endpoint to see what might've sparked the violence."

The elderly woman on their right made a dainty, high-pitched sound as she cleared her throat, turned and then smiled tightly at Eva.

"Sorry," Eva whispered. Here she was, a librarian, being shushed in a reading room. She looked around to see that most of the other patrons were looking at her and Myles.

While scrolling back to the paper for July 24, Myles paused over a last-page article on July 27 under the headline, "Tinkers' Victim Laid to Rest."

"'Tinker.' A dated term for a traveler, right?" said Eva.

Myles nodded. "Sometimes the word is associated with Irish gypsies. I'm sure in this case it's pejorative, or at least demeaning. Rootless, vagabond—those could be equivalents. Eva, would you pass me that notepad for a minute?"

Eva reached for a foolscap pad and handed it to Myles, who started jotting down notes. The story of the "Tinkers' Victim" was principally about the funeral and burial of the Reverend H. Carter Davies, a fifty-three-year-old Anglican curate from a small working-class parish in North Oxford. The man had led a modest life, but tragically gained notoriety by dying at the hands—according to the paper—of Irish tinkers who were encamped not far from the church house. The funeral was attended by scores of dignitaries, MPs, aristocrats—Queen Victoria sent a representative—and most of Oxford.

Scrolling a bit further to the previous day, July 26, revealed a short article on the discovery of Davies' body. Eva once again adjusted the magnifier.

The Anglican curate's body was found floating in the Thames about a half-mile south of the Irish encampment. The article described the body as "treated with great malice," recounting how the man had been stabbed up to twelve times, including in his head, and had been nearly eviscerated. The coroner judged that the curate had been killed very likely the day before.

"Okay," Myles said, scribbling on the notepad. "The curate was likely killed on Thursday, July 24."

"How sad," Eva whispered.

Myles nodded distractedly. "It doesn't say where he died, only that his body was found in the Thames."

"Does it matter?"

"I'm not sure, Eva. If the curate's death was the straw that broke the camel's back that summer, it was convenient for the mob that his body was found in the Thames, not far from the Irish encampment. And given that his parish wasn't that far away, it's possible he might've been walking along the Thames when the murderer found him."

At that moment a cell phone started chirping. The woman tsked loudly and readers fidgeted in their chairs. Eva rifled through her bag searching for the phone and muted it. She saw that the caller ID was "Principal Penrose," looked quizzically at Myles and whispered that she'd better take it. Myles turned to watch Eva weave quickly through the reading room with several "pardons," open the door and put the phone to her ear.

Myles turned to the issue from July 25, the day the curate's body was found. He spent the next ten minutes reading that day's edition, almost entirely devoted to the riots. There were articles about street fights and property damage, mostly in houses, factories and other buildings near the Irish encampment. Two Anglican churches were torched, though the fires were quenched before extensive damage had been done. No one was reported hurt. Not so for the counter-measure: a Catholic rectory on the Woodstock Road was burned to the ground, again without personal injury. An editorial that same day called for a united front by town and gown against the "Irish miscreants." Catholic leaders in the area attempted to intervene for peace but were either shouted down or assaulted by the growing anti-Irish throng.

Eva slipped quietly into the chair next to him.

"What was that about?"

"It was Simon Cole, calling on Penrose's behalf to ask how we were since that nightmare in the archives." Myles said nothing, continuing to turn the microfilm reader slowly. "He also hoped our trip to Collington was—how did he put it?—rewarding."

"You bet it was," Myles said, nudging her.

Eva stifled a laugh. "Hush. I simply told him that old Collington was very kind and offered us some valuable information about Lumen. I also asked Simon if he had any idea whether Moncrieff was a name associated with Christ Church College."

"What did he say to that?" asked Myles.

"He'll check the college records but he's doubtful they'll reveal much other than membership. But here's the interesting part, Myles. Simon said he'd found some ancillary bits about Lumen's leadership in the seventeenth century from the college library that he thought might be interesting. He'll send them by courier to Ignatius this afternoon. Very helpful, don't you think?"

"Absolutely...Look at this, Eva."

Myles pointed to an article nearly a week before the riots began. The body of a Miss Mazie Houghton, a seventeen-year-old kitchen girl at St. John's College, was found in the pre-dawn hours of July 18, three blocks from the college and only steps from the tenement where she shared a room with two other college housekeepers. She'd also been stabbed numerous times and her face and head were slashed with a butcher's knife, according to local authorities. Two articles that ran in the *Oxfordshire News* after Houghton's death began referring to the "Tinker Murders."

Myles jotted Mazie Houghton's name just above the Anglican priest's and gave the date of death as July 18 or 17.

The paper described the Anglican curate's murder as the third and Mazie Houghton's as the second in a series, so Myles and Eva searched in the previous issues for the first.

They found it in an article dated Monday, July 13. Henry Woodruff, a twelve-year-old public-school student, went missing on July 11. He lived with his parents, two brothers and a sister in a house on Holywell Street near Magdalen Park. He was last seen walking through the park to the Choir School at Magdalen College, where the young Woodruff was a chorister. His body was found by tradesmen early Monday morning at the bottom of a coal chute in the furnace room of Tompkins Textiles in east Oxford. The murderer or murderers heartlessly stabbed the Woodruff boy until he died from loss of blood. The coroner estimated that the boy was killed shortly after his disappearance on July 9, likely somewhere in the vicinity of the factory. His dead body was removed to the factory coke room, where there was scant evidence of blood. The boy's hands had been tied behind his back with a belt decorated, the article vaguely said, "with Hibernian symbols."

They scanned the previous week's issues and found nothing approaching the magnitude of the boy's murder—only a few reports of college burglaries and public drunkenness.

"Okay," Myles said, consulting his notes. "The Woodruff murder must be the first in the series. Let's assume that he died the day he was abducted, July 11." He checked the date the story of the boy's murder was published. "That would have been a Friday. Now, let's see...the maid at St. John's—"

"Wait a minute, Myles. How can you assume that the boy was murdered on the 12th when the body was found on the 13th?"

"Good question, Eva, and clearly I can't assume anything. But let's keep two things in mind. If this was the work of Lumen, they needed to be both covert and expeditious. They couldn't be hauling off captives, keeping them alive somewhere and then dispatching them. Both the curate and the maid were found dead not far from where they lived. It's only the boy, Henry Woodruff, whose body was discovered a fair distance from his home and even from where he was abducted. The factory's about a half-mile from Magdalen, where he was going to choir practice. There was something intentional about that murder and the body's location."

Myles made a few more notes. "Okay, so where were we?"

"Mazie Houghton," Eva said.

"Mazie...right. She had left college that night and was found very early the following morning. Since she was killed in the short distance between where she worked and where she lived, she likely died Thursday night, July 17."

"What possible motive could they have had?" Eva asked, lines furrowing in her brow. "It doesn't make sense."

"Not on the surface, maybe, and that's what the news reporters thought, too, in 1867. But we know that serial killers are methodical. Typically, they have an eye for particular victims and they're very purposeful."

"And the former Father Dunn would know this how?"

"I'm a fan of true crime books."

"So," continued Eva, "what about the priest?"

Myles looked up from his notepad and stared ahead into the microfilm reader. He then looked at Eva. "What did you say?"

"I said, what about the priest?"

Myles looked back down at the notepad and drew bold lines from various points across the page.

Eva continued. "You know, priest—the man in black, good for your soul, collars, cassocks and parish fetes."

"Holy shit!" Myles shouted, slamming his hand on the table.

The elderly woman searching for ancestors in distant shires brought a hand to her mouth, her face a portrait of unfathomable alarm. Everyone in the room turned abruptly in Myles' direction.

He leaned in toward Eva and whispered, "You're brilliant. I could kiss you right here." She gave him a questioning look as he grabbed her hand. "Let's get out of here, now."

57

At a Chinese restaurant across the street, a few late-lunch patrons awaited their checks, mostly students with backpacks. Myles and Eva sat down and ordered a pot of green tea.

"Now, would you mind telling me what that was all about?" Eva's voice was serious but her eyes hinted of mirth, enjoying Myles' recent display of bad form.

Myles missed the playful look because he was still poring over a jumble of figures, phrases and lines on his notepad.

"Sorry, Eva. I just knew we needed to be in a place where we could talk and not in hushed tones." He took a deep breath followed by a sip of tea. "Okay, first of all, we've got three murders that precipitated the Oxford riots of 1867, right? All, it seems, perpetrated by the same killer or killers."

Eva nodded. "Lumen, we think."

"Yes, *we* think, but not the 1867 *Oxfordshire News*. Three murders spread evenly over a two-week period, the boy on the 11th, the maid on the 17th and the priest on the 24th. A full fortnight."

Eva's eyes widened. "The number 14 on the manuscript. We thought last week it was about the number of lines in a sonnet, and so it is. But you think—?"

"Yes, the timing of the murders. Hopkins was making notes on that sheet of paper. And that's not the end of it, Eva. You referred to poor Reverend Carter as a *priest*. While that's true, the stories we looked at in the newspaper kept referring to him as a curate." Myles looked at her, his eyebrows raised.

"Okay, but I'm obviously not with you yet."

"Try this: 'Trinitas'—it's the Christian Trinity, but as we agreed last Saturday, it can be any set of three. What sets of three do we know occur in the poem?"

Eva leaned back and stared into the distance, while animated chatter in Mandarin wafted in from the kitchen in the back of the restaurant. She, like Myles, had long ago memorized the lines of the poem and was now running through them in her mind.

"The only one that comes to me just now is: 'acolyte, virgin, priest.'" She stopped and looked at Myles, a peculiar light dawning in her eyes. "The little boy—they called him a chorister."

"Pretty close to the altar, so let's call him an 'acolyte.'"

"And Mazie Houghton was described as an unmarried seventeen-year old."

"Again," said Myles, "it's an approximation, but Lumen wasn't being scientific about this. They were looking for an unmarried girl, a maiden, and were willing to assume rather than prove virginity. And third, the priest, killed by the same murderer. All three in a fortnight."

Eva allowed all of this to sink in. "So, we've got the trio of murders. I still don't know what this has to do with Hopkins. Why is he writing about it?"

"I'm not quite sure yet, but one thing's for certain. Hopkins had to know about the killings, as well as Lumen's involvement in them. Otherwise, why would he have bothered to hammer out a cryptic poem in the last days of his life? He wasn't a member of the prestigious club, but he must've known someone in it, someone who was willing to tell Hopkins about the murders."

"Maybe it was this Thomas Carrick, who had done something offensive enough to be expelled from Lumen…But then why didn't Hopkins go to the police?"

"We don't know that he didn't, Eva. Maybe his story was as unbelievable to the authorities in his time as ours is today. The crime was twenty-three years old by the time he wrote the sonnet, a world away in Ireland and approaching death. There's also the fact that Lumen was still around, still in Oxford, and any clear communication with regard to the crime of Lumen, the whereabouts of the Cuxham Chalice, or whatever Hopkins was hiding in the language of his last dark sonnet, would have put others at risk."

Myles' words trailed off as the questions loomed larger and more opaque. He tried to fend off frustration by reminding himself that he and Eva were closer than ever to understanding the poem. Moreover, if Jeremy had by any chance come as far as they had, he might be found with just a few more turns at the poem.

"And so," said Eva, "our presumed title, 'For an Oxford Jesuit,' is really an instruction from Hopkins, a sort of last will and testament. It never got delivered, as he'd hoped."

"Yeah, I guess that was a risk he was willing to take." Myles drained the small white cup of tea. "He wasn't taking into account the possibility that his poem might not be read closely until a century after his death, which brings us back to now. The nineteenth-century killings were blamed on the Irish, and Lumen succeeded in fomenting social discord that was met with devastating reactions from the authorities and the public against Irish immigrants. Look at what's happening today: a twelve-year-old boy and an elderly spinster are slaughtered, and the local Muslim community is scapegoated pretty successfully by whoever's perpetrating these murders."

Eva's eyes lit up with indignation. "Peter Toohey and Florence Ballard...our acolyte and virgin. The next victim, if the murderer is going by Lumen's nineteenth-century calendar, is to be a—oh my God, Myles!"

"Yes, a priest. If Jeremy started out on one of his 'errant Strands,' it may have turned into something of a nightmare."

Eva checked the calendar on her phone. "If Peter Toohey's death on May 1 begins the fortnight, then Sunday—two days from now—ends it."

"Which means we've likely got until sometime tomorrow to find Jeremy."

They stared at the table in silence while absorbing this chilling realization.

"Good God, Myles, *who is doing this?*"

"Someone who has exhumed a nineteenth-century crime to stoke twenty-first-century fear, bigotry and hatred." He shook his head. "As I think about our list of possible suspects from Guest Night, I can't see any one of them carrying out something like this. Penrose, Jacoby, Moretti, Cole, other guests hobnobbing in the SCR. It's unimaginable."

"You're right," said Eva. "It's inconceivable that any one of those people could do this. After all, we're not talking about an isolated crime of passion, but an elaborately planned conspiracy."

Myles nodded slowly, thinking. "Which means more than one person..." he said after several seconds. "You're onto something,

Eva. A conspiracy: a crime planned in secret by a group of people. This is the only explanation for what we're seeing." He paused for a few seconds to collect his thoughts. "Besides having the stomach for murder, it has to be someone who has some familiarity with Jeremy, maybe Hopkins, certainly the sonnet, along with esoteric archival information, connections in the Oxford community, the ability to abduct and possibly—here we're hoping—hold Jeremy alive and captive for days. All without being noticed. How could one person accomplish all this?" Though barely above a whisper, his voice had risen in tone and intensity as he unloaded the contents of his undigested thinking.

"I'm with you," said Eva, leaning in, "but this doesn't change our strategy. We can't focus on the perpetrator or perpetrators. We continue following where the sonnet leads."

"Agreed,' said Myles. "Our aim is to find Jeremy—hopefully alive. But all this underlines the danger inherent in what we're doing." He looked at her intently.

"Is it time to reconsider going back to the police?"

"I wish I believed that would help," Myles replied. "But we've tried and failed. We failed to convince them to take seriously the evidence rooted in a piece of nineteenth-century poetry. In a way I can't blame them. The whole thing feels insane. Going back to there and trying to explain the connection between Jeremy's disappearance and the two recent murders, based on the new evidence we've unearthed—"

"—is a fool's errand, I know." Eva's tone expressed a combination of anguish and resignation.

She looked at her watch and immediately picked up her bag. "I've got to get back to work. I'm afraid I've stretched a long lunch to the breaking point."

Myles reached across the table and took her hand. "I'm going to do whatever it takes, Eva. If he's alive, we'll find him."

Their eyes met and both nodded, determined in that gesture to slay, or at least subdue, the demons of doubt.

After he'd paid the check, Myles stood for a moment outside the restaurant. Eva made to go on, but turned around and walked back.

"Haven't had enough green tea?" she asked quizzically.

"Eva, I have no real proof for what I'm about to say, but I think Moretti has been shadowing me, us, maybe you for a few days."

"Really? You mean, he's in the restaurant?"

"No, at least not that I saw. It's all been peripheral. I'll sort of see him in a crowd on the street and then stop and scan, and he's not there. It's a feeling, really. I'm almost embarrassed to even mention it. If for no other reason than helping me see I'm not crazy, just keep an eye out for our Italian friend. He might be up to something."

58

After returning to Ignatius and doing an hour's work, Eva headed out to Banbury Academy, twenty minutes outside of Oxford, to pick up Sam. Her mind wanted to wander back to the night before and the early morning hours, to the pleasure and easy rapport she'd felt with a man she hardly knew. But reality forbade her from indulging such reverie. Another kind of rapport—currently more vexing and far more important in her life—now required her full attention. After tossing her backpack into the back seat, Sam plopped into the passenger seat and stared out the window.

"How was your sleep-over, love?"

"Fine," Sam replied distractedly.

"And how did the presentation go?"

"Fine," she repeated rotely before suddenly turning toward her mother.

"I've read through those books you got me, and I've decided that I'd like to practice Islam for a while. I mean *really* try it."

Eva said nothing for several moments while negotiating traffic exiting the school grounds. As she reached the stoplight at Banbury Road she turned to face Sam.

"Well, you sound definitive all of a sudden. Are you sure this is the right time—considering all that's going on around here?"

"Why not? I've been reading some books and pamphlets that Rabi gave me, like some bits of the Qur'an, along with some of the stuff you brought me. It's really cool. And deep."

Stopping the car to let a group of students cross, Eva glanced over at Sam and saw in her eyes the openness and optimism of a blossoming young woman. She also saw immaturity and vulnerability.

"Sam, I want you to have a strong sense of morality and ethics, compassion and forgiveness, and religion helps provide that for some people. Many people. But I also want you to have a sense of self and of limitless possibility."

Sam nodded. "I get it, Mum, but I can do both of those things. And why must you be so dead-set against Rabi?"

"This isn't about Rabi," said Eva, finally exiting school grounds and turning onto a main road. "I just think a boy you've known for such a short time seems an insufficient reason to take up a religion."

"Oh my God! All I'm saying is that I want to check it out, Rabi or not. I'm not about to formally utter the Shahada. I'm just exploring the faith because it seems to have so much beauty to it. Other people—most people, in fact—have religion or some spiritual foundation to their lives. I have none."

She stared pleadingly at her mother, who felt at a loss for words. "Sam, Rabi seems a bit confused—and frankly he scares me."

"Mum, we've both agreed, this isn't about Rabi. And besides, there's so much more to him than his faith. He's funny, smart, idealistic, and way more mature than other boys I've known or dated."

"What other boys have you dated?"

"You know, one or two..." Sam said trailing off without much conviction.

Keeping her eyes on the road ahead, Eva nodded slowly, trying to identify with her daughter. She remembered being young and in love, and she wondered if she was being unfair to her daughter— projecting her own experiences and failures. Still, Sam's budding interest in religion, especially Islam, had done nothing to allay Eva's concern about Sam's relationship with Rabi.

"I'll admit," said Sam, "I've been worried about him, too. He's been so defensive and, I don't know...preoccupied." She paused before turning to face her mother again. "But that doesn't mean I should give up on him."

Eva listened patiently before reminding Sam to stay focused on her goal: doing well in her A-levels and attending a top-notch university.

"You've been working toward that goal for years," Eva continued, "and you've only known Rabi a few months. You've got good instincts. Trust them. You're right to be concerned about him, and I hope you've told him how you feel. If he doesn't respect your opinion, well then that tells you a lot. As for Islam, let me think about it."

Sam was a sensible and intelligent girl, but, like most teenagers, she could be emotionally volatile, and on this subject, she had dug in her heels.

"I know what that means," Sam huffed as Eva maneuvered the car down Pixie Lane. "Why are you so set in your ways? You're so middle-aged! You're seriously going to forbid me to go to a mosque or read the Qur'an just like Dad forbade you to go back to school?" Her voice grew louder and more shrill.

"No, Sam," Eva replied calmly but sternly. "I'm saying don't ever alter your future for a young man you only *think* you know."

She immediately regretted saying it. It felt too heavy to lay on a seventeen-year-old in the midst of her first love.

Sam was sullen and silent during the remainder of the drive home. Eva had barely come to a stop in their driveway before Sam grabbed her backpack, got out, slammed the door and stomped toward the house.

59

Myles cursed when he felt the vibration from his cell phone, indicating a text message. It was the first time he'd exercised in days, and the run had provided a much-needed stress release and a chance to think clearly. His friend was very likely hours from being murdered, and Myles had no idea how to save him. The answer lay buried in Hopkins' sonnet—*but how? Where?* After his run, he'd sit down with the sonnet for the umpteenth time and not get up until he'd found some answers. The nagging question of why the hell Moretti was keeping tabs on him would have to wait.

He'd been running for forty minutes, during which his mind had gone back and forth between details of the poem and Eva. He kept replaying in his mind the night they'd spent together. He couldn't escape the euphoric sense of having surrendered himself to her, lost himself—in the sheer excitement of touching her hand, the yielding softness of her lips, the firm contours of her back against his hands, the mesmerizing timbre of her voice, and those disarming, steadfast eyes, as impermeable as they were inviting. It had been two long years since he'd been so open with a woman or felt anything like the thrill that was coursing through him now.

Slowing down to glance at the phone screen, he saw a number he didn't recognize and stopped along the side of the canal towpath to read the message.

Sir Stephen has some crucial information about the chalice. Come to the manor immediately and he will explain. His time is short, so do not delay! Helga Spinzel.

Myles stared at the message and frowned. He pictured Sir Stephen's forbidding nurse. How did she get his number? What would prompt her to reach out to him? More importantly, what did Sir Stephen have to tell him so urgently? He pushed the call back button and finally hung up after ten rings. Something felt wrong.

He started to phone Eva before remembering she told him

she'd be at a piano recital with Sam that night. He pocketed the phone and sprinted back to college.

After a quick shower, he bounded down the stairs, detouring to the kitchen for a banana and glass of orange juice, and then dashed across the quad. Upon entering the Jesuit garage, he cursed again. All the cars were taken. As he scanned the garage, his eyes fell upon something leaning against a far wall among disused rakes and bicycles.

"Oh God," he said aloud as he slowly crossed the garage.

The 1969 Norton Commando 750 Fastback, chrome front fender askew, dented black gas tank, bent exhaust pipe, and scratched-up helmet resting on the headlight—just the way he'd left it two years ago.

He heaved a sigh and let the air out slowly. He tentatively reached out and put one hand on the handlebar as he ran the other across the dusty dried-out leather of the seat. His senses were transported to that day in early June…the heat of the afternoon, the chuffing motor of a tractor in the near distance, and the smell of freshly cut grass from the field into which Pippa had been thrown and in which he knelt, cradling her bloody head and her limp and broken body.

The searing memory of Jeremy's face when Myles had told him the news brought him back to the urgency of the moment. He had to find Jeremy, and nothing could or would stop him, including his own resurgent grief.

He opened the gas tank and peered deep inside. Empty. Not surprising. He spotted an orange gas can in the corner, and lifted it. Enough to get him to a petrol station. Using the old foot-operated pump that still lay in the corner, he feverishly filled the flattened tires. After shaking bits of debris from the helmet, he strapped it on, then rolled the bike out of the garage. He straddled it and stepped down hard on the kick-starter. Nothing. He tried again and the engine roared to life. Its familiar sound and the vibration of the machine pulsing through his arms, legs and shoulders sent a rush of memory through him. He revved the engine, spinning gravel and rocketing down the narrow-cobbled lane and onto St. Aldate's Street.

Five minutes later he had fueled up and was flying northwest along the A44 toward Chipping Norton. He pushed the bike to full throttle.

As he cruised, he wondered more and more why Sir Stephen asked him to come back. Had he remembered something? If he had something to say, why not do so over the phone? Since it was likely about Lumen, the old man, of course, would be hesitant to say anything over the phone. And again, how did the nurse get his cell number? After the rush of emotion in the garage, riding again after so long brought Myles a strange kind of calm. The late afternoon sun played hide-and-seek with a handful of cumulus clouds, until 75 minutes later, when he pulled off the highway.

After speeding and leaning his way along twisting roads that cut through Cotswold hills and meadows, he turned onto a wooded lane. Moments later he passed between the stone pillars that marked the entrance to Collington Manor.

As the estate came into view from the curved driveway, he braked suddenly. Fifty yards from the house he could see that the large front door was ajar. Though he'd been there only once, it struck him as unusual. The gardener's truck was gone and no other cars were visible.

He watched the doorway for half a minute. No one.

He had an idea. Turning the bike around, he revved the engine and sped out the entrance, rode half a mile further along the wooded road, then turned the bike into the woods. Across a relatively even layer of leaves and pine needles he weaved quickly between the oak and pine trees that surrounded the Collington property.

Regardless of all that was happening, he felt a rush of adrenaline—even exhilaration—that recalled the dirt biking he used to do as a teenager around the hills south of Denver.

After a few minutes of riding and dodging trees, he stopped, killed the engine and leaned the bike against an unusual, gnarled oak that had a distinctive burl about fifteen feet up the trunk. By his reckoning, he was a little under a mile northeast of Collington Manor.

After fifteen minutes of rapid walking through the woods, the east wing of the manor house came into view through the trees. Under cover of the woods, he walked the perimeter of the grounds in a half-crouch. He studied the doors and windows, watching and listening for activity. Nothing.

He approached the house and peered in ground-floor windows until he came to the front door. It was still ajar exactly as it had been fifteen minutes ago.

He stood in the doorway and listened. So much for the Collington security system, he thought. The house was eerily silent except for the ticking of a towering grandfather clock that stood guard beyond the vestibule in the hall. After a full minute, he slipped into the house and pushed the big door shut.

He tiptoed through the foyer, looking in every direction. He walked down the long hall toward the study where he and Eva had met Sir Stephen the day before. This time the door was closed. He put his ear to the black oak panel. Nothing. He turned the ancient handle.

On the floor before the gaping hearth sat Sir Stephen and Nurse Spinzel, back-to-back, their heads slumped forward and their legs extended in front of them.

As he approached, a momentary sense of uncertainty gave way to a sense of horror. Their eyes bulged from faces an unnatural shade of purplish green. Around each of their necks was a dripping red ring.

"Garroted," Myles mouthed as he felt each wrist. No pulse, but the bodies were still warm. Their hands had been bound and tied together behind their backs where they sat. On the floor beside the bodies lay a cellphone along with the card Eva had given Nurse Spinzel. Myles noticed that Eva had written his mobile number beneath hers. Nothing else in the room seemed to have been disturbed, suggesting to Myles that the killer was known or trusted. Or maybe he persuaded the victims to think he was.

Either I was coincidentally just a few minutes too late, or—

Before he could finish his thought, Myles heard a siren. Then multiple sirens. Growing louder. He peered out the window and saw several police cars and vans rush up the circular driveway.

—or I've been set up.

His mind raced. Reason and logic told him to stay and explain the simple truth to the police. He'd received a message that Sir Stephen wanted to talk with him. He came straightaway and found the bodies. He had every reason to stay put.

But his gut told him to get the hell out. By all accounts, Jeremy's life was in the balance, and it was a matter of hours. Stopping to make explanations to the police would mire him in procedural detail—not to mention the fact that he was already on their shit list. Incredibly, in the short time he'd been in Oxford he had established himself in the eyes of the authorities as a hothead. He'd been warned to stay out of their hair. Myles had every reason to believe that finding him here was all they needed to take him back to Oxford and hold him for questioning. Or worse, throw him in a cell.

Deciding to get the hell out and making it happen were two entirely different matters.

He grabbed the card with the phone numbers and ran out of the room. He sped down the long hall to the front of the house and halted abruptly at the front door. He could hear the chatter of police scanners and someone yelling orders: "...and you three cover the rear entry points, then enter on my command..."

Just behind the enormous old door, mounted on the wall exactly where he hoped it would be, was a small white touchpad. A green light blinked beside a Cotswold Security emblem.

Myles removed the cover to find two thick columns of interconnecting wires. He'd seen systems like this dozens of times, since they sold replacement parts at the hardware store. On a few occasions he even helped customers problem-solve glitches. The question was whether or not the difference between US and UK voltage and frequency altered the wiring. He didn't have time to figure that out. He had to hope his trick would work.

He dried his sweaty hands on his pants, then carefully reached for a green wire on the left column and a red wire on the right column. He held his breath and pulled the wires forward.

"Through the door on three!" boomed a voice through a bullhorn just outside the door. "ONE!..."

Myles touched the exposed ends of the wires together.

"TWO!..."

Nothing. He tried again.

"THREE!"

The flashing green light turned red. Myles heard a series of loud *CLICKS* as the security system engaged the locks of every exterior door and window in the house. It wasn't perfect, but it would slow them down and buy him a few extra minutes. His only hope was a slim one. If it worked, he'd have Ilbert, of all people, to thank for it.

As he ran from the front door he could hear shouts of "We'll need the battering rams ASAP!" At the base of the stairway he paused to look left and right, trying to decide. He made his choice and bolted down the hall, opening the first door he came to. A library.

He ran to the next door. Throwing it open he saw a billiard table under an exquisite hammer-beam and vaulted ceiling.

Yes! he exclaimed to himself. The original chapel. The well-worn marble floor and wainscoting that rose to seven feet high were the only hints that it had once been a chapel. The arched ceiling had been painted an odd assortment of colors. If there had been stained glass in the old arched windows, it had been removed long ago.

He could hear the police hammering something heavy against the front door. Then another door somewhere else in the rambling structure. Furiously he pushed chairs and tables out of the way, then began running his hands along the wainscoting. Gently pushing and tapping, he listened for a hollow sound.

He had nearly made his way around the entire room when, in one corner, he came upon a curtain. He pushed it aside. What he thought would be a window turned out to be an old confessional. It had two doors, one for the priest and one for the penitent. He opened each, bent over and tapped the walls, his ear pressed against the wood. Nothing.

He knelt in the penitent's section, hoping for inspiration.

From somewhere in the house he heard a thunderous crack followed by a booming thud. They had succeeded in breaking down the main door. *Maybe I should go out, hands held up non-threateningly, and tell them my story,* What would he say? "It's ok, gents. I'm just an ex-priest looking for an old priest-hole, so I'm innocent"?

Not bloody likely.

He stood up and knocked on the rectangular wooden piece where his knees had just been. It sounded hollow. He tried pulling up on a corner of the board, but it was firmly secured to a short wooden base that was itself secured to the floor with metal clamps.

He stepped out of the confessional and looked around. The curtain. He reached up and yanked on it until it came tumbling down along with its metal rod. He slid out the rod and bent it in half around his knee until it broke. Using the sharp edge as a pry bar, he wedged it under the kneeler base. He applied enough force to pry the wood apart without breaking the rod. In a few seconds the rectangular kneeler pulled away from its base on one side.

Myles felt a rush of cool, dank air. Framed by the base of the kneeler was a narrow black hole.

He heard voices and footsteps from the hall and on the stairs as he reached for his cell phone and turned on its flashlight. He stepped into the opening and began squeezing his way through. About a yard down, his feet settled on what felt like a wooden ledge. The opening was narrower than his shoulders, so he had to tilt his head and left shoulder, lower his left arm first, and then use that hand to push upward on the frame beneath in order to force his right shoulder through.

As the door to the billiard room opened to the sound of police radios and voices, he reached up and replaced the rectangular board in its horizontal position atop the kneeler base.

His cell phone light revealed that he was on a sort of landing from which narrow wooden stairs descended steeply. The stairway was extremely low and narrow, lined with wood planks rather impressively assembled. Some of the planks had come loose and stuck out.

He hunched over and tested the first stair. Wobbly, but it held. He cautiously took the second and third. The fourth step gave way with a low, splintering sound. As he caught himself with his free hand, the voices from the billiard room grew louder.

After two dozen steps, the stairs took a 90-degree turn. The tightness of the space made this a tricky maneuver for Myles, who had to contort his body and extend his arms straight above his head. Voices and sounds from above grew louder, closer. After what felt like several minutes, he managed to inch and force his body through.

The rickety stairs gradually began to level off until they gave way to an earthen path. Dusty, dank and littered with dead rodents—and the occasional living one—the tunnel's construction and condition were unpredictable. His desire for speed was frustrated by the frequent need to crawl and squeeze through collapsed walls and tangles of tree roots.

The air was muggy and he felt increasingly sweaty. He had no idea where—or if—the low, narrow tunnel would open out. It wound to and fro, and despite the occasional help of his phone's light, he lost all sense of direction. From what little he knew of priest-holes, he guessed that it would lead toward the woods rather than the road.

After twenty minutes the tunnel began to shrink. The ground slope gradually upward, but the ceiling didn't. He duck-walked until that became impossible. Then he belly-crawled. Loose dirt cascaded down on him as his head, elbows and feet scraped the ceiling and sides. The flashlight now useless, he could see nothing. After several minutes, movement slowed to nearly a halt. He paused for breath, but his breathing was labored in the air thick with dust. His heart pounded and he felt claustrophobic. He considered turning back, but couldn't imagine how that was physically possible.

He had to press on. After another fifteen minutes of arduous crawling he was drenched in sweat. A tangle of tree roots abruptly stopped his progress. He aimed his light upward. Nothing but a mass of thick roots and dirt.

"Shit," he said.

In desperation he reached up and pulled at the roots. They barely budged. He grabbed hold of them and pulled harder. Some of the dirt that held them plunged onto his face. He wiped his eyes and pulled again. More dirt tumbled. He looked up again, and through the network of roots he now saw a plank. Then two, then three. It was a hatch of some sort.

Unable to gain any purchase on it to pull, he pushed. With little room to move and his arms tight above his head, he could muster minimal force against it. With his knuckles and fingers, he scraped and clawed at the dirt around the hatch's edges. After two minutes of vigorous work, he was able to get his hands behind one side and yank. On the third pull the hatch moved several inches, sending a spray of dirt and pine needles from above. And a rush of fresh air.

Myles chimneyed his way up the tight space and hoisted himself through the opening. Surrounded by trees and covered in dirt and sweat, he took deep breaths of the fresh air.

He could just make out the chimneys and roof of Collington Manor about a half mile distant. A steady stream of sirens and flashing lights told him that the bodies had been discovered. If they hadn't already, the police would soon enough begin searching the surrounding countryside for suspects, which meant Miles was by no means out of danger.

He looked at the sun's position and set off jogging what he believed was due east. With any luck he'd spot the unusual oak where he'd left the Commando, which he guessed to be no more than a mile away. Stopping every few minutes to scan the woods and treetops, in about ten minutes' time he saw the oak a hundred yards ahead. For the second time that day, he was relieved to see the old bike.

His relief was short-lived.

From behind the tree where the bike leaned there appeared a tall policeman. Looking around him, Myles realized he was surrounded by a dozen more, guns aimed directly at him.

60

Jeremy had no idea how long he had been there among the dead, nor even how many times his captor had visited him. His hold on reality, like his physical condition, was increasingly feeble and faint in this timeless hole. Consciousness was ephemeral, clarity tenuous. He could recall the occasional bottle of Gatorade or some kind of nutrient drink pushed against his lips, aggressive questioning, countless stinging slaps and, of course, the taser shocks, which had produced a raging fire scorching through his nervous system. Everything appeared through a gauzy veil, like the grim and ghastly figure he saw across the table each time his captor appeared with glow sticks.

As weakness and wooziness gained ascendancy, he felt an increasing kinship with his decomposed companion. He knew death was near and so began to contemplate the first of the four weeks that make up St. Ignatius' *Spiritual Exercises.* The goal is to "reform the deformed"—to recognize God's unconditional love and come to terms with one's failure to respond generously to that love.

Deformed. The irony almost brought a grim smile to Jeremy's face. He had never felt more deformed. Insignificant. Mortal. And he never felt more desperately in need of transcendent intervention. Yet instead of feeling worthy, he felt feckless and foolish. He wanted to open himself and receive that divine love—truly, *any* love—with open arms. But he couldn't even *move* his arms. He felt his chest heave as if he wanted to sob but his body was unable. *Maybe this is how it ends. Without dignity. Without freedom.* He began to recite the *Suscipe,* the prayer of surrender. *Take Lord, and receive all my liberty. My—*

"Wake up, mate! We're having a come-to-Jesus moment, you and I. Not the kind you were having just now, I'm afraid. I'll need your full attention. Drink this."

Jeremy felt the sharpness of a plastic bottle at his lips. As best he could, he swallowed the sickly-sweet fruit drink.

"Drink deep, Father Strand. You'll need those electrolytes to last another day."

Jeremy let go the allusion to his own mortality. At this point, death would be a relief. He just hoped Eva and Myles would be all right, although he was powerless to supply the information his captor wanted about the chalice. In his fractured state, he couldn't even conjure a decent story to buy time. But that voice...*Surely I know it from somewhere. If I could work out where, then maybe I could reason with the man...*

"I need to give you an update, Strand. You'll recall what I said the last time about how death can be messy?"

"Dear, God, please...you didn't harm—"

"No, the two friends you have in the world are still in it. I had them followed to Christ Church the other night. One of my company did his best to frighten them off the hunt, but their devotion to you appears unshakable. As touching and commendable as that may be, they followed it up by causing the deaths of two more innocents: Sir Stephen Collington and that cancerous German growth he called a nurse. Though it pained me to deviate from the plan, I couldn't take the chance that the old man was loose-lipped yesterday."

"Collington? The old man..." Jeremy, despite the infusion of Gatorade, struggled to keep awake.

"You're as sharp as ever today, Strand. Had your friends left the old man alone, I wouldn't have had to drive out there this morning and...dispatch him. The unfortunate nurse was simply in the wrong place at the wrong time. As for the American, I managed to lure him back to Collington and into the hands of the police. By the time they realize their mistake and let him go, he'll no longer be a thorn in my side. Nor will you, though for different reasons."

"Please, let me help you...I can help..."

"Yes, you can tell me the precise location of the Cuxham Chalice."

"I can't...I wish..."

"Yes, well, that makes two of us. Things don't always go according to plan—yours or mine."

SLAP!

"Stay awake, Strand! Collington wasn't part of the plan. He had to die because your damn friends elicited from him God knows how many details that he should have forgotten. Lumen in its last days and especially Lumen in its glory years: the Moncrieff tenure. He might well have been the greatest genius of social manipulation the English nineteenth century ever knew. Do you know the story?"

Jeremy could barely shake his head.

"It was a simple process of scapegoating. But recall what I told you the other day: plan, plan, and plan again. You kill someone on the right side and find a creative way to blame it on someone on the wrong side. That's the easy part. Genius lies in bringing it off successfully. You see, Moncrieff hated the Irish and the Catholics. I don't much care for your kind either, Strand. Here I don't mean Jesuit, though that's bad enough. I mean poofter. Still, your lot pales in comparison to the Muslims. What a great stain they are on England!"

The tenor of the voice kept vacillating erratically between rage and gravitas, agitation and pride. "Toohey was the first to be martyred for the cause of ethnic purity." He chuckled. "But isn't it delicious that the first to die was an *Irish* lad, and a Catholic altar boy at that? I love symmetry! Inflammatory? Absolutely. But I merely fanned the fire of anti-Muslim hatred and resentment that already burns within the hearts and minds of every true-blooded Englishman.

"Be honest, Strand. You know I'm right, just as Moncrieff was right. All I did was light the match. It's what leaders do. We light the way. *Lumen*. And, indeed, the lads are poised to take over. Once the third murder has been committed and your body discovered, then come more riots. And the counter-strife. And conservative ranters in Parliament. And the police and soldiers. And the various elements of gross discontent that hurl stones through perfect windows, even on good days. These will all unleash a holy terror upon the Muslim in Britain.

"But back to Collington, who was older than dirt. He knew the Moncrieff legend, but he also had information that would enable your bloody American friend and his dusky wench to connect Moncrieff and Lumen's glorious past with me. Maybe I should have had them killed at Christ Church Archives instead of merely scaring them off the scent. You see, Strand, Moncrieff was my great-great-great-grandfather. Yes, I am this great man's heir. This, and only this, is the reason why Lumen must have its chalice back. The timing is sensational." He glanced at his watch. "And speaking of timing, Dunn is cooling his heels in the clink right about now. Out of my hair for the duration of our triad, I should think."

Jeremy tried to rouse himself but could manage barely a breathy murmur. "How do you know what the old man told Myles? Were you there?"

"Well, of course I was there, silly man. And then I returned to end them. But I take your meaning. It's surprising what people will tell you when threatened with death."

"And all of this violence for a chalice? What do you…What do you know of…what a chalice symbolizes?"

"Oh, I know enough not to be fooled by old priests and their tales, Father. To me, your Eucharist is nothing more than play-acting about human sacrifice involving a body and some quantity of blood. The Cuxham Chalice was Lumen's founding treasure, given by Wolsey himself. He made Lumen the guarantor of England's purity at all costs. *At all costs.* Not until my thrice-great-grandfather's regime did that phrase reach its apogee and Lumen discover the true depth of its mission.

"My heroic forebear made the chalice the vessel of Lumen's darkest secret and noblest deed, committed on behalf of all Englishmen. The chalice, you may know, Strand, is a 'votive chalice,' a receptacle of more than altar wine. What better vessel, therefore, than this chalice that once contained Christ's blood to hold within it the bloody rebirth of Lumen *and* the reaffirmation of Christian purity!"

"Votive," whispered Jeremy. Nearly blacking out, he used every bit of his flagging strength to keep his captor here, where his only violence could be against Jeremy. The effort to remain conscious only exacerbated his aching light-headedness. "Please, stop this horror before other innocent people die."

"Once again, you haven't been listening, Strand. Killing innocents is the whole idea. Oh, it's possible that someday hence, I'll feel sorry for Toohey and Ballard. And you, and the happenstance that led me to you and to this hole in the ground. 'Tis a pity you couldn't help me unearth the chalice. I'll bring the lads round in a few months, when other things will have eclipsed your murder. Perhaps we'll find the chalice, perhaps not. In any case, England will thrive, its values and purity unsullied by the latest immigrant onslaught."

The voice walked from behind Jeremy and stood beside the skeleton. He brandished a knife nearly the size of Jeremy's forearm. His smiling face was illuminated in the light of the glow stick.

"It's *you*? But what—? Why…?"

"You may think you know me. But you have no bloody idea!" The man glanced at his watch. "Make a good Act of Contrition, as you Catholics say, Father Strand. Lumen's fortnight ends in a little more than twenty-four hours, which means your end is nigh."

61

"Damn!" Myles slammed his fist against the butt-smoothed wooden bench.

Three officers, including his old pal Sergeant Thornton, had interviewed him for two hours about the deaths at Collington Manor, showing little sign of believing his story, let alone his explanations of the connection between the Collington killings and Oxford's recent troubles. Instead, they reminded him of their warning not to meddle in police business and flatly denied him a phone call. He had no idea how long he'd been locked in this cell. Every passing moment was a bitter slap of failure, as it brought Jeremy closer to being the latest victim of the Lumen-lunatic psychopath.

Myles paced back and forth. When he tired of that he stopped and clutched the iron bars in his fists, hoping for a miracle and shouting for them to allow him a phone call. When nothing came of his hoping and shouting, he would sit, until he got up and did it all over again.

Hour after hour, images of the garroted and bloodied corpses of Sir Stephen and his nurse intermingled with those of his old friend's smiling, forgiving face. The surreally merged faces spun menacingly through Myles' imagination. Waves of guilt, sorrow and desperation crashed mercilessly in his mind—even, it seemed, in his soul. *I've let you down, old friend*, Myles thought as he pounded out the words on the cell bars. *Where are you and how can I possibly find you now? Are you hurt? Are you still alive?*

He felt the anxiety of his helplessness. He didn't know the exact time—they'd taken his cell phone when they brought him back to Oxford and processed him in the station—but he figured it must be close to ten o'clock, Friday, May 12. If Lumen or whoever was holding Jeremy kept to the two-week schedule begun with the death of Peter Toohey and continued with Florence Ballard's, then the "priest" of the Lumen trio was due to die before Sunday, the end of the fortnight. How much time did Jeremy have? How much time did Myles have? If he could make a call, at least he could alert Eva to events. But then, what could she reasonably do? Hell, what could Myles do? What did he have to go by? A possible location: Trinitas or Trinity, whatever that meant. A collection of obscure references in the sonnet: something—the chalice, maybe?—that was entombed. Something about a slype, a scroll.

"Damn it, Jeremy! Why didn't you tell me more?" he said aloud. Another spike of anxiety.

Myles knew he was in a holding cell, which meant that they'd soon transfer him to some other location in the jail or have to let him go for lack of evidence. But how long would it take to process the murder site at the manor? At least a day. And Myles had pretty much been caught red-handed, or nearly so, fleeing the house in the way a suspect might. At the same time, he knew they couldn't attribute to him any motive for the Collington killings.

His mind ran in this investigatory direction for a few minutes more, and he was keenly aware of how precious those minutes were. He knew he would be cleared, but he dreaded the thought that his freedom might come at the moment of Jeremy's death—or after. He pushed himself away from the bars in frustration and sat down on the bench.

He leaned forward, forearms on his thighs, head in his hands. The posture he had sometimes used in prayer. It was a posture of lamentation, but he struggled to make it one of hope. *God, get me out of here. Let me help my friend.*

Sometime later, Myles heard a key noisily working the lock of his cell door. He stood up as Sergeant Thornton opened the door and stepped in.

"I don't know who you are, Dunn, but you've got friends in high places. You've been released. Come this way."

Myles could hardly believe his ears. Thornton led him past cells, some of them occupied with late night revelers. Myles noticed a cell with two men seated on cots wearing Salam tunics.

"What time is it?" Myles asked, as he and Thornton stepped into an elevator.

"Eleven fifteen," he said curtly, avoiding eye contact with Myles.

"Who arranged for my release?"

"No idea. The order came down the chain of command at TVP."

Myles figured Tock must've intervened with his friend, Chief Inspector Hillary Stratham. He couldn't imagine any other possible arrangement.

Thornton took him into a small room with a Plexiglas window looking out onto the main lobby of the Thames Valley Station. He could see a number of people waiting to be either processed or dismissed. He didn't see Tock or anyone from Ignatius College in the crowd, and he didn't know what Chief Inspector Stratham looked like.

Another officer at a desk in the small room stood up when Thornton and Myles entered. He asked Myles to sign two forms on a clipboard for the return of his possessions—his wallet, cell phone and Ignatius College keys. The motorcycle was still being transferred from Collington, and he could pick it up tomorrow. Myles scribbled his signature twice and shot a glance again toward the clock. Thornton nodded for him to follow as the receiving officer buzzed them out of the secure room.

The lobby was noisy with chatter, mostly worried conversations. Myles turned to Thornton who simply nodded in the direction of the door.

"That's it?" Myles asked.

"Your ride's waiting outside the door," Thornton said. As Myles turned toward the exit, he heard the sergeant say behind him. "And for bleedin' sake, Dunn, leave police matters to the police."

62

Myles stepped out of the station to an idling black Mercedes. A uniformed driver opened the back door with a nod of courtesy. Myles slowed his steps to the car and bent down to peer into the back seat. There, sitting and offering a similar nod of courtesy, was Monsignor Moretti. He patted the black leather seat next to him. For a moment, Myles didn't know whether to get into the car with the Italian or run in the opposite direction. Moretti had been so consistently inconsistent during the time Myles had been observing him at Ignatius College that he really didn't know whether this was an invitation to freedom or yet another costly digression on his way to helping Jeremy.

"*Subito*, Dunn," Moretti said with mild irritation. Myles got into the car, and Moretti told the driver in Italian to take them back to the college. He quickly tapped the back of the headrest. "*Velocemente!*"

A thousand questions ran through Myles' mind as the car sped out of the police station and into the labyrinth of Oxford streets. "How...Why...?"

"We have little time, Dunn. For the moment you are"—Moretti cleared his voice as if about to make an announcement—"an agent of the Vatican Secretariat of State, and now possess full diplomatic immunity. At least, as I say, for the moment." He opened a valise on his lap and withdrew a passport with the seal of the Vatican City State emblazoned in gold. He handed it to Myles. "Your US passport, of course, remains in effect, but you enjoy a diplomatic status possessed by very few."

Myles stared uncomprehendingly at the passport and then at Moretti.

"Of course. You have questions. Let me explain, as much as I can at this moment."

Moretti went on to describe how a certain Father Slater had

been monitoring Myles' whereabouts in England and notified his superior upon learning of the arrest. Moretti had made several quick phone calls and one very lengthy one to his own superior, the Cardinal Secretary of State. He next spoke with British diplomats in Vatican City and London before finally placing a call to the Vatican's representative to Great Britain in London. The archbishop, a friend and seminary classmate of Moretti, had provided the Mercedes and its driver, a young Italian named Stefano.

"Do you know where Jeremy is?" Myles couldn't avoid the tinge of accusation in his voice.

"Do not mistake me as an enemy, Dunn," Moretti said as he pulled an iPad from a black valise. "I cannot say I share your friendship with Father Strand, but I share your concern for him, and not merely for his possible connections to the chalice."

"So, you actually believe there is a chalice?"

"*Certamente*, Dunn, and I believe with you that Strand knew more than he was telling and may have already found the treasured cup. In any case, that he is not here to tell us suggests that something dreadful has taken place. One thing I do not believe in—and I have no doubt you concur—is wasting time."

Moretti glanced at his watch as the car took another sharp turn at speed. "I will explain my office's interests in this matter on another occasion. For the moment, your work as 'special envoy' is to be immune from the interference of local authorities in order to search for Strand. He is in danger; we both know that."

To his own surprise, Myles allowed the evasion. He had known priests for a very long time and had even met his fair share of top brass like Moretti who were rarely transparent. Still, there was something in Moretti's words, maybe in his tone, that gave Myles pause.

Moretti picked up on it. "You are having trouble solving the riddles of that sonnet, no?"

Myles nodded distractedly. His mind took him to the manuscript copy sitting on his desk, where he needed to be hours ago. "Dr. Bashir and I are convinced that there's something yet in that manuscript that will lead us to Jeremy."

"*Ma*, if it were in Italian," Moretti said with a humorous fervor in his voice, "I might be able to solve it for you."

Myles let the humor pass and continued trying to read Moretti, searching for something in the man's face, voice. He made the decision finally to trust the Italian. He had gone to tremendous lengths to extricate Myles from an impossible situation, and whatever his motives regarding the chalice, Moretti could be his—and Eva's—only help now in getting to Jeremy.

Myles succinctly described what he and Eva had discovered from Collington, the dark legacy of Lumen and the nineteenth-century murders devised by Alec Moncrieff, and the realization that the secret society may have been revived in Oxford today. The most important revelation was that the current murders were being orchestrated and timed to follow carefully a script that had been written by Moncrieff a hundred and fifty years ago. But not entirely. Myles quickly shared with Moretti the origin story of the Cuxham Chalice in the murder of young Hugh of Lincoln and the blame that a few resentful Christians had placed at the feet of the local Jewish community—with devastating results.

Moretti was familiar with the blood libel story and, as it happened, had reached similar conclusions about the Cuxham Chalice and the Jewish community of Lincoln only in the last couple of days. Father Slater was proving an indispensable resource. "So, now innocent Muslims here in Oxford, and perhaps all of England—all through Europe—are meant to suffer vengeance over the murders of that boy and the old woman?"

Moretti let the question hang in the air unanswered. Another one, more important to him at the moment, needed to be asked.

"We are almost to Ignatius College, and you have much work to do before the night is finished. But in the intervening few moments, Dunn, I need to know something: Why did you end all of this—priesthood, the Jesuits, an academic career?"

Myles was taken aback by the question. He wanted to tell Moretti to mind his own business. Any question that didn't help unlock the sonnet or aid in finding Jeremy was useless.

Moretti could read the anger mounting in Myles and raised a pacifying hand.

"*Piacere*, Dunn. Indulge me for a moment. You know the world I come from, where power is too often everything. But why would you, a man destined for such greatness in the Church, leave it all, to do what—choose a life remarkable for its lack of consequence? This is not a question of orthodoxy, I assure you. That is none of my concern. But for the sake of more than you can know right now, I need to know something of the man."

Moretti grabbed the headrest in front of him for stability as Stefano took an abrupt turn into the cobbled road that led to Ignatius' main gate.

Myles peered intently at Moretti and spoke firmly. "Look, I'm grateful for you getting me out of jail. I'm still not sure how or why it happened, and I have even less idea why you're asking me this question. My focus is on finding Jeremy and bringing him home, not discussing a decision which is, frankly, none of your concern."

Seconds before the Mercedes came to an abrupt stop precisely at the gate, Myles reached for the door handle.

"*Bene*, but what do you need now?" asked Moretti as Myles hopped out. Moretti continued speaking through the passenger window, "to bring your friend home? How can I be of assistance?"

"You've already helped me. Thanks again. What I need now is to get back to that poem. We may have only a few hours to find him."

"One final thing, *dottore*. Forgive me for tripping you up in the chapel sacristy that first night you were at college. I'm sorry I impeded you then and will do everything now to speed your path."

With a look of mild surprise, Myles shut the door and strode through the main arch and into the college.

After watching Myles disappear, Moretti said something to the driver, and stepped out of the car. In a moment, the Mercedes slid away quietly into the black night as the Italian lit a cigarette. He took one long draw before flicking it onto the cobblestone just as Tom Tower, a short distance away, tolled midnight.

Saturday, May 13

63

Never before had he felt on the brink of failure. Never such a combination of urgency and inadequacy. Such need to act and yet stay calm and focused. His mind raced in multiple directions. Here he sat—many hours later than he'd planned to, needed to for Jeremy's sake—at the small desk in his room, perched on the edge of the squeaky wooden chair, head bent. Disturbed and fatigued from the ordeal at Collington and the lost hours in jail. He had to summon a rush of energy. To delve into and scrutinize once again the cryptic lines of verse.

He looked at the clock. 1:00 am. He shook his head rapidly. Stood up and gulped a glass of cold water. Sat back down.

He stared at the manuscript, which after all this time seemed to ask more questions than it answered. Grabbing a legal pad, he began listing them:

First and foremost: What did Jeremy see here that he didn't—or couldn't tell us—and where did it take him?

Why "For an Oxford Jesuit?"

Why the inverted acrostic *trinitas*? Was it a location clue—Trinity something—and was its inversion a downward direction: when you find trinity, go down?

What, if any, was the significance of the various manuscript markings? The stylized chalice was now an obvious link, but did any of the other markings serve Hopkins and the reader of the sonnet as clues?

What accounted for the radical shift—in tone and subject—between the octet and the sestet?

Was the poem purposely left incomplete? And why is it incomplete in the manner that it is incomplete? Myles thought again of those mystifying lines that began with a word or two at the end of the sonnet and then went nowhere. There must be *something* to those words, or why would Hopkins have bothered?

He then wrote the words "Hopkins" and "puzzle-master" and underlined them. How many puzzles could there be in the poem or on the page? If, as Tock had said in the SCR last Sunday, Hopkins was a puzzle-master, then everything on the page might be some sort of puzzle or clue. Why was Hopkins hiding and revealing at the same time?

He scribbled down all the word puzzles he could think of: acrostic, palindrome, cryptogram, anagram, jumble. He thought of an old game show in which contestants gradually revealed clues in the form of words and pictures. What was it? "Concentration." What was the term for that kind of puzzle? After a pause he scribbled the word "rebus."

The acrostic had come fairly easily, and maybe it was meant to, but they'd been stumped ever since. What if "TRINITAS" wasn't a clue, but simply a verbal-visual homage to the Holy Trinity? Jeremy had been convinced otherwise. If there was an acrostic and at least one sort of "rebus" in the form of the stylized chalice—the very same markings that appeared on the victims' foreheads—then it made sense that Hopkins had some sort of agenda beyond poetry and beyond the spiritual.

The acrostic made use of the opening letters of each line, and it did so by using a Latin word. Myles played around with the final letters of each line—"l" for "Grail, "e" for "foe," and so on—but came up with nothing in the octet, in English or Latin. Since the sestet was incomplete, it also seemed to be a dead end. He tried scrambling the letters of each of the final words of the octet. Again, nothing.

Maybe Hopkins intended to provide a more complete set of

clues in the form of puzzles but simply ran out of time. Clearly, the poem was incomplete. But maybe he completed what he *needed* to for his purposes. Whatever they were.

Myles decided to focus his energies on the more incomplete and elusive part of the sonnet, the sestet:

> Unbaptise th'nointed twelve; in boldness fly! He
> Cowers not who rights, but routs the fiendish jackdaws, sets
> Holy justice alight: guilt-in-gilt unscroll.
> Whet...
> Ah, my brother...
> Embrace thereby the truth 'tween hell and heav'n.

Two features stood out: every line contained at least the first word, and the final line was the only complete line. He held the manuscript at arm's length, then held it up to the light, and finally close to his eyes. Something struck him: with the possible exception of the final line, the first word of each line was either larger than the rest of the line or maybe a bit more noticeable than the accompanying text. As if those six first words had been written with greater emphasis. Why had he not noticed this before? Was he imagining it? Was it significant?

He wrote down those first six words: "unbaptise," "cowers," "holy," "whets," "ah," "embrace." He considered palindromes but saw none. Jumbling the first letters in a kind of anagram style produced gibberish. He tried jumbling the entire word, starting with "unbaptise." Again, nothing that made any sense. Next was "cowers." Unless Hopkins had concerns about "escrow," this, too, led nowhere. Similar results followed with the other four words.

Myles got up, went to his sink and splashed water on his face. He rested his hands on either side of the basin and stared in the mirror at his dripping face. He felt physically and mentally depleted but saw in his reflection something entirely unexpected: desperation. He hadn't even begun to process the horrific events at Collington Manor or the rage he felt being incarcerated. Without having remembered taking a deep breath, he let out a long sigh. He returned to his chair, wiping his face with his sleeve as he sat.

He stared at the words again. *Think, Dunn. Think! It's a poem whose secret identity seems to hinge on "trinity." Maybe "trinitas" points downward...or maybe to a "three" motif. Let's divide the six lines—i.e., the six first words of the sestet—into three pairs of two.* He opened his laptop, ran a quick search for an "anagram generator" and started typing in various combinations of words from the sestet, beginning with "unbaptise and cowers." The results were unimpressive, to say the least: "rub pee wainscots," "pun sees crowbait" and "tea cups brownies." He shifted to "holy" and "whets," which yielded such gems as "hotly hews," "why hotels" and "the shy owl." A good pub name.

Rather than three pairs of two words, maybe it made more sense to scramble and unscramble two sets of *three* words. He retyped "unbaptise" and "cowers" but added "holy" and began unscrambling the sum of their letters—in other words, "unbaptisecowersholy."

He quickly decided to set aside the hundreds of results containing four or five words, since none of them made sense as a phrase—such as "warehouses ply bin cot." Instead, he focused on three-word results. The results still numbered in the hundreds, but he was able to eliminate most of these rather easily—such as "whereabouts nosy clip" and "cartwheels buy poison."

Ten minutes later he had produced a list of three-word phrases that at least made sense. In five more minutes he narrowed this to a shorter list of phrases that seemed intriguing, for one reason or another:

Absolution creeps why
Eucharist bows openly
Censurable whoso pity
Chasuble sinewy troop
Bishop unseat crowley
Obeisance worthy plus
Incurably weeps sooth
Absence worth piously
Broaches went piously

His attention was especially drawn to any religious or ecclesiastical terms such as "ablution," "absolution," "Eucharist," "bishop," and "chasuble," though none leapt out as an obvious clue.

As he reread the list, he stopped at "bishop unseat crowley." It was the only result that contained an imperative verb: "unseat." If "TRINITAS" was a locative clue, then any other clues embedded in the poem might also be directional. He stared at it and felt sure he had heard or seen the name "Crowley" before. Something with Eva. He put a line through "bishop Crowley unseat" and wrote "unseat Bishop Crowley." He couldn't place the nagging sense of familiarity and put a question mark next to it.

He repeated the unscrambling process with the letters of "whets/ah/embrace," again focusing on results that contained three words. The results were less promising here and produced no ecclesiastical or religious terms. He found it noteworthy that the word "breach" had appeared as possibilities for both sets of three words, so he spent several minutes contemplating the possibilities. Finding nothing promising, he continued to type other word combinations and generated a slew of three-word anagram results, including "chase what ember," "bare what scheme," and "chasm the beware."

The list contained several active and imperative verbs: "chase," "watch" and "thrash." "Bare what scheme" intrigued him because of its implied sense of revealing a hidden plan. The word combination that stood out, however, was "chasm the beware." He crossed it out and rewrote as "beware the chasm." Though unexplainable, it was the sole result that made grammatical sense. That it was a warning seemed significant to Myles, though, again, he had no idea what chasm to beware of. He circled it and put a question mark beside it.

Maybe he was getting somewhere. He had to think like the poet. He had an acrostic—TRINITAS—and possibly a set of two anagrams, though what they were he couldn't say. Maybe Hopkins figured that the acrostic, more apparent than the anagrams, would be discovered first. If there were anagrams embedded in the sestet, as Myles now suspected, they must make sense in relation to the acrostic—"trinitas," or trinity.

He slapped his hand on the desktop. "Let's go!" he shouted. His adrenaline pumping, he turned to the last line. With the previous two lines barely begun, why did Hopkins complete that line? Was it of particular importance to him? To the poem's message? Something was missing, some vital piece of information. A direction? A clue?

Myles picked up his phone and pressed Eva's number.

"Myles, do you have any idea what time it is?"

"Sorry, Eva, I—"

"And where've you been? I called and texted you a few times this evening, or I should say *last* evening."

"Long story, Eva. I'll fill you in later. What's pressing right now is something I've discovered."

He told her about the probable but inconclusive anagrams.

She shared his excitement. "This is a breakthrough," she said hopefully.

"Feels like a discovery without a payoff. Not yet, at least. Right now it's pointing us nowhere and every minute is crucial. *We're missing something*. Do you think Jeremy knew about this?"

Eva heard the frustration in Myles' voice and sensed the fear that lay beneath it. "I don't know. I can't imagine so. Maybe we need to step back from the poem for a moment."

"I keep thinking: Where did he go? What else did he know that led him to take off in the wee hours after Guest Night? If he knew about hidden anagrams, let alone the significance of them, then he was doing a damn good job deceiving us."

"Agreed," said Eva. "Let's be honest, he likely would have let something like that slip at Guest Night. He seemed hardly able to contain himself." She paused. "Something else must have come to him, some other bit of information."

"Or someone," said Myles. "Not during dinner—we've already replayed that conversation *ad nauseam*. Is there anyone he saw, anyone he spoke to who might have given him some kind of idea?"

"About what, exactly?"

"Anything, really: about 'trinitas,' which he knew about, of course. Or Lumen. Or something else about Hopkins…or some detail of the manuscript."

Eva yawned. "I kept my eye on him until I left, though I didn't monitor his every word. But maybe we still can," Eva said with a sudden burst of exhilaration, "at least in retrospect. I should have thought of this before."

"How? What?"

"I'll be there in ten minutes."

64

Myles met Eva in the parking lot and greeted her with a peck on the cheek. She took his hand and they walked hurriedly to the library's back entrance. At three in the morning, the entire college was still and lightless. Even Celia Frick and her cooks wouldn't be there for another hour to open up the kitchens.

"So, what's your idea?" asked Myles as Eva reached into her bag for her college keycard.

"In his divine wisdom, the Master saw fit to safeguard the college art collection by installing security cameras in various locations, including, I think, the Senior Common Room."

"I knew Ilbert was paranoid, but I didn't know he could afford it. And I never thought I'd be grateful for it."

"I know, right?" said Eva.

Moments later they were inside the library and staring at the screen of Eva's office desktop computer. Myles stooped down next to Eva, who sat on the edge of her desk chair as she keyed in her college password.

"Though I've never tried to access it," said Eva, "the CCTV footage is uploaded hourly into the library's digital archives."

Within two minutes Eva had accessed the security archive and pulled up the files for the Senior Common Room on Guest Night. Their faces inches apart, they watched as the video rolled. The view took in the entire SCR, including the doorway. They watched guests gradually file into the room shortly between 8:45 and 9:15.

"It probably makes most sense to begin at the time when you leave," Eva said. Myles nodded in agreement, and she forwarded the video until the digital time in the upper left corner of the screen read 11:55. After a few minutes of viewing, they saw Myles speak with Jeremy, then leave the SCR. Jeremy chatted briefly with a group that included Father Ilbert and several guests. Sarah Penrose touched Jeremy on the sleeve, and the two of them stepped aside.

Once they were off to the side, Penrose spoke animatedly to Jeremy with a look of grave concern with the occasional smile sprinkled in. The camera angle made it impossible to read Jeremy's expression, but the few times he began to speak up Penrose interrupted him. After several minutes, Simon Cole appeared in the frame and said something privately to Penrose, after which she excused herself and left the frame.

About twenty minutes later, Jeremy pulled aside a lanky man with a shock of red hair and wearing a university gown, and the two spoke privately in a corner.

"Do you know who that is?" asked Myles.

"I think it's Barry Goodall, professor of architecture at St. Cat's. I can verify that." After pausing the video, she pulled a blue booklet from a shelf behind her desk and rifled through the pages of photos. "Yes, that's him." She held out to Myles a photo of Barry Goodall listed under the Architecture Faculty, St. Catherine's College.

She resumed the video, and they watched Jeremy speak animatedly for a few minutes, followed by a back-and-forth in which Goodall did most of the speaking while Jeremy appeared rapt. After several minutes, during which Jeremy had set down his drink, he shook Goodall's hand and left the room in a hurry.

Myles and Eva looked at each other.

"We've got to call him," said Myles, standing up and looking at his watch. "Hell, it may already be too late for Jeremy."

"Let's use my office line," said Eva reaching for her phone. "If he sees that it's a university number, he may be more likely to pick up."

With the phone on speaker, she punched in the mobile number listed under his name in the Directory.

After several rings, a groggy voice answered. "Hello?"

"Professor Goodall, this is Eva Bashir, Librarian at Ignatius College. Please forgive the hour, but it's an emergency involving Father Jeremy Strand."

"Jeremy Strand? Who...? Do you know what time it is?"

"Again, I apologize, but as I say, it's an emergency. We think Father Strand may have been abducted after Guest Night last Sunday, and you may have been the last person to speak with him. We have reason to believe his life is in danger, and time is of the essence."

"'We'? Are you with the police?"

"Yes, she is," broke in Myles impatiently, giving Eva a look and holding up his hand. "This is Myles Dunn, another colleague of Father Strand. Dr. Bashir and I have, indeed, been working with the police trying to ascertain what's happened to him."

"Well, I didn't—"

Myles pushed through Goodall's stuttering defense. "Listen carefully. You spoke with Father Strand last Sunday night."

"Hmm…Strand? So many clerics that night."

"It was late that evening—nearly midnight—in the Senior Common Room," said Myles. "You'd remember this particular priest."

After a silence, Goodall spoke again. "Rather a furtive chap? Fond of his Port? The chalice priest?"

"Yes, that's him," said Myles. "Now think carefully. Can you tell us what you spoke about?"

"Oh, good heavens," muttered Goodall. "I don't know…between the port and the single malts, one's memory grows rather muddled…let me see…"

"Focus, damn it!" cut in Myles impatiently. "Did he say anything about trinity or *trinitas*?"

"No…he didn't," said Goodall, in a tone somewhere between flustered and appalled. "But I did."

"What?" Myles and Eva said together.

"Father Strand was asking about medieval architecture, about slypes, of all things." He spoke more quickly now. "Wanted to know what exactly they are and whether there are any in Oxford."

"Dr. Goodall, please, what did you tell him?" asked Eva in a decidedly gentler tone than Myles.

"He had the idea that a slype is a covered passage usually found in a medieval monastery or church, connecting the transept and the chapter house, that sort of thing. While that is the strict definition, I told him that slypes were a somewhat looser concept than that. You see, a slype can be merely any covered passageway of any shape, size or purpose."

"What about trinity?" asked Myles, his patience wearing thin.

"As I told Father Strand, theoretically, there may be a semblance of a slype in any number of Oxford locales."

"What about something that would have been in ruins in the late nineteenth century?" asked Eva.

"The list is short," said Goodall. "Of the four renowned monastic houses of medieval Oxford, Osney and Rewley would have been gone by then. The third, St. Frideswide's, of course, is still active. The fourth was Trinity in Godstow."

Myles frowned. "Based on what you're saying, there's no slype at Trinity Church. We were just there the other day."

"No, I didn't say 'church,' did I? There's a slype, though not much of one anymore, at the old priory cemetery not far from the church."

"The priory?" said Eva.

"Mm. It hardly counts as much of one nowadays. Nineteenth-century archeologists and engineers removed the remains, and neighbors trucked most of the stones away. They're in miles of Oxfordshire property walls now, I should think. But you'll find the foundations of a rather handsome slype, oh, less than a hundred yards from Trinity. North and east of the church, through the woods. Been there myself some time ago, and I must say it's—"

The line went dead.

65

"Crowley was the name we saw a number of times at Trinity Church," said Myles in the passenger seat as Eva sped north along a deserted Banbury Road.

"So we've no idea," said Eva as she blew through a red light, "what 'unseat Bishop Crowley' refers to, let alone 'beware the chasm,' but we think it must be in the priory ruins. And we don't know where they are in relation to the church we explored a few days ago." Eva's voice betrayed her doubt.

"I know what you mean. Still, this has to be the place," Myles said emphatically. "If Jeremy was asking about slypes, then he must have realized, or strongly suspected, that Hopkins used the word as an architectural term and used it as a second locative clue in the sonnet."

"If Jeremy learned enough from Goodall on Guest Night to propel him out to Trinity in Godstow, then he had to have been there before."

"Yes! That explains it. The morning Jeremy went missing, I found a collection of photos on his desk—seemingly random and unconnected images of grass, earth, rocks, weeds and crumbling stonework. They didn't make any sense at the time. They might have been from anywhere. But I assumed they were some kind of record of Jeremy's rambles around Oxford, looking for any evidence that seemed to connect with the sonnet. I'll bet at least one of them was taken at the ruins we're about to see."

"If he thought 'slype' was important, he never mentioned it to me."

"Nor to me," said Myles. "But he might not have yet been aware of its significance. Hell, he probably thought it was nothing, at first. A dead end. He was merely being thorough, amassing information, tracking down possibilities, following hunches. Until a somewhat boozy question to an architecture don flipped a light bulb in his head." He couldn't help feeling proud of Jeremy for his dogged nature, for the kind of trust he was placing in Hopkins and his poem.

As Eva downshifted and leaned into a sharp left turn, Myles put his right hand on the dashboard for support. It was the middle of the night and there was hardly another vehicle on the road. The city lights of Oxford lay behind them now, and streetlights, houses and businesses were few and far between. It felt like they were careening headlong into darkness, a metaphor not lost on either of them.

"Let me get this straight," said Eva, exiting the main road. "There was a priory associated with Trinity Church, and the church and the priory each had its own cemetery?"

Myles nodded. "Yeah, piecing it all together, it seems the church in the early centuries was an accommodation to parishioners north of Oxford. After the Reformation it became an Anglican parish, long after the original priory had fallen into ruins. The parish would have had its own cemetery, but so would the priory. That's where the monks, and perhaps our Bishop Crowley, would have been buried. And who knows how old the cemetery is. Medieval churches and monasteries were sometimes buried on older ruins—altars, crypts, charnel houses, even pagan shrines."

"If Hopkins wanted something found, why be so cryptic about it?"

Myles shook his head. "It's hard to say, Eva. He couldn't have been playing a game. Too much was at stake. Somehow he learned late in his life that the chalice was endangered or maybe that something about the chalice had to be vindicated. There has to be more to this chalice than its value as a rare work of art."

"Maybe having it in hand, like we think Hopkins did, can give us a clue as to the 'holy justice' he was aiming for," said Eva, quoting from the sonnet.

"Yeah," said Myles, "and that justice can come about when the reader—presumably the so-called Oxford Jesuit—exposes the guilt represented by or contained in the golden chalice. That must be what 'guilt-in-gilt' refers to."

"And the 'unscroll'?" asked Eva.

"Not sure," said Myles thoughtfully. "We'll find out if we ever get our hands on it."

"What we do know," said Eva, "is that it had something to do with Lumen."

Myles nodded. "And if we find the slype, I think we can trust that it'll lead us to something to do with Bishop Crowley. 'Unseat' might require moving a throne or something. Maybe a monastic cell? Or wine cellar? Or crypt. We'll have to see. As for the 'chasm'…again, it'll be some directional clue that we have to hope we figure out once we're there."

"Wherever 'there' turns out to be," added Eva. "Who are you calling?" she asked as Myles was punching numbers into his phone.

"Police—specifically, Hillary Stratham. I got her direct number from Tock. We're up against a brutal, calculating murderer. We should let someone know where we are and what we're doing."

"Good idea, but the police haven't exactly been receptive to our line of inquiry."

Myles nodded. "And it may be fruitless, but if something happens to us, Stratham is the one I want to know about it."

A moment later he left a voicemail describing their whereabouts, what they expected to find and, in a calm but insistent tone, succinctly expressed the gravity and urgency of the situation. He also added, "If you need any confirmation of anything I've said, contact a Vatican official at Ignatius College named Monsignor Moretti. He can vouch for me."

Myles closed the phone and saw the look of bewilderment on Eva's face. "I'll explain later," he said.

In less than five minutes, Eva made a breakneck turn into the church parking lot before breaking to a hard stop. Before stepping out of the car, Myles pulled two sturdy flashlights from his knapsack and handed one to Eva.

"Courtesy of the college storeroom," he said.

He had pulled up an aerial Google map on his phone and showed it to Eva, who leaned close into him. "See this clearing in the woods a little to the northeast of the church? These must be the ruins of the old priory, where the slype is. Looks like a hundred yards or so from the parking lot."

Myles studied the map image. He then stared into the pre-dawn dark all around them.

"There's no indication of a path. I'm not sure what—or

who—we're going to encounter, so keep one hand on the flashlight and hang on to me with the other." He squeezed her hand gently.

Eva nodded and grinned. "Lead the way, cowboy."

Using the flashlights as a guide through the darkness, they walked briskly. Once they had crossed the church cemetery, they stopped at the border of the woods.

"I think if we just head in here and walk roughly straight ahead," said Myles, checking the map one more time before pocketing it, "we'll spill out onto the ruins. If we come to the river, we know we've gone too far to the west."

Leaves and branches were dripping wet from rain the day before. Moonlight and flashlight glinted off tree bark and the occasional stone.

Compared to their first visit by daylight, the darkness, far from disorienting Myles, heightened his senses. The smell of mildew and moisture and the faint drone of croaking frogs hinted that the river was less than a quarter mile away. The scent of Eva's hair and the touch of her hand stirred fleeting images of the night they spent together. With everything else that was rushing through Myles' mind, he felt grateful to have Eva here. But he was instinctively protective toward her and concerned not to put her in harm's way. This feeling heightened his vigilance all the more.

Though overgrown with bushes and weeds, the many mature trees with minimal ground cover beneath them meant that Myles and Eva could navigate a bramble-free, albeit circuitous, path. The footing was spongy and uneven. The ground sloped generally downward as they approached the site of the priory ruins and what must be the remnant of an ancient cemetery.

After fifteen minutes of snaking their way, with frequent stops to check their bearings, the woods opened up to a relatively level field dotted with small trees. Scattered all about the clearing were irregular heaps of stone amid high and untamed grasses. Something living scampered out of the shadows of one heap and into the dense wood nearby.

They swept their flashlight beams back and forth to get a sense of the scope of the ruins. Myles guessed it covered about an acre and a half. The only sound to be heard was a soft breeze soughing through the tall grass. There was a palpable isolation about the place, and not just because of the hour. Both were keenly aware of it, wordlessly acknowledged with a mutual squeeze of their hands.

"Where shall we start?" she whispered.

They decided simply to begin at one end of the ruins and work their way systematically across. They had little to go on but Jeremy's cell phone photos, nearly useless at this hour of the night, and their general understanding of what constituted a slype. They quickly developed a system where Eva directed the light onto anything Myles was pushing against, lifting or heaving along the way.

"Until tonight," Myles muttered after twenty minutes, "I had never regarded the phrase, 'leave no stone unturned,' as anything more than a hackneyed metaphor. We have to do this quickly, Eva, but methodically. This late in the game, I don't want to miss anything that might give us a clue to where Jeremy is. *If* he is here."

"Oh, Myles—he's *got* to be here!"

For forty minutes they encountered and thoroughly examined several intriguing configurations of stone and suggestive recesses in the ground. But no slypes. They crossed a ten-foot stretch of stone-free earth that led to another section of what appeared to have been a significant structure. Several heaps of stone lay strewn and piled indiscriminately. Closer inspection with the flashlights revealed the low remains of what could have been parallel walls separated by a narrow space.

Myles squatted down and shone the light along the stones. He walked slowly over the grassy space between the foundations of walls. It was nearly impossible to follow because the parallel lines of stone intermittently failed or disappeared altogether.

As they proceeded, perhaps twenty feet, the two rows of stone became more intact. Instead of stones half-buried under grass and weed, this clearly indicated the remains of parallel walls.

"A slype?" asked Eva.

Myles nodded. "Look at this," he whispered excitedly. He directed Eva's attention to the ground a few feet beyond them.

The tall grass and weeds immediately adjacent to the rows of stone they'd been following had been trampled. They stooped to examine the ground. The trampled area continued for twenty more feet until the slype became blocked by a mass of brambles wedged between the walls.

Myles carefully reached both hands deep into the twisted mass and pulled. The whole thing came out easily, and he tossed it aside. In the space where the tangled mass of brambles had been the earth was noticeably sunken.

"Careful here," Myles said, pausing Eva with his hand as he tested the ground with one foot. He could feel something solid beneath the grass. They both dropped to their knees and felt around.

They looked at each other. They both felt the edges of a board. It felt cool and moldy.

Myles wedged his fingers underneath the wood and tugged. It came away, revealing another two similarly moldy but solidly intact planks. Myles yanked them out and tossed them into the grass behind them. One thing was certain: all three had recently been pulled out of the surrounding earth.

Myles turned back to Eva. His eyes followed her astonished expression to the downward beam of her flashlight: a narrow stone staircase leading into the earth.

As Myles was about to descend, Eva put her hand on his arm. "In spite of myself," she whispered, "I'm guessing we don't want to call out for Jeremy."

"Agreed," said Myles. "There's a chance that there's nothing and no one down there. If he is here, it isn't voluntary. We don't want to alert anybody but Jeremy."

With Myles in the lead, they descended the long stairway. There were no handholds, and the upper steps were unstable with loose stones. After a few steps the going got marginally easier, though blacker. After a dozen steps they came to a floor. Cold stone under their feet.

They played their flashlights on the walls for a full minute. They found themselves in a sort of labyrinthine crypt with chambers, right and left along a narrow passage.

Myles' heart thumped in his chest. He was glad to feel Eva's hand gripping the back of his jacket as they slowly moved through. It felt cool and dank. Myles' head brushed the claylike ceiling. The stone walls were cracked but essentially intact and stable. There was no sign of human presence, no litter or debris. The place seemed eerily uncluttered except for the occasional skeletal remains of rats and other rodents.

After a few minutes of measured exploring, Myles stopped and pointed. The prints of hard-soled men's shoes in the packed earthen floor.

"Jeremy's?" Eva whispered.

Myles put his shoe beside one of the prints and shook his head. "Too big for Jeremy."

Short corridors fanned out from the main entrance, leading to doorways that opened into several chambers of roughly eight feet square. Like a catacomb, the walls were lined with niches, all of which were empty.

After examining three chambers, they came to the last room.

"Jeremy!" they both exclaimed at once.

66

Tied roughly to a wooden chair pulled close to an oblong table, head slumped down onto his chest, sat a barely recognizable version of their friend.

They rushed to him. While Eva gently held his head, Myles tore away the binding from his wrists and feet. On the floor behind Jeremy's chair lay a black gym bag with a dozen or so glow sticks tied together. She pried one loose and snapped the light.

Myles looked up immediately as Eva gasped and instinctively stepped back. Only at that moment did they notice what was seated in a chair on the other side of the table from Jeremy. A human skeleton, its skull tilted back grotesquely so that its empty eye sockets stared at the ceiling.

"I'm not sure," said Myles, "but I wouldn't be surprised if that's Thomas Carrick, late of Lumen."

He stripped away most of the nylon rope from Jeremy's arms and legs, then stabilized his friend's limp torso. Eva took a bottle of water from Myles' rucksack and tried to coax some drops past the priest's parched lips. Beneath the thickened gray-brown beard, he looked pale, thin and haggard. Dried blood was smeared across his forehead and at the base of his skull.

"Jeremy," Eva whispered, inches from his face, trying to revive him.

"That rope was tight," said Myles. "He can't have much feeling left in his extremities."

"We need to get him to a hospital," she said with a look of concern.

"Agreed," said Myles, "but let's try to get some more water in him and see if we can revive him."

She nodded, and they both began rubbing their friend's hands, arms and ankles. His breathing was regular but he was barely conscious.

"Jeremy, who did this to you?" Eva asked, tears running down her cheeks.

He was unresponsive. His entire body lax and chilly to the touch. After several minutes, he opened his eyes slowly. It didn't last. He faded in and out of consciousness.

"Let's get him on the table, Myles."

"Good idea."

Myles hastily took off his jacket and stuffed it in the rucksack, which he then rolled up and handed to Eva. He pulled the table a foot or two away from the corpse. Sliding one arm under Jeremy's knees and the other across his back and under his arms, lifted his limp friend from the chair and gently laid him face-up on the table. Eva placed the rolled-up rucksack under his head.

Myles scanned the room with his flashlight. It appeared to be the largest of the crypt chambers that they had found, the terminus of the subterranean maze. On three walls were carved-out recesses. Once tombs, now long-pillaged and empty. The fourth wall was blank except for a prominent memorial engraving of a medieval bishop. Myles could see no other doorway leading out of the crypt.

"Myles," said Eva, who had been continuing to coax water into Jeremy to little avail, "I'm going back up to find a signal and call for an ambulance."

He followed her flashlight beam out of the main crypt and into the connecting passageway. He then turned to Jeremy and bent down to speak in his ear.

"Jeremy, we're going to get you out of here." Myles had begun to work his arms again under his friend to prepare to carry him, when he felt a faint grasp of his hand.

Myles stopped and swung around to face his friend. "Jeremy!"

"Myles...please, please...not yet. So close...find it. Find it here..." His eyes slowly closed and his hand went limp again.

Myles felt Jeremy's pulse. Faint but regular. He whispered, "I'll give it as long as it takes for an ambulance to arrive, brother, and then we're out of here, chalice or no chalice."

Myles opened another few glow sticks and placed them on the ground closer to the tomb wall. He played the stronger flashlight around the crypt again. He steadied on the memorial slab. The figure was arrayed in miter and crosier with pontifical vestments and seated in profile on a bishop's throne.

The first of the two anagrams: "unseat Bishop Crowley."

There was no specific indication that this was Crowley, but it had to be.

"Now," Myles whispered in the dank space about him, "how to unseat him?"

He stepped close to the slab and appreciated how massive it was. The engraved image, chiseled out of stone, was as tall as the wall. One hand holding the flashlight, Myles ran the other over the carved lines.

"Unseat," he muttered to himself as his fingers swept the surface of the carved throne. No gaps or cracks. He pulled a pocketknife from his knapsack. He began scraping the blade aggressively along the carved perimeter. A seam! It ran along the edges. Too small to wedge his fingers in, let alone get any purchase to pull or try to wiggle loose any bits of the stone.

Focusing his efforts on a six-inch line of the seam, he continued to scrape, using the flathead screwdriver blade on his knife. Bits of stone gave way. Now he could wedge his fingers in deep enough for a handhold. He tried wiggling and pulling the stone. No movement. He wedged his fingers in until they hurt and tugged. Nothing. Once more, pulling with all his strength. Still no movement. Not enough purchase.

He stepped back and stared at the carving. He turned suddenly at the sound of approaching footsteps.

"It's me," said Eva before Myles could see her, and then as she entered the crypt, "Any progress?"

"Not really," he said. He shook his head and let out a frustrated puff of air. "How about you?"

"Yes, an emergency vehicle is on the way. They should be here soon." She stood by Jeremy, holding his hand and again offering water.

Myles returned to the memorial sculpture. "What does he mean by 'unseat'?" He reached forward and once again ran his hands along the carved outline of the chair.

Then it occurred to him. *A pivot hinge.*

He leaned directly against the carved back of the *cathedra*, the bishop's throne, and pushed with his hands. The chamber immediately echoed with the grating sound of stone against stone. It stopped. He stepped back and led with his shoulder. He leaned

319

heavily into it, his body nearly horizontal as he drove with his legs. The entire Crowley slab pivoted slightly around an invisible centerline.

He glanced at Eva, whose mouth was slightly open in disbelief. He took a deep breath and held it, then pushed again. As the side where he was pushing—the side of the slab depicting the high back of the chair—moved inward, the other side pushed outward into the room. Sure enough, it moved on some ancient version of a pivot hinge, most likely an iron rod that ran down the center of the massive slab.

He picked up the flashlight, which had been resting on its side to provide enough light to work by, and aimed it into the space. He saw a short, crude staircase that descended steeply into black.

He glanced over at Eva, still watching over Jeremy. "How is he?"

"Still in and out," she said. "Not ready to move yet."

Myles nodded. "I'm going to check this out. Keep your ears peeled for an ambulance. They'll need some guidance to get back here."

She nodded. "Be careful." She watched Myles turn his body sideways and disappear into the dark opening.

67

Stooping and following the beam of his light, Myles gazed down at irregular stone stairs. They led into a small chamber about six feet by six feet with a height of about ten. The stone of the steps was in rough shape, but not enough to deter him.

The first step was unbroken and felt pretty solid. The second showed several cracks and shifted slightly under his weight. The third give way beneath his foot.

Eva heard a muffled exclamation of "Whoa!" followed by the sound of scraping and crumbling rock.

"Myles, are you all right?!"

No reply.

His body was suspended in mid-air, his fingertips clinging to cold stone. "Yeah," he lied in a strained exhale. He swung his right leg around and up onto the step below, then pulled himself up and back onto what felt like only marginally more solid stone. The whole stairway felt like it could give way at any moment.

He grabbed his phone, which had luckily fallen to the side rather than straight down with him. He aimed it into the void that had nearly swallowed him.

"Holy shit," he muttered as he peered into the abyss. "It must be twenty feet to the bottom. That explains the other anagram."

Myles jumped from where he stood down to the floor of the small chamber. The air felt even chillier and heavier than in the chamber above. He scanned all around with his flashlight beam. The floor was littered with chunks and piles of stone, along with rodent droppings and the odd bone fragment. An ossuary, Myles realized. A sub-crypt. Likely the most ancient place in these entire ruins.

Come on, Hopkins, Myles thought. *Help me out here.* The acrostic "Trinitas" had gotten them to the old priory and then down into these ruins. The anagrams had gotten him safely to this ossuary. Now what? A third puzzle?

Nowhere could he see writing. No verbal clue as to where the Cuxham Chalice might be "entombed." The words might not be here, but what about that last line of the sonnet, the stand-alone one that gave nothing further in acrostic or anagram? It must hold some other kind of clue and not a linguistic one:

Embrace thereby the truth 'tween hell and heaven.

The only telling features of the chamber appeared on the eastern wall in the form of painted murals. The badly damaged reds and blues nevertheless still leapt brightly from the pale stone. The murals had been painted around several openings in the wall where monks' bones were deposited. In addition, the shifting earth had created its own crevices and holes. Myles studied all of it. The colorful details, chevron shields, a coat of arms. A castle flanked by two prominent pennants snapping in an imaginary breeze and manned by knights in armor, frozen in motion and time.

His eye kept returning to the pennants as his mind replayed the sonnet's final line. Two pennants...hell and heaven...an Oxford Jesuit. What is a pennant? A flag, a banner...a standard. *That's it: a reference to the meditation of the Two Standards from St. Ignatius' "Spiritual Exercises"!*

He scanned the wall and fixed on one of the crevices high up and slightly to the right of center, between the "two standards." He stepped forward and reached for the crevice. Too high even for Myles' six-foot height. He searched the rubble floor. A stone about a foot high was at his feet as if intended for a step-up. He bent down and shimmied it into position directly beneath the pennants and their crevice. He stepped up and reached his hand into the opening. Nothing but small rocks and the crumbling earth of centuries.

"Oh, damn, no," Myles' voice echoed in the chamber.

He reached in a second time, moving his hand around the black space. Far to the right, his long finger touched something. Something soft. A thin fabric. He strained on his tiptoes and reached a fraction further in. The fabric surrounded something hard and heavy. He took hold of it and pulled it out.

What was left of the tattered cloth fell away in his hands, but there was enough to suggest a once fine, burgundy-colored velvet pouch cinched with a silver knotted tie. Myles carefully pulled away remaining bits of the fabric. Stepping off the stone, he picked up the flashlight from the floor and balanced it on a stone outcropping of the muraled wall.

He held up the treasure with both hands: *a resplendent golden chalice inlaid with jewels.*

His hands began to tremble and he forced himself to be steady. He beheld the awe-inspiring craftsmanship, the finely etched images of church spires illuminated by amethysts and emeralds. He knew he was holding a fable, now made real.

Eva's voice. He froze and listened.

"Eva?" he called.

Nothing.

Poised on the balls of his feet near the bottom of the steps, Myles observed the flickering shadow of a figure framed by the pivoting doorway. Eva appeared, in silhouette. Immediately behind her loomed another figure. His hand held something shiny to Eva's throat. The flashlight trained directly behind her blinded Myles to the person's identity. He could hear Eva's rapid, shallow breaths. Myles kept his deliberate and steady.

He trained his light now onto the face that slowly appeared in the doorway. The man with one hand aiming a flashlight at Myles and the other pressing the gleaming ten-inch blade of an ornately carved knife against Eva's throat came into view. Ignatius College sub-bursar, John Brooke.

Eva winced in pain.

"Light off," commanded Brooke in a voice as steely as his unyielding grip around her neck. He wore his usual unremarkable black suit.

As he flipped off his light, Myles felt every muscle in his body tense. If any possibility presented itself, he would lunge for Eva and take her captor by surprise. The trouble was, they stood several feet above Myles. Moreover, Brooke's flashlight was aimed directly at him, so Eva and Brooke appeared as only a splintered glow through Myles' squinting eyes. Any wrong move and Eva—or all three of them—could fall into the pit.

"Why don't you take the knife away from her throat," he said coolly.

"I want the prize," said Brooke. "Give it to me!"

Myles realized that even with the flashlight, Brooke couldn't see the chalice he held at his side and in shadow.

"You have no idea what I'm holding to her throat, do you, Dunn?" Brooke's voice had grown breathless and edgy. "It was used by the Ottoman Turks in 1453 when they conquered Constantinople and put an end to the Byzantine Empire, perhaps the greatest of countless Muslim atrocities. You see," he continued, like an imperious and impatient Oxford don addressing a recalcitrant first-year undergraduate, "they've been infiltrating and slaughtering Christian kingdoms for centuries."

He removed the blade from Eva's throat and held it in front of her. The arm that held the flashlight yanked her head backwards against his chest. She let out a small yelp.

"But this knife has been something of a convert, one might say. It was one of Lumen's original treasures and passed down to me from my great-grandfather's father, Alec Moncrieff. The last *Praeses*. The last one with balls, anyway. Until now." His voice became solemn. "The perfect weapon for a latter-day blood libel, don't you think? Or hadn't you figured out that's what's been going on? To incite blame upon the Muslims. God knows they deserve it—and more."

Brooke gritted his teeth in anger. In a sudden movement, he pressed the shimmering blade hard against Eva's neck, drawing blood.

Myles instinctively moved up to the next step, poised to leap. "Let her go, Brooke."

Brooke took a step back and shook his head. "I'm sure, Dunn, that you wouldn't want to be responsible for the death of a woman you care for."

Myles remained motionless, his eyes on Brooke and his mind calculating.

"By tradition," Brooke continued, "this knife has been painstakingly honed, so much so that it stings when it pierces the flesh, as young Peter Toohey or ancient Florence Ballard would tell you if they could. Very little pressure and it will sever her jugular. And inscribing flesh with the tip is at once effortless and exquisite. A much more effective implement for writing—or making—history than a pen or a keyboard."

"Lumen was a noble fraternity, at one time," said Myles agreeably, as if to appease the madman. "I can see why you'd want to revive it, especially a man of your pedigree."

"What would you know about brotherhood or pedigree? Left the military. Abandoned the Jesuits. Or did they abandon you? Damaged goods and all that." He tsked. "How the mighty American has fallen. You'll soon be more damaged, I'm afraid. Your friend and this little brown tart will both perish because of you."

He pressed the edge of the blade harder against Eva's throat, drawing more blood and eliciting another cry of pain. Tears now ran openly down her face.

"You don't have to do this," said Myles in a calmly persuasive tone. "You're not a slave to history. None of us is."

"What do you know about history, about worth, enduring value? You're an American. You could learn a thing or two from me about pulling oneself up by one's bootstraps." Brooke's tone was subdued with a hint of a quaver, like one barely containing rage.

"It's all about outsiders and insiders with you, isn't it?" said Myles, changing tack and buying time. "Who can be part of the club and who can't. Who's allowed in and who isn't. But for people like you and Moncrieff, simple exclusivity wasn't enough. Hell, even overt prejudice wasn't enough. You wanted ultimate control over people's lives. And deaths."

"My noble lineage took a tumble after Moncrieff, and the odds were always against me. No one gave *me* a helping hand." He spat at Eva. "Government and feeble-minded, soppy people like you were only interested in minorities, refugees, the needs of the brown-skinned. I was never given a 'leg up.' So I made a plan. And I taught myself to fit in..."

"Tell me, Brooke, were you bullied as a kid? Are you doing all this because you didn't get enough attention?"

Even through the murk, Myles could see the man's face morph in an instant from smug to saturnine. "Shut up, Dunn."

Myles persisted, taking another step up. Picturing Jeremy lying on the hard wooden table, brutalized and barely breathing, and now hearing Eva's shallow gasps and seeing tear-stained dribbles of blood falling from her neck and smeared across the front of her blouse, it took a kind of strength Myles didn't know he still had to maintain external calm. He wanted to thrust himself upward at Brooke's legs and then tear him apart. He knew better, though. Such a move could end badly. To gain the upper hand, he needed to make his adversary lose control. Get him off-balance in every sense. He fired a verbal fusillade, his staccato delivery so aggressively muted and monotone that it would have made Joe Friday proud.

"What was it, Brooke? Did you resent the fact that kids who didn't look like you were more popular? Or lived in better houses? Did better in school? Weren't you smart enough to go to university? Just what made you into the morally bankrupt scum that you are?"

"Shut up! NOW!"

"Or were you just too weak? Lazy? Obtuse? Too unimaginative to succeed on your own, without falling back on your sick, twisted ancestor? Are you just too mediocre, Brooke? Is that why you did it?"

"Enough! If you don't stop..." Brooke pressed the knife harder against Eva's throat. She drew in her breath sharply.

Myles raised his free hand, palm forward, in a placating manner. He had to play this just right. "Let her go, Brooke." He then held out the chalice with his other hand. "You can have this."

As Brooke's flashlight caught the chalice, his eyes became immediately transfixed by it. After a moment's hesitation, he jerked Eva back from the Crowley doorway and shoved her to the floor behind him. Myles heard her body hit the hard ground.

Brooke burst through the doorway. He stopped himself after descending one step. He transferred the flashlight to the hand that held the knife, then reached out his free hand.

"Now, hand it to me," he commanded, his voice faltering ever so slightly.

To Brooke's evident surprise, Myles slowly backed down and away from the base of the crude stone stairs.

"Aren't you curious to see where it's been hidden all these years?"

"What do you think you're doing?" said Brooke in disbelief.

Myles stood in the center of the chamber. "So many holes," he said, gesturing with his free hand. "And it's so easy to get confused about which one is which. The trouble is, most of them aren't just little niches. This is an ossuary—a charnel house—where bones would be dropped into these holes. Some of them, I imagine, run to great depths. One of them doesn't, though. It's been the resting place for the Cuxham Chalice since 1867."

Brooke continued to stare at Myles. "Stop your lecturing and bring the chalice to me NOW. I can still slit the throats of your two feckless friends here."

"Oh, I don't think you'll do that," said Myles. He held up the chalice so that it sparkled in the light of Brooke's flashlight. "Because if I drop this into the wrong hole, you'll never retrieve it." He stepped to the wall and inserted the chalice deep into one of the holes.

"No!" cried Brooke as he sprung forward and down the stairway.

His next step, however, was his last. The slim remnant of stone gave way beneath him. He disappeared with a short "Ahhh!" Then came a dull thud, followed immediately by a scream of pain.

Myles took his flashlight out of its resting place in the muraled wall, He stepped forward to the edge and peered down. Some twenty feet below lay Brooke, his body grotesquely contorted, surrounded by human bones. Half of the huge knife blade protruded upward through his right shoulder.

"Help me...out of...here," bawled Brooke, as he stared up at Myles.

"You'll be helped out as soon as the police arrive, Brooke. And thanks for testing out the depth of that drop."

With great care and the chalice in hand, Myles navigated what remained of the stairs back up into the crypt. Eva was on her feet, holding her hand to her neck wound. Myles put the chalice on the table next to Jeremy and went immediately to Eva.

"Let me look at it," he said, putting one arm around her. "Are you all right?"

She smiled. "It's superficial—I'll be fine."

Jeremy made a noise and they quickly stepped to the table.

Eva took his hand as Myles held out the chalice.

"Here it is, old friend," Myles whispered.

Jeremy opened his eyes and smiled through tears. The hand that Eva wasn't holding he extended to Myles.

"Help me up, Myles," he whispered hoarsely.

Myles got Jeremy in a sitting position on the table; Eva stood with her arm around Jeremy's back, helping to support him. He tried saying something, but neither Myles nor Eva could make it out.

"What?" they both asked.

"It's inside," he managed to say.

Myles and Eva exchanged confused glances.

"What's inside, Jeremy?" Myles looked into the cup, searching for engraved words but saw nothing but smooth gold.

"Turn it over...the base..." Jeremy's head bobbed toward his chest as he struggled to remain conscious. "It's inside."

Suddenly Myles understood. He inverted the chalice, held the node in his left hand and attempted to turn the faceted base clockwise with his right. *Guilt-in-gilt unscroll*, he thought. The base gave slightly. He pushed it as it pivoted on one of its angles.

There, rolled tightly inside the stem of the chalice was a piece of parchment.

He looked at Eva, whose eyes caught the dance of light off gold. "The point, Eva—the small circle in Hopkins' scrawled chalice. This is what it stood for, this scroll!"

Myles carefully pulled the parchment scroll from the chalice. He set the chalice on the table, then unscrolled the parchment. He beheld four lines penned in elegant Victorian cursive:

We, the Light of Oxford, Lumen Mundi, for Britain's Sake do bind ourselves in Honour and Secrecy, to the deaths of Righteous Ones, even as of Old, to cleanse the Realm of its Impurities.

Myles then read the names of the three victims he and Eva had found in Oxford news articles from 1867. Below the three were arrayed the individual signatures of Lumen, beginning most prominently with Alec Moncrieff. Myles counted eleven, not twelve. Thomas Carrick, the sole member of Lumen ever to be cast out of the prestigious group, was not among the signatures.

"It must have been Carrick," Myles said, "former treasurer of Lumen and thus keeper of the Chalice, whose murder had been payment for his refusal to partake in the crimes and sign this document."

Eva nodded in understanding. "This is what Hopkins was so desperate to tell the world."

Myles wound the scroll up and placed it back in the stem of the chalice and turned the base back into place.

They could hear the sounds of sirens approaching. Another howl of pain came up from the ossuary pit.

"Eva, let's see if we can get Jeremy up into some fresh air." He motioned toward the pit. "He's not going anywhere until the police arrive."

He stuck his head through the pivoting doorway and took one last look down. "Oh, and by the way, Brooke, beware the chasm."

Tuesday, May 16

68

Never had Myles been so relieved to be in a hospital room. Over the past few days he had endured a slew of meetings and interviews at the highest levels of law enforcement and government. Chief among these were sessions in which Myles apprised local and national authorities of all the evidence, contemporary and historical, against John Brooke as well as Lumen in the nineteenth century. Brooke was recuperating in an Oxfordshire prison hospital, awaiting arraignment on charges that ranged from kidnapping, torture, and murder to conspiracy and domestic terrorism.

Much to Father Ilbert's dismay, Myles had refused countless media requests for interviews to discuss his role in solving the murders and recovering the Cuxham Chalice. True to character, the Master had been eager to capitalize on the sensational aspects of the story, which he deemed a public relations opportunity for Ignatius College—and himself.

Myles sat in a chair at Jeremy's bedside. The recovering patient's IV had been removed an hour before, but he still had a distended white bandage on the back of his head. Because of the concussion from repeated taser strikes and blows to the head, he was told to expect fatigue, headaches, and disorientation for days, if not weeks.

"Sounds like an extended aftermath of Guest Night," Jeremy had joked to the neurologist. He was regaining his sardonic and self-effacing sense of humor.

In the four days since he had been at the Radcliffe Infirmary, recuperating on IV fluids and sleep, he had been allowed no visitors until today. When Myles appeared just after the IV's removal, Jeremy was sitting up sipping juice and nibbling at a sandwich.

Far more interested in information than nourishment, he peppered Myles with questions about his and Eva's every movement after his abduction.

According to Myles, it now seemed clear that Brooke had overheard the Lumen table talk at Guest Night, as well as the later conversation with Goodall and then followed Jeremy out to the priory ruins. The police had only a few days ago found Jeremy's bike in the river near Godstow Bridge, where Brooke had undoubtedly tossed it. Myles then delved into a day-by-day accounting of events after Jeremy's disappearance. Though he occasionally needed Myles to slow down and repeat things, Jeremy took great interest. When Myles mentioned Collington, Jeremy confirmed that he had stumbled across the name in a 1950s Oxford yearbook citing members of the last coterie of Lumen, though he hadn't had a chance to follow up on it.

Jeremy slowly processed the information as he tried to piece together both the nineteenth-century narrative and the one that had just concluded. When Myles told him that a turning point in their investigation came with the discovery of the name Carrick in the Lumen Register, Jeremy looked puzzled.

"It's all making sense now, Myles, but it's also hard to believe that John Brooke was that monster in the crypt. He seemed a likable enough chap on the few occasions I spoke to him at college. But I can't quite see his connection to Hopkins."

"Carrick *is* that connection," said Myles. "In the Register his name was crossed out, no doubt by Moncrieff, the *Praeses* in 1867 who masterminded Lumen's transformation from a wealthy secret society into a murderous, scapegoating purveyor of blood libel."

Jeremy nodded slowly, as if struggling to recall something. "I remember Brooke ranting about some ancestor. Could that be…?"

"Yes," Myles confirmed. "Alec Moncrieff was Brooke's direct ancestor through his mother. And we think Brooke added to his prescribed murder plan protocol—acolyte, virgin, priest—because he knew that Collington was the only living person who might recall that Moncrieff's daughter married a man named Brooke."

"I have a groggy recollection of him telling me that he killed the old man," said Jeremy, "and blaming you and Eva for forcing his hand and disrupting his plan." Jeremy shook his head, fighting back tears.

"He's a lunatic," remarked Myles with a doleful grin, "but he's a principled lunatic. His plan was strict adherence to his great-great-great-grandfather's timeline and pattern of murder: virgin, acolyte and priest. This doctrinaire attitude is likely what kept him from killing Eva and me, or having us killed, when we were shot at in the Christ Church Archives. He thought that would dissuade us from our search and did everything short of killing us."

Jeremy nodded slowly. "He fancied himself Moncrieff's true disciple and the scion of all things Lumen."

"Whatever grandiose delusions he may have had or family stories he told himself, the guy's a terrorist," said Myles flatly. "He was raised in Leeds by a single mother and grew up lower middle class economically and undistinguished in every other sense. Police are still piecing together his background, but he seems to have been a sullen, disaffected kid, and at some point in his late teens, he found some old family papers in a trunk and learned about Moncrieff. From that point on he was a true believer, committed to doing whatever it took to emulate Moncrieff. He moved to Oxford, got a low-level job at Brasenose, where he did well and worked his way up to sub-bursar. Over the past year or two he's been grooming susceptible undergrads. After learning about your research into the chalice, luck was on his side and he landed a job at Ignatius. His modus operandi was publicly to blend in, be a chameleon, and privately to pave the way for a new Lumen in the manner of Moncrieff.

"At his flat," Myles continued, "the police discovered a walk-in closet that he'd converted into a sort of Lumen shrine. Among the items they found were Moncrieff's journals, in which he alludes to his search for a damning document that had been misappropriated by a traitor. There was even a list of Oxford undergraduates, evidently arch-conservative kids Brooke was grooming for the awakening of Lumen. One of them was dispossessed of a Glock 17. The police are interrogating each of them now."

Jeremy shook his head in dismay. "Yes...I knew there were others assisting Brooke and I pleaded with a few of them to free me, but they were silent. Hell, Myles, half the time down there, I wasn't sure what was real." He leaned his head back on the pillow and closed his eyes to dismiss the ghostly images of the crypt. "So, finding the chalice ended up becoming a family legacy, a fanatical mission that Brooke took up. But why? I can understand it's a valuable object, but why the particular fervor—by Moncrieff and Brooke—to find it and keep others from doing so?"

"Because of the damning evidence we found—or, really, you found—in the base of that remarkable chalice," explained Myles.

"A votive chalice," said Jeremy. "I suspected that and Brooke knew it. Now, it makes sense how he did."

"He was right about that, at least," said Myles. "I did some looking into it, and liturgical historians believe that only a handful of such chalices were ever made, most in England in the thirteenth century and all lost or destroyed well before the Reformation—until now. They were also called reliquary chalices because that little secret chamber at the base served as a kind of mini-reliquary meant to hold some bits of saints' bones or other body parts." He shook his head in wonder. "Not all that surprising, I guess, given the popularity of relics back then. But still, that pivoting base is a pretty damn cool mechanism. Even Tock had never heard of it."

Jeremy looked pensive. "And the body in the crypt—that was Carrick, we think?"

Myles pulled out his phone and flipped to a photo. He held it up to Jeremy. "When the forensic people removed the skeleton, they found this on the chair."

"A cufflink?"

"Look at the initials."

"TC." After a moment Jeremy's eyes opened wide. "Thomas Carrick. That decayed corpse at the table was Hopkins' dear friend..."

"Moncrieff seems the likeliest suspect for killing Carrick. Moncrieff was, of course, obsessed with recapturing the chalice, not only because of Carrick's betrayal, but also because the evidence in the chalice would've been the end of Lumen and the whole murderous lot. I figure Moncrieff or one of his thugs intercepted Carrick in the crypt, tortured him to death, and left him there."

Jeremy nodded slowly. "And Moncrieff didn't know about the sub-crypt, the one you discovered beneath Crowley's tomb."

"Apparently not," said Myles. "But Hopkins and Carrick knew of it and the old ossuary dating probably to the priory's origins. In fact, the crypt you found, courtesy of 'trinitas' and the slype, doesn't appear on any ordnance survey map of the county. Had you not gone looking for the chalice, Jeremy, the crypt might never have been, well, disinterred."

Jeremy looked out the window and smiled slightly. After a moment, he turned back to Myles. "So, the chalice was the symbolic heart of Lumen. And after refusing to participate in the murders and being expelled from Lumen, Carrick stole it...Why, exactly? In an attempt to demoralize Lumen and stop its heinous deeds?"

Myles nodded. "Who knows? But I like to think it was to derail the sinister direction that Lumen had taken under Moncrieff's leadership by removing the group's talisman—the chalice. And he likely knew about the scroll inside and may have planned to turn it over to the authorities once he had the chance. Knowing what Moncrieff was capable of, Carrick took a huge risk in running off with the chalice."

"And Hopkins himself must have taken a chance, too. How exactly did he learn the location of the chalice? And what prompted him to write the sonnet years later, just before he died?"

Myles shook his head. "We'll probably never know for sure. Carrick must have told Hopkins where he hid the chalice or intended to hide it. Clearly, Hopkins knew enough about both chalice and its dark storage in order to write the sonnet. But I doubt that Hopkins knew that his friend had been killed, though he must've suspected it later in life. The combination of what he knew—the murders, the sacrilege of a holy vessel being so misused—and what he may have feared—his friend's horrible fate, Moncrieff's vengeance and determination to find the chalice—all must have haunted him. Finally, his imminent death may have infused that long accretion of knowledge and fear with a sense of urgency."

Jeremy let out a long sigh. "It had to be an unbearably lonely burden to carry for Hopkins. And it had to have contributed to the dark mood that hung over him during his years in Ireland, the darkness that helped produce some of his greatest sonnets."

"I think it certainly explains why Hopkins wrote this poem, our fragment. In those final days he felt desperate to make a connection with someone, someone who could right the wrong—even if it was someone he didn't know, a Jesuit brother in some distant future."

"Our fragment was a dark sonnet, after all," said Jeremy. "The product of a dark night of the soul, a crisis of belief. A poem composed at death's door, from a place of utter aloneness. But instead of self-pity, Hopkins sought justice."

They sat in awed and sober silence, each contemplating the poem's tragic and heroic provenance. Myles watched Jeremy doze off and left the room for a cup of coffee.

"Myles, Thomas Carrick's body—it's been properly buried, I hope?" Jeremy asked as Myles handed him a cup of coffee.

"Certainly, close to it. Of course, his remains are still evidence—of more than one crime—but it was mentioned in a recent news briefing that the body would be returned to the Carrick family for the burial now of a hero rather than a traitor. And speaking of heroics," said Myles finally, "you're redeemed after all, both your soul and academic pedigree."

"Hmm. Redeemed? I suppose so, though that feels rather grandiose. Was I in need of redemption?"

"Aren't we all?" Myles chuckled. "In any case, this means a new lease for your career. It's a huge discovery. You'll be on all the talk shows. Time for a new wardrobe."

Jeremy grinned sheepishly. "I won't deny feeling excited about it all—and relieved! But you and Eva deserve most of the credit."

Myles shook his head. "I think I did here what I needed to do. I just want us to stay in better touch. I'm committed to that."

"Myles, this conversation has all been about me! How are you?" he asked, pushing himself up in the bed.

Myles leaned back in his chair. "Being back here was tough in many ways. I dreaded seeing you because I knew I'd have to face down my greatest fear: taking responsibility for Pippa's death."

"Oh, Myles. You can't—"

"No," interrupted Myles. "I can. And must." He leaned forward, resting his elbows on his knees and wringing his hands. He took a deep breath and let it out slowly. "She'd be alive if it weren't for me trying to show off. I robbed you of your sister. I can't apologize to her, but I can to you. I'm so sorry." His voice cracked as he added, "You have no idea how sorry I am."

His friend reached out his hand and Myles grasped it and squeezed. "I think I do know," said Jeremy. "And I also know this: Pippa lived the way she wanted to live, on life's precipice, hanging on with full heart and full commitment like she hung onto you leaning into that curve."

Jeremy rubbed the tears from his eyes before continuing. "When you showed up a few weeks ago, I made it harder for you to be here and to say what you needed to say to me. I know you loved her. After she died, I was so wrapped up in my own grief that I never told you how sorry I was that you lost your future wife and the beautiful, adventurous life you two would have built together. I accept your apology wholeheartedly for...what happened. And for not being in touch. But it's a two-way street, and I need to apologize to you." He paused. "I'm sorry, Myles."

"No need," said Myles, shaking his head slowly. "I never told anyone this. Just before we crashed Pippa shouted in my ear, 'I won't let go!' For the first year after being back in Colorado I hung onto that. I took it as a sign that she was still hanging on and that I had to do the same. After a while, helping my mom and Cora, having time to get outside my head and do real work, spend time with people who weren't academics, that pressure I put on myself began to ease. Just a little. I feared returning to Oxford, but it's actually been good—for several reasons."

In response to a knock on the door, both men turned to see a smiling Eva holding her bag and a vase brimming with flowers.

"And here's one of those reasons," exclaimed Jeremy, extending his arms for a hug.

Myles stood up, and Eva walked to the bed and hugged Jeremy, then set the vase on the bedside table.

"Oh, aren't they splendid!" said Jeremy. "I *love* peonies! You're *such* a sweetheart."

Myles rolled his eyes and smiled. "Should I put on a Lady Gaga playlist to go with those?"

They all laughed as Eva sat down in a chair that Myles had pulled close to the bed. He noted the light scarf she wore to hide the small bandage on her neck. After she had caught up on how Jeremy was doing and feeling, she pulled out an iPad. "Have you seen the latest news?"

"I've just been filling him in," said Myles.

"Probably not this news," she said excitedly. She held up her iPad to show them the headline from the London Times: *Treasured Chalice Restored to Rightful Owner*. "I just got off the phone with Sister Pax. She and the sisters at St. Clare's have the Cuxham Chalice."

"What?" said Myles in disbelief.

"That's brilliant, but why does she have it?" asked Jeremy.

Eva explained that the night of Jeremy's rescue, the chalice was taken into police custody, and from that point higher government officials intervened.

"It's amazing how quickly this has happened," Eva continued. "Cuxham Abbey, the Benedictine abbey in Lincoln for whom the chalice was made, has long been out of existence, but what kind of nun is Pax?"

Jeremy admitted the question was loaded, but he and Myles said at the same time, "Benedictine!"

"Correct!" said Eva. "And St. Clare's is considered the only surviving daughter house of ancient Cuxham. As such, the convent inherits the Cuxham Chalice."

"This is amazing news!" said Jeremy.

"Unbelievable," Myles added, looking pleased but pensive. "How did this happen?"

"The article only mentions 'high-ranking government officials' without going into much detail. But it's sensational!"

"Does it say what Pax plans to do with it?" asked Jeremy. "With all the press, I can't imagine the chalice being safe there."

"She's already put it in the hands of the British Museum, which is more than eager to purchase it. You know Pax—savvy, practical, no-nonsense and charitable. Listen to this quote." Eva looked down at her tablet. "'Oh, we've no use for such a bauble. It's an embarrassment that the church was ever associated with such riches. But with the proceeds, think of all the good that can be accomplished in the community.'"

"The convent won't be hurting for money now," said Jeremy. "Who arranged this?"

"I've no idea," said Eva. "Nor does Pax. But you figure, with something like this, people of considerable power have to get involved."

She looked at Myles, who shook his head in wonder and smiled but seemed lost in thought.

Wednesday, May 17

69

Jeremy returned to Ignatius College on Tuesday, well enough to move about on his own. Still, the doctors cautioned rest and the Jesuit was surprisingly compliant, agreeing to limit his movements to meals and a few hours in the library. An early Tea that day was set aside as a special welcome-home for the Literature don. Since Jeremy had become something of an Oxford celebrity following his ordeal with Brooke, the college anticipated a well-attended celebration, so Tea was convened in the Dining Hall.

Festivities commenced at three o'clock and the hall was overflowing. Spring bouquets decorated every table and the college *schola* sang a selection of May madrigals. The domestic staff felt the pressure of the relatively impromptu occasion. Ivy Cassidy ordered urns of tea set out with silver trays full of seasonal cookies and cakes, and Celia Frick, never loath to delegate, was cracking the whip with conspicuous relish, much to the dismay of her student workers.

Eva had overseen the collection of donations for the purchase of a new bicycle for Jeremy. Myles suggested it should be fitted with limited range capability, designed to seize up fifty yards from college.

Felix Ilbert, in the least dyspeptic gesture Jeremy had seen from him in years, amiably presented the Hopkins scholar with a gift on behalf of Ignatius College: a beautifully reproduced and framed copy of Hopkins Fragment 24.

Approaching 4:30, the party had all but ended. A few tables had stragglers, mainly students looking for any excuse not to get back to end-of-term essays and exam preps. The housekeeping staff had been snapped-to by Mrs. Cassidy. Eva wanted to tidy up some business in the library before she went home to Sam, and Jeremy had been easily talked into returning to his room in the Jesuit Wing for a quiet evening. Myles volunteered to secure the new bike in the college garage. It was Myles and Tock who remained alone at the Master's table engaged in conversation.

"Joy and celebration today, and yet so much sadness lingers. Peter Toohey, Florence Ballard. All Oxford—including Brooke himself." Myles looked at Tock skeptically. The old priest continued. "Yes, there's room for pity even for him. Right here in our midst, and we had no idea. 'Twas ever thus: darkness around us, darkness within. None of us is above it, Myles. No one exempt or immune."

Myles sat thoughtfully, watching the last few students depart the hall in smiles and laughter.

Tock gestured towards the grim portraits of past Jesuit Masters that hung in the hall and towards the guests filing out beneath them. "In our company, we've many fathers and brothers, sons and daughters and sisters. Our brother Gerard from the nineteenth century paid us a visit here, across the great distances of time and place." He mused silently for a moment. "He wouldn't be the first misunderstood Jesuit, our Hopkins. Any who love him, as I do, regard him best as a poet of great faith, a man who suffered and sought in his own way to make sense of it all, dark sonnets notwithstanding. Indeed, therein may reside his greatest contribution. But who on earth would have thought of Hopkins as a *hero*?"

"You're right, Tock. God knows, when I first read his poetry, I pigeonholed Hopkins as a moody, unfulfilled aesthete with a brilliant turn of phrase. But now, I think most people as close to death as Hopkins had to be when he wrote that sonnet would've just given up and left to others the unfinished business of their lives. Hopkins had to rally against incredible odds in those final days in Dublin, to do what he could, holding together in his fevered mind poetic artifice and careful secrecy."

"And what do you make of that secrecy, Myles? Couldn't Hopkins have sent a letter to some trusted soul in London and been done with it?"

"I don't know, Tock. Why the cryptic language, all that subtlety and wordplay? The only thing that I can think to explain it is that Hopkins took the chance that somehow the chalice was still in the crypt where he and Thomas Carrick used to study. And if Lumen was as brutal to Carrick as it seems they clearly were, what other people might have been in danger, or under Lumen's surveillance? Hopkins must have sensed this and did what he always did: put it to verse, in hopes that it would find its way into the hands of someone who could do what he, nearing death, could not." He paused, as it came to him. "In his darkest hour he turned, pen in hand, to a dark sonnet."

The old man bowed his head and nodded slowly. "And out of that darkness has dawned a new light." After several seconds, he continued, his voice low and measured. "Hopkins' trust that his poetic puzzle would find its way into the hands of a brother who could actually *do* something about it was an act of surpassing faith. But any act of faith, whether faith in the Divine or in another person, is a risk, a question. We await the response of the other, and often that 'answer' isn't the one we were pursuing. But in all my years, I've found that the answer is whatever we truly needed, not what we wanted or were desperately searching for." When he finished he raised his head and looked at Myles.

"I'm not sure I follow, Tock."

Tock reached toward Myles' hand and tapped it once. "You, Myles Dunn, are that 'Oxford Jesuit' brother to whom Hopkins addressed his sonnet. It was *you* he needed to parse his tattered poem." Tears of gratitude and wonder welled in the old man's eyes. He read Myles' reaction. "I do not say that, my boy, to embarrass or to flatter you. And I do not say that you shouldn't have left the Jesuits. Your life is in God's hands—it always has been, you know that. But you would have done nothing with that poem-puzzle were it not for the love you bear your brother still, Jeremy. You would not have gone after him had you not felt that kinship. And you would never have found the chalice amid all those bones and death had you not known in your heart the wisdom of our father, Ignatius. You are the Oxford Jesuit."

Myles was quiet for a long time. Indistinct, busy sounds came from the kitchen, and from the windows high in the hall bells chimed from Tom Tower ringing the half-hour. Myles could not bring himself to say anything in response to Tock's words. But he smiled and held the hand that had just tapped his.

"And isn't it something, Myles, that the third and greatest

question that Hopkins posed to his hoped-for Oxford brother had to do with discerning a fundamental choice: which do I choose, the standard of Christ the King, or that of some worldly potentate? Under whose banner, whose standard, shall I live?" The old priest shook his head and chuckled softly. "I shall never think of the Exercises in quite the same way again. Which brings us to you. Which standard? Whither goest *thou*?"

Myles took some moments to respond. "That's the question, Tock. The simple version of an answer is back to Denver, to my family and a job that has to be a bridge to something else. And that something else becomes the more complex version, which is just another question. Oh God, I'm beginning to sound like Hopkins. I guess I'll know it when I see it."

Tock nodded gravely. "I believe you will. It will come, this next thing. Meanwhile, embrace the unknowing, the mystery. The numinous. I don't need to tell you that God can reveal Godself in anything, and that goes for the humdrum routine of selling nuts and bolts and whatever else you have in that hardware store."

Tock clapped his hands together and smiled widely. "You remember the lines, Myles. Go ahead, recite them!"

"What are you talking about, old man?" Myles laughed.

Tock played along. "I'll start you out:

Glory be to God for dappled things—
For skies of couple-color as a brinded cow;
For rose-moles all in stipple upon trout that swim;
Fresh-firecoal chestnut-falls; finches' wings;
Landscape plotted and pieced—fold, fallow, and plough;
And all trades, their gear and tackle trim."

He paused and let Myles finish the Hopkins sonnet:

"All things counter, original, spare, strange;
Whatever is fickle, freckled (who knows how?)
With swift, slow; sweet, sour; adazzle, dim;
He fathers-forth whose beauty is past change.
Praise him."

The two men stood up and embraced each other.

70

Myles squinted into the last rays of afternoon sun as it hovered just above the dome of Radcliffe Camera. Not for the first time, he would miss this ancient city—the way its spires and finials caught the light but also held the darkness. Like the Colorado mountains, it represented a place he once called home but also a place of dislocation.

His gaze returned to the poised and prepossessing woman across the table. Eva had suggested this restaurant on Turl Street for their final goodbye, and Myles returned her radiant smile with a wistful one of his own. She wore a white sundress and strappy sandals, Myles khakis and a colorful short-sleeve sport shirt. They'd had dinner and talked about the many forms of poetic justice that had been attained before their eyes by virtue of Hopkins' sonnet: Jeremy's recovery and the rehabilitation of his career, Sister Pax's sensational windfall, Lumen's exposure and Brooke's downfall and likely fate. One subject they avoided was Myles' departure the next morning. They had spent the night together two nights ago, and Myles kept replaying their tender and impassioned love-making. He already felt the absence of this enchanting woman from the life he was about to resume.

She could read the sadness beneath his smile and reached across the table to take his hand.

"So, are you packed and ready to go?" she said.

"Mostly," he said, relishing the gentle caress of her fingers on his palm. "Packed, I mean. As for ready to go…" He looked at the sky. Cirrus clouds flecked the blue expanse like fanciful brushstrokes. "Tock calls me a searching soul, but I never thought of my searching as aimless. Until recently."

Eva nodded knowingly. "There's an important distinction, isn't there, between, on one hand, constantly striving to reach the elusive horizon and, on the other, a lifelong journey that leads us out of ourselves and back to who we are. The former is dizzying, the latter challenging and affirming."

He stared at her, marveling at her unassuming wisdom and wishing he could know more of it. "For most of my life I was a risk-taker, maybe even an adrenaline junkie. My faith kept it all real, kept me grounded. Then one day—while living in this city—I realized that I didn't know what I believed. My whole life changed."

"I wonder if it did."

He looked at her quizzically.

"In the past couple of weeks," she explained, "I've seen a man who values loyalty and threw himself into the unknown with fervid intensity." In response to his slightly confused look, she nodded. "It's admirable, infectious...and a tad irresistible."

Myles reached his other hand toward hers and stroked it pensively. As he looked intently into her eyes, he watched them fill with tears and felt his own do the same. "It's so beautiful right here, right now," he said quietly, "that it makes me wonder why I'd want to be anywhere else."

Eva leaned forward. "What was it you told me your father used to say to you—'Dunn is never done'? I've learned that we can't have everything we want. It sounds hopelessly basic, but I keep having to relearn it."

At that moment Eva's face lit up in a broad grin. Myles turned around in his chair to see Sam appear hand-in-hand with Rabi.

As they approached, Myles and Eva both stood up.

"Hey," said Sam to her mom. "Hello, Myles."

"Hi, Sam, Rabi," said Myles, offering them chairs. "Join us?"

"Thanks, but we can't stay. We've just come from Pax's place," Sam said excitedly. "The interfaith service in St. Giles' Square was absolutely brilliant. Pax gave a speech, as did Rabi's imam and the mayor, who called for an end to Muslim scapegoating."

"Brilliant," said Eva.

Eva pointed to a book Sam was holding behind her back. "What's this?"

"It's the Qur'an." She looked at her mom with timid defiance. "I told Rabi I'd help him with his application to Oxford Polytechnic in exchange for helping me learn more about Islam."

"Sounds fair." Eva smiled as she looked at Sam, but Myles could see the unanswered questions in her eyes. Turning to Rabi, she said, "Ox-Poly, eh? What subject?"

"Engineering."

"Good choice," said Myles with a slight grin. "I hope you like math."

Rabi managed a grin. "I do."

"Mom, you didn't forget about the movie, did you?"

"Of course I didn't forget," replied Eva. She turned to Myles. "Iranian film night at the Phoenix."

"You should come, Myles," said Sam enthusiastically.

Myles held out his palms in a gesture of gratitude. "I'd love to, but I'm afraid I can't."

"He's traveling back to the States tomorrow morning and I imagine he has plenty to do," said Eva.

"Oh, that's right," said Sam. "Bummer." She studied the two adults' faces. "Maybe another time."

"Thanks," said Myles.

"My car is just up the block, love," said Eva to Sam. "You two go on ahead and I'll be along in a minute."

"Safe travels," Sam said to Myles.

"Thanks," he replied with a smile. "Good luck on your A-levels."

Just as Sam and Rabi turned and began walking away, Myles said, "*As-salamu alaykum.*" Rabi stopped and turned to face Myles, who continued, "*Atmana laki kul Al Saada.*"

Rabi, with only a hint of a smile, put his hands together and made a slight bow. "*Jazak Allah Khairan.* May Allah reward you with blessings." He turned and strolled away hand-in-hand with Sam.

In response to Eva's mystified smile, Myles said, "I wished him peace and—"

"And happiness, yes I know," she said. "I haven't forgotten all my Arabic. The question is, how did you become that fluent? And don't tell me it was spending time in Afghanistan."

He looked at her and sighed. "Well, that's a long story, and you've got movie plans." He took both her hands in his. "But I'll tell you what—next time we get together to rescue a mutual friend, unearth an ancient relic and foil a sinister plot, I'll tell you all about it if you're still interested. Sound like a plan?"

"More like a dodge," she said with a grin. "But as you say, I've got two young lovebirds waiting for a ride."

For the next few moments they stood facing each other, eyes locked in silence.

Finally, Myles leaned forward and kissed her on the cheek. She put her hands on either side of his waist and gently pulled him closer. Their faces inches apart, they held each other's gaze for several silent seconds with smiles of gratitude and affection, tinged with the sobering acknowledgment of what might have been. She reached a hand up and touched it lightly to the scar along his jawline, then to his cheek. Then she raised herself on her tiptoes and kissed him on the lips.

As he watched her walk away, instead of pushing against the rising tide of regret, he remembered Tock's counsel and let the pain wash over him.

Thursday, May 18

71

Myles zipped up the duffel bag he'd packed in Denver two weeks before and tossed it on his bed. He included in his belongings both the picture of Pippa and his old copy of the *Spiritual Exercises*. A few minutes earlier in the college computer room, he had printed out his boarding passes and said a glad goodbye to a few students working on papers. His flight from Heathrow was scheduled for departure in four hours, giving him plenty of time to hop a bus at Gloucester Green for the airport, clear immigration, and then on to Denver by way of Chicago.

Earlier that morning he had placed the Host that Rabi had found at the murder site on the main altar of Martyrs' Chapel. He figured the college sacristan, perhaps with a shrug, would know what to do with it when he found it. In any case, the culprit had been found and this particular piece of evidence needn't be placed in some plastic bag and kept with the Thames Valley Police indefinitely. And Myles liked the symmetry of it all: Brooke had likely stolen the Host from the college's sacristy to begin with.

He placed the Vatican passport on the desk with the intention of dropping it off at Moretti's room as he was leaving. He still wondered at the gesture. *Why give me something of such consequence when its effect covered only a few hours?* He shrugged and then tucked his boarding passes into a luggage sleeve, walked to the window, opened it and stretched out into the quad. As he'd done on his first day back, he inhaled deeply the sun-drenched spring air and admired, beyond the dorm rooftops of Ignatius College, the spires and towers of Oxford, the steeple of St. Mary's Church—Newman's church—and the finials of All Souls College. He thought of Eva,

Jeremy and Tock and how he would miss them. He thought, too, of his former life as a Jesuit and priest and felt buoyed with gratitude at the mystery of it all—and just a little deflated at having to leave.

As he turned from the window he saw Monsignor Moretti standing in the open doorway, his knuckles raised and poised to knock. Tucked under his right arm was the same black valise he'd had in the Mercedes. Myles registered a quick shift from a kind of native suspicion he'd harbored for the Italian since their first meeting to that breadth of gratitude he'd felt at the window.

"Monsignor." Myles reached for the Vatican passport on the desk. "I was just about to return this to you with my thanks. I might still be in the slammer if not for you."

"The *what*?"

"Never mind. Please, come in."

"I cannot stay too long and I know you must leave soon, but I must have a word with you."

Myles grinned. "I wonder if it has anything to do with how a certain thirteenth-century chalice worth a small country's GDP wound up in the hands of some old Benedictine nuns."

Moretti smiled enigmatically. "It is true: someone well-placed had it sent there."

Myles nodded with a knowing grin.

Moretti continued. "As you know, I have some connections with various departments and ministries of state. I knew about the sisters and their unspoken claim to the chalice before I left Rome to come here a month ago." Myles couldn't hide his surprise. "The provenance of the chalice, as you now know, was not so difficult to trace. It was originally given to the monks of Cuxham by the goldsmiths' guild of London—Jews—in partial payment for the completely fictional crime of their Lincoln brothers in the death of the young boy, Hugh. Of course, we both know the murder was blamed on Jews, but the goldsmiths of London had not the... historical perspective we now enjoy. In any case, it was for those Jewish goldsmiths a costly effort to placate the mobs who wanted more blood, even after the deaths of so many..."

Myles was impressed to see on Moretti's face a look of genuine sorrow, as if the man had traveled through many stories of misfortune, crime and deprivation and that this was merely the latest.

Centuries old, it still touched, if distantly, on the ruined lives of innocent people.

"The chalice's restoration," the Italian summarized, "was a simple act of justice."

"This doesn't sound like the typical work of the Vatican Secretariat of State," said Myles.

"And that is why I am speaking with you, *dottore*. My official position at the Vatican is as an Under Secretary of State, a modest diplomatic post which takes me to any country with official ties to the Holy See. But that is part-time only." He paused. "May I sit?"

Myles gestured toward the desk chair and sat on the edge of the bed.

After closing the door and taking a seat, Moretti looked at Myles intently. "What I am about to tell you only four people in the world know: myself; my Dominican Secretary, Father Ian Slater; the Secretary of State, Cardinal Zampelli; and the Holy Father. You will be the fifth."

Moretti allowed the significance of his statement to hang in the air between the two men.

"Twelve years ago, with a substantial inheritance from my father, I proposed directly to the pope a very different kind of Vatican enterprise. In order to be effective, perhaps even prudent, it needed to be secret." Moretti laughed lightly at what he'd just said. "*Ma*, but what office in the Vatican is not in some sense *segreto*? The point is, since that time I have devoted ample resources to seeking out lost or stolen religious artifacts, not unlike the Cuxham Chalice."

"And most of this is for the Vatican Museum, I suppose?"

"Not at all. What I do—what this covert office hidden under layers of bureaucracy in the Vatican is meant to do—is to right certain wrongs. As we have done here with the Benedictine sisters." Myles arched an eyebrow as Moretti continued. "Sometimes we realize that a supposedly stolen piece is no more than a fiction, as we initially thought about the chalice. But more often the object is both real and located somewhere it should not be, and so it becomes a matter of justice. Do you see?"

"Monsignor, you have my admiration, and I assure you that what you're telling me will remain *segreto*. But why tell me at all?"

"Because, Dunn, I am getting old. And these"—he briefly

lifted a pack of *Nazionali* cigarettes from his jacket pocket before slipping it back in—"may have done their damage." He was unsurprised when Myles started shaking his head. "No, listen more. I have watched you these past weeks and have come to see in you a most unusual combination of gifts: courage and physical strength, ingenuity, tenacity, skepticism and expertise in world religions. All qualities I once possessed."

"Monsignor Moretti, I don't think—"

Moretti's hand was up again. "*Momentito.* You were an Army engineer as well as an officer engaged in special communications. A singular conjunction of skills, no?"

Myles let several seconds elapse before responding. "Things needed building, but rarely in a straightforward way. Since I spoke passable Arabic and less than passable Pashto, my presence proved useful." Intending to be laconic rather than vague, he spoke in a matter-of-fact tone and demeanor that Moretti construed as veiled.

The older man nodded, as if acquiescing to the evasion. "Of course, I do not know the specifics of your work, nor do I need to. I also beg your forgiveness for prying so deeply, but at first it was a matter of my own assurance that you were trustworthy as far as the Cuxham Chalice was concerned. Then it took on a more professional interest regarding my office and its work." He studied the American's face and found there a quizzical curiosity. "The work I do transcends parochial boundaries and concerns, transcends religion, transcends even the Vatican. Yes," he chuckled, "even that. This is why I asked you the question a week ago in the car about why you gave up your life as a Jesuit priest. My question had little to do with faith and everything to do with motivation, character, fortitude. And readiness."

He paused momentarily and looked directly at Myles.

"Dr. Dunn—Myles—you know how to find things out, and you are not afraid to do whatever is required. That is the kind of man I need."

Myles said nothing as he cocked his head and frowned.

Moretti reached into the black valise and withdrew a red diplomatic pouch. It bore the arms of the Vatican City State in gold. "The details are important, of course, but all I wish for you to do now is to read this. What is your Jesuit word? 'Discern'—yes, discern this as a next step in your life's work."

He held the pouch out to Myles. After a long, assessing stare, Myles slowly reached over to Moretti and took the packet.

Glancing at the desk, Moretti added. "Please, keep the passport. I hope it will be of further use to you." Moretti promptly stood up, walked to the door and put his hand on the knob. Turning, he said to Myles, "*Adio e molto grazie, dottore. Buon viaggio,* Myles."

Then he was gone.

Myles stood for a full minute trying to make sense of the previous thirty. He then slid the red diplomatic pouch and passport into his carry-on bag. He had an hour and a half to get to Heathrow.

Thank you for reading *Dark Sonnet.*

If you enjoyed this book, please help other readers discover *Dark Sonnet* by leaving a short review where you bought the book. Thank you.

Authors' Note

The two of us met at Oxford University sometime in the last century and lived at Campion Hall for two years, along with other students, Oxford dons and Jesuit priests. Since that time, we've worked out various ideas for Myles Dunn and his explorations, real and metaphysical, including *Dark Sonnet*. There's much of Oxford in these pages that's real: venerable colleges like Christ Church, All Souls, Balliol and Trinity all exist; visitors to Oxford will find an amiable English bitter in historical pubs like the Turl and The Head of the River. Campion Hall (not mentioned in *Dark Sonnet*) is indeed one of Oxford's six Permanent Private Halls, but it's not meant to be the prototype for the fictitious St. Ignatius College. Cardinal Wolsey, was the actual founder of Cardinal College at Oxford which would, after the Reformation, grow into Christ Church College. Neither Lumen nor Wolsey's foundation of the group is historical.

Two other real-life characters—the Jesuit poet, Gerard Manley Hopkins and his spiritual director, St. John Henry Newman, later cardinal—walked Oxford's cobbled byways in the mid-nineteenth century. Whether or not they met at Oriel College is unknown. While the reader will encounter Hopkins' elegant and often challenging verses throughout these pages, and while a handful of his poems have come to be called "terrible" or "dark" sonnets, the one that draws Myles deeper into our mystery is our own invention, as are all other nineteenth- and twenty-first-century characters. While there are thousands of medieval artifacts that sit in church sacristies and museums all over the world, the Cuxham Chalice is not one of them. Monsignor Moretti's secret Vatican office is not a real one, but then, if it were a secret, how would we know? Finally, and most assuredly, any similarities a reader might find between the fictional characters of *Dark Sonnet* and real persons, living or dead, is merely coincidental.

Tom McCarthy
Bill Dohar

Acknowledgements

One author's debt to friends and relations who advise and support the creation of a book can run to great lengths. With two authors, this gratitude becomes very hard to control. We've been at this book for some time, and so many helped get us to an Acknowledgment's page. Included among these are Catherine Dohar, Maryam Paulsen, Betsy Kehres, Cynthia Burns-Coogan, Kim Pizinger, Dan Kelly, Suzanne Boyle, Dr. Ron Isetti, T.H. Linton, Robert Dohar, Lucy Iglesias, Philip DeCosse, Moira McCarthy, Anne Grycz, Tim Iglesias, Marty McCaslin, Byron Russell, Ellen McCarthy, Maggie and Gary Arbino, Dr. Hervé Kieffel, Tim Jessen, Christopher Dohar, Dr. M. Michèle Mulchahey and the late Fr. Paul Crowley, SJ. Dr. Tom Powers gave the manuscript a careful and sage read, and Rev. Professor Joseph Amar assisted with the Arabic. Clare McCarthy, M.D., provided invaluable insight into how the human body is affected by various kinds of assault and physical trauma. Roger Freet of Folio Literary Management believed in the book from the start and offered many helpful suggestions in plot and character. Jane Dixon-Smith of JD Smith Design gave us a masterful cover and formatted the text, and illustrator Stefan Salinas brought our Hopkins sonnet to life.

About the Authors

Tom McCarthy and **Bill Dohar** have been lifelong students of language and mystery.

Tom is the literary half of this writing duo. After graduating from Georgetown, he earned a Master's degree in English at the University of Oxford and a PhD from Harvard, where he was appointed Lecturer in History and Literature and won a teaching award and a Mellon Fellowship. For five years he wrote a monthly column in *America* magazine on the interplay between intellectual and spiritual life which formed the basis of a book entitled, *From This Clay.* Other books include *Relationships of Sympathy: The Writer and the Reader in British Romanticism.* He teaches interdisciplinary courses on urban consciousness, nineteenth-century poetry, Dickens, Modernism, political speech, borders, wilderness and death. He and his wife divide their time between Minneapolis and Tucson.

Bill is a medievalist who specializes in popular religion and the history of pastoral care. He studied history and theology at the University of Notre Dame, earning master's degrees in both fields. He went on to Toronto where he earned both a licentiate from the Pontifical Institute and a PhD from the University of Toronto. He spent two years at Oxford while researching his doctoral dissertation. Bill is the author of *The Black Death and Pastoral Leadership* and co-authored with John Shinners, *Pastors and the Cure of Souls in Medieval England*. Bill is a former Catholic priest who lives in San Francisco and teaches in the Religious Studies Department at Santa Clara University.

Made in the USA
Monee, IL
13 September 2022

13886647R00201